lora leigh

taken

 st. martin's griffin ✿ new york

for love lost and love found
and all the memories in between

TAKEN. Copyright © 2014 by Lora Leigh.
"Reno's Chance," by Lora Leigh. Copyright © 2005 by Lora Leigh. First published in *Honk If You Love Real Men*, 2005.
"For Maggie's Sake," by Lora Leigh. First published in *Real Men Do It Better*, 2007.
"Atlanta Heat," by Lora Leigh. Copyright © 2008 by Lora Leigh. First published in *Rescue Me*, 2008.
"Night Hawk," by Lora Leigh. Copyright © 2010 by Lora Leigh. First published on www.heroesandheartbreakers.com, 2010.
"Cooper's Fall," by Lora Leigh. Copyright © 2009 by Lora Leigh. First published in *Real Men Last All Night*, 2009.
"Sheila's Passion," by Lora Leigh. Copyright © 2012 by Lora Leigh. First published in *Legally Hot*, 2012.

www.stmartins.com

Designed by Anna Gorovoy

Library of Congress Cataloging-in-Publication Data

Leigh, Lora.
  [Short stories. Selections]
  Taken / Lora Leigh.
      pages cm
  ISBN 978-1-250-04545-4 (trade paperback)
  ISBN 978-1-4668-4408-7 (e-book)
 1. Man-woman relationships—Fiction.   I. Title.

PS3612.E357A6 2014
813'.6—dc23

                    2014008533

St. Martin's Griffin books may be purchased for educational, business, or promotional use. For information on bulk purchases, please contact Macmillan Corporate and Premium Sales Department at 1-800-221-7945, extension 5442, or write specialmarkets@macmillan.com.

First Edition: July 2014

10 9 8 7 6 5 4 3 2 1

taken

also by lora leigh

contents

reno's
chance

prologue

it wasn't a party she wanted to go to, but Raven had promised her best friend Morganna that she would be there. Being there meant she would, of course, run into Reno. Reno, with the softest gray eyes she had ever seen, the most luscious buff body God had ever given a man. As she left the bathroom, her body washed, scrubbed, lotioned, and perfumed, she assured herself it wasn't for Reno.

But she knew better.

Her body knew better.

She wanted to come up with an excuse to stay home, but she knew she wouldn't. It had been weeks since she had seen him and she missed him.

They were friends, she told herself. She was allowed to miss him. It didn't mean anything. Just because her heart hammered in her chest at the thought of seeing him, her breasts became swollen, her nipples hard and tight, it didn't mean anything except he could turn her on.

That was all it meant.

She threw herself on the bed, turning on her back to stare at the ceiling overhead. It wasn't the ceiling she saw, though. She closed her eyes and it was Reno she saw. His head lowering, his lips so full and sensual, taking hers.

She was shocked at the moan that passed her lips, the heaviness that filled her body, the liquid warmth she could feel between her thighs. His hands were broad, callused. How would they feel moving over her naked body, cupping her breasts as his fingers, then his tongue, rasped over her nipples?

She licked her finger and thumb, moving it to her nipple, mimicking what she thought he would do, and had to bite her lip to keep from crying out at the pleasure.

"Yes," she whispered instead. "That's what I want, only better."

And it *would* be better. His fingers would be hotter, rougher, more demanding.

Her legs shifted on the bed as her hand moved down her midriff. *Pathetic,* her mind jeered.

She could fantasize, she told herself fiercely. That's all it was, just a fantasy.

She touched the bare flesh between her thighs and a broken sigh fell from her lips.

God, she wanted him.

And she could have him. She knew she could. He had been chasing her for nearly two years now. Every time he came home, he watched her with a promise swirling in the stormy depths of his gaze. And that didn't count the stolen kisses, the knowledge that one day soon, he was going to start chasing her in earnest. She knew it was coming. Knew she could fight him only so long.

If she fought him at all.

He made her hot, wet. Her fingers slid across the dewy flesh, gliding along the silken juices that eased their way until they rasped against her swollen clit.

"Reno," she whispered his name, her breathless voice sounding as hungry as her body felt.

But it was Reno she saw. His touch, his fingers that stroked the sensitive little bud that kept her on the edge of pleasure, her release a strangled breath away as she imagined his lips covering hers, his tongue licking, stroking, probing. She gasped, her fingers moving faster, more firmly against her clit as she felt her release peaking.

"Yes, take me." Her head tossed on the pillow, her fingers pushing her pleasure higher. "Now, Reno. Now."

She imagined him moving over her, his cock, broad and engorged with lust, sliding through the wet folds, pushing forward, stretching her, taking her. . . .

Her hips arched as the explosion tore through her, pleasure singing through her body as she whimpered in need. But it wasn't enough. It was never enough. The release, despite the pleasure, was tinged with a hollow emptiness, a knowledge that nothing could match the real thing. That if Reno were with her, taking her, she wouldn't be whispering—she would be screaming.

Her hand fell back to the bed as she took a deep, weary breath.

He was all she wanted in the world, had ever really needed.

And he was the one man she could never allow herself to have.

chapter 1

"need a ride?"

Raven McIntire stiffened in shock at the raspy, dark voice behind her. She turned slowly, her breath halting in her throat at the sight that met her eyes.

Reno Chavez. Six feet three inches of tough, powerful muscle and finely honed strength. Thick, midnight black hair cut close to his head showed off the strong, harsh features of his face. Brooding gray eyes, high cheekbones, lips that drew the eye time and time again. He was a well-built, powerful male animal and he knew it. Even more, Raven knew it, and had been hopelessly drawn to him for years.

How did you fight the man your heart ached for? The one who had been your best friend, your confidant, your protection as a teenager? The first man you ever fantasized about, and the only one that made you hot enough to whisper his name in the dark safety of your bed?

It wasn't easy, but she had been managing it. Well, sort of. He did manage to sneak the odd, knee-weakening-make-her-want-to-beg kiss whenever he had the chance. She had sworn she wasn't giving him any more chances after the last one. But she was still standing there, staring up at him like a lovesick fool.

He tipped the bottle of beer to his lips and drank, his eyes locked on hers as she stared up at him in fascination. A woman couldn't help but be fascinated by him and she was no exception.

The only difference was, she liked to think she was smart enough to stay away from the bad boys and keep on the safe side of the emotional court.

"I called a cab." She lifted the cell phone she held in her hand as she flashed him a bright smile.

Reno had always been a bad boy. A devil-may-care charmer who had stolen her heart when she was no more than a teenager and continued to hold it. Even now, after he entered the one career that made him off-limits to her. She knew the perils of loving a Navy SEAL, and was terrified of the cost of giving into the seductive war he had been waging on her for the past year.

He continued to watch her as her gaze flickered nervously to the street. She was standing on the porch of his sister Morganna's house, having ditched the party nearly a half hour before. She wasn't a party girl, no matter how she tried to pretend for her friend's sake at these little get-togethers.

She wore the short, flirty black skirt with its low-rise waist and the matching, snug, sleeveless top with its high-rise hem. Her tanned belly was bare clear below her navel, the little diamond navel ring she wore glittering in the overhead light of the porch. And there was no mistaking the fact that he noticed. His gaze kept drifting down, his eyes heavy-lidded, making her belly tingle in response.

It reminded her too much of the touch of his lips, his hands moving over her back. The last few times he had been home after assignments, he hadn't let a chance to touch her go by. He was trying to seduce her, and Raven knew it. Knew it and had no idea how to combat it.

"Stop looking at me like that, Reno," she ordered him, frowning as his gaze lifted to hers again.

"But I like looking at you, Raven." A grin tilted one corner of his mouth as he stared down at her. "I like looking at you a lot. Did I ever mention how much I miss the days when you flirted and teased, instead of running from me?"

She snorted indelicately. "I bet you do. You have enough women chasing after your tight butt. You don't need me." She glared at him suspiciously. "How much have you had to drink anyway?"

"Not near enough," he sighed as he reached out, pulling at a curl that fell over her shoulder. The action had her heart racing, her womb clenching in hunger. "Do you realize this is my first night home and my bed is occupied? I went to find the earplugs to drown out that crazy music and crash for a few hours. But I think the bed is going to need delousing first."

His lips twisted with a grimace, though his gaze was rueful as he stared down at her. And he did look tired, exhausted, in fact. Raven knew he wouldn't be likely to sleep here until tomorrow night, not if his bed was in use.

She crossed her arms under her breasts, knowing that what she was about to do was dumb. Really dumb. But if she had a weak spot, it was Reno. It was a weakness she fought continually, but a woman could only be so strong. And she didn't have a chance against an exhausted, vulnerable Reno.

"Look, if you mean it about the ride, I have an extra room. You can crash there until you're rested enough to delouse your bed," she offered. Hell, she couldn't see the man suffer. He fought for God and country. It just wasn't right.

He tilted his head slowly, those gorgeous gray eyes of his softening marginally.

And she was softening, as well. All she could remember was the touch of his lips, his hands, the heat of that hard, corded body the last time he had been home. What he made her feel was dangerous, addictive.

"You don't have to do that, Raven. I'll toss Morganna out of her bed."

"Good luck." She snorted at that one. "Last chance, Reno. My cab should be here in the next five minutes, and if you don't have me on the road by then, I'm taking my offer back."

A grin quirked his lips. "You drive a hard bargain, Raven. My bag is still packed," he said lightly. "I'll go grab it and my keys. Stay put."

Evidently, the lure of a quiet bed was too much to resist. She sighed as he turned and reentered the house, his tight buns flexing beneath his jeans as he moved. Damn, that man was packed from head to toe. He was definitely male candy and she had a horrible sweet tooth.

She throttled a purely female groan of frustration at the thought. He couldn't have a clue just how hard she had lusted after his male form over the past years, or how hard denying him over the last few months had been. The only thing that had saved her from drowning in her own drool was the fact that she knew he was way more man than she could handle. That had been forcibly brought home to her just after her eighteenth birthday, nearly seven years before, when she surprised him by bursting into his bedroom in her excitement to see him. Reno was six years older than she was, a grown man, sexual and intense, even then.

She shivered at the memory. She had shuddered, eyes wide as she stared at the curvy blonde tied to his bed.

"Perv," she had snapped before turning and literally running.

He had been naked, aroused, hard and thick and long and tight . . . and hard and thick and long . . . She closed her eyes and clenched her teeth as her clit began to throb and her pussy spilled its slick juices along the sensitive folds between her thighs. She wasn't going to think about it, she told herself fiercely. If she did, she would never get any work done tonight.

"Let's go." He stepped outside, his duffel bag slung over his shoulder, the keys to his pickup in his hand.

This was stupid, she told herself silently. But she couldn't stop the rush of pleasure as his hand settled in the small of her back and he urged her to the side of the street. Callused and wide, his fingers nearly spanned her lower back, the strength in them sending a thrill shooting through portions of her anatomy that she wished weren't nearly so responsive.

He led her to the wide, double-cab, black pickup she had admired earlier. She should have known it was his, she thought in resignation. It was as strong as he was. A man's vehicle.

Opening the door, he gripped her hips before she could do more than gasp, and lifted her into the seat. Eyes wide, surprise whizzing through her, she stared back at him, aware that her response to the action must be plain on her face. Dammit, she was supposed to be playing it safe.

"Scoot in," he whispered as his hands slid slowly from her bare waist, and he stepped back, his hand going to the door.

Drawing in a deep breath, she swung her legs into the truck, moving in just enough for him to close the door. Her flesh tingled where he touched her, heated and ached for more.

"Dumb, Raven," she whispered to herself as he loped around the truck. "Really dumb."

He opened his door, tossed the duffel bag in the back, and stepped easily into the cab. He had no problem navigating the height from the street because his legs were so damned long, she thought irritably.

The truck pulled from the curb as she sat nervously, staring out the window, calling herself every kind of fool she could think of. This was kind of like the lamb inviting the wolf into its pasture, she thought in disgust.

"Thanks for the bed, Raven," he said softly as he turned at the corner, his voice sending shivers down her spine.

That voice should be illegal. Someone should put duct tape over his lips and a sign on his body that declared him dangerous to the female sex, because that's exactly what he was.

"Not a problem." *Liar, liar,* she raged silently. There wasn't a chance in hell she was going to get any work done with him in her house.

She tugged at her skirt as his eyes strayed to the bare flesh of her lower thighs. Dammit, she knew this skirt was a bad idea. It was sexy and fun and showed her body off to its best advantage. And Reno was definitely taking advantage of all the bare skin flashing.

She could feel his gaze flickering over her legs, her profile, and though he kept both hands carefully on the wheel, she could almost feel them coasting over her body instead. Callused and warm, rasping against her flesh as she arched to him.

She clenched her teeth, pushing the vivid fantasy back as she restrained the shiver that would have worked over her body. Flames licked just beneath her skin, sensitizing her flesh, reminding her why she didn't have a love life. Because she knew, clear to her soul, that no other man could make her want him as intensely as Reno could. Without a touch, without a word. Hell, he didn't even have to be in the country.

Pathetic. Stupid. Reno was so far out of her league that they didn't even exist within the same reality. He was a warrior, a fighter; his world consisted of blood and death while hers existed within the security he helped create. And to be honest, he terrified her. The needs and desires she had when she thought of him, the fantasies that taunted her in the deepest part of night, and the sexual hunger she could feel building within her were too intense, too damned strong.

"Here we go." He pulled into the parking lot, swinging the truck into the empty space in front of the town house. "I really appreciate you letting me stay over."

She glanced up at him. Damn, he did look tired. But still sexy as hell. She was such a lost cause where he was concerned.

"Not a problem," she said again as she gripped the door handle and swung the door open. "Come on and get settled in. I have to work some tonight, but I'm pretty quiet on the computer."

She pulled her key from the minuscule purse she carried at her hip. Behind her, she was aware of Reno moving silently. How the hell did he do that? There wasn't even the sound of his shoes on the pavement.

She unlocked the door, flipping on the light to the small living room as she led the way in.

"Come on up. The bed is made and everything, so you can crash whenever you want to."

She moved up the stairs, uncomfortably aware of him following her. She could feel her butt burning. Oh God, was he looking at her butt? Unconsciously she clenched the cheeks of her ass, then forced herself to relax. Dumb. Dumb. Dumb. He hadn't even touched her and she was ready to rape him. This was so pathetic.

She opened the door to the spare bedroom, the one directly across from her own, and stood aside as he brushed past her. His arm slid over her breasts as her breath caught in her throat. She barely managed to throttle a hungry moan at the contact.

"Well. Good night." She had to get away from him. She had to close him up, get him out of sight.

He dropped his duffel bag to the floor and turned to face her, a slow, predatory move that reminded her of a wild animal or a hunter on the prowl. Why did she feel like the lamb?

He smiled then. A wry quirk of his lips, really, as the gunmetal color of his eyes gleamed with amusement.

"Good night, Raven," he said, his voice huskier, deeper.

The sound echoed in her pussy, her very wet, very aroused pussy. This was not good. Not good at all. She escaped the room, now heavy with his male presence and the predatory lust she saw reflected in his gaze. Morganna had warned her that Reno wouldn't wait long before pushing for what he wanted. He had made his intentions clear to her, informing her in that brisk, no-nonsense voice of his that he wouldn't let her run from him much longer.

And she had most likely just played into his hand.

Raven gritted her teeth as she paced the living room, pushing her fingers through her hair and again calling herself every type of fool she could think of. She was no match for Reno, and she knew it. How was she supposed to fight him? Hell, he was every woman's fantasy come to life, and he was now flat in the middle of her home, right across the hall from her bedroom, his hard body aroused. Yes, she had seen that bulge pressing against his jeans, the way his eyes darkened as he watched her, the determination in his gaze.

Reno was through playing, and Raven had a very bad feeling she wasn't going to get far resisting him. But what bothered her even more was the fact that she wasn't entirely certain she wanted to resist him. And that scared her more than anything.

It was her own fault, she reminded herself with harsh criticism. The day she had turned nineteen and learned that he wasn't staying home after his tour in the Navy was finished, that he was actually taking the BUDs training to become a SEAL, she had been enraged.

Not Reno. Not the man she had pinned all her dreams on. She couldn't lose him as her mother had lost her father. As she had lost her father.

"Don't go. I'll do anything," she remembered whispering tearfully, staring up at him, her hands on his chest, all her naive beliefs that her love for him would keep him with her, filling her.

He had smiled that crooked little grin she loved so well as he touched her cheek and lowered his head. She knew he had meant the kiss to be light. To be comforting, rather than exploding out of control as it had.

"I'll be back," he had sworn. "I will, Raven. For you."

She had slowly backed away from him, shaking her head, as her lips throbbed from the kiss that had sent a swelling wave of hunger rushing through her.

"If you go, I won't be here." She had choked on her tears, her fears. "I won't be here for you."

"You'll be here," he had whispered then, his voice immeasurably gentle, confident. "Just as I'll be back, Raven. You'll be here. And once I have you, baby, I won't let you go."

She had made certain he never took her. That he gained no

more than the stolen kisses he managed to get when he caught her unawares. That he took no more of her heart than he already possessed.

She was going to drive him insane.

"Damn woman," he growled.

She had been running from him for years, and he had been aware of it.

But he had made up his mind on a cold winter's night as he lay alone in his bed, smiling like a fool over a teasing remark she had made one evening. He had made his mind up. Raven was his, and she was going to stay his.

She had been too young then, only seventeen, unaware of how sexual he was, of how dominant he could be. He wanted the woman he saw emerging within her, not the child she still was.

At the time, he was on leave from the Navy and knew the course he wanted his life to take. As soon as possible, he was heading for SEALs training and a military career. It would be years before he could have her. Years, he knew, before she would be mature enough to accept loving him, despite the career he had chosen. But when he had told her his plans two years later, her reaction had only reinforced his belief that she needed to mature first.

She was mature now. And stubborn. Stubborn enough that he knew, if he waited any longer, she would slip out of his grasp forever. With each year, she set herself more firmly against him, more determined that he wasn't the man for her, simply because the career he had chosen was the same one that had made her parents so miserable.

He wasn't going to let her run any longer. She was stronger than her mother whether she knew it or not. And he knew damned good and well that she loved him. Otherwise, he would have had a lover to deal with, rather than just her stubbornness. And dealing with her just might end up driving him over the edge of frustration.

His cock was throbbing and that flirty little black skirt she was wearing wasn't helping matters. It barely covered her ass, showing her long, beautiful legs to advantage, and at the same time baring her lower stomach like a feast to a starving man.

Long, golden brown hair, thick and filled with riotous curls, fell down her back, while her blue eyes watched him with wary arousal. She tried to hide it, but it was there, just as clear as the press of her tight, hard nipples against the snug, matching top.

The flush of her creamy cheeks, the soft part of her pink lips. She was a temptation he wasn't going to deny himself much longer. He had waited too long as it was. What good did it do a man to fight the endless wars, to survive the wounds and the loss of friends when there was no warmth left in his life? Only fantasies. And it was time to make the fantasies come to life.

His dream of being a SEAL, a warrior, had been fulfilled. It eased that pit of fury he felt each time he heard of the injustices that plagued the world. Now he had his biggest dream to fulfill. That of possessing Raven, heart and soul.

He was in her home. That was the first step. Undermining the enemy's defenses was best done from inside, as SEALs had proved more than once. Slipping under the wire, undetected, silently setting up the explosion to come.

And she *would* explode.

He grinned at the thought. Of making Raven so hot, so wild, she went up in flames in his arms.

Damn, he could feel his balls drawing tight against the base of his shaft, his own release begging for freedom. He had a limited amount of time to make this work. For the time being, he was on leave, but that would end the minute his team was needed. He might have a few weeks, at the most, to work with.

And if he didn't touch Raven soon, feel her lips under his, her body pressed against him, then he was going to be a candidate for the asylum.

He shifted his shoulders in an effort to relieve the tension building there. He was exhausted. He had expected to come home and rest at least one day before putting his plan into motion. Instead, he found his bed occupied, his sister in a frenzy, and the object of his obsession standing before him like the most erotic fantasy he could have imagined. Damn that skirt.

Reno was an ass man and he knew it, and Raven's ass had tempted him for years. Perfectly rounded, taut and tempting. Her breasts were his second favorite. Full, rounded globes, her nipples pressing hard against the material of her shirt.

Son of a bitch. His cock was so damned hard, he would never manage to sleep tonight. He shook his head at the arousal beating through him and Raven's obvious determination to close him out of sight. He knew his sister's best friend better than she thought. She wasn't working, no matter what she said, so he had no problems whatsoever disturbing her. He was a man on a time limit, and he wasn't given to being wasteful with his time.

Anticipation surged through him as he strode to the bedroom door and opened it quickly. The stairs were just to his side as he turned the corner and started down them. He heard her voice, lowered, a feminine hiss of fury as she talked on the phone.

"Dammit, Morganna, the man is exhausted. He has shadows under his eyes and his face is almost dead gray. What the hell were you thinking? You knew he was coming home. He told you he was coming home."

Reno stopped halfway down the stairwell, his head tilting as something melted in his heart. He actually felt the muscles of his chest, his heart, expanding then relaxing at the realization that she was ripping his sister's ass over that party.

"I don't care how pissed off you were at Clinton. That's no reason to treat Reno like that. For God's sake, he needed to sleep and you let your friends take his bed. What kind of sister are you? . . . Well you shouldn't have had the party to begin with. Smack Clinton around. Having a party is not going to get his attention, you nitwit."

Actually, it would, but Reno saw no reason to point that out.

Her brother Clint would make his move when he was ready and not a minute before. He was just as stubborn as Raven. Maybe more so.

"Get his bed replaced, Morganna. He cannot stay here. . . ."

The hell he couldn't.

"Don't give me excuses. I want zero excuses. I want a phone call in the morning saying his bed is ready for him to occupy. Period. Or I swear to God I'm going to tell Clinton all about your lurid little fantasies that you force me to listen to."

Lurid fantasies? He grimaced. He did not want to know about his baby sister's lurid fantasies. It was time to cut this conversation short.

Sighing silently, he moved down to the next step heavily, allowing her to hear him practically stomp down the stairs. When he rounded the closed-in space to the small living room, she was off the phone and staring at him with wide eyes. It was the cutest sight. Wariness and hunger reflecting in her deep blue eyes, her breasts moving hard and fast, peaked with hard little nipples as she watched him nervously.

"You're supposed to be sleeping," she snapped, a frown forming between her brows. "I hate to hurt your feelings, Reno, but you look like something the cat dragged in."

A smile tilted his lips. She made him smile, made him want to linger in the warmth she filled him with.

"I feel like something the cat dragged in." He agreed with her there. "Am I disturbing you?"

Her shoulders lifted in a defensive shrug. "Not really." She cleared her throat nervously. "I was just yelling at Morganna. Unfortunately, I think she's too used to it. She wasn't paying much attention."

"That's Morganna for you." He watched as her gaze flickered over him, touching him with curious, hungry eyes before being forced away, staring at every point in the room, except him.

Damn, he loved how shy she could be. How sweet she was. How prickly she could get. He figured he had loved Raven all her life in one form or another. But what he felt for her now consumed him. The plan he had set in motion tonight was risky, and he admitted it, he was taking a chance, but he was damned tired of waiting for her to realize how much they meant to each other.

She was watching him warily now, biting her lower lip nervously as her gaze flickered over him again.

"You're acting like I'm going to pounce on you, Raven." He moved closer to her. He wanted to touch her so damned bad, it was killing him.

Stopping in front of her, he reached out, one finger twining in a tight curl that fell across her shoulder. Her breath caught, a flush washing over her face.

"Aren't you?" she snapped. Fiery, accusing, Raven was nobody's fool. She might be stubborn, but she was smart as hell. "Every time I turn around, you're trying to grope me."

He spread his hands out innocently. "I'm just standing here talking to you, baby. If I was going to pounce, you'd be flat on your back on that couch rather than standing there deliberately provoking me. And as I recall that last kiss, you were groping right back."

It had been right after his last assignment. He had returned home a week late to find Raven sleeping on the couch, having evidently waited with Morganna until he arrived.

How was he supposed to resist her? Years of fantasies, of aching hunger, and there she was, a temptation to his body and to his heart that he couldn't ignore.

She hadn't sniped at him or tried to run from him. Sleepy, seductive, she had lifted to him, her lips opening eagerly for his kiss when he knelt beside the couch. He would have had her in his bed minutes later if Morganna hadn't interrupted them when she did. That kiss, her eagerness for him, and the soft breathy sound of her voice as she whispered her pleasure had sealed her fate. She was his woman.

She frowned darkly. He frowned right back at her.

"I am not provoking you," she informed him imperiously. "You're tired and disagreeable. And I really think you should head on to bed and go to sleep."

She wasn't running from him, but he could see the indecision in her eyes, the sweep of arousal and emotions filling her. She wasn't going to back down easily, and she wouldn't give in without a fight.

"I should be," he agreed, his voice rough. "I really should be, but this is a hell of a lot more important right now."

His head dipped down before she could move, if she intended to move. Her eyes widened, her lips parted, and he caught the gasp that escaped her throat.

Bombs exploded in his head. Fire rushed along his nervous system until it centered in his aching cock. She was ambrosia. She was the elixir of life.

His arms circled her, tight, as he restrained his need to eat her alive. His lips moved over hers, his tongue spearing deep as a shattered moan escaped her throat and her hands tightened at his waist before moving to his back.

He could taste coffee, mint, and woman and the alternating flavors exploded on his senses, going to his head like the strongest narcotic. Reno bent over her, surrounding her; he wanted to draw her into every cell of his body as her lips opened, her tongue met his, and his senses flamed. Sweet, velvet heat. The taste of her went to his head, the feel of her causing his erection to pulse and pound with a hunger barely leashed.

"Reno?" Her voice was dazed as his lips slid to her cheek, to her neck.

Her head fell back as his teeth raked her shoulder, her body becoming liquid, pliant. His. He allowed his hands to move, rather than holding her to him, roaming her back instead, pulling at the short length of the skirt until one hand could smooth over her bare buttock. *Bare? Fuck!*

His hand clenched on the curve as she trembled against him, a thin wail of pleasure escaping her throat a second before she jerked out of his arms.

"That was damned unfair." Raven stared back at him, shock and pleasure racing through her system as she fought to make sense of the impulses that still pounded through her body. He made her drunk, made her greedy for more of his kiss, his touch.

Oh God. That kiss. Her hand rose to her lips, her fingers feeling the swollen curves as her shoulder tingled from the rasp of his teeth.

Dammit, she was supposed to be denying him, not falling into his arms like a wimpy sex kitten. But it never failed; he touched her and she melted. She lost her mind, her sanity, her ability to remember the fact that Reno would never let her escape with any part of her heart intact.

He was watching her with blatant hunger. There was no apology, no attempt to hide the lust that burned in his eyes and darkened the features of his face.

"Who said I was going to be fair?" he growled, coming closer, looming over her as she backed into the entertainment center behind her. "Raven, are you wearing panties?"

Heat flooded her face, her body.

"Yes!" she gasped. "I am. Dammit, Reno, you aren't supposed to kiss me like that."

Like he was starving for the taste of her, ready to consume her at a moment's notice. How was a girl supposed to keep her sanity when a man stripped her control with no more than the touch of his lips?

"Why?" His voice was dark, incredibly deep. It vibrated in the pit of her stomach, causing her womb to spasm in need as her pussy creamed heatedly. The panties in question were going to be soaked if this didn't stop.

She breathed in deeply, striving for control as he moved closer, pressing her into the shelf of the entertainment center as she felt the length of his erection pressing into her lower belly.

"Do you know how long I've waited for you, Raven? Since you were seventeen, teasing me, tempting me to take what I couldn't have. You're not a kid anymore. You're a woman."

She couldn't handle this. How was she supposed to fight him *and* herself? Especially when she wanted him so desperately?

"Find Gina what's-her-name," she snarled back, remembering the day she had burst into his room to find him naked, preparing to take another woman.

"You were a kid. I was a man, Raven. You are not a child any longer."

She shook her head. This wasn't happening.

He was destroying her defenses. He was going to break her heart.

"You tied her down," Raven gasped. She didn't want to be tied down. She really didn't. No matter how many times she dreamed about him tying her to his bed, torturing her with his touch.

"Mmm," he murmured against her lips, his tongue stroking over them slowly. "Yes, I did. Just like I want to tie you, Raven. Stretched out on my bed, unable to do anything but feel me. Feel me now. I'm dying to touch you."

His hands slid to her buttocks as he lifted her, notching the hard length of his cock against the swollen pad of her pussy as her clit throbbed in pleasure, in need. Her hands gripped his shoulders, her nails biting into the fabric of his shirt as, helplessly, her legs parted, her thighs gripping his outer legs as his hands held her closer, his fingers massaging the flesh of her ass as she shuddered in his arms.

She couldn't get the picture out of her head. Her tied to his bed rather than Gina Delaney. Her legs spread for him, the bare folds of her cunt wet and glistening as he came to her, his cock like a living arrow preparing to impale her.

"Reno. Reno, wait. . . ." His lips were at her collarbone, his tongue stroking the sensitive skin as he thrust slowly against her, stroking her clit into full blazing life.

Every cell in her body was screaming for his touch. Her breasts were swollen, her nipples . . . God, her nipples were on fire.

"Ah, Raven," he whispered, lifting her closer, pressing deeper between her thighs as she shuddered, her thighs clenching, her hips moving against his, rubbing his shaft against her clit as she fought to breathe through the incredible sensations. "Baby, I don't know if I can let you go now."

"We have to wait." She shook her head, struggling against him and herself as she felt the hands at her rear parting her flesh, sending a heated strike of pleasure whipping through the tight, forbidden little entrance there.

"Wait for what?" he growled. "For another excuse to run? You run every time I come home, Raven. How am I supposed to seduce you when I can't even find you? Dammit, the waiting is over."

chapter 2

okay, a command, given in such a sexually rough, dominant voice should not have the juices spilling from her pussy like warm honey from a comb. But it did, and they were, even as he picked her up off her feet again and moved quickly to the couch, laying her down as he loomed over her.

His face was savagely cast, his cheekbones high and sharp, his lips full and hungry. She could feel every erogenous zone in her body perking up and taking notice of the commanding male form that had her in his grip.

"Reno, this isn't boot camp," she protested, even as she tried not to moan when he pressed her thighs part, his hands gripping her hips, holding her still as her skirt pooled inches above the decent line.

Could he see the crotch of her panties? Were they as wet as she suspected? She shuddered at the thought of him seeing the proof of her desire.

"Hell no, it's not," he growled. "Damn good thing, too, baby.

I'd have to punish you for insubordination first thing. I might any-way. . . ." His voice dropped, becoming raspier, sexier. "I could really get into spanking that pretty little ass, Raven."

No. No. No spanking. So why were the cheeks of her ass clench-ing as though it might be fun?

"Pervert," she gasped instead as his head lowered, his lips pressing over her navel as his tongue curled around the small dia-mond navel ring and tugged.

Her hips came off the couch, a high, broken cry leaving her lips as her hands gripped his head. To pull him back. Yes. Make him stop. So why the hell was she holding him closer, her fingers clench-ing in his hair as reality began to recede?

It was so fucking sexy. She had never known anything so erotic as Reno's lips on her stomach, his tongue flicking over the ring as his hands moved to grip her thighs, parting them further, sliding high.

She shuddered in his grip, her knees bending, her skirt rising above the crotch of her panties as his fingers smoothed over the flesh of her inner thighs.

"Perfect," he whispered as his lips began to move higher. "There you go, baby, just lay there and let me make you feel good. Do you know how much I've wanted to just make you feel good? Make you burn for me?"

His tongue swiped over a nipple as he neared her breast. Even through the material of her short tank top, the sensation was in-credible. Hot enough to send the blood surging through her body, her nipples hardening further as an unfamiliar burst of heat surged from her nipple to her pussy.

"Feel good?" His voice was a rough growl as she stared up at him.

His hand hooked into the stretchy fabric of her top and began to lift it.

Raven whimpered. She couldn't help it, and the helpless sound of arousal infuriated her. She heard her own hunger, her own

weakness in the sound. The complete inability to deny the whiplash of emotions and erotic pleasure that seared her senses. Her
hands gripped his wrists, but she couldn't whisper the words she
knew it would take to stop him. All she could think about was his
tongue licking over her ultrasensitive flesh, sucking her into his
mouth, stroking the intensity of pleasure higher.

"There we go, baby," he crooned as she released his wrists, allowing him to pull the material over her head and toss it aside.

God. She was practically naked in front of Reno Chavez. His
stormy gaze was eating her up, his hands trailing incredible shards
of pleasure over the sides of her breasts as he watched her with a
lust-filled expression.

"Reno . . ." She whispered his name, terrified to believe it
was actually happening, he was really here, his hands moving
quickly over the buttons of his shirt and stripping it from his
shoulders.

She reached for him. She couldn't help it. All that tanned, hard
muscle with the light arrowing of short, dark hairs was too much
to resist. She sat up, barely noticing the surprised pleasure in his
expression an instant before her breasts raked over his chest. Her
hands gripped his neck and she pulled him down to satisfy the
overwhelming need for his kiss.

Within seconds he had her flat on her back again, but she had
what she needed. His chest sliding over her nipples, his tongue
plunging into her mouth, twining with hers as her hands roved his
shoulders, her nails raking, her sensuality taking over as her greatest
fantasy began to come true.

It wasn't smart. Holding her heart back from him would be the
hardest thing she had ever done in her life. But she needed this.
She needed him. Once and for all she needed to exorcise the ghosts
of her own fantasies. She had known since she was no more than a
teenager that Reno was her greatest weakness. And now she knew
he could destroy her.

She moaned in protest as his hands pulled at her arms, bringing them from around his neck as he gripped her wrists in one hand and stretched them over her head, his eyes lifting as he watched her with narrow-eyed hunger.

"Stay." His voice was impossibly dominant as he issued the sensual order. "Keep your arms up, your hands right there. Don't make me tie them, Raven." Then he smiled, a slow, intensely erotic curve of his lips that had her fighting to breathe. "Or is that what you want?"

To be tied up? Hell no! But she couldn't get the thought out of her head. As she clenched her hands, keeping her arms in place, she could almost feel the restraints holding her, sending her imagination flying until she felt him move.

"Oh God. Reno . . ." His fingers released the little purse at her side, then slid the zipper of her skirt down.

"I want you naked, Raven," he told her firmly. "If you intend to say no, baby, you better do it now."

No. No. No. No. Her head was screaming the word, but it wouldn't come to her lips. Instead, she gripped the armrest of the couch, shuddering as he eased the skirt over her thighs, moving away from her to strip the material completely off her body.

"Sweet mercy," he whispered as he stood by the couch, staring down at her.

Raven knew the point of no return had already been reached. There was no turning back now and she knew it. She didn't want to turn back.

She watched, breathing harshly as he toed his sneakers off, and his hands went to the waistband of his jeans. As though in slow motion, she watched: the metal buttons were flicked open and the jeans parting, revealing the dark material of his snug boxer briefs.

Seconds later, hooking his fingers in the waistband of the briefs, he peeled off both jeans and underwear; the thick length of his erection, the purplish head bulging, heavy veins straining against satiny flesh, was free.

"I want to touch you," she whispered, her gaze locked on his cock. "Please, Reno. I need to touch you." Her mouth watered with that need.

"Later, baby," he groaned. "If you touch me now, I'll lose it."

He knelt on the floor then, spreading her legs until one rested on the floor, the other, knee bent, still on the cushions of the couch. Leaning forward, his tongue flicked out to lick over her nipple before drawing it into the incredible heat of his mouth.

"Reno. Oh God. Reno. It's so good. . . ." She writhed beneath him, unable to keep from watching, her eyes locked on his lips as he drew her nipple into his mouth. His tongue rasped it as he sucked it deep, sending sharp fingers of lightning-hot sensation rushing straight to her cunt.

It was incredible. Unlike anything she had known before. Anything she could have imagined.

He growled, the sound vibrating through her, throbbing through her clit and causing her hips to arch with an involuntary violence.

"Easy, baby," he whispered, kissing his way to the other mound, his tongue licking over the tip before he drew it in as well.

"So good," she whimpered. "Reno, I don't know if I can stand it."

She was arching to him, trying to press her flesh deeper into his mouth, willing to beg if that was what it took as she watched him tug at the peak, his cheeks working rhythmically with his tongue to make her crazy.

"You can stand it, baby." His voice was deeper, more sexual, as his lips began to drift down her stomach. "I've dreamed of eating you like candy."

He was going to kill her. She was certain of it. She stared at him, dazed, out of her mind with the sensations spearing through her like wicked fingers of fire as his lips trailed to the elastic band of her minuscule thong.

"So pretty," he whispered as his head lifted, his hands moving to her inner thighs, spreading her legs further as his lips smoothed over the crease between her leg and the heated flesh of her cunt. "So sweet and hot."

"Oh sweet God . . . Reno . . ." His lips capped over the hot mound, covered by the silk of her panties, as his tongue pressed against the tortured nub of her clit.

She tried to close her legs, to clench against his head, to hold him in place while she rubbed against him and rocketed through space. His brief chuckle was her warning that he wasn't going to allow that. His hands tightened on her legs, holding them in place as his tongue prodded at the tormented, nerve-ridden flesh.

"Reno, really. I swear. I don't think I can take it," she cried out desperately. "I've waited too long. Fuck me now."

He jerked up as he stared back at her, his eyes nearly black as his gaze clashed with hers. The groan that tore from his throat was tormented as his hands ripped the panties from her and he moved quickly over her.

She felt the broad head of his cock part the swollen folds waiting below. She was slick, incredibly wet, as he pushed against the hungry opening of her vagina.

"Damn, you're hot," he whispered as he lifted her legs, bringing them to his hips, holding her still as he pressed closer, grimacing as the crest penetrated the snug opening.

"Now, Reno," she begged shamelessly, her nails digging into the couch as she strained closer. "Please. Now."

A throttled groan left his chest as he surged inside her, hard and deep, forcing his way past unused muscles, as the fierce, thick length of his cock impaled the tight sheath.

Raven's eyes widened as a shocked cry of pain left her lips. She struggled beneath him, her hips writhing as her hands flew to his chest, pressing against him as she fought to adjust to the fiery, involuntary stretching of her vagina.

"Fuck!" He stared down at her in shock, his hands at her hips, flexing, gripping her tight as his erection throbbed almost violently inside her.

"Reno." She tried to smile as she forced herself to relax. She had read about this. It was supposed to hurt the first time. She knew it would hurt the first time. Everyone said it would. She had to relax.

She felt her pussy ripple around him as she concentrated on the muscles there, forcing herself not to clench tighter around him, but to allow the flesh to accommodate him, to clasp him snugly rather than fighting against the penetration.

"You should have told me." He was panting above her, the struggle for control obvious on his face. "Dammit, Raven, you weren't supposed to be a virgin."

Her eyes narrowed. She could feel the pleasure building now, the tension gathering in her clit, in her womb, the release that had tormented her since his first touch.

"And you're not supposed to be an asshole, but you are," she gasped. "Now finish it, dammit."

She flexed around him, moaning at the incredible sensation, the snug fit, the feel of him inside her, a heavy thick weight pressing against delicate, sensitive nerve endings.

A strangled scream left her throat as he began to move. The short, incredibly firm strokes made her crazy. She couldn't stand it. She strained against him, her hips meeting his as she fought for breath.

He was being careful. Dammit, she didn't need him to be careful. This was her first time, her first real climax, her first everything. She wanted it all.

"Harder," she panted, twisting against him as her fingers gripped his shoulders. "Do it harder."

"I don't want to hurt you, Raven." His voice was more an animal growl than a groan. "Dammit, wait."

"No." Her head thrashed against the cushions. "Harder, Reno. Fuck me. Fuck me like we both need it. Do it now."

As though her words triggered the desired response, he moved over her, bracing one elbow at her head, tucking the other beneath her rear to lift her to him as he nearly pulled free.

The hard stroke of his cock over the tender nerve endings had her arching closer, eager for more, a second before his control disintegrated.

Raven held on to Reno as he began to ride her hard and deep. She was shocked at her own cries, primitive, desperate—but even more shocking was the pleasure ripping through her.

The pressure building in her clit as his pelvis stroked against it was almost painful. His hips lunged against hers, driving his erection to the hilt inside her over and over again as she felt her mind begin to unravel. She couldn't survive it, surely no one could take such pleasure and ever be the same again.

The sensation built in her womb, her clit, the overfilled recess of her pussy as she felt the muscles there tightening, the tension coiling. . . .

"Raven." His head lifted, his gaze spearing hers as her eyes drifted open. She was so close. So close. "Are you protected?"

The words barely registered; the meaning was lost to her.

"What?" she gasped. She needed more. She tightened further as his cock surged inside her with a rhythm that left her fighting just to hold on to her sanity.

"Protected, Raven," he groaned, his hand tightening in her hair as he forced her attention to him. "The pill. Goddamn, anything. Are you protected?"

Protected. The pill. Thank God her doctor had prescribed them to regulate her monthly cycles. "Yes . . . ," she wailed as the pleasure began to clash and career inside her. "The pill. Yes. Oh God, Reno, harder. Harder . . ."

He gave it to her harder. Bracing his knees on the couch, the hand at her hip clenching with bruising strength, he gave her what she needed.

"Fuck. Come for me, Raven. Come now, baby. . . ."

There was no need for the harsh command. She was holding onto the edge, desperate to fly to the center of the shocking heat consuming her. She didn't come. She didn't release. She dissolved. She fragmented. She exploded. She lost herself as the pleasure became a white-hot conflagration that ripped through her soul and sent her flying to space and beyond.

She was only distantly aware of him looming over her, driving harder, deeper, as a new, surging flood of heat inside her sent her higher. All she knew was perfection. Merging. A complete, terrifying release that kept her floating as the pleasure slowly receded, leaving her limp and wasted beneath him. And certain that nothing would, or could, ever be the same again.

chapter 3

it was one o'clock in the morning, there wasn't a chance in hell Morganna was conscious enough to even answer the phone, let alone understand Raven's bitching. And the man slowly easing from her body looked like a sated demigod as he sat on the couch at her feet.

Uncomfortably aware of her nudity, Raven hauled the thin blanket from the back of the couch as she sat up herself, pulling it around her almost desperately. She could feel his eyes on her, watching her with that eaglelike glare of his.

"You should have told me." He sighed then, running his hands over his hair as he breathed out roughly. "You weren't supposed to be a virgin, Raven."

She turned and gaped at him in disbelief, nearly speechless at his comment and the irritable tone of his voice.

"Well, excuse me, Mr. Experience," she snapped in reply. "What does my being a virgin have to do with anything anyway? What was I supposed to do, excuse myself and go get fucked by someone else before you had your turn?"

He grimaced before turning his head to look at her. And she really wished he wouldn't look at her that way. All satisfied and sated and considering another round.

"I wouldn't try it now if I were you," he grunted, reaching out to touch her hair as she pulled back from him. "I wouldn't be happy."

"And your happiness matters, of course." She rolled her eyes at that.

She ached in places she had never known existed. A deep, pleasant ache. She wanted to curl up on the couch and sleep for a week, to relish the bone-deep feeling of completion that she couldn't extinguish. Damn him, he should come with a warning sign.

He didn't answer, merely watched her. And that was more nerve-racking than the sound of his voice. He could always do that to her. Look at her as though he saw into her soul, or he was a part of her soul. She shivered at the thought.

"I'm going to bed." She pushed herself to her feet, wondering if she could actually walk now. "God, I must have been insane."

She wavered as she stood, forcing her legs to steady, wishing she could force the ache building in her chest to go away as easily as she made her legs obey her. Holding the blanket to her tightly, she made it the first step.

"I don't think so." He stood up, placing himself in front of her, giving her an up-close view of that gorgeous chest as he did so.

She could feel their combined juices easing from her pussy now, dampening her thighs, reminding her of the pleasure of moments before. That memory sent a shiver racing down her spine and a coil of heat building in the pit of her stomach again.

His hands gripped her upper arms, his fingers caressing her sensitive skin as she lifted her gaze to his.

"Reno." She swallowed tightly. "We need to think about this. I need to think about it."

She couldn't deal with him now, she had to make sense of this, she had to find her bearings. This was Reno, for God's sake. She had known him all her life, lusted after him since she was fifteen and shed tears for him while he was on assignment. This was the only man who could break her heart, who could destroy her soul.

He snorted in reply to her desperate words.

"Yeah, like I'm going to give you a chance to come up with excuses to run from me."

The world spun around her as he lifted her into his arms, turned, and headed for the staircase. She clutched his shoulders, fighting to force back the melting sensation in the center of her chest. He was carrying her, with little or no effort. Taking the stairs quickly and moving into her bedroom.

"I'll help you shower."

"I don't need any help showering." The panicked sound of her own voice shocked her.

He moved into the bathroom. "Then I want to sleep with you, Raven. Just sleep. I want to hold you close and feel you breathing against me." He set her on her feet, his hands cupping her face, lifting it until he could stare down at her intently. "I'm not going to let you go tonight."

She shivered. She tried not to, but she couldn't help it. She had known he was bossy, dominant, a man who knew what he wanted and how to get it. She just hadn't expected that phenomenal will of his to turn on her in quite this manner.

"You forget, I've run for a reason." Her hands gripped his wrists as she stared up at him.

"We'll break each other's hearts, Reno."

She could see the exhaustion marking his face, clearer now than it had been before. A haunting hunger filled his gaze, and Raven knew in the bottom of her soul that she wasn't going to deny him. For now . . . for this moment . . . he needed her. Surely, for the short amount of time he would be here, she could protect her heart. Couldn't she?

"This is a good idea, Raven." He lowered his head, his lips whispering over hers. The kiss was soothing, calming. Emotions raged just beneath it, subtle, but intense. Emotions she refused to delve into.

"One of these days, your bossiness is going to get you into trouble," she warned him as he pulled back, a small smile playing about his passion-swollen lips as he moved away from her to adjust the water in the shower.

She could do it. She took a deep, fortifying breath. It was too late to turn back now, anyway. She could have tonight, enjoy his touch, his laughter, the qualities that made him so very unique to her. And when he left, she could let him go without the tears or the rage or the fear. She was strong enough. She didn't have to love him.

"Come on, baby." He stepped into the shower, his hand catching her wrist as he pulled her in after him.

"Do you ever ask for anything?" she asked as he sheltered her from the spray and began soaping a washrag.

His smile flashed, filled with amusement and warmth.

"When I have to."

Raven frowned at that.

"All of you macho SEAL-types are so damned bossy. Reminds me why I steered clear of them."

Her brother Clint was a SEAL; most of her friends' brothers were in one part of the armed forces or another. They were all bossy, domineering men who forged their own paths, whether in life or in love. They left, and sometimes they never returned.

"You weren't steering clear of me, Raven," he told her then, his hands incredibly gentle as he pressed the washcloth to her chest and began to wash her. "I just let you think you were."

She snorted mockingly. She would argue, but that washcloth felt so good, rasping over her flesh, washing away her thoughts as easily as it did the sweat from her body.

She tilted her head back, allowing him to have his way. She had fantasized about this too much, and unfortunately, he was better than the dreams had ever been.

"You should be falling on your feet," she whispered, the sound of her voice punctuated with a gasp as the cloth moved between her thighs, cleaning her slowly.

"Maybe," he growled, "I should rest."

He knelt in front of her, spreading her legs as he lifted one, propping it on the small shelf at the side as the washrag moved over the bare flesh of her pussy.

"Damn, Raven. Do you know how pretty you are? Silky and soft, and so responsive to my touch." He shifted, allowing the spray to rinse her as he dropped the cloth, using his hands to help dispel the suds there.

Arousal built within her quickly. She knew what he was going to do and she didn't know if she could bear it.

His fingers moved over the narrow slit, parting her swollen flesh as she fought to get her bearings, to breathe. If she could just breathe, she could maintain her control.

"I've dreamed of tasting you . . ."

Oh God.

"Fucking you with my tongue, sucking that pretty little clit into my mouth . . ."

She felt her juices gathering, weeping with sensual abandon from her sensitive cunt as her head rolled against the wall of the shower. The explicit, diabolical words made her weak, made her long for him to do it with every fiber of her being.

Her hands braced against the wall and the shower door. She couldn't touch him. If she touched him, she would beg, plead for him.

"Reno . . ." Her thin wail filled the shower stall as his tongue swiped through the slit, circled her clit, then disappeared.

Her eyes drifted open as she stared down at him, her legs weakening at the erotic sight of him kneeling before her, his tongue moving in again, circling her clit as he stared up at her.

Not fair. Oh God. She couldn't stand it.

Her hands moved involuntarily, her fingers digging into his scalp as she parted her legs further, pressing him closer.

"More . . . ," she panted. "Lick me more."

He hummed in approval, his tongue dancing in the slick cream that began to coat her as her hips tilted further.

"Oh yes," she moaned. "Like that, Reno. Lick me all over."

She was trembling, watching him, feeling his tongue circle her clit, lick along the narrow valley, circling the sensitive opening of her vagina, teasing her with the threat of a sensual thrust into the suddenly hungry depths. His hands were at her buttocks, spreading them open, sending chills racing up her back at the flare of heat that invaded the tiny entrance there. The sensations were building, pulling at her, ripping away the veil of distance she tried to maintain as he teased her with his tongue.

"Reno, do it," she whispered desperately as his fingers slid lower, parting the folds of her pussy as his tongue teased and tempted. "Please. Please do it."

"What, baby?" he whispered wickedly. "Tell me. Whatever you want, I'll give you."

Her eyes fluttered; her knees weakened. His tongue stroked, taunted, yet never gave her what she knew would throw her over the edge. She wanted it inside her. She wanted to feel his tongue shoving hard inside the snug depths of her pussy as she watched him. Watched him eating her like he loved it, lived for it.

"Do it," she cried out fiercely. "Dammit, Reno, stop teasing me. Please."

He flickered over the opening, licking at the juices falling from her as she shuddered at the pleasure. So much pleasure.

"Fuck me with it." She thrust her hips closer, her hands pressing against his head, her gasping moans turning to a shattered scream when he did as she begged. His tongue plunged deep, filling her, pumping inside her as her orgasm took her by surprise, hurtling her into a rapture she could only give herself to.

"Son of a bitch!" He was on his feet, lifting her, bracing her against the wall a second before he wrapped her legs around his hips and plunged deep inside her.

Shocking. Burning. He filled her to overflowing and then made her take more. Delicate tissue parted, clenched, hugging him heatedly as he began to move, sending her flying again, ripping away, layer by layer, the shields around her soul.

"Ah God, Raven baby . . . so tight . . . so hot . . . hold me, baby. Hold me and mean it."

She couldn't do anything less. She held on to him as though her life, her very heart, depended on it. And in a way, she knew it did. He was filling her soul, the one thing she had sworn she would never allow to happen, was happening.

Her legs wrapped around his waist, tightening, her arms around his neck locking in place, her lips searching blindly for his as she convulsed again, jerking in his grip, trying to drive him deeper, harder, as the world rocked around her in a release that seemed never-ending.

Reno pumped inside her, hard and fast before his groan filled her senses and the heat of his release filled the hungry depths of her pussy. She milked him, moaning in exhaustion as the tremors of release shuddered through her again, leaving her limp, ragged in his hold as his arms tightened around her.

Moments later, she was only distantly aware of him pulling free of her, cleaning her again, then himself, before he shut the water off and dried them with quick, economical movements.

A smile curved her lips though, as he picked her up in his arms and carried her to her bed. Curling against his chest, his hands buried in her hair as his arms surrounded her, sleep overtook her. Warm, sheltered, free of the teasingly erotic dreams that used to haunt her, she slept in her warrior's arms.

Reno stared into the darkness of the bedroom, Raven's warmth tucked close to his heart as he sheltered her against his chest. She slept naturally, easily. Not that he expected the battle to be over by any means.

A sleepy smile quirked his lips. He'd better rest tonight, because he had a feeling that come morning, she would be just as prickly as ever. Not that he intended to let it do her any good. He was a part of her, whether she wanted to admit it or not. Just as she was a part of him.

And being a part of Raven was like being reborn. Never had he known anything as sweet, as hot, as soul-fulfilling as being her lover.

He had warned her, the night Morganna had interrupted them, that her days were numbered. He wasn't waiting any longer to claim what he had known for years was his.

She shifted against his side, a murmur of pleasure leaving her throat as his hands rubbed lightly down her back, and she settled against him once again.

"I love you, Raven." He whispered the words he knew she didn't want to hear. Gave them to her while she slept, knowing that, for now, it was the only way she would accept them.

"Reno . . ." His name as it left her lips filled him with pleasure. Even sleeping, she knew where she belonged.

chapter 4

she had slept with Reno Chavez.

She hadn't just slept with him, she had been taken by him. Held by him. Fucked senseless, to be honest, she snapped silently.

Raven leaned on the kitchen counter the next morning, her head cradled in her arms as she waited for the coffee to finish, for the rich fragrance teasing her senses to become an elixir that would hopefully clear her head. Bring her sanity back. It would be really nice if it could turn back time.

She moaned pitifully.

She couldn't even claim she'd been drunk; she hadn't so much as touched a beer while at Morganna's. She had been stone-cold sober until Reno kissed her. Until his hands stroked her body, bringing her nerve endings to life and a ravenous hunger clawing at her womb.

She pressed her thighs together at the memory, hating the feel of her loose shorts rasping against her flesh. She wanted Reno's hands. Even the loose shirt was uncomfortable on her sensitive body. She could strip it off. She could undress, go to him. . . . She gritted her teeth in mental refusal.

She was not going to think about it. She was not going to relive each and every slow slide of his cock inside her vagina, stroking the pulsing nerves there, stretching her, filling her, making her burn. . . .

Her fists clenched as she rolled her forehead against her arm.

She couldn't have made a bigger mistake if she had actually put effort into coming up with one. Sleeping with Reno was tantamount to jumping from a plane without a parachute. It wasn't just risky; it was suicide to her emotional well-being.

He had been hardheaded as a boy, bossy as a young man, and now he was so firmly dominant, it was enough to make her teeth clench. What happened to the nice young man who put Band-Aids on her knees and bought her ice pops from the corner store? Why did he have to become the big tough SEAL who insisted on a career that risked his life every time he went to work?

"Dumb. Dumb. Dumb," she muttered as she lifted her head, staring at the slow stream of black liquid that ran into the carafe.

"When are you going to break down and buy a real coffee-maker?"

She stiffened at Reno's amused voice, refusing to turn and face him, to stare at that incredibly sexy body. The same one that had risen over her last night, pushing between her thighs as he filled her with the hard, broad flesh of his cock. She shivered at the memory.

"This one works," she mumbled. And it had been her mother's before she died five years before.

There was no way she was going to consider facing the day without coffee. She needed it. It was essential. Otherwise, she was going to melt into a puddle of aroused goo before she ever managed to push Reno out the door.

He grunted noncommittally behind her.

"We'll get a coffee grinder later and some fresh beans. I'll make you some real coffee."

Turning her head slowly from the shelter of her arms, she stared back at him. Over six feet of lean, smooth, hard muscle. Damn him. He wasn't wearing a shirt. His chest, with its smattering of hair, was displayed in all its dark glory, muscles shifting, tempting, encouraging. . . .

"Don't you have a bed to buy or something?" She straightened quickly, jerked a cup from the hook on the wall, and prayed the dark brew would hurry. She had to clear her head, or she was never going to make it through the day.

"Are you trying to run me off, Raven?" She could hear the grin in his voice, see it when she glanced back at him.

"Yes," she snapped desperately. "I am. I can't deal with you this morning. Go torture Morganna."

Like she thought for a minute that he was going to do that. She should have known better, she told herself frantically. He had warned her that last time, when he woke her with a kiss, looming over her like a tide of passion, that her days were numbered. She had tried to convince herself he wasn't serious. She should have known better.

"I don't think so, baby. Do you think I'm going to let you run me off this soon?"

Uh-oh.

She blinked back at him as his expression hardened, his gray eyes turning stormy. She knew that look, and it did not bode well for getting rid of him.

"How soon, then?" She slammed the cup to the counter and jerked the pot from under the small stream inching into it to rapidly fill the cup.

She brought the cup to her lips and sipped too quickly. The hot liquid burned her tongue, but it did nothing to erase the remembered feel of his touch.

"Damn, Clint was right, you're a grouch in the morning," he stated as he moved to the pot himself, causing her to back away quickly. If he touched her, she was a goner.

"I'm always a grouch." She frowned as he poured himself a cup of coffee. "And that's my coffee."

He lifted his brow mockingly. "I know a cure for your grouchiness."

The wicked smile playing about his mouth had her womb convulsing in arousal. Damn him. Damn him. She could feel her body preparing for him, aching for him. Even more frightening was the fact that it felt right. His presence in her kitchen wasn't as upsetting as it should have been. It felt comfortable, impossibly natural. She hated having people around her first thing in the morning, but Reno was different. Which meant he had to go.

"As soon as I finish my coffee, I'm throwing you out." There was just no other answer.

She moved to the table, cradling the cup lovingly as she inhaled the scent. Sanity resided there surely.

"You'll have to grow quite a bit first, darlin'." He wasn't amused; he wasn't smiling. He was staring at her from determined, intense eyes.

"And don't call me darlin'."

He leaned against the counter, his bare ankles crossing as she glanced at his feet. Dammit, even his toes looked sexy.

She sipped the coffee, remaining silent. There had to be a way to get him out of her apartment, short of calling the police. And what was she supposed to tell the police? Excuse me, Officer, but I let him fuck me last night, so of course he thinks he has rights now.

She rolled her eyes at the thought. Of course he thought he did. She knew Reno. There wasn't a chance in hell he had even considered a one-night stand. He was her brother's best friend. Her best friend's brother. He was playing in earnest.

Panic flared at the thought of that. *Oh hell.* She looked up at him wildly, taking in the small grin quirking his lips and the way he watched her. As if she were his.

"It was just sex."

He laughed. Asshole. He sipped his coffee and grimaced.

"I'm definitely going to have to show you the fine art of preparing coffee," he drawled. "This stuff isn't going to help your attitude at all, Raven."

"My attitude is not the problem. You are," she informed him through gritted teeth.

"I invited you over to sleep. Not come in and take over," she said, feeling desperate as she got up from the table. "You weren't supposed to . . . to—" Her face flamed. "—do what you did."

"What did I do?" His eyes widened, almost innocently. She could see the knowledge glowing there, even as the sweatpants he wore began to tent in the front from his erection.

She swallowed tightly at the sight of it. Her mouth was watering. Oh God, why was her mouth watering? Why were images of going to her knees and pulling the waistband clear of that thick flesh suddenly torturing her? And her mouth was watering. Weak, Raven, she accused herself firmly. You are so weak.

"That," she said, her hand waving toward the erection. "That's what you did last night. You seduced me."

"Seduced you?" He was clearly laughing now as he glanced down at the tented material. "With my cock? That was seduction? Baby, all I did was kiss you. You kissed back."

"Well that was enough," she sniffed. "Now it's time for you to get dressed and leave."

He set his cup down on the counter, his eyes narrowing, and trepidation skated down her spine. She knew Reno. Knew his looks, his moods, and his stubbornness. She knew when he was about to do something he knew was going to piss her off. And he had that look now.

"Come here." His voice was deep and rich like black velvet.

"What?" she said, staring at him warily.

"I said, come here," he growled. Raven shivered in reaction. Her pussy was gushing at the sound of his voice. She was so easy.

"No." She crossed her arms over her breasts, hoping to hide the telltale rise of her nipples. Damn, they ached for his touch, his mouth, his tongue flickering over them.

His brow arched.

"You know," he said conversationally. "I'm dying to watch the bare flesh of that pretty little ass turn red. Get over here, Raven, or I'm going to see just how fast my hand can make it blush."

Reno watched as Raven's eyes flared, the blue darkening, filling with arousal and heat as she stared at him with wild-eyed panic. He wanted to chuckle, but he had a feeling it would push her further into retreat. As though he was going to allow that.

He mentally shook his head, watching her trying to rebuild her defenses to keep him out.

Poor Raven. It didn't matter.

Nothing was going to diminish the heat and the hunger between them.

"You did not just threaten to spank me," she suddenly snapped, blinking in amazement as she watched him.

"Yes, I did," he said, refuting her statement blandly. "Now come here." He pointed his finger directly in front of his feet.

Anger sizzled in the air. Pure feminine fury heated the room as her arms dropped slowly to her sides and her cheeks flushed with emotion.

"How dare you order me around!" She was seconds from stamping her foot. Damn, she made him hot when she flamed like that. "This is my house, Reno," she said, pointing at her chest, her own eyes narrowing. "My kitchen, my house, and you're leaving."

Reno studied her before quickly coming to a decision. She was trembling with anger . . . and panic. He didn't want to push so hard and fast that he lost her. So he'd leave, but he wouldn't be gone for long. He'd give her a bit of time to miss him, but he would be back. Besides, there wasn't a chance he could stay away long, not after having had her, feeling the heat of her pussy gripping his cock, the sweet tight muscles rippling around him as she came, holding her satisfied body next to his afterward.

He straightened, watching her closely. She stiffened, her foot moving back as though to retreat before she quickly checked the motion.

"Raven, come here," he said more gently.

If possible, her eyes widened even more in panic at his softer tone.

He was very well aware of the risk he was taking. Convincing Raven to open her heart was fraught with danger. Not the physical kind, but the emotional kind. She had seen the result of her mother's life with her Navy SEAL father. The long absences, the fights when he returned home, her mother's inability to accept the danger her father faced and her father's refusal to deal with the situation in any way except to take more missions, to stay away longer, until finally he hadn't returned. He had been killed while on a mission, leaving her mother to deal with her guilt, and Raven to face the world without a father.

Her lips tightened defiantly before she stalked over to him.

"Now what?" she snarled up at him.

"This."

He lowered his head. He didn't touch her except with his lips. He gripped the counter behind him with both hands, itching to grip her instead. No force, no demand, nothing but the arousal whipping between them, making him crazy, making her hot enough to sear.

Her lips opened on a strangled gasp, her hands reaching for his waist, her fingers curling against his flesh as his tongue surged deep inside. Slanting his head, he pressed closer, groaning when his erection cushioned against her stomach as she rubbed against him, a whimper of lust escaping her throat as he nipped at her lips, stroked them with his tongue, then delved inside for the sweet nectar of her passion.

When she was soft, pliant, molded to his body as her tongue tangled with his, he slowly drew back.

"Reno . . ."

Her soft gasp of protest had him gritting his teeth as he fought every instinct inside him screaming to take her to the floor, to convince her, to force her to admit what she was so obviously denying.

Instead, he drew in a hard breath and stepped away from the temptation of her sweet body. God, she had no idea how hard it was to step away from her, to leave her as aching as he ached for her. But he couldn't, wouldn't risk losing her. If he carried through now, took her to her bed as he wanted to so desperately, then it would weaken not just his resolve, but the inroads he had made into making her realize what they could be to each other.

"Now I'll go." He turned and walked out of the kitchen. "I'll see you in the morning, Raven. I'll bring the coffee."

chapter 5

raven stomped around the house for hours, cleaning what didn't need cleaning, cursing men, their arrogance, and their damned alpha, dominant, gung-ho, hero complexes. She had cursed both Reno and her brother Clint for years for the very things that made them so special. They were warriors, determined to protect, to make a difference. And they did make a difference. But he was still being arrogant. Relationships weren't war zones.

"There is no relationship, dammit," she muttered furiously, stepping out of the shower and drying off quickly before fluffing her hair.

She was not going to sit around tonight and wait for him. She had waited for him too many nights, pacing the floor with Morganna, chewing her fingernails if they knew he was on a mission, shedding tears when he was later returning home than he had told his sister he would be. She and Morganna both waited for that black government car that would bring the horrifying news of a death.

Now, she was supposed to sit around the damned house and torture herself over feelings and emotions she knew she was never going to be rid of.

She loved him.

Dammit, she did love him but that didn't mean she had to like it.

She jerked the red silk and lace thong panties and bra from her drawer and pulled them on, knowing they looked good on her. Sexy and hot. They made her feel wicked and wild. Almost as wicked and wild as Reno made her feel.

Biting her lip, her hands moved slowly, cupping her swollen breasts as her thumbs rasped over her distended nipples. She closed her eyes and could almost feel him touching her, making the heated burn ignite fiercely in the depths of her womb.

He wasn't supposed to do this to her. Make her miss him so desperately, make her wish she could accept as easily as he did. But he wasn't the one who would be left to pace the floors, to fill with anger. And that was the part that terrified her. She didn't want to be like her mother, always angry or depressed, terrified when she heard the sound of a vehicle coming up the drive.

Reno and Morganna's parents had died six years before in a car accident. Together. There had been no government condolences, no questions were ever answered regarding how they died. Where they died. The questions Raven's mother had asked every day until her death.

She plucked the sexy little black dress she loved so much out of her closet as the past ate at her soul with a hollow ache. The dress fell halfway down her thighs, the thin straps barely covering the bra straps as the bodice draped over her breasts. The shimmery black silk felt good on her, looked good on her.

She paired it with the high-heeled, black strappy sandals and drew in a deep breath before shoving keys, cash, and ID into a minuscule purse and heading downstairs.

She wasn't married. She didn't have to sit at home and pace the floors and she damned sure didn't have to worry about Reno Chavez or his perceptions and arrogance. Let him sit and brood if he wanted to. She was going to play.

She was bored out of her ever-loving mind, but she wasn't going to admit it to Morganna, who had joined her on her little evening adventure.

"Reno's going to be pissed" was Morganna's only objection to the night's activities as they walked into the small club, the pulse of the music surrounding them, the smoky atmosphere dim and not nearly as appealing as Raven tried to pretend it was.

"He'll live," she snapped. "Your brother is entirely too dominant, Morganna. And I'm still pissed at you for letting your friends use his bed."

"Of course he's dominant," Morganna laughed as they made their way through the crowd to the back of the club and a lone empty table. "He wouldn't do what he does if he wasn't. Admit it, Raven, it's one of the things you love about him."

It was one of the things that terrified her about him.

"No, that's what you love about Clint." She took her chair and looked around impatiently for the waitress. "I like my men a little safer. You know, Morg, the 'stay at home and hearth' type of guy?"

She waved the waitress over, impatient to get on with forgetting about Reno and his arrogant my-way-or-no-way attitude.

"You like fooling yourself is what you like," Morganna laughed after they gave the waitress their drink orders. "But you go right ahead. I like watching Reno in action. He's smooth. Clint should take lessons."

Raven directed a dark look at her friend.

"Drop the subject. I'm here to have a good time, not to talk about Reno."

She danced with the first man who asked, not the up close, slow and sway, but a fast hard beat that filled her veins and allowed her to ignore the memories threatening to overwhelm her senses.

She sat out the slower dances, a rare occurrence for her, which only made her angrier. But she couldn't stand the thought of another man holding her, not yet. God, how pathetic was that, she wondered as she moved to the hard beat echoing through the club.

She swayed in time to songs, her hair flowing down her back, caressing her upper shoulders, reminding her of Reno's touch. She closed her eyes and saw his face, only to snap them open and glare at her present partner.

She glanced across the room and her heart shuddered in her chest as she swore she caught a glimpse of him moving through the crowd. No one could move like Reno, with a male predatory grace that drew the eye and had women panting to rub against him like cats.

Shaking her head, she pushed the suspicion away.

She didn't know why she was letting this affect her so drastically. The physical attraction had bloomed between them for years now. She had known that she would eventually end up beneath Reno in bed; she just hadn't expected the raw power of it.

She moved back as the rawboned, broad young man she was dancing with reached out to clasp her hip, flashing him an irritated frown when he pouted back at her. She wasn't in the mood to be groped. She wanted to dance, expend the energy pulsing in her body, and forget about the one man she knew would be cemented in her brain forever now.

As the band paused, preparing to strike up another number, a hard hand suddenly gripped her wrist, pulling her around as she gasped in surprise.

Oh hell. Reno was pissed.

She stared up at him, aware of the immediate hardening of her nipples and their ultrasensitivity against the lace of her bra. Between her thighs, her clit began to throb with the same furious, hard beat of her heart.

"Well, fancy seeing you here," she yelled out above the music as he began to drag her across the dance floor. "Let me guess, Morganna called you."

"Morganna shows good sense at the oddest moments." His head turned, eyes narrowed on her as he began to pull her out of the crowd. He stalked across the room, heading for the shadowed corner of her table. Rather than being pushed into one of the chairs there, she found herself flattened against the wall as his head lowered, his lips at her ear.

"What are you doing here?" She stared up at him defiantly. "I don't remember inviting you."

"No, you were too damned busy running away from me," he snapped.

She should have told him then and there she didn't want him, didn't need him, but the words wouldn't come out of her mouth.

"Jealous, Reno?" She was breathing harder, her nipples pebbled and pressed tight against her dress.

"Not jealous at all," he assured her tightly. "You wouldn't let another man touch you, would you, Raven? You know who that sweet little body belongs to, don't you?"

"Yeah." She smiled slowly, aware of the drowsy passion that reflected in her expression. "Me."

He nipped her ear firmly, sending shudders racing through her. "I'm going to paddle your ass for that one."

"Oh, spank me." She gave a mock shiver, her voice sarcastic despite the tremors of trepidation skittering up her spine.

She gave a startled jerk as he imprisoned both wrists in one hand, holding them above her head as the other moved to the back of her thigh, running up the skirt of the dress to cup one rounded cheek of her ass firmly.

The feel of his hand, callused and warm, had her breath catching in her throat. The implied threat in the action should have pissed her off, at the very least should have made her more nervous than aroused.

"Oh baby, I *will* spank you." To prove his point, his hand moved back before delivering a light, warming tap to her flesh. "You have no idea how well I'm going to spank that pretty little ass. If you wanted to play the vixen, sweetheart, then you knew where I was. You could have come to me."

Her head fell back against the wall as his fingers slid beneath the edge of her panties and trailed down the narrow crevice separating her buttocks.

"I wanted to forget about you, not run to you," she snapped breathlessly, fighting herself and the weakness that struck her knees as his fingers probed ever closer to the slick curves of her cunt.

She could feel her flesh heating further, the thick juices coating her pussy, preparing her for him as her mind filled with the erotic images of the night before. Reno coming over her, parting her thighs as he slid between them.

Her breath hitched in her throat as her vagina spasmed in greedy hunger.

"We're going to discuss that one as well, darlin'," he growled at her ear, pressing his hips against her lower stomach, letting her feel the thick erection behind the fly of his jeans. "We're going to discuss all your little bad habits, in depth." Two fingers plunged inside the weeping entrance of her cleft, stretching her sensitive flesh as he pushed her to the edge of climax.

The music surrounded them, the awareness that anyone could be watching. Not that they would see much the way Reno had positioned her.

"Reno . . ." Her gasping wail was low, a throttled cry of need as his lips slid to her throat, his teeth raking as he took gentle nips, then soothed the little fire with the warmth of his lips and tongue.

"Damn you, Raven." His voice was rough, the edge of control apparent in the husky baritone. "You're pushing me too far, baby. Only you would refuse to settle back and see where the hell this could go. Why do you want to push me?"

He thrust his fingers in her weeping pussy, holding her on the edge of sanity as she fought to keep from screaming out her demand that he take her. There and then.

"I'm not pushing you," she gasped. "You keep pushing. . . . Ah God, Reno." She had to bite her lip to keep from begging as he slid his fingers from her, panting as his lips continued to caress her neck, his breathing heavy and labored.

She stared up at him as he pulled back from her, lowering her arms, but still holding her wrists prisoner with his powerful hand.

"Show-off," she accused darkly as her gaze flickered to her bound wrists. "Why didn't you just bring the handcuffs?"

"Don't tempt me." His smile was all teeth. Predatory, intent. "Now come along like a good little girl, Raven."

She frowned at the heavy mockery in his voice. He might be a bit more than pissed, she thought, which only caused her own temper to rise. He had no right to be angry with her; it was her choice how she spent her time, not his. And she would be damned if she would put up with this attitude because she decided to spend time dancing rather than waiting around on him.

"Hey, dude, you got no right to be hauling her out of here." The big boy from the previous dance stood in their way, bringing Reno to a slow stop.

Raven glanced over his shoulder, wide-eyed. The younger man wasn't as tall as Reno, but he was thick and heavy, built like a damned linebacker and staring at Reno like a bull on a rampage.

"Sorry, dude, but the lady belongs to me." A normal rational man might have paid attention to the warning in Reno's voice, not to mention the savage look on his face.

"I didn't see no brand, asshole." The younger man swayed drunkenly in front of him, causing Raven to stifle a groan of mortification.

Reno would never let her live this one down, and neither would Clint, once he got wind of it. Dammit, why did these things have to happen to her?

"You just didn't look in the right place," Reno informed him, his voice deep, deadly. "Count yourself lucky. If you had, I'd have to rip your throat out."

Raven's eyes widened. This Reno was scary. He looked ready to fight, to defend, to claim.

"Uhh, Reno, let's just go." She pushed at his arm, aware of the grip he still retained on her wrists.

"Tough little man, aren't you?" the boy laughed, and Raven

groaned miserably. The other man had to be drunker than she thought, to even consider insulting Reno so rudely. Besides, Reno was at least six inches taller than the other man. Sometimes wider did not mean better.

Before she could do more than gasp in surprise, she was free, and Reno had the boy by the throat. Slowly, he took the younger man to the floor as beefy hands wrapped around his wrists and brown eyes began to bulge at the lack of oxygen.

"Don't mess with me, boy," Reno growled mercilessly. "Or my woman. Period."

When he released the younger man, Raven glared at him.

"You're insane," she said, slapping at his arm with enough force to sting her hand as he stared back at her in surprise. "Your woman, my ass! You are a bully, Reno. A macho, self-serving, arrogant SEAL bully and I'll be damned if I'm going anywhere with you."

She turned and swept through the crowd, her face flaming in embarrassment and fury, even though her body was still heated, throbbing.

My woman.

Something inside her had melted when he rasped the words, his tone thick with possessiveness and male fury, while another part screeched in horror. He had claimed her. It wasn't just sex to him, he was serious about this, and that point had just been driven forcibly home. Not that she hadn't been aware of it already. But now, she knew it down to her soul. All her dreams, hopes, and fears were tied up with one man. With Reno.

She was screwed.

chapter 6

reno stayed carefully behind Raven's car as he followed her home, his hands gripping the steering wheel.

She was right. He had been pissed, jealous, and riding the fine edge of his control; otherwise, he would have handled the younger man with a bit more discretion. Truth was, he wanted to kill that kid for daring to try to come between him and Raven.

He wiped his hand across his face as he fought his raging emotions. Never had he felt the adrenaline pumping through his system as it was now. His cock was harder than it had been at any time in his life and the urge to fuck Raven until she was too exhausted to fight back was nearly overwhelming.

She was driving him insane, not that he had expected anything less from her. He had known that stealing her heart wouldn't be easy, and binding her to him even harder. She looked at him and saw her parents. The father who left to fight, the mother who screamed and raged and drank too much while he was gone until the day he returned in a casket.

It was the danger of the job that some women couldn't handle. And he would have worried that Raven couldn't handle it, if he didn't know for a fact that each mission Morganna knew he was on, she and Raven waited out together. Laughing, joking, calling him names, and insulting him to hell and back, as reported by his sister. But she handled it. Just as Morganna helped Raven handle Clint's absences. They had a support system they had relied on most of their lives.

She was stronger than she thought was, Reno reflected, as he pulled into the driveway behind her car. He watched, eyes narrowed as she flounced out of the car, that little black dress flirting with her upper thighs as it whipped around her in a cloud of silk.

More slowly, Reno got out of the truck. Slow and careful, he cautioned himself. He had lost it at the club. Hell, he had nearly fucked her in that dark corner for everyone to see.

"Go away, Reno," she snarled as she unlocked the front door. "I don't want to see or talk to you."

At least she didn't try to slam the door in his face. She pushed into the house, leaving it wide open for him. Reno controlled the smile that wanted to touch his lips. She could yell until hell froze over, but he knew her. Inside out and upside down, he knew her, loved her, and he would be damned if he was going to let her find excuses to throw him out of her life.

"Aren't you tired of being such a coward, Raven?" he said as he followed her inside, closing and locking the door behind him.

She whirled around, the long, sleek golden brown curls that made his hands itch fanning around her slender body.

"Me? A coward?" An imperious thumb pointed into her chest. "I'm a realist, Reno. Unlike you, I prefer to see the truth rather than the pretty lies you want to feed me."

He crossed his arms over his chest, slowly. "When, Raven, did I ever lie to you?"

"Every time you touched me," she yelled back at him, thinking of the past two years, the teasing kisses and flirtatious touching.

"Pretending it was something light, something friendly. You want it all, don't you, Reno?"

"Hell, yes!" he snapped, facing her across the room, knowing if he got too close, there was no way he could keep from touching her. "I never pretended any different, Raven. You were the one who kept running, who kept refusing to face facts. You're the liar, Raven, not me."

"I never lied to you." Her hands swiped through her hair, frustration and pain evident on her face. "I told you I couldn't handle you. I couldn't handle the kind of relationship you want from me."

"Fuck that," he growled. "I don't want just a damned relationship with you, Raven. I want forever. And you knew it all along."

Raven stared at him wide-eyed.

"No . . ."

"Yes, by God, you did," he bit out. "You'd flit around, teasing and flirting, a little kiss here and there, a pet and a pat, and you thought that would be enough to hold me off. Now you're finding out otherwise and it scares the hell out of you."

Determination straightened her shoulders and glittered in her eyes. "I want you to leave." Her voice was rough, ragged with emotion. "Leave and don't come back, Reno."

A mocking smile twisted his lips. "Yeah, I guess you do." He crossed his arms over his chest again, restraining the need to hold her, to promise that everything would be okay. "If I leave," he continued, "you'll keep hiding your head in the sand, pretending that somehow, some way, if I'm killed in action, then it won't hurt. You'll survive it without a bottle in your hand and your heart will remain intact."

He watched her pale, the color leaching from her face as she stared back at him in shock.

"Do you really think you can do it, Raven?" he asked softly. "Do you think it won't hurt? Do you think you have your heart packed away nice and tight where nothing or no one can break it?"

"Stop." Her voice shook, breaking his heart. But her rejection hurt worse. It seared his soul.

He moved toward her then, gripping her shoulders before she could evade him, staring down at her as he fought his own raging emotions.

"Will it work?" He wanted to make her see the truth. "Look at me, Raven. If I die tomorrow, will it hurt any less than it would if we had a year or twenty together? Will you lay me in the ground any easier?"

"Oh God!" She shuddered, her eyes filling with tears as she stared up at him in misery. "I couldn't stand it. Don't you see, Reno? I couldn't stand it if something happened to you."

Those tears. He couldn't handle her tears. God, don't let her cry—it made him want to kill someone. And since he was the one causing the tears, that didn't leave many options.

"You don't understand," she said, dashing away her tears. "What if I'm like my mother? I don't have the courage to face that."

"The hell you don't," he said, and swooped down, taking her lips, forcing her head back against the wall as he took the kiss, as he needed to take her heart. Fully. Completely. And her response was everything he knew it could be, everything he knew she kept hidden inside her soul.

Her lips opened, her tongue reaching out for his, suckling him inside the warmth of her mouth as she lifted to him, pressing the hard tips of her nipples into his chest as her arms wrapped tight around his neck, her hands gripping his head.

With a ragged growl, he pulled her closer, lifting her into his arms and turning for the staircase. If this was all he could have, then he would take it. But by God, he would show her. If it was the last thing he managed, he would show her exactly what she was throwing away.

chapter 7

the expression on his face was like none she had seen before. Powerful, dominant, the hard planes and angles tightened into sharp relief as he moved.

"Reno." The protest was halted by the simple means of his lips covering hers again as his hands gripped the rounded curves of her buttocks, pulling her up and flush against the thick cock ridged behind the fly of his jeans.

Heat flared instantly, spreading from her pussy through the rest of her body as her hands gripped his shoulders and she arched closer. She couldn't imagine never knowing this again, never being held by him, loved by him.

Twisting in his grip, she fought him for the kiss, as desperately hungry for him as he seemed to be for her. His hands clenched the flesh of her rear, pulling at the curves until an erotic, sharp little tingle pierced the small entrance of her anus at the separation of the flesh.

"Feel it, Raven. Feel how sweet and hot it is. That doesn't just go away, baby; it haunts and eats at the soul and makes you so fucking hungry for it, you think you'll go crazy without it. That's how I've been. That's what tears at me every minute we're apart. Needing this. Your taste, your touch."

She stared up at him, knowing she couldn't refute his words. The memory of those brief, heated kisses in the past, his arms surrounding her, had tormented her. She needed him, needed him until it terrified her, but it made her aware of the weakness of her heart and the battle she was losing to hold it aloof.

Then the world spun around her as he lifted her in his arms, ignoring her instinctive protest as he strode across the room and quickly upstairs.

"Reno . . . you're taking over again," she gasped as he stepped into her bedroom, lowering her feet to the floor before pulling her back against him once again.

"I'm not taking *you* fast enough," he growled, bending his head as he tilted hers back, catching her lips in a kiss that stole her objections, just as it stole her breath.

He chuckled, the sound rough and strained as she worked her hands between them, moving for the buttons that held his cock prisoner. She wasn't going to stand there, allowing him to control her, to dominate her so easily. She couldn't deny the pleasure, but she could make him just as crazy as he was making her.

"No, no. Bad girl." His hands caught hers as he turned her around quickly, pulling her back against his chest as one hard arm locked around her waist. "Look in the mirror. Look how pretty you are, Raven."

She blinked at the image in the large mirror that sat atop the chest. Reno's hand moved along her shoulder, lowering the strap of her dress down her arm until the draped bodice fell away from the swollen curve of her breast.

The red lace of her bra showed up clearly against her pale skin, the picture reflected back at her was one of a forbidden taste of sensual excitement. He stood head and shoulders above her, staring down at her as he stripped the dress from her upper body, his lips moving over her neck and shoulder as the material dropped to the floor.

Raven stared into the mirror, seeing him as he surrounded her, a broad, powerful male animal intent on possession. His gaze met hers in the mirror, his gray eyes nearly black, his expression tight, the skin stretched tight across his high cheekbones, the fight for control blatantly evident.

She felt the breath lock in her chest at the image he presented. Boldly, unapologetically male. Possessive. Dominant. He held her and meant it.

"Such a pretty little bad girl," he whispered then. "Do you know what happens to bad girls, Raven? Bad little girls who refuse to admit what they see staring them in the face?"

She almost came from the sound of his voice alone. She felt her womb convulse, stealing her breath and her senses as his hands smoothed up her waist and cupped her engorged breasts in a firm, heated grip. Devilish thumbs rasped over the peaks, sending flares of brilliant heat washing through her.

The sight of those broad, darkly tanned hands cupping the swollen mounds of her breasts was highly erotic. He was so strong, yet his grip was firm, gentle. There was no pain, no sense of force, just pleasure and hunger and need that spread from those hands to her body and left her trembling in arousal.

"You really are a pervert." Unfortunately, it was turning her on more than it should.

"Oh baby, you have no idea," he whispered, his eyes, so filled with emotion and lust, meeting hers in the mirror as he loosened the catch of her bra. "But I intend to show you. I'm about to let you get very well acquainted with every perverted fantasy I've ever had about you."

The bra dropped to the floor.

Raven gasped at the sight of the bare skin as his fingers, the backs of his fingers only, traced the curve of her breasts, rasped over the hard points of her nipples. Electric pleasure sizzled though her nerve endings, sending pulses of sensation whipping over flesh. She could feel her juices easing past her vagina, dampening the bare folds of her pussy as she pressed closer, rubbing her buttocks against his erection.

He wasn't the only one who could tease. She might not have his experience, but her arousal made up for it. She needed him, needed his touch, his kiss, the flames of pleasure that surrounded her and struck into the core of her being as he held her.

"Vixen," he growled roughly, pressing his cock tighter against her rear. "You keep teasing me with that little ass and you'll get more than you bargained for."

Her eyes widened as she blinked at his image in the mirror. He looked serious.

"You wouldn't." She arched against him as one hand slid down her stomach, his palm cupping the heated contours of her pussy through the lace and silk of the thong that seemed more a tease than any actual covering.

She stared at the image they made—sexual, hungry. His hand cupped her possessively, his fingers curving between her thighs, rasping against the material of the panties over her swollen flesh.

"Don't bet on it," he growled at her ear. "But first, I have to show you how I punish bad little girls."

She had only a second to gasp in shock as he lifted her from her feet, backed to the bed, and sat down heavily before pressing her over his legs.

"You wouldn't! Dammit, Reno!"

His hand landed on the upraised flesh of her butt, sending sensation shooting to her clit. She jerked, shocked, amazed. She had known, that first time he spanked her so long ago, that a little pain could be an incredible turn-on. But this was different. His bare hand applied to her naked ass sent her flesh blooming with heat, and her pussy spasming in pleasure.

"Beautiful." His fingers trailed over the rounded flesh before his hand lifted, falling again on the opposite cheek with the same devastating effect.

"Reno, this isn't a good idea." Her pussy was creaming furiously as she shuddered in his grip.

He slid his fingers under the silken strap of material that ran between the cheeks of her rear. "Are you sure, Raven? I think it's a very good idea."

Raven groaned as she felt the silk of the thong rasping over her cunt, caressing the swollen nub of her clit as she writhed on his lap. Just when she thought he must have surely forgotten his previous intentions, his hand rose and landed on her bare butt again, causing her womb to convulse as she felt her juices flowing from her pussy.

She was quivering, shuddering with a fiery pleasure as he spanked her with an erotic precision that had her screaming out with each strike against her flesh. The pleasure whipping through her body seared her from the inside out and left her gasping, nearly screaming in arousal.

"Reno, this isn't fair." She moaned, jerking against him as one blow nearly threw her into orgasm, the pleasure-pain was so intense.

"No, Raven, what isn't fair is your denial." His hand landed again, making her burn as she screamed out beneath the fiery lash. "What isn't fair is aching for you, loving you, and having to fight you every damned step of the way—" Smack! "—when we both—" Smack! "know—" Smack! "exactly how you feel. . . ."

She was arching back to his hand and begging for more, so close to climax, she could feel it shuddering through her, clenching in her womb as he suddenly lifted her, tossing her to the bed as he rose to his feet.

Rolling to her back, Raven came to her knees aggressively, baring her teeth in an arousal so deep, so hot, she knew it was burning her out of control. Before he could loosen the first metal button of his jeans, her fingers were there, pushing his out of the way, loosening his jeans until the rigid length of his cock jutted through the open fabric.

Thick and heavily veined, the flared head broad and ruddy, it was a treat Raven couldn't refuse any longer. Her eyes lifted, meeting Reno's stormy gaze as her head lowered, her tongue swiping over the small pearl of liquid that collected on the tip. His fingers threaded through her hair as her lips parted, covering the hot flesh with greedy hunger.

Her lips and mouth moved on him as her fingers enclosed the silken length. He was like iron encased in silk, hot and heavy, an erotic weapon of such sensual destruction that she was left helpless in the face of their combined needs.

Her mouth enclosed him, tightened as her tongue flickered over the sensitive head and she began a smooth, firm, sucking action that had a harsh groan ripping from his throat as his fingers tightened further in her hair.

A sense of power filled her, a heady feminine thrill that she held such a sensual, sexual force in the very palm of her hand. It was exhilarating, shattering, more arousing than anything she could have imagined.

Her mouth moved on him in ever increasing demand, feeling the hard throb of blood just under the flesh, feeling the thick erection pulse and throb as he groaned her name in a thick, guttural tone.

One hand moved to the heavy sac just below the straining shaft, her fingers cupping the taut flesh as her other hand stroked the length that her mouth couldn't consume. She moaned around the fullness that thrust demandingly between her lips, hungry for the heat and taste of him.

"Enough," he suddenly growled, his hands tightening in her hair as he pulled back.

But not before he spilled a few precious drops of semen on her tongue. Hot, salty, male, the taste sent her senses spiraling as she fought his hold, eager for more.

"That's not fair," she gasped as he held her out of reach, his hands catching her wrists to keep her from tempting him further.

"Of course it is." He turned her quickly, pushing her upper body to the bed as he raised her hips, coming to his knees behind her. "Especially when I intend to do this."

In one smooth, fierce stroke he filled her. Raven arched, a strangled scream escaping her lips as she felt his cock fill her to overflowing, powering into her with a force and pleasure that left her helpless.

He filled his hands with the smooth flesh of her rear, separating it as he began to move, creating a brilliant shaft of electric sensation as he parted the entrance to her anus. His thumbs smoothed down the crease until he reached the point where he filled her. There, his fingers slid in the slick cream that flowed easily from her body. He smoothed it back, dampening the little hole over and over again as she bucked beneath him, the pleasure so intense, she wondered if she could survive it.

One hand held her buttocks spread as the other began to spread more of her juices back along the crevice. Below, his cock thrust slow and deep inside the sensitive, hot depths of her pussy. He was making her crazy, moving so slowly, teasing her with alternate deep, fast strokes, then slow, easy ones. All the while his fingers played at the tiny entrance above, relaxing her, easing her.

"Do you want to throw this away, Raven?" The question was delivered in a hard, possessive voice. "This as well as everything else we've ever shared?"

"No!" She couldn't stop the protest, the need that filled her. Not just sexual, not just the hunger for the biting pleasure of having his cock fill her. But something more, something that went deeper, that grew more intense each time he touched her. It wasn't just sex, no matter how desperately she wished it were.

"Good girl," he whispered, thrusting harder inside her, thrusting against delicate tissue and nerves as she cried out at the pleasure.

She was gasping, crying, begging for more when she felt his hand tighten on her hip. The thumb massaging her anus paused for just a second before it began to push inside with slow devastation.

Raven's back arched, a strangled scream escaping her throat as the piercing pleasure-pain shot up her back before arrowing back down to strike the core of her womb as he began to fuck her in hard, deep thrusts. He stretched her, filled her, thrusting inside her in counterpoint to his thumb as it raided the tender entrance of her ass.

The dual penetration broke the last threads of her control, both physical and emotional. A shattered wail escaped her throat as she clamped down on him, exploding with a force that drew every muscle taut as it shuddered through her body in hard, heavy pulses of release.

Behind her, she heard him groan, felt him swell inside her, then felt his explosion, the hot splash of his semen filling her, branding her. She collapsed beneath him, groaning heavily as his thumb slid from the tight grip of her anus. Seconds later, she heard him breathe in heavily as his cock slid free of her wet vagina and he collapsed on the bed beside her.

"Hell, we're going to kill each other at this rate," he panted as he pulled her into his arms, one hand smoothing back the perspiration-damp hair that fell over her brow.

Raven opened her eyes, dazed, relaxed, knowing she was losing the emotional battle she was fighting, and fighting to make sense of it. He wasn't giving her a chance to think, to consider, to come to terms with the emotions tearing through her heart.

"It hasn't changed anything," she whispered then, watching his eyes darken with emotion. "How am I supposed to deal with this, Reno, when you keep clouding my mind with sex?"

"I'm not clouding your mind, baby." He then pulled her closer in his arms as he sighed deeply against her hair. "You're clouding it yourself. Either you want there to be an 'us,' or you don't. Think very hard before you make that decision, Raven. Fear can be dealt with, but you have to face it before you can defeat it."

She frowned.

"I love you, Raven." He tilted her head back, staring down at her, his eyes dark, filled with emotion, with a savage intensity that clenched her chest and brought tears to her eyes. "That won't change in a day, a week, or a century. But I won't destroy myself chasing after you. You have to decide what you want, and once you do, you have to stick to it. Either way it goes, there's no going back."

chapter 8

"we really should get out of bed," Raven muttered drowsily the next morning as Reno smoothed his hand over the rounded curves of her rear and watched her quietly.

She lay on her stomach, her head turned away from him, the long tangled locks of her dark hair flowing around her. Reno trailed his hand from the rounded flesh of her buttocks to her back, his fingers tangling in the rich mass of curls. She looked so delicate, small and tempting as she lay beside him, exhausted from their love-making.

This was the picture he would keep in his mind of her. Her beside him, tired and replete, her hair fanning over her back as he touched her, stroked her.

He kissed the curve of her shoulder, allowing himself to breathe in deep, to fill his senses with the scent of her.

"Did you hear me?" she mumbled as she lifted her shoulder against his lips.

Reno smiled at the irate drowsiness. He could hear the threat of laughter in her voice, despite her tone. She liked to play at being tough, unemotional, but he could hear the threads of feelings that she tried to hide.

"I hear you, grouch." He raked his teeth over the flesh he was caressing, smiling at the faint shiver that gripped her body. "You're just a coffee hussy. You think you're going to convince me to fix you some."

Soft laughter greeted the accusation.

"Guilty." She rolled to her side, dragging the sheet around her as she glanced up at him.

Something in his chest expanded, threatening to steal his breath as he stared down at her. Her angel's face staring up at him, those dark, sleepy eyes staring at him from the flushed expanse of her face. She had the power to steal his breath, and often did.

He held her close, his arms tightening around her as she cuddled against him hesitantly. He could feel her breasts pressing against his chest through the sheet she had pulled around her like a shield. But at least she wasn't running.

"I really need that coffee, Reno." Her voice was languid, as lazy as the hand that played almost unconsciously through the mat of hair on his chest.

"You gotta pay for it first." He grinned as she sighed with exasperation.

"You should be tired," she grumped. "*I'm* tired. You didn't even let me sleep last night."

"Of course I did." He smiled against the top of her head as he pushed the sheet away impatiently. "You slept between two and seven while I made some calls and reenergized with a snack."

"You eat too much." Her casual tone was spoiled by the tensing of her body when he mentioned the phone calls.

He wasn't going to let her ignore who and what he was. That wasn't going to help when the next assignment came up. That, unfortunately, he knew would be sooner than he had expected.

"I have to keep up my energy," he whispered as he pressed her to her back, pulling the sheet away from her as she watched him, her eyes darkening with arousal.

"How pretty," he sighed as his hand smoothed down her stomach, feeling the muscles ripple beneath his fingers as he moved unerringly to the heat between her thighs.

Her breath caught, her eyes widened as he cupped the damp, bare flesh there. He loved that look, surprise and arousal, a hint of confusion, as though she hadn't yet figured out why the pleasure was so intense.

His head lowered to capture the sweetest lips he had ever kissed as his fingers played erotically in the hottest, silkiest folds of flesh God had ever made. Raven just felt different from any other woman. She tasted different; she smelled different. Everything about her was so unique, so soft and sweet and spicy that it sent his senses spinning. She was addictive. She made his head spin, made his heart pound out of control, and his hands ache to hold her forever.

For now, his fingers parted the swollen folds between her thighs, caressing her gently as she gasped beneath his kiss. Her hands clenched his shoulders, dragging a groan from his chest as pleasure whipped through him. He tightened against the surge of lust that nearly overwhelmed his senses.

She arched beneath his hands, her hips pressing closer, the swollen bud of her clitoris rubbing into his palm as she tensed beneath him. Reno raised his head, staring down at her intently, seeing the wash of heated hunger suffusing her face as she stared back at him in bemusement.

He slid a finger slowly past the tender opening of her vagina, watching her mouth open as a cry escaped them. God she made him crazy.

His cock twitched in anticipation as he thrust his finger inside the heated depths of her cleft, massaging and caressing the silken tissue that rippled beneath his touch. Her breathing was harsh now, thready little moans escaping her throat as her head tilted back, her eyes closing while her hands moved down his chest, her nails raking over his flesh.

"What are you doing to me?" she moaned, writhing beneath him as he slid another finger inside her, working her muscles slowly, easily, feeling the slick cream of her arousal coating his fingers as she clenched around them.

"Loving you," he whispered as he read the dazed pleasure consuming her expression. "Do you feel me loving you, Raven?"

He thrust in harder, deeper, finding the ultrasensitive mass of nerves, so that when his fingers pressed into it, rotating subtly, she cried out with sensual abandon, arching closer, her hips pumping against his hand as the muscles of her cunt convulsed around his fingers.

"There you go, baby," he whispered, forcing back his own driving hunger to watch hers. "Let me love you, Raven."

He twisted his fingers inside her, sliding nearly free before driving deep again. He watched her face, relished the ecstasy that consumed her even as his own hunger bit deep into his loins. He was dying for her. He would die for her.

Filtering the overpowering lust was the incredible love he had always felt for this woman. She was so much a part of him that he could never imagine life without her now. Couldn't risk that she would turn away when the job became a reality rather than a distant thought.

Gritting his teeth, he quickened his fingers inside her, pushing her over the edge, watching her dissolve as he pulled free and slid quickly between her thighs. She was still convulsing, the muscles rippling and clenching as he positioned the straining length of his cock and pushed inside her.

"Oh God, Reno," she cried out beneath him, her legs rising to circle his hips, her arms wrapping around his neck as her eyes opened, the deep blue burning with emotion and pleasure as she stared up at him. "Don't let me go. Please don't let me go."

"Never, baby. I'll never let you go," he swore deeply as he lowered himself, bracing his weight on his elbows as his hands clasped her head, staring down at her as he began to move inside her with quick, long strokes that sent frissons of sensation shooting up his spine.

She was so tight, so hot. Clenching around his flesh with rhythmic strokes that had him groaning roughly as his hands clenched in her hair.

"Reno . . ." Her nails bit into his shoulders as she stared up at him, her expressive face filled with confusion, with love, with such arousal, it had his scrotum drawing up tight as warning tingles of release began to sizzle at the base of his spine.

"Yeah, baby?" He was fighting for control. Just a few more seconds, he thought desperately. He could feel her tensing further beneath him, her own explosion nearing. "Tell me what you need, Raven," he said, panting. "Anything you want, baby, it's yours. Anything you want."

He watched her eyes turn liquid, tears filling them, but never spilling over as the emotion in her gaze intensified.

"I need you." Her legs tightened around him as the words whispered from her lips, hesitant, filled with longing. "I need you, Reno."

He lowered his head again, his lips whispering over hers as he felt her rising, felt the impending explosion moving through her.

"You have me, Raven," he whispered against her lips. "Forever, baby, you have me."

He pushed inside her harder then, deeper, his strokes increasing until he was jackhammering inside her, exploding with her, his soul dissolving and merging with hers until he had no idea where Raven ended and he began; all he knew was that he would never, could never, let her go.

Raven walked into the bedroom that afternoon, coming to a slow, careful stop as she caught sight of Reno packing the duffel bag that had lain nearly empty since the first night he had spent with her.

He was dressed in the camouflage fatigues, black boots, and dull green shirt that were trademarks of his job. As she watched, he lifted his holster and the deadly weapon it contained and packed it carefully.

He was leaving. No warning, no time for her to prepare for it. She stared at him, fighting the building dread that rose within her.

He flashed her a strained smile. "I should be back in about a week. Command called about an hour ago. There should be a car to pick me up soon. I'll be at the base tonight, before we head out first thing in the morning. I left you a present in the kitchen."

She swallowed tightly, shoving her hands into her jeans pockets as she pushed back the emotions roiling inside her. Fear, pain, desperation. They hadn't had enough time together, less than a week, not even long enough to build up the memories to hold her through the long, empty nights.

"Sure." She smiled back, certain she came off as perfectly relaxed as if he had told her he was heading to the corner store. She would not be like her mother. She would not send him away, worried, stressed, uncertain about her state of mind. "Be careful."

She leaned against the wall, memorizing his face. The curve of his lips, his dark, stormy gray eyes, the strong arch of brows.

He watched her carefully, his expression concerned. Tense.

He shrugged his shoulders as though shifting some invisible weight.

"I'll be back," he said again.

She smiled back at him. "Of course you will."

He seemed to relax then, at least marginally, the smile on his face curving more naturally. This was who he was. He was a warrior. You can't tame the wind, and you can't housebreak a warrior. She had to accept that.

"I love you, Raven," he said then.

I love you, Raven. I love you, Raven.

The words rebounded through her soul.

She drew in a hard, deep breath. "Did you get everything packed?"

She moved quickly to the dresser, opening and checking drawers. "Clint is always leaving his stuff strung around the place when he visits. I swear, he's a slob. I pick up after him for a week after he leaves."

Nerves were jumping beneath her skin as she fought to hold on to her composure. She wasn't going to cry, she wasn't angry, but she was suddenly realizing how much more she stood to lose than she ever had.

"Raven." His hands landed on her shoulders, holding her. "I love you."

She stilled, then turned to him, staring up at him desperately as he watched her. Something inside her was splintering, fragmenting. What was it? She wasn't angry as her mother had been when her father went on assignment. Raven had been through this too many times with both Reno and Clint. Admittedly, she didn't have as much to lose then as she did now, but this part she knew how to handle. Didn't she?

"Don't you go and get yourself hurt, Reno," she fairly snarled up at him. "I won't be happy."

His off-center smile had her heart clenching with love.

"I'll make sure of that," he whispered, his voice quiet, almost saddened as he watched her.

His head swooped down then, his lips catching hers as her breath caught in her throat. Her throat tightened and something in her chest exploded as his kiss consumed her. Her arms went around his neck as she lifted to him, helpless, aching, as his arms jerked her closer, his hands nearly bruising as they roved over her back and shoulders, imprinting his touch into her soul forever.

A horn blew outside. Once, twice.

He pulled away from her, turned, grabbed his duffel bag and stalked from the room. Seconds later, the front door slammed and he was gone. Raven stared at the window across the room, the shards of sunlight cut across the bed, small motes of dust dancing in the air.

The silence was oppressive, heavy.

She forcibly held back her tears, the pain. She could survive this. She wasn't angry, but God she missed him already.

As she stared at that bright swath of sunlight, a memory broke free, surging past her defenses. She had been young, so young. Barely ten as she lay on her bed that weekend, listening to her parents scream at each other. Her father had to leave again, another mission, another fight. Her mother was crying, begging him not to go. His voice had echoed with his frustration, his own anger. He had to leave. It was his job. No, her mother had screamed, it was his mistress, and she wouldn't share him. He might as well not even come back.

He hadn't come back. A black car and two military counselors had arrived instead. Her father had died in an unknown country, and he was never returning. He wouldn't come home. She wouldn't hear her parents arguing ever again, or sit on her father's lap while he read her stories. He would never tickle her again or call her his dark angel. He was gone forever.

Which was worse? The worry or the loss? She had always wondered that. Especially with Reno. If she let herself love him, which would be worse? Never having him or knowing there would never be another chance?

She moved from the bedroom, down the stairs, and to the kitchen. The soft noises coming from the other room warned her of what to expect, but nothing could contain the rush of emotion when she stepped into the room.

The box sat by the door, barely large enough to contain the ball of fluff attempting to break free. Attached to the side was a note, written in Reno's distinctive scrawl.

To keep your feet warm until I return. Love, Reno.

"Until you return," she whispered, staring at the golden retriever pup as it began to howl pitifully for release.

"Well, little guy," she whispered, kneeling beside the box as she touched a soft silky ear hesitantly. "At least we'll have each other."

She drew him from the box and stepped outside, feeling the late summer heat on her face, the breeze whispering over her damp cheeks. But they weren't. She'd promised herself she wouldn't cry.

But the tears fell as she cuddled the pup, staring into the brilliance of the late summer sky.

"I didn't tell him I love him," she finally admitted, the pain exploding in her chest as she realized Reno was right. There was no hiding from it. No hiding from him. She loved him, and she hadn't even told him.

"It's an easy in and out." Reno faced his men in the small conference room, standing in front of the large monitor that displayed the target they were being sent in to hit. "We have two hostages to rescue and a laptop used by the cell commander. Laptop is priority. We'll go in quiet, set the explosives, grab the laptop and the hostages, and run. Pickup will be waiting on us here." He pressed the button that switched the picture to an area nearly ten miles from target. "Two Black Hawks will be waiting to fly us out to a waiting ship."

He lifted the stack of files on the desk beside him.

"Read this carefully. We have intel reports on entrances, exits, weak spots, and so forth. We'll meet with the assist team when we reach the ship and finalize plans there."

"The cell commander is wanted for war crimes, Major," Ace spoke up, his deep voice echoing in the small room. "Are we just after the laptop or his head as well?"

"The assist team will be in charge of that," Reno informed him. "We'll be going after the hostages. But you don't take chances. The opportunity is there to take that laptop, you get it. We stick with our target op and adjust as we have to."

"And pop the bastard if we get him in our sights," Joker, the explosives expert of the team, spoke up. He wasn't joking. This particular terrorist commander was brutal, without mercy. He wouldn't be shown any.

As Reno opened his mouth to dismiss the men, a sharp knock had his head lifting as the door opened.

"Major Chavez, we have a situation that demands your presence," an MP snickered from the doorway. "General says now."

Frowning, Reno nodded to Ace as he handed the files to him to distribute to the other three men and made his way to the door.

"Situation?" he asked warily.

"Situation, sir, of a very delicate sort." The MP nodded, amusement dancing in his eyes. "This way, sir."

As they neared the general's office, a frown worked between Reno's brows at the sound of an irate female voice.

"General, I don't care how busy he is. You were my father's best friend and I'm not above pulling strings. If I don't see him before he leaves in the morning, I promise you, I'll be making a visit to your wife, your daughter, and your son. They like me." The voice was husky and filled with feminine fury.

He heard the general's voice, low, soothing.

"I'm not in the Army, General," she said. "I don't need rules quoted to me. I need strings pulled. I want to see him. Now."

A grin tugged at his mouth as the MP chuckled.

"She's been ripping on the general for an hour," he whispered as they neared the door. "Want to bet he chews on you next?"

Reno grimaced but something in his heart was loosening. He wouldn't bet against the MP, but he would bet it just might be worth it.

He knocked on the door lightly.

"Enter." The general's voice was frustrated and clipped.

Reno stepped in, saluting smartly, then turned to stare at Raven.

She was cuddling the puppy he'd bought her like a baby. Her face was wet with tears, her deep, deep blue eyes filled with misery.

"Raven?" He stepped toward her, pulling her and the puppy into his arms as he stared back at the general. "What's happened?"

"Major, I'll leave you to talk to Miss McIntire." The general sounded stern, but Reno caught the soft look he cast at Raven. "We'll talk later."

"Yes, sir." Reno nodded as the general left the room and he turned his attention to the pup wiggling between them.

"Raven? Baby? The puppy is going to be smashed," he whispered as he gripped her arms, pushing her back enough to release the wiggling little mass. "What's wrong? Is Clint okay?"

The tears rolled silently down her cheeks. There were no sobs, just a hitch in her breath as she stared up at him.

"I forgot." She hiccupped then. "You left, and I forgot to tell you. . . ."

She shuddered as her voice broke.

Reno moved to the couch, pulling her to his lap as she cuddled against his chest.

"I love you," she cried desperately. "God help me, Reno. I don't want to lose you. I can stand anything but you leaving, maybe being . . . hurt . . . ," her breath caught, "and not knowing I love you."

Reno closed his eyes, his arms tightening around her, his heart exploding with joy. She knew she loved him. That was all that mattered.

"It's okay, baby," he groaned, kissing her forehead gently as her head tilted back, the wealth of long silken curls flowing over his arm. Her hand lifted to his face, her lips trembling as he wiped the tears from one silken cheek.

"You knew all along, didn't you?" she whispered then. "That I loved you."

"All along," he agreed with a smile.

His lips lowered to hers, moving over the soft curves, nibbling at the damp softness as the feel and smell of her sent his senses rioting.

"Hell, if I fucked you in the general's office, he would court-martial me for sure," he sighed, smiling down at the seductive softness in her expression.

"Yeah. He probably would." Her smile trembled, but it was still there.

"Wait for me, Raven," he growled, his voice husky, deep, knowing every day away from her would be hell. "I'll be home. Wait for me."

"Always, Reno." She kissed him. Her head raised, her lips moving against his with incredible passion and loving heat. "Always."

chapter 9

three months later

"you are in so much trouble."

Reno tossed his duffel bag to the corner of the bedroom as he stalked inside the room, his brows lowered into a dark frown as Raven reclined back on the bed, her knee bent, her naked breasts thrusting forward in invitation as his hot gaze raked over them.

Damn he looked good. The camouflage pants made his legs look sexy as hell, planted apart as they were, the bulge between his thighs filling out the front of the material.

"Oh really, Reno, it wasn't so bad." She rolled her eyes at his miffed state. "It was just a little present."

She restrained her smile as he dug his hand into his pocket, no small feat with that erection tightening the material. Her mouth watered at the sight of it. He had been gone for nearly two weeks this time. Too long as far as she was concerned, and she was wet and hungry for him. The adult toys he had been so kind as to teach her to use the last time he was home did little to bank the fire that thinking of him caused.

She blinked as the small velvet box landed on the bed beside her. She almost had to bite her lips to keep back her smile.

"Is this a proposal?" She arched a brow as she glanced back up at him.

Oh yum. He was undressing. There went the shirt, revealing the golden expanse of his chest, muscles rippling beneath the sun-darkened flesh.

"I'm going to spank your ass," he grunted as he bent to unlace his boots. "Do you want to know where I was when that box dropped out of my duffel bag, Raven? I was in the middle of communal quarters, sweetheart, with three different teams. Can you imagine the fun those men had at my expense?"

She lifted the box, opening it, and grinned at the sight of the wedding set she had found in his dresser drawer just before he was due to leave. The short letter she had wrapped around it was missing.

Who's hiding now? she had written.

He had been so very careful of their relationship over the last three months, never pressing her for anything, but she had seen how he had steadily cemented his presence into her life.

His clothes now shared space with hers. His guitar was residing under her bed, and his prized trophies from high school and college had made their way to her small shelf downstairs. He even had his own computer desk for the laptop he often worked on. This was his home. He hadn't asked to inhabit it, he had just moved in, just as he had taken her heart, a little bit at a time. But he never mentioned taking it further, never pushed her, though she could tell he wanted to.

She looked up as his pants cleared his hips and his erection sprang free. Thick, the broad head flushed to a near purple hue, it looked intimidating, ready to conquer. She was more than ready to be conquered.

"Turn over," he growled.

He had that intimidating, dominating look on his face now. The one that made her cream furiously and made her blood pressure shoot through the roof. She loved it when he looked like that, and she loved what resulted.

"Do I look crazy to you?" She flipped the box closed as she watched him mockingly. "Why buy the cow, Reno, if you're getting the milk free? I think perhaps you should sleep in the spare bedroom tonight. Better yet, Morganna's not having any parties this weekend. Maybe she can spare a bed."

She moved to get off the bed, knowing the game and loving it. She saw that twinkle in his eye. The happiness that tugged at his fiercely controlled lips and the lust that flushed the hard cheekbones of his face.

Her feet barely touched the floor when she felt his arm hook around her waist, dragging her back to the bed as he flipped her onto her stomach in one smooth, economical move.

She screeched in mock protest, struggling against him as she felt his muscular legs bracket her, holding her to the mattress.

A second later, his callused palm landed on her rear with stinging force. Heat whipped through her buttocks, sizzled along her nerve endings, then down to her clit with vicious force.

"Reno, that's cruel and unusual treatment." She bucked against his hold. "There's laws against this."

He smacked the other cheek, causing her to wiggle fiercely as her vagina began to ripple in desperate need. Damn him, he knew what this did to her.

"Your proposal sucked, Raven," he drawled lazily as another blow landed, making her moan at the border between pleasure and pain.

"It beat yours," she cried out, pressing back, feeling the tip of his erection as it slid against the crease of her damp thighs.

He was hard and hot, and her body was starving for him. She pressed back again, moaning heavily as two more strikes landed on her upraised ass, making her clench at the fire blooming there.

"I was wooing you," he half snarled.

He was always like this after a mission, more dominant, so eager for her that he took her breath away.

"You call that wooing?" She was panting now. His hips shifted, pressing his cock against her eager entrance as she fought for that first hard thrust. "I could die an old maid waiting on you." The next smack landed with burning force on her ass as she felt her womb contract almost violently.

A second later, her back arched as a hoarse scream tore from her throat. The full, heavy length of his cock surged inside the slick, tight confines of her vagina, triggering an explosive climax that left her shaking in reaction, shudders of pleasure vibrating through her entire body.

"Oh, you're not done yet, baby." He slid free of her, flipped her to her back, and lifted her legs as his head lowered.

His tongue attacked the sensitive folds with ravenous greed, licking around her straining clit as his murmurs of approval hummed against her flesh. Deep, penetrating thrusts of his tongue had her lifting her hips in supplication moments later, only to have him retreat to torture the burning nub above once again.

He was voracious. A sensual, sexual demon intent on draining her of every last vestige of resistance against him. Not that the resistance was anything more than feigned. She loved this side of him, provoked it often, and gloried in his possession of her.

She could feel her heart hammering against her chest as her hands lifted from the bed, her fingers moving for the aching tips of her breasts, knowing he was watching. It inflamed her all the more to know that she could push him over the edge, that she could make him as crazy with need as he made her.

He was her lover, her heart and her soul.

She pinched at her nipple as she heard him groan roughly, tugging at the tender points as her eyes opened, her gaze meeting his as his tongue circled her straining clit. He would make her come again, make her scream for him. He always did.

She could feel perspiration gathering on her body as the heat inside her began to build. Her muscles tensed, her breathing became broken whimpers of agonizing need until his mouth covered the erect little clit, his tongue flickering as he sucked it firmly.

She screamed for him as she exploded. Rocketing into the stars with a force that left her dizzy as she felt him thrust inside her, hard and deep, penetrating her to the very core before his hips began to move with furious thrusts.

It didn't take him long. The need was too great; the absence had been too long. He pushed her into a final, exhausted orgasm before giving in to his own, groaning harshly as he buried inside her, his cock jerking in reflex as he spilled his semen in the gripping depths of her pussy.

Seconds later he collapsed beside her with an exhausted sigh, pulling her to his chest as they both fought to bring their breathing under control.

"I need coffee," she muttered sleepily, burrowing close, her hand going to the scar on the right side of his chest.

The bullet he had taken there could have taken his life if it had been a few more inches toward the center. It had been a close call. A terrifying one, but she had survived it without recriminations. When he came home, she had babied him and loved him, and treasured every day she had with him after that. She vowed she would never waste their lives as her mother had hers.

"Coffee hussy," he chuckled into her hair. "What do you do when I'm gone?"

She breathed out pitifully. "I suffer, Reno. It's a tragic, horrible sight to witness. Poor Morganna even feels sorry for me."

She shivered as his hands caressed her back, one running low to her hips before smoothing over her buttocks.

"You're marrying me." His voice suddenly hardened. "Notice, I'm not asking. I'm telling you."

"I already proposed, big shot. You dropped the ball. Remember?"

He grunted at that. "Minx. The men are still laughing over that note you left. Don't you know I'm fearless? I never hide."

"Coward." She yawned, unconcerned, nipping his chest as her lips closed. "Do you know how mad I got when I found that box? It's a good thing you were getting ready to leave that day or I might have had to hurt you."

He gripped a handful of hair, tugging her head back as she stared up at him, her legs smoothing across his as she felt his erection growing, pressing against her lower stomach.

"I love you, Raven," he whispered then, his voice no longer filled with amusement, his gaze velvet soft as he watched her. "Forever."

"You took a hell of a chance, Reno," she whispered. "I didn't know myself how much I loved you. What if I hadn't realized?"

A smile curved his lips. "I would have fucked you into submission."

She rolled her eyes, one hand pressing against his shoulder as though to push him away.

"Get serious."

"Withheld the coffee?" he suggested darkly.

She stared up at him in some concern then. "You wouldn't do that."

"Oh yes I would have," he growled. "But more importantly, I wouldn't have given you a moment's peace. You're mine, baby, and I don't let go of what's mine."

He kissed her then, a kiss filled with promise, heat, and magic as her heart dissolved within her chest and flowed into his. It wouldn't do him any good to let her go, she thought, because she had no intention of releasing him.

"I love you, Reno," she whispered against his lips again. "Forever."

for
maggie's
sake

chapter 1

maggie samuels was pale. Too pale. The freckles across her creamy cheeks and along the bridge of her nose stood out clearly, emphasizing the frail, delicate look of her features. Her lush lips trembled, her wide green eyes were shocked and filled with unshed tears.

And he wanted to save her. Joe Merino stared through the two-way glass, his hands pushed into the pockets of his slacks as he watched Maggie wrap her arms across her chest and stare unseeing back at the detective questioning her. Detective Folker had been questioning her for hours.

Her husband had been dead less than a week, a husband who had supposedly adored her. Who lived for her. The same man who had supposedly been Joe's friend. And now, Maggie's life was being threatened as well. Because of that same man.

Joe knew he shouldn't give a damn. From all accounts, she had gotten herself into this; he should let her get herself out of it. That's what his head was saying. His heart was saying something different.

His heart was assuring him that there was no way Maggie was involved. He had slept with this woman at one time, held her in his arms, and watched her as she climaxed. The woman he had known couldn't be cold-blooded enough to be involved with this. But then again, he had never suspected for a second that Grant was part of Fuentes's organization. That he had helped rape and torture many of the young women that Fuentes had kidnapped.

And now, here he stood, days after Grant's death, trying to harden himself to the threat that someone else he cared for could be involved in the horror that that operation had turned into. That his own life could have become such a mess.

He had let his bitterness, his distrust of women after his wife's deceit and death five years ago, stand between him and the woman he knew belonged to him. Hell, he had known it at the time. Each time he thought of forever with Maggie, the memory of Bettina's death hung over him like a haunting specter. She had died leaving him. She and her boyfriend, high on drugs, had run the car they were in over an embankment, killing them both. He hadn't been able to hold on to the woman he married, the woman who swore to love him. And two years later, there he had been, falling in love with Maggie.

Joe watched Maggie now, his jaw clenched, his back teeth grinding, as the past threatened to swallow him. Two and a half years before, Maggie had belonged to him for a few short months. But he hadn't taken what he knew could be his. Maggie had walked out of his arms, and months later had walked into Grant's.

The problem was, he hadn't stopped loving Maggie.

He stared into the interrogation room, fighting to ignore the tightening of his chest, the regret and the rage and the lust. He had been fighting the lust for two and a half years. A hunger that never slept, that never eased, for a woman he could never have again. A woman who, it appeared, was involved in her husband's illegal activities.

He ignored the gut-clenching feeling that she couldn't be involved, that she was innocent. It was the same reaction he'd had when he began to suspect there was indeed a mole within his team.

He had begun the investigation on all the team members, except Grant. He had shared his suspicions with his friend, discussed the best way to flush the traitor out. And Grant had sympathized, become angry on Joe's behalf, and pretended to help.

God, he had been a fool. Just as he was being a fool again, wanting to believe in Maggie when the evidence against her was mounting.

"Mrs. Samuels, your husband was working for Fuentes," Detective Matthew Folker told her, not for the first time, his plump face and hazel eyes appearing almost kind as he watched her. "Your neighbors have seen him." He pointed to Diego Fuentes's picture. "As well as his nephew Santiago Fuentes, and his brother Jose, at your home. Surely you overheard something?"

Maggie shook her head, the silken fall of her deep red hair caressing her shoulders as her lips trembled again. He knew how Maggie reacted when she was hiding something. Her lips didn't tremble. Her lips trembled when she couldn't understand the pain she felt or the events unfolding. Her lips had trembled when she had seen another woman on his arm, and her face had gone that same pasty white.

"I saw them. They came to the house several times over the past months. . . ."

"You met with them," Folker accused, his voice benign, confident.

"I didn't meet with them." Her voice was thin, filled with fear. It sent a surge of fury racing through Joe. Was she lying? The evidence said she was. But the evidence had come from Grant. And they all now knew how reliable Grant had been. Even two and a half years ago Joe had known he knew Maggie better than he knew his best friend. He had acknowledged it, and it had scared the hell out of him.

"Agent Samuels left evidence that you were involved in his illegal activities," the detective repeated. The accusation had been voiced a half-dozen times in the two-hour-long interview.

"God. No," she whispered, as a tear slipped free and she shook her head again.

"There is proof you were involved. Pictures, Mrs. Samuels, as well as written notes. We're prepared to be lenient here. Give us the pictures and audiotapes Agent Samuels made of his meetings with the Fuentes family and we'll forget your part in this."

She shook her head again, her breathing jerky as she stared back at the detective.

"Mrs. Samuels," Folker sighed, pushing his hand over his balding head as he stared back at her, a glimmer of compassion in his eyes. "Would you like to call your lawyer? We do have evidence that you're involved. If you're frightened . . ."

"I don't know anything." Her hands tightened on her upper arms, her fingernails biting into her own flesh as a sob echoed in her voice. "I don't need a lawyer because I didn't know what Grant was doing. We've barely spoken for months."

"Mrs. Samuels, it's too late for this game." Folker slapped the table in frustration. "Look at the damned pictures." He pointed to the pictures of the young women murdered over the past two years; the morgue shots were horrendous. "Look at them, Maggie. He helped do this. You helped . . ."

"I didn't do this," she screamed back, tears washing over her cheeks as she stared back at the detective. "I didn't know. I don't have anything to do with it. I swear to God I don't. Please . . ."

Maggie lowered her head, her shoulders jerking from the sobs she was fighting to hold back, as Folker leaned back in his chair and looked over his shoulder to the mirror behind him. The disapproval in his gaze was heavy. He didn't like what he was doing to her, what he had been ordered to do. Detective Folker didn't believe Maggie could be involved. And, Joe admitted, he couldn't fully believe it himself.

Joe turned his head to the district attorney standing beside him, as well as the federal prosecutor observing the interrogation.

"I don't think she knows, Mark," he sighed wearily. "At least, not that she's aware of."

"Santiago and his uncle Jose will be out of jail before the day is out," Mark Johnson murmured. "We couldn't deny bail at this point because of the threats the judge has received. Our only chance is to trap them in this. If she walks out of this office without giving us the information, she's dead."

"We can't protect her, Agent Merino," Andrew Jordan, the federal prosecutor sent to oversee the interrogation, spoke up. "She's our only hope at this point."

Joe breathed in, slow, deep. As he stared at Maggie he saw Grant, his face twisted with hatred as he prepared to kill Morganna Chavez when he couldn't get her to the exit of the club and to Fuentes. The attempted kidnapping, the drugging of the women before her, the rapes, the death of Agent Lyons. It all lay at Grant's feet, and now at those of his wife Maggie.

"Are we certain she could have had access to the information?" Joe asked as he crossed his arms over his chest, ignoring the instinctive demand that he go to her, hold her, take the fear out of her eyes.

"We're certain she lived with him for two years. She would have seen or heard something, even if she wasn't involved. We've found too many lies in those damned journals to take his word for it," Johnson grunted. "Word on the street is that the price is already on her head, though. And Grant would have tried to cover his ass. He had the evidence, I suspect; the question is where."

"And if she doesn't know anything, consciously or subconsciously?" Subconsciously, yeah, he was betting she knew something. Consciously? He couldn't make it work in his own mind. Maggie would have never been able to live with the rapes and deaths of those women. It wasn't possible.

"If she doesn't, she's dead anyway. We can't do anything to protect her if she doesn't cooperate," Jordan answered.

"She trusts you, Joe. She asked for you when we brought her in this morning."

There was a question in the district attorney's voice, one Joe heard clearly. The DA was well aware of the fact that Joe and Maggie had been involved in an affair. Grant's irrational journals had been filled with furious entries raging over the fact.

"What do you want me to do?" Joe steeled himself against the denial raging inside him. He couldn't interrogate Maggie. It would destroy them both.

"We need that proof, Joe. Without it, the nephew and the brother will walk and the Navy will never find the mole responsible for the death of that Navy SEAL and the young women that drug destroyed." Johnson sighed.

Joe wanted to trust her, he wanted to hold her, to take away her fear and promise her everything was going to be okay. She was his best friend's wife. . . . His jaw clenched. No, Grant hadn't been his friend—the illusion of friendship, of brotherhood, had been a game, nothing more.

In the days since Grant's death, the depth of his treachery had slowly been revealed. He had been on the take for years. More years than Joe could have imagined.

"You know me, Matthew." Joe heard Maggie's whisper clearly through the glass. "I wouldn't be involved in this."

Joe never would have thought she would be involved in this, but then again, he never would have believed Grant would betray him. The evidence supported her involvement. For now he had no choice but to go with the evidence, the tangible proof rather than his emotions. Because his emotions couldn't be trusted. Because Maggie's life depended on her knowing something, whether she realized it or not.

"Maggie, we have evidence." Matthew laid his arms on the table as he leaned forward. "Evidence that you were at the house during the meetings, that you know where the photos and recordings are hidden. Lying isn't going to help you."

"I'm not lying to you." She smacked the palm of her hand on the table, that Irish temper finally coming to the fore. "I don't know what you're talking about, Matthew, and I'm not telling you that again. I didn't know what Grant was doing."

Despite the temper, she was trembling. He could see the fine tremors racing over her body, echoing in her lips.

"I'll take care of it." It was a promise Joe made not just to the DA, but to Maggie.

He was a fool. No greater fool had ever been born than he was at that moment, and he knew it.

Johnson watched him silently. Joe could feel the other man's gaze on him as he stared through the two-way mirror at Maggie.

"How?"

"Fuentes already put a price on her head. She's as good as dead without protection, until we can get the evidence she's hiding. I'll take her to a safe house, see if I can wear her down."

"If that doesn't work?" Andrew Jordan's eyes were narrowed as Joe stared over the district attorney's shoulder at the older man. Andrew Jordan was a sparse, tall man, with hawklike eyes and a jutting, pugnacious chin. He was the terror of the capital and a bulldog when it came to the cases he prosecuted.

"What do you want, Jordan?" He fought the anger welling inside him. "Arresting Maggie and terrifying her isn't going to help anyone at this point, and it won't get the evidence against the Fuentes gang. According to Grant's journal, his marriage to her was less than perfect. She wouldn't protect him."

"She wouldn't be the first woman to follow the money, Merino. You know that," Jordan pointed out, clearly referring to the rich bastard his first wife had died with.

It was well known that Joe refused to touch the money his parents made available to him. He used the inheritance his grandfather had left him, but his parents' money he had never touched. Not because of any anger or animosity toward it or his parents. There was none. He loved them, as interfering and broody as they could be. But he didn't want their money. With the inheritance he had, and his salary, he had more than he needed. More than Bettina would have needed if she hadn't gotten hooked on drugs.

"If Maggie wanted money, she wouldn't help kill to get it," he snarled. "Give me a week, maybe two. Let me see what I can learn."

"She has to go voluntarily," Johnson warned him. "We can't make it official."

"She'll go."

Maggie had trusted him a long time ago. Once, she might have even loved him. He accepted the guilt from the past on his shoulders. That didn't mean he would allow more lives to be lost because of Grant's hatred and greed.

"I'll leave it in your hands then," Jordan murmured.

Mark Johnson nodded then. "Keep me up to date, Joe, and hurry. We need this information now."

Maggie had been telling herself for a week that she would wake up, that this was all a horrible dream, that any minute she was going to wake up and it was all going to be over. But, as she sat in the interrogation room and stared into Matthew Folker's suspicious gaze, she realized she wasn't going to wake up. It wasn't a nightmare, it was reality.

Where was Joe? The question kept racing through her mind, tearing through her emotions. She hadn't thought Joe would desert her, that he would allow Detective Folker to question her without his presence. They had been friends once, more than friends.

Then again, he had loved Grant like a brother, and had never realized how much Grant hated him. But Maggie had known. For two years she had listened to Grant rage about Joe. The petty jealousy and fury Grant felt toward the other man had begun frightening Maggie within months of their marriage.

"Maggie, let me help you." Matthew leaned closer, his hazel eyes compassionate as he watched her. "We're not interested in prosecuting you, not if we get that information. Otherwise . . ." Otherwise, they would hang her out to dry on whatever trumped-up evidence Grant had left.

"So, it wouldn't matter to you if I *had* been a part of this?" she accused, as she waved her hand toward the pictures before her, the morgue shots of the young women who had been killed because of the horrible drug Grant had helped to distribute. "As long as you get whatever Grant had hidden, then you would just wipe the slate clean?"

"I give you my promise, Maggie. The DA will put it in writing . . ."

"Then you're a fool," she screamed, jerking to her feet as she grabbed the nearest photo and slapped it beneath his face. "*You* look at her, Matthew. She was savaged. And you're willing to let go someone you suspect of being capable of helping in it?"

She was shaking so violently she could feel the very core of her threatening to shatter apart. She couldn't fight her tears any longer, or her rage. She wanted to leave here, she wanted to go home, and then she wanted to find whatever the hell it was she was supposed to have and throw it in Folker's face.

"Sit down, Maggie." He sat back in his chair, calm, remote.

She had known the detective for nearly ten years now, since she had come to the station with her father when he worked with the paper. It was as much her world as the newspaper office was.

"Don't tell me to sit down." She shook her head furiously. "I did not do this, Matthew. Not in any part." She pointed a shaky finger at the pictures between them. "And if you had the evidence you say you do, you and that son-of-a-bitch Jordan would have arrested me while he was spitting his accusations in my face earlier."

The door opened at that second. Maggie jerked around, her heart exploding in her chest at the sight of the man standing there: tall, remote, his brown eyes so cold and hard they were like chips of dark ice.

"No, Maggie, they wouldn't have arrested you," Joe told her softly. "Because I won't let them. Now get your stuff together and let's get the hell out of here."

Out of there? To where? She had thought he would be her salvation, that if anyone believed in her, Joe would. But as she stared into the cold hard depths of his eyes, she was terribly afraid that Joe didn't believe in her any more than anyone else did.

chapter 2

one week later

maggie stared into the misty morning of the South Carolina mountains and contemplated mistakes. Past mistakes, present mistakes, and how they would lead into the future. She was twenty-eight years old, and she might not live to see twenty-nine. The choices she had made in the past two and a half years had led her to this mountain, this cabin, and the man she couldn't forget.

She had been such a fool. Two and a half years before she had walked out of Joe Merino's life, believing she had left in time to save her heart, to go on and to find happiness with someone else.

He hadn't loved her. They were damned good in bed, but he had made it clear he didn't want or need her in his life. Real clear. Another-woman-on-his-arm-type clear.

She curled her feet beneath her, tucking her body tighter in the rocking chair that sat on the weathered wood porch of the cabin Joe had brought her to a week before.

That had been the beginning of her downfall into hell. She had broken all ties to Joe Merino two years and six months before. Several months later, she had met Grant Samuels. Six months after meeting, they had married.

She should have known better. The moment she learned Grant was in law enforcement, she should have run. But Grant had been a detective with the Atlanta Police Department at the time, and Joe had been an agent in the DEA. They might have known each other, but it had never occurred to her that they had been as close as they were. And Grant had kept the secret until only days before their wedding.

She should have broken off the engagement the day she learned Grant and Joe not only knew each other, but were supposedly best friends. And she would have, except Grant had pleaded with her, swore he loved her, and the wedding had been only days away.

Grant had claimed he had known about her and Joe, and hadn't told her who he was because he had been terrified of losing her. That much would have been the truth, considering how easily he had used her, how he had intended to use her.

She had loved Grant. Or she had thought she did. Within months she had learned that the man she loved didn't exist. Grant had married her because he believed Joe cared for her. She had been a trophy, something to torment Joe with, and nothing more.

She had tried to leave him. Three months after their marriage began, she had walked out, only to learn the true nature of the man she called her husband and the information he had gathered to ensure she never divorced him. Information that would destroy her father.

And now here she was, still fighting to escape the hell of a marriage that had been doomed from the start. Older, wiser, and more certain than ever that Joe Merino would end up breaking her heart, if Grant's deceptions didn't end up getting her killed first.

Where would he have hidden the information Joe needed so desperately? Information that would seal the government's case against the remaining Fuentes family? Hell, did he even have the proof his journal had stated he had? Everything else in that damned book had been a lie.

Oh, he had really managed to mess her life up completely. The journal claimed she knew the location of the proof he had taken against the Fuentes family: Pictures and videodiscs of Santiago and Jose Fuentes along with Roberto Manuelo, the cartel general who had been killed the night Grant had tried to kidnap a female DEA agent, and had coordinated the drugging and rapes of over a dozen women in the past two years. The location of the lab where the drug was created and even the identities of several influential political figures involved with Fuentes.

In the past week, Maggie had learned exactly why the police department was so eager to drop any charges they could bring against her in return for the information they were looking for.

So why couldn't the bastard Grant have just written it in his journal with all the lies he had written against her? He could have included some truth in it, just for a change of pace.

She pushed her fingers through her hair, the circles in her mind exhausting her. There were no answers, and the cold suspicion in Joe's eyes was killing her. He had changed since Grant's death. Since he had been forced to kill Grant, rather. There was an edge of unrelenting ice in his expression, in his eyes, that hadn't been there before. Amusement had always lurked in the chocolate brown gaze, sensuality; playfulness had always curved his lips.

Even when they had argued, when she had walked out on the relationship they had, there had been regret, sadness, softness. There was none of that now. This wasn't the man she had given her heart to.

So why was he protecting her? Why did he give a damn? Those were questions he had refused to answer since their arrival at the cabin, questions that garnered no more than a cold silence.

At this rate, she was going to have frostbite before the month was out.

"You're a sitting target out here."

Maggie flinched at the sound of his voice from the doorway. The dark sensuality of the tone couldn't be hidden, no matter how coldly furious he might be. It throbbed just beneath the ice and sent heat curling through her system.

She hated that. She hated the response to him, unwilling and unwanted, that she had learned she had no hope of controlling.

She stared into the forest, watching the mist rise like a veil of dreams above the treetops to meet the heat of the rising sun.

"If the Fuentes family knew where I was, then they would have already struck." She shrugged her shoulders, wishing she had worn a bra beneath the loose T-shirt she had slept in.

Her nipples were hardening, her breasts were swelling, and this was no time for it. She could feel the steadily rising sense of expectation building within her. She had spent a week with Joe, alone, and the tension was only growing worse by the day.

"You aren't showing much faith in my protective abilities," he grunted.

"Of course I am." She kept staring into the forest; she wasn't about to watch him. Watching him only aroused her further. "I'm sitting here watching the dew meet the sunrise, in plain view. See, I trust you to know I'm well hidden."

"You make about as much sense now as you ever did." His voice turned surly. "Come inside, I have coffee ready."

Yeah, she had smelled it for the past half-hour, tempting, strong, teasing her senses. Rather like Joe did.

This was not going to work.

"You're sitting out here pouting," he accused, when she didn't move to follow him.

"I don't pout, Joe," she reminded him. "I think."

"You think too much then," he growled. "Now get your butt in the house. Maybe the coffee will even out your temper."

She clenched her teeth. She was not going to argue with him. Arguing with him was a pointless exercise. It was like beating her head against a wall. She only ended up hurting herself.

"I don't have a temper." She was restrained. Hell, he was still alive, wasn't he?

"Uh-huh." Was that amusement she heard in his voice?

After a week?

She couldn't help herself, she turned and looked at him and her senses went into overload. He wasn't wearing a shirt. The leanly muscled contours of his hair-matted chest brought back memories better forgotten. Memories she had never forgotten.

The warmth of him as he came over her, his thighs parting hers, the feel of his cock nudging against her sex, filling her slowly, riding her fiercely.

Maggie shivered as her vagina clenched with a sudden spasm of hungry need, a clenching of lust as the heated dampness began to prepare her for a touch that certainly wasn't coming. She jerked her eyes from his chest and lifted them to his face. Beard-roughened, the darker growth contrasted with the dark blond, rakishly cut hair that framed his face. The two days' growth was nearly black, and gave him a piratical appearance that was too mouthwatering for words. It just made his lips appear sexier, more lickable. And she really wanted to lick them.

"Come on, Maggie. Coffee and breakfast. Then we can talk." He held his hand out to her, the ice that had filled his eyes for the past week thawing, warming.

Maggie licked her lips nervously, feeling her heart racing in her chest, her nerve endings sensitizing. She rose from the chair, though she ignored his outstretched hand as she watched him warily. He was like a damned chameleon, and the abrupt changes were throwing her off balance.

"So where's the prick I've spent the last seven days with?" she asked as she moved around him to enter the cabin, feeling the walls closing in on her as he stepped in behind her.

He had a habit of that, sucking all the space out of a room until nothing remained except him. At least, that was all she was aware of. The warm, cheery tones of burnt reds and soft desert browns of the living room were lost on her. The couch was wide, comfortable. Joe liked making love on couches. Floors. Coffee tables. Kitchen counters.

She stepped back quickly, giving him plenty of room as the corner of his lips kicked up in a grin.

"Same cautious Maggie," he said, as he moved past her and headed to the kitchen. "How long did it take me to get you into bed the first time?"

"Not long enough," she stated. "And I am not having sex with you again, Joe." Yeah. Right. Her body was all in agreement on that one. In another second, the dampness building on the folds of her sex was going to start dampening the fleece of her pajama bottoms. If it wasn't already.

"We're sleeping in the same bed . . ."

"That's not my choice," she argued, as he glanced over his shoulder, casting her a wicked look. "You wouldn't let me sleep on the couch."

"Sure you can." He shrugged his tanned shoulders negligently. "But it's going to be an awful tight fit with both of us there."

That was pretty much his stand on it seven days ago. She followed him slowly into the kitchen, admiring the tight contours of his rear beneath the snug jeans he had only zipped, not buttoned. Yeah, she had caught that little detail out on the porch.

"How much longer are we staying here?" She finally asked the question that had been hovering on her lips for days. "When are you going to give up, Joe?"

"When the Fuentes family is dead." He padded to the coffeepot, lifted the carafe, and poured the liquid into waiting cups.

His answer shocked her. Before, his answer would have been once a culprit was behind bars, not dead.

"I just want to know how they managed bail," she sighed, moving to the kitchen table as he turned back, the coffee cups firmly in hand.

"One of Fuentes's lieutenants paid off the judge. We have the money and evidence in hand. Judge Gilmore was none too pleased with the offer. He could take the money and let them out, or his grandchildren could suffer the consequences. We opted to go with the bribe, taped it, and now have the money impounded in a safe location until it's needed. All with Jose's and Santiago's fingerprints."

She couldn't have been more surprised if he had said he was Santa Claus.

"And that's not enough to lock them up for a while?" she asked, amazed.

"We need it all, Maggie. We want them locked away forever, if they're smart enough to live until the trial. I don't want them out on a technicality. And I don't want families murdered to get them there."

Maggie stared back at him suspiciously. She had been questioning him for a week now, and he was finally giving her the answers she wanted: Why?

"If I'm suspected of being part of this, then didn't you just put several people in danger by telling me?"

His gaze was hooded as he glanced back at her before shrugging. "I don't believe you're part of this."

Oh yeah, she really believed that one at this late date.

"So I'm here why?" she questioned him as he set the coffee in front of her. "And they are still out on bail for what reason?"

"We need that proof Grant hid and the Fuentes family still believes you have that." Joe took his seat across from her, watching her steadily. "You don't know where it's at; that means your life is still in danger. And the Navy needs that mole. There's too much at stake here to risk a trial on what little evidence we have of the two aiding and abetting Diego. If we want to shut down this cartel and that drug, then we have to do it here."

Ahh, so the truth was emerging, perhaps.

"You're using me . . ."

"Hell no!" Anger flashed across his expression. "You are not bait, Maggie. No matter what you think. I told you I'd protect you, and I meant it."

And she didn't trust him, not even for a second. Fear raced down her spine as she stared back at him, suddenly wondering to what lengths he would go to in capturing the Fuentes men. But she knew the lengths he would go to, she reminded herself. He blamed the Fuentes family for what happened to Grant, rather than blaming Grant himself.

"And this information the federal prosecutor thinks I'm hiding?" she asked, not bothering to hide the mockery in her voice. "Have you just given up on it, Joe?"

He tilted his head as he regarded her for several seconds. "You don't know where it's at. That's a dead end."

"Oh, you are so good." She would have cried if it didn't hurt so damned bad. The truth was there in his eyes, the suspicion, the calculation. Others might not have recognized it, but Maggie saw it and knew it for what it was. "Do you really expect me to swallow that line of crap, Joe? Do you think I'm that stupid?"

"On the contrary, you're not stupid at all. Suspicious," he chided her with a quirk of amusement. "But not stupid."

Maggie ignored the coffee sitting before her, the smell of it suddenly as unappetizing as the lies passing his lips. Standing slowly to her feet, she stared back at him impassively, fighting to hide the pain exploding inside her.

"You've changed, Joe," she whispered. "I never pegged you for a liar. An asshole and a prick maybe, but not an out-and-out liar. Congratulations, you did the impossible. You made my opinion of you sink lower than it was two and a half years ago."

Turning on her heels, she moved to stalk from the kitchen, to put distance between herself and his games, his lies. She hated lies. She hated herself. Because she wanted to believe him, she wanted to trust in the arousal and the warmth that had heated his eyes, just as she wanted to believe that he could trust in her, just once. She was a fool.

"No, you don't." She came to an abrupt stop as he jumped from his chair, his hand reaching out to catch her upper arm as she moved to pass him.

The shock of his flesh touching hers, the heat and strength in it, nearly drove the breath from her body.

"Let me go." She jerked against his hold, feeling the anger growing inside her, the hurt burning through her heart.

"I won't let you go, Maggie," he suddenly snarled, jerking her around, as his free hand buried in her hair, his fingers locking into the strands. He jerked her head back and stared into her eyes fiercely. "I won't let you go and I won't let you die. Lie to me all you need to. Fuck it. I'll get Fuentes in the end, if I have to kill him to do it. But I won't let you go."

"You don't have a choice." She pushed against his chest, desperate to escape him, to break free of the hard temptation of his body. "I don't belong to you, Joe, not anymore . . ."

"By God, you always belonged to me. Always."

Before she could stop him his head lowered, his lips covered hers, and time came to a stop. There was only Joe's kiss. His lips moving against hers, his tongue licking, piercing her lips, moving between them in a fierce, dominant kiss.

Her fingers curled against his chest, then spread out, nerve endings soaking in the feel of him, remembering, relishing the rasp of the short, crisp hairs on her palms, the fiery warmth beneath his flesh.

Against her lower stomach she felt his erection pressing intently through the material of his jeans. His arms enfolded her, his kiss intoxicated her.

"Joe," she whimpered as his lips slid to her cheek, to her jaw. "Don't do this."

Don't make her feel again. Don't make her ache for all the things she knew she couldn't have. Don't make her love him more than she already did.

"I dreamed of you." The arousal and the anger pulsed in his

voice as he nipped at her ear. "For more than two years, I remembered what it was like to feel you beneath me, to hear the soft little catch in your voice when you came beneath me, the feel of your body tightening around me. I remembered, Maggie, and it drove me insane."

She whimpered at the pain that enveloped her, the raking fingers of need, regret, and sorrow that filled her.

"This won't fix the past." She tightened her fingers on his biceps, feeling the power and the tension that vibrated in his body. "It won't solve anything, Joe."

He wanted to punish her. She could feel it pulsing in the air around them, feel it in the rake of his teeth along her neck, the nipping little kisses, and the press of his erection against her.

Even as her head screamed out a warning against his touch and the probability of heartbreak down the road, she felt herself relaxing, leaning into him, the response he had always commanded from her leaping through her system.

"I know one thing it will definitely solve." One hand slid down her back, gripped the swell of a buttock, and lifted her to him.

Maggie moaned at the feel of his cock notching between her thighs, his lips at her neck, his tongue licking erotically at her skin. Blood pulsed hot and fast through her veins, heating her flesh, sensitizing her nerve endings, as lust began to spike the air around them.

Hunger surged through her. More than two years of aching, of needing, of suffering the restless, shadowed dissatisfaction that edged at her mind, culminated here. In Joe's arms. His touch. His kiss. It was the drug she had never recovered from, the one very likely to destroy her.

chapter 3

the feel of her lips beneath his, her body pulled against his, was heaven and hell. Memories swamped him, and following close on its heels was a lust that tightened in his balls and sent hunger slamming through his system. This was Maggie. Redheaded, fiery, a need he had never exorcised from his heart. A hunger he couldn't forget. No matter how hard he tried—and he had tried, for two and a half years he had tried. He was tired of denying himself.

His lips moved over her jaw, back to her lips, and he stole the words he could feel rushing past them. A denial, the cautious, intuitive part of her that had always driven him crazy. There was only one way to silence it, one way to steal beneath her defenses and make her melt in his arms.

"Maggie," he whispered, lifting his lips until they ghosted over hers. "Let me love you . . ."

"You son of a bitch!"

He was unprepared for the raging fury let loose on him. A redheaded mini tornado that kicked, slapped, and threw herself at him like a force of nature intent on destruction.

"Dammit, Maggie . . ." He grabbed her wrists, only to let go as she kicked at his shin.

Jumping back, he stared at the aberration confronting him. Her red hair was wild, waves of fiery splendor cascading to her shoulders, her cheeks flushed, her green eyes brilliant with tears.

"I can't believe you!" Her fists were clenched at her sides as her breasts rose and fell with the quick pace of her breathing. " 'Let me love you,'" she mimicked him. "You know about as much about that emotion as Grant did. Zero, Joe. Nada. And you can kiss my ass."

"Give me the chance." He narrowed his eyes on her, letting a mocking smile curl his lips. "If you had put the bitch on hold for a minute, I might have gotten around to it. And the next time you compare me to Grant, you might find that sweet ass spanked rather than kissed."

"Lay a hand on me and I'll charge you with assault," she yelled back. "You had your chance to love me, Joe, and you blew it."

"Like hell," he snarled, sexual tension and raging anger rising inside him. "I loved you every damned chance you gave me, Maggie. Completely. Neither of us could move after we were finished."

"You fucked me," she corrected him brutally.

Joe flinched at the explicit wording, something dark and inexplicable rising inside him to deny it.

"And what did you do, Maggie? I hardly think it was love; you married the man you believed was my best friend six months later."

"I didn't know until he brought you to the wedding rehearsal." Her gaze was filled with disgust as it raked over him. "I nearly broke the engagement then, and I would have if he hadn't begged me not to. I knew." Her laughter was tinged with bitterness. "God, I knew better. I should never have listened to him when he swore to me that my relationship with you didn't matter. That he hadn't known about it."

The pain in her eyes made him pause. Maggie had never been

much of liar, at least not before her marriage to Grant. She wore her heart on her sleeve, loved or hated with equal intensity. A person didn't have to guess where he stood with her.

"He knew about our relationship," he informed her, watching her closely. "He knew the night you walked out on me, and he knew why."

Her lips parted for a second before closing firmly, tightening into a bitter line. There was no surprise there, though, only remembered pain. Grant's lies couldn't surprise her anymore, only her own stupidity at the time still had the power to hurt her.

"Yes," she finally admitted. "He did. He knew about our relationship and he used it the entire time we were married. Too bad I didn't know any better before the vows were spoken."

"Why did you marry him?" That question had haunted him, had driven him to drink more nights than he could count.

"Because I thought he loved me," she threw back at him fiercely. "And I thought I loved him. I thought he was honest, that he wanted more than the quick fuck his buddy had decided was all I was good for."

"Say that word again and you're going to regret it, Maggie," he snapped.

"What? Fuck?" she sneered. "What's wrong, Joe, does it offend you to know what a complete bastard you were?"

"I know well how damned stupid I was." God knew it had been driven home night after lonely night for two and a half years. "But you were never just a fuck."

"Oh, you loved me?" she asked mockingly. "Yeah, sure you did, Joe. Even while you were parading Miss Big Boobs around on your tuxedoed arm for a night out? Did you think I had forgotten that one?"

Miss Big Boobs. Fake boobs maybe, not that he had checked. The woman in question, Carolyn Delorents, had been the daughter of a suspected drug kingpin. He had been on assignment. Nothing more. An assignment he hadn't told Maggie about.

"I haven't forgotten," he growled. "And you would never listen to explanations."

"Explanations come before you spend the night with another woman hanging off you, not after," she pointed out sarcastically. "And I didn't want explanations. The fact that you did it, without telling me, was enough."

"We weren't married . . ."

"I was falling in love with you," she cried out. "You knew it. You knew it, and rather than telling me I was wasting my time, you let me find it out at an event I was covering for the paper. You didn't tell me anything."

"I didn't know you would be there."

"Which only makes it worse." She swiped her fingers beneath her eyes before blinking back her tears. "I've paid enough for our affair, Joe."

She turned, stalking from the room before he could stop her. Following her, he caught the bedroom door before she could slam it closed and moved slowly into the room.

"Explain that comment." Suspicion uncurled in his stomach. He had tried to convince himself that Grant had been good to her, that he had loved her. Through the past two years he had never imagined she had been anything but worshiped.

"He married me because he was convinced you cared about me." Her eyes flashed with pain and anger. "Three months after our marriage I left him, Joe." Mockery twisted her features. "Only to be forced back. He blackmailed me with a mistake my father made when first starting the newspaper. He wasn't about to let me leave, to lose the one thing he had to torment you with."

"Why didn't you tell me?" He forced back his anger, his disbelief.

"Blackmail, Joe. You understand the concept, right?"

"I understand the concept." He held on to his control by a thread.

She wasn't lying. He knew Maggie. In that moment he realized that he knew her better than he had ever known anyone in his life. And he couldn't make himself believe that she was lying.

"He left me alone for the most part, as long as I played the role," She sniffed back her tears as she sat slowly on the edge of the bed. "We had separate bedrooms. He never tried to touch me. He got off on hurting you. He hated you." She shook her head, confusion filling her voice. "I never understood that."

Joe met her gaze as she lifted her eyes to his, watching him with such perplexed anger that it caused his chest to clench.

"Did he ever say why?" He had never really known Grant—Joe realized that now—but a lifetime of believing in the friendship he thought they had was hard to put behind him. He had trusted Grant above anyone else in the world, even his family. Grant had been the brother Joe had never had. At least, he had thought Grant was. Separating himself from those memories sometimes felt as though he were separating a part of his soul from his body.

"Oh, he had plenty of reasons." Weariness washed over her expression. "The promotion you got and he didn't. Something about bullies in school. But I think most of it came down to the fact that your family was stinking rich, according to him. That bothered him most of all."

And Joe had never known. That was the hardest part for him. He had never suspected that Grant had hated him so thoroughly.

"I loved him like a brother." And he had, since they were boys. "That's why I didn't stand between you when I learned who he was dating, then marrying. It's the reason I left it alone, Maggie. I thought you deserved someone to love you, and I thought he loved you."

She stared back at him for long moments, remnants of anger glittering in her dark green eyes.

"Such sacrifice," she snorted, the sound causing him to clench his teeth against the frustration eating at him. "You should apply for sainthood, Joe."

She rose to her feet once again, moving slowly around the

bedroom before stopping on the far side and turning back to face him.

"What did you think I was going to do now? Fall back into your arms as though the past two and a half years never happened?"

"I could have handled it." He shrugged tensely. "I never forgot, Maggie—"

"Then forget now."

Joe read the wariness in her eyes.

"Have *you* forgotten, Maggie?" He moved toward her slowly, dying to touch her, to taste her one more time. "Did you forget how hot I could make you? How hot and wet you got for me, baby?"

He didn't touch her as he moved to her; he stared into her eyes, feeling the needs rising inside him as fiercely as they reflected in her eyes.

"This isn't going to get us anywhere," she whispered, her hands clenching the material at the front of her shirt. "I won't let you do this to me again."

"That's what I swore about you a week ago," he admitted. "That I wouldn't get so hard for you that the only thing that mattered was getting you beneath me, burying my cock so deep inside you I didn't know where you ended and where I began. That I wouldn't ache for you, that I wouldn't need to hear that soft little cry you make when you come for me."

"That you wouldn't use what I felt for you to try to trap me?" she suggested mockingly, causing him to grit his teeth in frustration.

"I wouldn't use the sex against you, Maggie." Would he? He was telling himself he wouldn't, but he knew he would push her. She had to know where that information was, if only subconsciously.

"You would use any weapon against me that you could find," she threw back at him as she edged away.

Joe followed.

"You were married to him for two years," he said softly. "You may have hated every minute of it, but you were there, in that house with him. There had to have been something he said, something he did . . ."

"And you think I haven't thought of that?" she spat out. "That's all I've thought of, Joe. Because if I could give you that damned information you want so bad, then I'd be free. Of you, of Fuentes, *and* of Grant. Trust me, no one wants you to have that information more than I do."

"You want to leave me that bad, Maggie?" He moved behind her, leaning in close, careful not to touch. "I remember a time when you found excuses to stay in my bed, to remain at my place."

"And I remember a time when you found excuses to escape," she reminded him, stepping away again, but not before he saw the little tremor of response that washed over her. "You didn't want what I had to offer before, Joe, and now, whatever you're offering, I'm passing on."

He watched her move across the bedroom and enter the bathroom. Unhurried, her slender body shifting beneath the loose clothes she had worn to sleep in. Her head was lifted, her shoulders straight, and the pride that was reflected in her stance caused a grin to edge at his lips.

He wondered if she knew she moved against him in that big bed each night. More often than not, her head ended up on his shoulder, a shapely leg thrown over his, and her hand lying directly over his heart. Just as she had lain when she had shared his bed so long ago.

And each night his control withered further away as his cock became more demanding. She could argue until she was blue in the face, and sometimes she could, but he knew what he felt each night. Hard nipples pressing against his side through her T-shirt. Her hands touching him tentatively, as though he were a dream.

He was a fool to let her go the first time, and he could be playing a bigger fool now. Only time would tell. And that was why he'd brought her here, he reminded himself. If she was lying, he would find out. If she was telling the truth . . . then he would protect her with everything he had. If she was telling the truth, then he would never let her out of his life again. She would be his. One way or the other.

chapter 4

men sucked. they were the root of every problem any woman could ever have. They were the reason for bras, the need for makeup, hair stylists, shaving legs, and high heels that made the arch feel like it had a steel rod slammed up it. They were picky, arrogant, argumentative, and so damned certain of themselves it made her grind her teeth in fury.

And Joe was the worst. He always had been. He didn't argue, debate, or consider anything; it was *his* way, however he had to make certain it came about. And once again he was working her. She could feel it.

He watched her now in a way he hadn't all week, eyelids lowered, his expression brooding, thoughtful, calculating. His dark eyes rarely left her, and she could feel the sexual hunger thickening in the air around him. He had a look when he was aroused to the point that the sex would be hard and brutally satisfying. And he was getting that look.

"Stay away from me," she ordered, as he moved close to her

that evening, brushing against her as she stacked the dishwasher with dinner dishes.

His male grunt did little to calm her nerves. Nothing he could do, though, could calm her nerves. He wasn't the only one aroused after a week of enforced confinement, of nights spent in the same bed with him, feeling the heat of his body.

She was dressed in jeans and T-shirt, and a bra, but the layers of clothing did absolutely nothing to stem the needs that only grew. She remembered nights, hours on end that he would take her, throwing her into one orgasm after another, leaving her breathless, exhausted as the sun rose beyond the windows of his apartment. He was inexhaustible. And the memory of it was killing her.

"You've changed," he remarked as he stood back from her, propping himself against the counter as he watched her. "You were never so confrontational before, Maggie."

"I was never in danger for my life before," she reminded him, flashing him a short glare. "It does change a girl's perspective, Joe."

"You're going to be fine." A quick frown edged at his dark blond brows as he watched her. "We'll figure out where the information is and we'll take Fuentes down."

"One thing you never lacked was confidence." Maggie closed the door to the dishwasher before setting the power and flipping it on.

"There has to be someplace Grant hid things. What about his other journals?" he asked her. "We only found the current one, it began six months before. Where did he keep the others?"

"I have no idea." She shook her head as she breathed out roughly. "I spent as little time around Grant as I had to. I didn't question him, I just wanted him to leave me alone, so I left *him* alone."

"Did he mention a safe deposit box?"

"Joe, these are all questions the detective asked me at the station," she reminded him abruptly. "If he had one, I didn't know. I never cared about his journals, his friends, or his comings and goings. If I had suspected for a moment what he was up to, I would have paid more attention. But I didn't."

"Men like Grant like to brag."

"Grant bitched, accused, and went into paranoid delusions." She shook her head at his perception that Grant would tell her anything. "Everyone was to blame for everything that had gone wrong in his life, except him. I assumed his journals were filled with the same crap, so I never gave them a thought."

He was silent then, but she could feel his eyes on her as she wiped down the counter and the table before pulling out the Swiffer to go over the floor.

She could feel the little tremors of response building beneath her flesh as he watched her, she could almost feel his eyes raking over her snug jeans, the press of her breasts beneath the T-shirt.

Minutes later she propped the Swiffer back in its place before turning and heading for the living room. She was aware of Joe following her, stalking her like a damned animal. As though he could sense her arousal and was debating the best way to act on it.

Let me love you, he had whispered earlier. He had no idea how those words had ripped through her heart. She had dreamed of him loving her, had believed he was beginning to until she covered that damned party she had no idea he had been invited to. Because he hadn't told her. Hadn't invited her. Oh no, he'd had one of his society women on his arm, decked out in silk and diamonds and platinum blond hair.

Had he slept with her?

She couldn't let herself think of that. Even now, two and a half years later, the thought that he would take another woman so quickly after having shared a bed with her had the power to rip her defenses to shreds.

"You can't ignore me forever, Maggie."

She stopped in the middle of the living room, breathing in deeply before turning to face him.

"I'm not trying to ignore you, Joe."

His eyes were brilliant with lust, the same look that had had the power to bring her to her knees during their relationship. Literally.

He tucked his hands into the pockets of his slacks and stared back at her silently, as her gaze flickered to the action. The heavy bulge between his thighs sent heat burning through her body. Her vagina ached, echoed with emptiness, as her nipples pressed hard against the material of her bra.

She swallowed tightly as she felt the need for oxygen increase.

"Did he please you in bed?"

The question took her by surprise.

"Excuse me?"

"Grant." He frowned back at her. "Did he please you in bed? Did he make you scream and beg for more, even when you were too exhausted to take more?"

Her eyes widened at the flicker of anger in his eyes.

"That's none of your business—"

"The hell it's not," he snapped. "I went crazy for two and a half years wondering if he pleased you, knowing he shared your bed . . ."

"Stop it, Joe. This isn't going to get us anywhere."

"I'll know." He kept his voice low, even, a sure indication that he wasn't going to let the subject go.

"No, you won't." She lifted her chin as she stared back at him, her fists clenched at her sides as she fought to maintain her control. "Because I'm not answering you."

Shame filled her at the thought of revealing the truth. She had known on her wedding night that the mistake she had made in her marriage was more severe than she had expected. Grant's lust had sickened her, his spoken perversions filling her with disgust and fear.

"His journal was pretty in-depth concerning your sex life," he informed her then. "He was quite descriptive."

Maggie felt herself pale. "We weren't having sex then. I hadn't shared his bed since the first months of our marriage, I told you that."

"Why?" He moved closer, stalking her like a predator.

"That's none of your business, Joe. Let it go." She watched him closely, warily, uncertain as to how he would react.

"You're a very passionate woman, Maggie. I can't imagine you denying yourself, or cheating on your husband to attain satisfaction."

"I like sex, so automatically I had to be fucking someone?" she snapped out furiously. God save her from hardheaded men.

"That wasn't what I said."

"Yes, Joe, that was what you were saying." She waved her hand back at him in a gesture of frustration. "What did you do for the last two and a half years? We both know you weren't a virgin when you came to my bed. How many women have you had since me?"

"No one."

The answer had her flailing for a response; instead, she could only stare back at him in shock.

She stared back at him silently as he came closer, his expression dark and intent as he watched her.

"You tormented me, Maggie."

She shook her head desperately. "Don't play with me like this, Joe. Please." She was willing to beg. She had left him, believing he didn't hold her heart. Now, two and a half years later, she admitted the truth she hadn't wanted to face then. She had loved him then, and that love had never died.

"I'm not playing with you, Maggie." His hand covered her cheek as she lost her breath. The sound of her tremulous gasp would have been humiliating if his touch weren't so warm, so needed. "I'm trying to save us both this time."

She was panting for air, certain her shaky knees would give out before she found the strength to move away from him.

"Do you remember what it was like?" he asked her gently.

Maggie stared back at him, dazed, uncertain, as his lips lowered to breathe a kiss against hers.

"All night long," he whispered over her lips. "I would fall

asleep, still buried in your body, still hungry for you. Do you remember that?"

"I remember seeing you with another woman." She forced the
words past her lips. "I remember you staring at me across the room,
your expression as cold as ice. That's what I remember, Joe."

His jaw clenched. "You can forget that."

"No, I can't forget that." She pushed away from him slowly,
fighting back the regret as she did so.

"I didn't sleep with her, Maggie."

The tension tightening his body had her stepping back further.
She could feel the certainty that he was at the edge of his control.
Once he slipped past the veneer of civility, denying him wouldn't
be an option. The hunger in him called to her too fiercely, pulled
at her too desperately. When Joe began coming after her in earnest, she would be lost, and she knew it.

"It doesn't matter that you didn't sleep with her," she told him
softly as she moved to the couch. There was no way in hell she was
heading to the bedroom. "It's not about the woman, Joe, it's the fact
that you did it. You weren't as invested in me as I was in you, otherwise you would have told me about the party. You would have told
me about your date."

She curled into the corner of the overstuffed couch, drawing
her legs up until they bent to her side and gave her a measure of
protection against the throbbing heat between her thighs.

He hadn't moved from where he stood, other than to turn and
follow her progress across the room with his eyes. She knew
what he was doing, what he had been doing all day. Trying to
push her buttons. From the first words out of his mouth that morning, when he accused her of pouting, to now, he was trying to
work her, to get what he wanted without giving any of himself in
return.

That wasn't enough for her now. She wanted as much in return
as she had to give, or she wanted nothing at all. And giving all of
himself wasn't something she thought Joe would do easily. He

faced her, his jaw flexing with tension, his brown eyes raging with frustration and arousal.

"Why didn't you tell me, Joe?" She tilted her head when he said nothing. "What would you have done if you'd seen me on another man's arm that night?"

"I would have torn him apart," he snapped.

"Your date left with all her hair and teeth intact," she pointed out gently.

"And you never came back," he growled. "You wouldn't answer my calls. By God, you didn't want to hear explanations."

"No, I didn't," she admitted sadly. "The explanation should have come before the reality of it kicked me in the gut, Joe. I watched you that night, pretending you didn't know me, that I was nothing, as you danced with another woman. . . ."

"I never took my eyes off you."

"Or your hand off her," she reminded him.

"It was a fucking case, Maggie," he snapped, a grimace contorting his face. "Do you think I wouldn't have told you if I thought you would be there? After I saw you it was too late; I couldn't jeopardize the case."

"I cover the society page, Joe," she yelled back, infuriated with his logic. "You should have known I would be there. You should have warned me."

"How?" He pushed his fingers restlessly through his long hair. "What the hell was I supposed to do, Maggie? I was in the middle of an operation, I couldn't just tell you what the hell was going on."

"You could have warned me you had a job to do. That's all I needed." She jumped to her feet, anger surging through her. "I knew you worked for the DEA, Joe. I wasn't stupid or incompetent. I wouldn't have asked questions, but I would have been warned. Why the hell do you think you walked out of that party with all appendages intact that night? I didn't strike out just in case you were working, rather than trying to fuck Miss Big Boobs hanging on your arm."

"Then why are you still so pissed?" He was genuinely confused. "Why did you avoid me, Maggie? We could have worked this out."

"Because you didn't warn me, Joe," she reminded him with false patience. "Because you expected more from me than you were willing to give, and every damned message you left on my phone proved it."

"What?" He frowned back at her in confusion. "I asked you to call me."

"You demanded I call you. You informed me, more than once, that I was being silly, childish, petulant," she sneered. "No, Joe, I wasn't. I expected no more from you than you would have from me, and you weren't willing to give it. You would never have tolerated seeing me with another man; why did I have to endure seeing you with another woman? No warning. No explanation. No nothing."

He was silent, staring back at her with narrowed eyes and stubborn features. His arrogance was one of the things she used to admire, that complete male self-confidence that drove her crazy and turned her on all at the same time.

"I didn't expect that from you," he ground out. "I would have explained."

"The explanation was too late." She tossed her hair back before smiling tightly into the growing anger in his dark eyes. "I'm not arguing this with you any longer, Joe. My relationship or lack thereof with Grant is none of your business. Just as your job and what it requires of you is none of mine. You're here to do a job. To protect me, and to find out if I know where Grant hid your precious proof. Stick to the job. You're good at that."

With that, she stalked from the living room into the bedroom and slammed the door behind her. She really prayed he took the hint and left her alone. The hurt and anger she had buried when she had left Joe were rising inside her now. The lack of outlet over the years, and her determination to hide from her feelings for him, had kept her safe from the repercussions. Now the pain was flowing through her, the remembered shock and heartache when she realized how little she had meant to him, slammed into her with a force she hadn't expected.

She deserved the same love she was willing to give, and her marriage to Grant had taught her that she wasn't willing to settle for less. Especially not from Joe.

chapter 5

the bedside clock read two in the morning before Joe heard the deep, even breathing that indicated Maggie had slipped off into sleep. Within minutes, as she had every other night, she rolled from the edge of the bed to the middle, and her slender body tucked in against his.

He gritted his teeth against the arousal pounding between his thighs, and knew Craig wasn't going to be happy to be pulling the extra hours of watch that he would be stuck with in the morning.

Maggie was unaware that Craig was watching the outside of the cabin. The other man slept through the day, then took up watch at midnight until Joe moved onto the porch each morning to indicate he was awake and on the job. Joe was getting up later every morning, though. Sleep was becoming harder with each successive night.

As Maggie shifted against him demandingly, he lifted his arm, allowing her to settle against his chest before he let himself hold her close. She felt right in his arms, but hell, she always had.

How many times had she slept against him like this? How

many times had he awakened in the middle of the night, just to listen to her breathe, to feel the softness of her hair as he held her close?

He stared up at the ceiling, his lips compressing as he remembered the accusations she had thrown at him earlier that evening. Had he really expected more from her than he was willing to give?

Maybe he had. He had been so busy assuring himself that what they had was just an affair, that the volatile little redhead wasn't getting beneath his skin, that he had missed the fact that she was firmly entrenched in his heart.

That was why he had jerked her out of the interrogation room when she had been brought in for questioning. That was why he couldn't accept that she had been part of Grant's criminal activities, despite the proof—pictures of Maggie handing Diego and Santiago Fuentes several envelopes at an upper-class restaurant, pictures of her greeting them at the door of their home, and exchanging small talk at several parties she had attended for the paper.

She had told Detective Folker she was unaware of what the envelopes contained. That she had run the errand for Grant simply because it was easier than fighting over it, and she had been going into that part of the city anyway.

The journal Grant had kept held pages and pages of accusations against Maggie. Implying that he had begun betraying the agency and his friends because of her spending habits, because of her determination to always have more.

But Maggie hadn't dressed any differently than she had before her marriage to Grant. There were no expensive clothes, no fancy jewels, and she had never driven the new car Grant had bought her. So where was the money Fuentes had given him?

He buried his fingers in Maggie's hair as he tried to work through the questions. After a week with her, his suspicion that she might have been involved was dissolving beneath his hunger for her and the knowledge that if money had been what Maggie was after, then she would never have cut him out of her life as she had.

He had money. A DEA agent's pay sucked, but his family was one of the most influential in Georgia, and his trust fund would see any children he had into old age if they were careful. Not to mention what his parents would one day leave him. If Maggie had been after money, then she had missed a much easier opportunity than marrying Grant and becoming involved with the Fuentes family.

Instead of trying to snag him for marriage or money, Maggie had left him. Not that Joe claimed anything as his own. Money was accessible if he needed it. But his parents' money wasn't his own, and he refused to touch it. Still, that wasn't the reason she had been so furious. She hadn't forgiven him for not warning her before she saw the daughter of the man they were investigating on his arm.

He had been there to get information. He had gotten the information, but he had lost the girl. His girl. Was he willing to lose her again?

A soft moan slipped past her lips as she moved against him again, her lips pressing the bare flesh of his chest. Joe clenched his teeth against the heated pleasure of her soft little tongue stroking over the flat, hard disc of his male nipple.

Could he survive another night of her in his arms without touching her? God, it was getting hard. She was like a little kitten, pressing to get closer, her fingers curling against his abdomen, her nails raking his flesh and sending a flash of clenching sensation to seize his balls. Sweat popped out on his forehead and along his chest and thighs, and his cock tightened further.

His erection was so damned hard, so sensitive, he bit back a tortured groan as the crest flexed against the material of his sweatpants. And there was no relief. He sure as hell wasn't going to try jacking off with her in the bed with him, and doing it any other time was out of the question. Besides, the hollow release gained from the act wasn't what he needed. He needed Maggie, her sweet, tight pussy enveloping him, burning him as he possessed her.

"Joe." His name whispered past her lips, that sleepy little plea he remembered from the past, the throb of hunger in her voice that had once had him turning to her, slipping easily inside her as he awakened her fully to his touch.

Instead, he now lay still, tortured, tormented, as her silken hand moved over his stomach, caressing, raking her short nails over his flesh, and sending agonizing bursts of pleasure through his cock.

He breathed in slow and deep as her teeth raked over his nipple, a murmur of feminine pleasure vibrating from her throat as her hand moved lower.

Joe lifted his arm, his free hand gripping a slat in the headboard behind his head as he fought for control, as anticipation began to spiral inside him. He knew her like this. Drowsy, when she would awaken in the middle of the night, hungry for him, all kittenish and relaxed. And he wasn't about to fuck this up. No way in hell. In those brief minutes between asleep and awake, Maggie had the most amazing habit of forgetting if she was pissed off with him. If she didn't remember it right now, he wasn't reminding her. Uh-uh. Was not going to happen.

"Maggie." He couldn't stem the hoarse groan that left his throat as her fingers played with the elastic band of the sweats.

He could feel his mouth drying out as anticipation began to build, his erection flexing in need as her fingers began to move beneath the band.

"Hmm," she murmured against his chest, her teeth sinking against his flesh in a sensual, warning little bite, as he parted his thighs and let her have her way.

Hell no, he wasn't reminding her of nothin'. If he did, then she was likely to turn away, to be embarrassed or angry. Whichever, it meant she would stop touching him, that the blazing heat of her hand wouldn't . . .

Son of a bitch!

His hips jerked violently as she moved again. Slender fingers tried to encircle the raging shaft as she shifted against him again, her lips moving lower on his chest.

Oh hell, he knew what was coming. He remembered this well, and if she came to her senses while his dick was in her mouth, then she was likely to get violent.

But it wasn't like he was encouraging her, he assured himself as he lifted his other hand to the headboard, determined not to guide her head lower. Hell no. He wasn't going to stop her. She was a grown woman. If she wasn't going to remember she was pissed, then he was not reminding her. Wasn't going to happen.

He fought to breathe as he stared in dazed pleasure at the ceiling above the bed, nearly panting in lust as her fingers pushed his sweatpants down, struggling to guide the material over the erection.

"Good," she mumbled with a soft smile against his flesh, as the cloth finally slid beneath the thick, iron-hard flesh rising eagerly to her touch.

Her fingers wrapped around him again, stroking slowly from his balls to his crest, as his hips arched involuntarily to her caress. Her fingers were like living silk as they rasped over the sensitive flesh. Her lips and tongue were hungry, heated as they moved below his chest, kissing, licking, taking sensual little nips from his flesh.

It always amazed him in the past when she would do this. That her need could so overtake her in those moments when she awoke that nothing mattered to her but being with him. Touching him. Tasting him. Destroying him with her hunger.

She was destroying him now. He ground his head into the pillow, bit back a violent growl that she hurry, and fought to enjoy as much as possible before she remembered she was supposed to be mad at him.

Two and a half years. He hadn't had a woman since the last night Maggie had spent in his bed. And God, he had missed her. This was why no other woman had shared his passion, because he knew no other could compare to what he was finding at this moment.

Knowing he was making an even bigger mistake, he moved his gaze from the ceiling, looking down the line of his body, as the dim light that burned past the partially closed bathroom door fell on Maggie's head as he watched her move lower. Lower.

"Sweet heaven. Maggie, baby," he panted.

He couldn't take much more. He was shaking, sweat pouring from his body as she moved to his abdomen, her tongue painting a path of fiery need across his flesh.

Closer. Ah, God, her tongue was so close. It was torture, the worst sort of agonizing pleasure, to have her silken tongue so close and yet so far away from his engorged erection.

Her fingers stroked his burning cock as her tongue came within inches, inches. He was shaking with anticipation, sweat building on his body and running in small rivulets down his chest as he fought to hold on to his control.

"Maggie. God, baby. Tell me you're awake." His hands clenched on the slats and he blinked back the sweat dripping to his eyes as he told himself to stop her. To put an end to the sweet torment before she took a bite out of him that he might not recover from. Maggie could be amazingly fiery, both in passion and in her fury.

He could move his hands. He could grip her head and force her to stop. But he was terrified that if he let go of the death grip he had on the bed, that rather than waking her as he pulled her from him, he would awaken her as he filled her mouth instead.

"God. Damn, Maggie." His ragged cry filled the darkness as her tongue swiped over the head of his cock. The hardened flesh flexed, then spurted a hard stream of pre-cum to her waiting lips.

Shit. That wasn't supposed to happen.

But her murmur of appreciation was followed by burning ecstasy. Her mouth enveloped the thick head, her tongue swirling around it, probing at the small eye as she greedily consumed him. Arching to her as another curse tore past his lips, he thrust deeper, feeling her lips tighten on him, her tongue lashing at him.

Ah God. He had to stop this. Didn't he?

How? How the hell was he supposed to find the strength to make her stop?

"Maggie, baby . . . please . . . ," he groaned harshly as she began to suck him with slow, tight strokes of her mouth.

Nearly to her throat, only to retreat, her tongue laving with quick little licks before sinking down again, her lips meeting her fingers as she stroked the lower portion of his shaft.

She was going to destroy him. Tonight, she would steal his soul and there wasn't a damn thing he could do about it. Once he spilled into her mouth there would be no returning to sanity. There never had been. He felt like an animal; reality receded and nothing mattered but spreading her thighs and both of them fucking into exhaustion.

"God yes." He blinked again against the moisture stinging his eyes as his hips moved to her suckling mouth. Thrusting in and out, his scrotum tightening until pleasure was near pain and the need to come was torture.

"There you go, sweetheart," he panted. "Hell yes. Suck it, baby. Suck it so deep and good. Your mouth is heaven, Maggie. Paradise."

He strained in her grip, desperate to reach deeper, to thrust harder. He fought the need to climax, his head thrashing on the pillow as he fought it with every ounce of control he could hang on to.

She was unaware of what she was doing. Surely she was. She had gone to bed furious with him, hadn't she?

Then she moved again, sliding between his thighs, one hand cupping the tight sack beneath his cock as she took him deeper, moaned, and her eyes opened in drowsy sensuality.

There was no shock. Green eyes stared back at him with drugged lust as her entire mouth caressed him, flexed around him, and he was lost. She knew what the hell she was doing. Just as she always had.

A hard growl tore from his lips as he drove hard against her grip and lost the last threads of control. He felt his semen exploding into her mouth, her lips moving as she consumed him, accepting his release as her hands stroked, caressed. Her tongue milked at the underside of his cock, urging more of the creamy release to her mouth as she moaned in rising hunger.

"I tried." His hands tore from the slats of the headboard. "God help us both, Maggie, I tried . . ."

chapter 6

she was so weak. Maggie cursed her weakness even as she let Joe bear her to her back on the bed. He was her weakness. His lips on hers, the sharp, fierce kisses that left her drugged as his hands pulled at her shirt. He lifted only enough to drag the material over her head and toss it aside before he was back.

Cool air rippled over the tender, aching tips of her breasts only a second before Joe's heat enveloped her once again. He had that power, the power to warm her, to fuel a fire inside her so hot, so desperate that nothing mattered but his touch.

Maggie opened to him, her hands clutching at his back as the rasp of his chest hair stimulated her sensitive nipples and stole her breath with the pleasure. So good. It had been so long. Too long without him, without his touch. She had sworn she wouldn't let this happen, but her own dreams and hunger had stolen her will.

She had dreamed of him every night that they had been apart. Aching dreams. Dreams of anger or of lust. Dreams of reunion or of parting. It didn't matter which, she looked forward to each one, to touching him, to seeing him, if only in those dreams.

But this hadn't been a dream. When she slowly awoke, forgetting for a few brief moments where they were, and the trouble she was in, Maggie had touched him. Her hand sliding over his abdomen. Her body heating with need. Just as quickly reality had tried to intrude. But Joe was there, tense but quiet beneath her touch, letting her lead.

He had never done that before. Never had he lain back and allowed her to set the pace of any part of their lovemaking.

Having that control had broken her resolve. That and her own hunger. God, such hunger for him. She couldn't bear the longing whipping through her, the emotions tearing into her heart, filling her soul.

As she moved between his thighs she had expected him to dominate the act, to move her head as he wanted it, to hold her to him as he took over the pace. Instead, his ragged voice had encouraged her as he arched to her. His hands had gripped the headboard, his body tight, tortured with need.

And now she arched to him. As his lips moved from hers, to her neck, then her breasts, his hands pushed at the pajama bottoms she wore.

Heat built around them until Maggie felt perspiration coat her flesh. Reaching for him, a whimper left her lips as he caught her hands and stretched her arms above her head.

"Hold on," he growled. "It's my turn now."

Her fingers latched onto the slats behind her as she watched him with dazed fascination. The expression on his face was one she had never seen, not at any time before. Savagery tightened it as hunger lent a dark cast that sent a shiver racing down her spine. He wanted her, wanted her with a depth and a strength she had never seen in him before.

His head lowered over a breast again, his lips poised just above the hard point rising eagerly toward him. His gaze lifted, meeting hers in the dim light of the room as his tongue extended to lick over the stiff peak, demanding that she watch. That she see the naked lust and pleasure tearing through him, as it tore through her. Sensation whipped through her, jerking her body violently upward as a cry left her lips.

"Joe. Don't tease me. It's been too long."

Years too long. An aching, sorrow-filled lifetime since she had known his touch.

"I know how long it's been." His voice was raspy, deep. "Every day, every hour, I counted with my need for you, Maggie. I'm a very hungry man now. Let me relish what little time my control will allow me here."

He turned his head, rubbing his rough cheek against the sensitive flesh of her swollen breast. Maggie bit her lip as she panted for air and shuddered beneath the caress.

"I love your breasts." His hands framed the hardened mounds, his thumbs raking over her nipples as the hard bursts of pleasure had her whimpering in rising anticipation. "Such pretty, flushed nipples." He lowered his head, his lips covering the hard tips, his tongue flickering over them with rapid, hot strokes. "So sensitive and easy to please. I love pleasing your nipples, Maggie."

Maggie's hands tightened on the headboard, as her gaze dimmed and pleasure rocked through her. It was so good, the slow worshipping of her breasts. She remembered that well, how he loved making her nipples hard, then driving her crazy as he made them more sensitive by the second.

Which was pretty much what he was doing now. Laving each with his tongue, raking them with his teeth, only to come back to suck at them firmly, one by one, until she swore she was going to climax from the intense pleasure of that alone.

"Beautiful." He breathed the word from one nipple to the other before giving each a parting kiss and moving lower.

As he touched her, Maggie could feel her heart melting, her soul reaching out to him. There was a difference in his touch, it was gentler, almost reverent. As though the time spent apart had hurt him as much as it had hurt her. Was she being fanciful? Probably.

But God, she loved him. She always had. And for just this one night she would let her heart have its way and convince her that he loved her as well. Just a little bit. Just enough to sustain the dreams she had kept hidden, even from herself.

"Joe . . ." The pleasure grew, wrapping around her until she knew she wasn't going to be able to bear much more. The agonizing arousal tearing through her clenched her womb, throbbed in her vagina. She was desperate for release, for his possession.

"I have to taste you again, Maggie," he whispered, his voice whisky-rough as his hands moved to push the pajama bottoms further down her thighs and over her knees.

With an impatient kick, Maggie discarded the bottoms. Arching her back, she lifted closer to the tormenting lips moving along her torso, then her abdomen. With hot licks and slow kisses, Joe had her stretched on a rack of lust nearly too intense to bear. The pleasure was burning through her nervous system, creating a vortex of need, hunger, and intense blinding arousal so deep it became the very center of her existence.

She needed more.

As he lifted himself between her thighs, his hands parting her legs and lifting them until her knees bent, Maggie could only watch in rising anticipation. Breathing was nearly impossible as she waited for that first touch, that first blinding, intimate kiss.

"I dreamed of this, Maggie." He moved his hand until the backs of his fingers were feathering over the short curls that shielded her sex. "Touching you, tasting you again. Did you dream of me, baby?"

His thumb rasped over her clit and she jerked in pleasured response.

"You know I did." The dreams had kept her going, had kept her hoping through two years of a marriage that had turned into hell.

She wasn't in the mood for games now, though. She needed to orgasm, needed that sharp brutal edge of lust to dissipate as it only did after Joe brought her to climax.

"Hmm, were your dreams this good?"

His head bent, his tongue swiping quickly through the drenched slit of her sex, as her hips arched violently and a cry tore from her lips. Electrical impulses of lava-hot sensation tore through her body, leaving her hovering on the edge of climax as Joe retreated.

"Don't stop." Her head thrashed on the pillow. "Joe, don't stop."

"I don't want to rush it." His voice was strained, his breath hot against the damp flesh between her thighs as he blew against the sodden curls.

His tongue licked over her, teasing the swollen bud of her clit before going lower. With wicked, knowing licks, he outlined the sensitive entrance to her vagina, his tongue flickering over it as she lifted to him, only to retreat teasingly.

She would never survive his teasing. She knew how he teased, knew how long he could hold off as he made her hotter by the second. She was more desperate now than she had ever been for his touch. The teasing wasn't going to happen, because she would never survive it.

"Rush it. You can go slow later."

She released the slats of the headboard, and before he could catch her hands, her fingers were tangling in his hair and pulling him to her desperate flesh.

She heard a growl a second before his lips covered the aching, burning nub between the sensitive folds of her pussy. Sucking it into his mouth, his tongue licked with a driving rhythm, as a thick male finger worked deep inside the pulsing depths of her vagina.

Oh yeah, that was what she needed.

Pleasure exploded inside her, brilliant shards of white-hot lightning sizzled over her nerve endings, burned through her flesh. Her clitoris swelled beneath the assault, her body tightened, and seconds later the orgasm that tore through her flung her into ecstasy.

She was unaware of the tight grip she had on his hair, or his grip as he forced her fingers free. All she knew was the rapture flying through her, and the feel of him kneeling between her thighs seconds later.

Opening her eyes, she arched her hips to him as he rolled a condom quickly over the straining cock rising between his thighs.

He was powerful, all sleek flesh and rippling muscles. His chest was heaving with the effort to breathe as he secured the protection, then moved into position between her thighs.

"How do you want it?" His voice was strained. "Fast and hard, or hard and fast?"

The limited choice would have amused her, if she wasn't so damned desperate for the coming penetration.

"How about hard and fast?" she moaned. "God, I don't care, just do it, Joe. Now . . ."

She screamed at the penetration. It was hard. Fast. In three strokes he had buried himself to the depths of her needy pussy. Coming over her, his arms tucked beneath her shoulders, his elbows holding the majority of his weight from her as he began to move.

"Hell yes. Take me, baby. Take all of me." The harsh demand, voiced in a tone desperate with pleasure, had her breath lodging in her chest.

All of him. She needed all of him. His body, his heart.

"Joe. Oh God. Joe." Her fingers clenched on his shoulders as her legs lifted, wrapping around his pounding hips and locking in the small of his back as he drove her to insanity with the pleasure burning through her.

"There, baby," he crooned, as his head lowered to her neck. "So sweet and tight." His voice was guttural, throbbing with lust. "I could fuck you forever, Maggie. Never stop. I never want to stop."

The fierce rhythm was too much to contain. Nerve endings untouched in more than two years rioted with the intensity of the sensations stroking over them. Explosions of nearing orgasm began to ripple through the tender tissue, as Joe groaned roughly at the further tightening around his plunging erection.

He liked that, she remembered. The way she tightened around him before climax, the feel of her racing toward completion.

"Come for me, Maggie." He nipped her ear erotically. "Come for me, baby, let me feel you milk me. Now, baby. Now."

He moved faster, impossibly deeper. Maggie felt the sensations splinter inside her as a stronger, harder orgasm gripped her. She couldn't scream, there was no breath to scream, no strength to fight the rolling explosions tearing through her as Joe's male cry filtered through her mind.

He tensed above her, driving deep in one last plunging thrust, before she felt the convulsive throb of his cock inside her, felt him spilling himself into the condom he wore.

"Maggie. God, Maggie. I missed you . . ."

Her heart clenched at the words, at the emotion she fooled herself into believing she heard. She loved him. She had always loved him. In that moment, Maggie knew that nothing and no one would ever replace Joe in her heart.

chapter 7

"did you really love him?"

Joe's question wasn't unexpected. Hours after the lust and hunger had burned itself down to a dull glow, sleep had stolen their strength. Now, awake, he held her, her back against his chest as she watched the day lighten beyond the bedroom window.

He wasn't confrontational this time, not as he had been when he questioned her about Grant before. He was quiet, reflective. Unfortunately, it was also when he was at his most dangerous. And she was very aware of the fact that right now he had no intentions of allowing her to brush the subject away. And maybe it was time to face it, to face the truth of the mistakes she had made.

"I thought I did," she finally answered. "I wanted to, until a few weeks after the wedding. Had he been the man I thought I married . . ." She paused. She didn't want to break the fragile peace between them.

"You would have," he answered for her.

He sounded accepting. There was no anger in his tone, he

wasn't tense. She hadn't expected that. In the past two and a half years she had seen Joe only once, at her wedding, where he had been best man. It had been hell. The moment she whispered her vows to Grant something had shattered inside her soul.

She should have walked out then; she admitted that to herself long ago. When the vows had stuck in her throat, and the tears had flowed, not from happiness, but from sadness, sorrow, she should have turned and walked out.

But she hadn't wanted to hurt Grant. She had cared for him deeply.

"I could have," she amended. "If I had let myself."

"Would you have let yourself?"

That question no longer haunted her. At first it had, in those first weeks when she had questioned herself so deeply, before Grant had shown himself for the bastard he was.

"If he had been the man I thought he was." Admitting it to herself was the hardest part. "Then I would have loved him." She would have lived her life loving two men, rather than just one.

"You wouldn't have." His answer had her jerking in his arms, turning until she could face him.

"I married him," she pointed out, ignoring the dark look he flashed her. "I cared for him then, Joe. Deeply."

"You cared for him, you didn't love him." His broad hand cupped her face, his thumb caressing over her swollen lips gently. "You would never have loved him, Maggie. Because you loved me."

She breathed in roughly as she stared back at him, remembering the nights she had ached for him, dreamed of him. The nights she had cried for him.

"I cared for him," she repeated. "He wasn't the man I thought he was, so I wasn't given the chance to love him."

She felt him behind her, hard, erect. There was no demand in him though, at least not yet. He smoothed her hair back from her face as he watched her patiently, his gaze velvet-soft, flickering with emotion.

"Wouldn't have mattered." The arrogance that suddenly stamped his features moments later had anger simmering inside her. "You loved me, Maggie. You still love me. You married Grant loving another man and you know it."

She gritted her teeth. She was not going to argue with him. Arguing with him got her nowhere.

"Stop it, Joe."

His smile was patronizing. "You knew when you married him that you didn't love him. You loved me. Admit it."

"Why? So you can gloat? So you know you've won?"

"Oh baby, I already know I've won," he growled. "I just want to make certain you know it."

"I know you have got to be the most infuriating man I have ever met in my life," she snapped, jerking out of his embrace as she moved from the bed. "You just can't help yourself, can you, Joe? Being an asshole is so deeply ingrained inside you . . ."

"I loved you, Maggie."

His calm, quiet announcement shut her up. She stared back at him in surprise, her eyes wide, the elation she would have once felt overshadowed by more than two years of pain.

"You loved me?"

Maggie watched as Joe flicked the blankets back and moved to the opposite side of the bed. The muscles in his back and lean buttocks flexed as he rose to his feet before turning back to her.

He was aroused. The hard length of his erection jutted forward demandingly. Muscular, hard, and proud, the sheer power in his body had always commanded her attention.

"You seem surprised," he grunted. "I haven't had a woman since you left my bed. Do you think it was from choice?"

Of course it wouldn't be. Joe was highly sexed, a creature of lust when it came to his pleasure. That didn't mean it was love. Did it? Or could it?

"I think I'm very much afraid you're playing one hell of a game with me," she admitted the possibility to herself. "You terrify me,

Joe, simply because you hold the power to destroy me in the palms of your hands. And if you've already judged me guilty, you wouldn't hesitate to use whatever weapons you could come by. Even lying."

His eyes narrowed on her; the distance of the bed between them suddenly seemed much farther and much more difficult to cross than it had been even days before.

"You're right," he finally answered. "If I thought you were lying, if I thought you were involved, nothing would save you, Maggie. But I haven't lied to you. I don't believe you were involved."

"You've just suddenly found all this love for me that wasn't there two and a half years ago?" She jerked her long shirt from the floor and pulled it on with shaking hands.

"It was always there, Maggie." He didn't bother to pull his sweatpants on, he just stood facing her, aroused and proud and so damned confident she wanted to throw something at him.

Her smile was mocking as she shook her head slowly. "I don't believe you, Joe."

A frown jerked between his brows. "Oh, really?"

The dangerous undertone of his voice wasn't exactly a comfortable sound.

"Really." Maggie ignored the nerves building in the pit of her stomach as she faced him.

She had never truly challenged Joe, not in anything he said or the parameters of their relationship. Confrontations weren't her first choice in solving anything, but as she stared back at him she realized that this particular confrontation had been coming since he had taken her from the police station.

"You don't want to do this right now, Maggie," he warned her quietly. The velvet softness of his voice was a sure sign that his temper was rousing.

"I don't want to push you, period, Joe." She turned from him, bending to pick up her pajama bottoms before putting them on. "It's not worth the heartache you can deliver. But I stopped believing in fairy tales two and a half years ago." She turned back to him, fighting the need to believe him even as she doubted him. "Especially yours."

She didn't expect his sudden response. Joe always handled himself calmly. Coolly. He never lost control. Until that moment.

The change came over his expression so suddenly that Maggie had no chance to react. From one second to the next the easygoing facade was stripped. His dark eyes narrowed, the flesh along his cheekbones tightened, and he had vaulted onto the bed, crossing it in one step before he was in front of her.

Turning to run wasn't really an option, but she tried anyway. With a squeak of alarm she turned and tried to jump for the safety of the bathroom, only to feel the manacle of his heavily muscled arm wrap around her waist as he pushed her against the wall.

"You stopped believing in my fucking fairy tales?" His voice was a hoarse snarl at her ear as she felt her heart rate increase, the blood suddenly thundering erratically through her veins. Not from fear. There was no fear as his hands literally ripped the T-shirt from her body and flung the scraps aside, all the while holding her in place as she struggled against him.

"Are you crazy?" she yelled out, more from shock than any other emotion. Where the hell had *this* Joe come from? She could feel the anger, the lust, and more. Some added edge to his touch that had her heart leaping in hope.

His hands were gentle despite their commanding strength, his body controlling her, even as it stroked against her. This was no act. She could feel it in his hands, in the sudden, dominant hunger blazing in the air around them.

"Believe in this fairy tale then, damn you," he snarled at her ear as the straining length of his cock pressed into the crevice of her buttocks. "You want reality, by God? This is reality, Maggie. I can't bear another woman's touch, and knowing you slept in that bastard's bed ate into my guts like fucking acid. My best goddamned friend, and all I wanted to do was slip into his bed and fuck his wife until she screamed my name and begged me for more. Is that enough reality for you?"

She was panting for him, in the space of seconds just as aroused, just as hungry for him as he obviously was for her. She could feel the pulsing, driving lust in the engorged length of his throbbing erection as he moved back, then spread her thighs further apart.

"You make me fucking crazy."

One hard, desperate thrust filled her with his flesh, took her to her tiptoes, and had her crying out his name.

"Joe, please . . ."

"Yes," he snapped, his voice thick with lust. "Joe. It's Joe, Maggie. It's Joe fucking you and it's Joe that's going to make you come. Come for me, baby. Oh God . . . Maggie."

He stilled as she felt him inside her, bare, the latex barrier he normally wore no longer there.

"Shit. Oh hell, Maggie, you feel so fucking good."

He was lost. Joe knew he was lost and there wasn't a damned thing he could do about it. The bitterness and pain in her voice and her expression as she doubted the emotions that had tortured him for so long, had broken his control. Control he had built for his own sanity, control he had sworn he would never lose with Maggie.

But there he was, his dick buried full length inside her, as bare as hell, throbbing with the need to spurt his semen inside her. No condom. Some primal instinct inside him screamed out the denial as he clenched his teeth and fought to pull back, only to return in a thrust that ripped the breath from his body.

"Oh fuck, it's so good," he whispered at her ear as he held her hands to the wall, shifted his hips, and stroked the brutally tight tissue clasping him. "Maggie, baby. You're so sweet and soft. So hot . . ."

He didn't know how to let her go. He knew he should, he needed to. This was a risk he shouldn't be taking, a risk he should have never allowed. But he couldn't release her. God, he couldn't let her go.

"Joe . . ." There was a sense of wonderment in her voice. The cynicism was stripped away, the doubt gone. Innocence filled her tone, the same innocence he had heard the night he took her virginity.

Hell, he had been just as shocked then as he was now by the sound of it. A woman nearly twenty-six years old should not be a virgin in this day and age. But Maggie had been. She had laughingly told him she was just waiting on a man who could do more than make her tingle. One who could make her desperate. And he made her desperate.

She made him desperate.

"It's okay, baby." He was panting with the effort not to come, not to fill her with the raging release drawing his balls tight. "Oh God, Maggie. Tell me it's okay. Tell me it's okay."

He had to move. She was so silky soft, slick, tight, gripping him and moving with him as he moved in short, hard strokes that sent radiant pleasure racing down the shaft to clench in his scrotum. He was shaking, literally, with the pleasure tightening along his cock. It was agonizing, blistering, the most sensation he had ever known in his life.

"Joe, please . . . harder. Please."

Her hips were twisting against him, her internal muscles milking him. Hell, it wasn't as though she were the first woman he had taken without a condom. There had been others. A few. But it had never been like this. She was so slick, so tight, that the soft sucking sounds of their movements were killing him.

The effort not to come had him drawn on a rack of torturous pleasure. He was going to pull out, he assured himself. He was.

"Are you on . . . the pill? The pill, Maggie." *Please, God, let her be on the pill. Let her be protected.*

She shook her head, even as her pussy tightened on him. His hips slammed against her, driving him in deep, hard, before he forced himself to stillness.

He couldn't breathe for the need to come.

"Move." He was at the point of begging. "Get away from me, Maggie. God, do it now. I can't do it."

He loosened his grip on her hands, but he couldn't pull free of her. Hell, where had his control gone? Where was his good sense? If he spilled inside her, she was going to get pregnant. He knew she would. Some instinctive knowledge tightened his gut, flared in his chest.

She didn't move away from him, she moved closer. Her hips shifted as her fingers splayed against the wall.

"Baby . . ." He stared at the side of her face, her cheek was pressed into the wall, her eyes opening with drowsy, sensual pleasure. "I'll come inside you, Maggie."

Her breath caught. He saw it, saw the flush that mounted her cheeks, felt the further tightening of her pussy as her excitement mounted.

"I'll give you my child, Maggie. My baby. Is that what you want?" He wanted it. Oh God, he wanted it so bad. His baby growing beneath Maggie's heart, sheltered by the woman who owned his soul.

Her doubt didn't matter. He loved her, and he was man enough to admit he had been a fool to ever believe Maggie would have aided Grant in any way. This was his woman. She had always been his woman.

He had dreamed of her for over two years. Dreamed of her back in his life, in his arms, her body growing heavy with his baby. God, he wanted that. Wanted to tie her to him in the most elemental way, in a bond that could never be broken.

"I love you, Maggie," he whispered again as he lowered his lips to her cheek and a fierce involuntary motion of his hips had him thrusting against her again.

It was heaven. Ecstasy. The feel of her surrounding him, clasping him so tightly he could barely breathe for the pleasure.

"Joe . . ." Emotion thickened her voice as her fingers tightened around his. "God, please don't hurt me again. Please, Joe . . ."

He saw the tear that tracked down her cheek, glimpsed the ragged fear and emotion that filled her eyes. And he knew the pain she feared, that he would let her go, that he would hide the need, the hunger, the desperation he felt for her again.

There was no hiding now. Not now, not ever. He was instinct, a male claiming his female, more animal than man, as he fought to hold to him the one person he knew he could no longer survive without.

"I'll not let you go again, Maggie." He was on autopilot and he knew it. Hated it. Only Maggie could do this to him, and that was why she had terrified him two and a half years before. This was why he had let her run when she had believed there was no hope for the emotion she needed from him.

"Oh God, Joe. I can't live without you again." She was moving against him, gripping him, writhing against him. "I've always loved you, Joe . . ."

Sanity disintegrated beneath her words. His head lowered, his lips covering the sensitive point between neck and shoulder as he began to move. Hard. Fast. Deep. He was fighting to breathe, feeling her tighten around him, hearing her cries in his ears, and finally feeling her dissolve around him.

Sweet and tight, the hot clasp of her cunt began to milk at his erection, long contractions of pleasure that had him slamming inside her, his back arching, his neck tipping back as he felt his semen pouring from him. Thick, hard jets of ecstasy spurted inside the flexing depths of her pussy as he cried out her name. He heard his own voice, guttural, unnaturally hoarse, as he tried to drive deeper inside her, to fill her womb, to tie her to him in the most fundamental, primal way possible.

She was his. Only his. And for Maggie's sake, not to mention his own, he hoped she realized that.

chapter 8

maggie was stepping out of the shower hours later, her body pleasantly sore and aching, a delightful reminder of Joe's loss of control and the feel of his semen spurting inside her.

As she dried, she rubbed the towel over her belly slowly, thoughtfully. She had always wanted children, had dreamed of having Joe's children. The knowledge that life could be growing inside her now sent an exciting shiver up her spine.

She had never allowed herself to hope, or to dream, that this could actually happen. But in the hours since that first shocking display of primal domination, Joe had done nothing to regain that control. No sooner than he had spent himself inside her, he had her back in the bed, moving over her, and claiming her again. And he hadn't stopped until morning was well on its way and a hunger for food had driven them to the kitchen.

They had showered together, though Joe had finished quickly and rushed to leave the small shower stall, swearing that if he didn't get away from her, he was going to kill both of them taking her.

Maggie smiled at the thought as she dressed, pulling a pair of silken panties up her sore thighs before easing into her bra, and then jeans and a T-shirt.

She had a feeling that anything requiring much exertion was going off her to-do list for the day. Which meant that the hike she had been thinking of talking Joe into was definitely out.

Sitting on the small stool in the corner of the bathroom, she pulled on her socks before rising and padding into the bedroom. She slid her feet into laceless sneakers before moving for the closed bedroom door and pulling it open.

Stepping through the doorway, she came to a stop as first Joe, then Craig, moved from the kitchen. Both men were carrying coffee cups and had their weapons hanging on their belts. Joe had been armed for the past week, she knew, but never so blatantly.

"Maggie." He paused just inside the living room, his brown eyes watching her worriedly. "Come on in, honey. Get some coffee."

Craig shot him a startled glance at the endearment.

"Is everything okay?" she asked.

Craig Allen was part of the DEA unit Joe had commanded before Grant's death. He had been unaware of her involvement with Joe before her marriage, just as everyone else had been.

"We have some information." His expression wasn't comforting, but at least he wasn't pretending they were strangers.

Unconsciously, her hand dropped to her stomach as she fought the nervousness rising inside her. Joe's eyes followed the movement, his nostrils flaring as his cheekbones flushed with lust. Response trembled up her spine, sending a small tremor through her body as he watched.

Maggie swallowed tightly, drawing her gaze from Joe to Craig, who watched them both suspiciously.

"I can do without the coffee for now, then." She breathed in deeply, feeling an insidious sense of disaster building in her chest.

"Come here, baby." He obviously didn't care what Craig saw or thought.

He crossed to her, drew her into his arms, and kissed her cheek comfortingly.

"It's going to be okay," he promised.

Maggie glimpsed Craig's expression. Surprise definitely, and suspicion. But the cold calculation that lurked behind both made her nervous.

"What's going on?" She let Joe lead her to the couch, sitting down nervously as Craig took the chair across from them.

"Your house was trashed yesterday." Craig wasn't one to beat around the bush, either.

As he sat down, his hazel eyes watched her closely, looking, she knew, for a guilty, frightened response.

"It was Grant's house." She shrugged. "If they just got around to trashing it . . ."

"It wasn't trashed in the typical fashion," Craig broke in. "The carpet was ripped through in most of the rooms and pulled back. We've had a team going through it, but we've found nothing beneath any of it. We got there before every room was hit, but we've found nothing, and we know whoever went through it didn't find anything."

"The carpet?" She shook her head in confusion. "Why rip away the carpet?"

"They were looking for hidden pockets in the floor," Joe said as he curved his arm around her shoulders, his fingers rubbing at her arm in comfort.

She glanced at him with a frown, shaking her head. "That doesn't make sense."

"The carpet could have been carefully cut to blend in with the nap of the material, but could be pulled away to access a hidden safe or loose boards in the floor where objects could be hidden," Joe explained.

Maggie glanced back at Craig. He was watching her closely, doubtfully. He thought she knew where the information they were looking for was hidden. God, she wished she did.

"Did you check all the rooms after you saw where they were looking?"

Craig nodded shortly. "We had a team stripping carpet all night last night. We found nothing."

Maggie rubbed her forehead. Where would Grant have hidden that information?

"It could have been a lie," she finally whispered, turning to stare at Joe dismally. "The journal was a lie, Joe. He could have lied about the information."

"He had it, Maggie," Craig informed her coldly.

She couldn't sit still. She had fought to calm the fear rising inside her for the past week, to take one day at a time and pray the information would be found. Rising to her feet, she paced across the living room, listening distantly to Joe and Craig discussing the search the night before.

The house Grant had been so proud of would be a mess. The two-story brick colonial design had been a major buy for him. He had bragged about that house incessantly. Because it was better than Joe's. Because as much money as Joe's family obviously had, they weren't real fond of sharing, because Joe's house was so much smaller, so much less classy. She remembered how he would laugh about that. How Joe's house, right down to the dank, unkempt basement, was so much less superior than the one Grant had managed to buy.

She paced to the edge of the room, turning back to stare at the two men as they continued to talk. Joe was frowning thoughtfully, his eyes narrowed as Craig explained the areas searched and how in-depth it had gone.

Grant wouldn't have hidden anything in his own house. He would have known that was the first place they would look. He was smarter than that. He was demonic. He would have found a way to hurt Joe, even in this. She was actually surprised he hadn't tried to frame Joe instead of her.

"We found several hidden caches of cash. Some drugs." Craig

was shaking his head. "And some more journals. Man, he was sick, Joe."

Maggie watched Joe's expression even out, become distant. Grant had nearly destroyed a part of Joe. The two men had been friends for most of their lives. Joe claimed him as a brother, a confidant. He hadn't known the cruel, bitter side to Grant that she had.

"Any clues in the journals?" Joe leaned forward, balancing his elbows on his knees as he watched the other man.

"Pretty much what we found in the others." Craig shrugged. "Different topics, same shit." He shook his head wearily. "We really didn't know him, did we?"

Grant had often laughed over that. How the others didn't really know him, had no idea how much smarter he was, how he could always stay one step ahead of them. Especially Joe. Poor dumb Joe, he would snicker, who would never know how easy he was to fool, how easy it was to use him. Right down to the car Joe had treasured. The '69 Mustang Joe cherished . . .

The Mustang. Grant had hated that car. He always sneered when he spoke of it, with an edge of smug satisfaction.

That taunting, self-satisfied gloat had always entered his voice.

She turned from the two men slowly, praying she appeared casual as she moved into the kitchen, toward the coffeepot. She didn't know Craig well enough, and she could be wrong. And, oh God, if she managed to lead Joe to the information after all, he was never going to believe that she had nothing to do with Grant's illegal activities.

She pressed her hand to her stomach, breathing in deeply when she paused by the counter. If he didn't believe in her, he would never have dared to risk a pregnancy with her, she thought with a surge of hope. Joe was very family-oriented. Even though he had many disagreements with his family, she knew he loved them and she knew he was fiercely protective of them.

She hated this. Hated the position Grant had placed her in. He was so lucky he was dead; if he weren't, Maggie believed she would have been tempted to kill him herself at this moment.

As she reached for a coffee cup she heard the two men in the living room moving for the front door.

"Let me know what Johnson says," Joe was saying as the front door opened. Maggie knew the "Johnson" in question had to be the DA she had met at the police station.

"Will do, and you watch your ass," Craig grunted. "Hopefully this will be over soon."

"Hopefully," Joe answered just before Maggie heard the door close.

She left the cup sitting on the counter in front of the coffeepot as she waited. Within seconds, she felt him. First, it was just an impression of strength, of warmth, then his arms were coming around her waist and his lips were pressing into her hair.

"What's wrong, Maggie?" His voice was husky, the dark undertone of arousal threading through it.

She breathed in roughly.

"Grant wouldn't have hidden that information at the house." Her heart was racing in fear. "It would have been too easily found. He didn't work that way."

"I figured as much." He kissed the top of her head again before pulling away and allowing her to turn and face him.

Meeting his gaze wasn't easy, but she did. She found the dark chocolate depths of his eyes filled with warmth and a question. The suspicion she had feared wasn't there, but that did little to temper her other fears.

"What did you remember, Maggie?" He tipped his head to the side, watching her closely as she clenched her fingers together in front of her.

"You're so sure I remembered it? Not that I already knew it?" She was slicing her own throat, and she felt the breath strangling in her throat from it.

A small smile quirked his lips.

"I deserved that," he admitted with a small nod of his head. "I'm not stupid, baby. You lived with him for two years. It's only logical that you may have heard of something that you'll eventually remember."

"Not that I was working with him?"

"Maggie." He reached up to push the strands of hair that had fallen over her face back behind her ear. "I don't believe you were involved with this, so let's stop tiptoeing around each other and finish this up. If you've remembered something, then let me know. We'll get this taken care of, get the danger off your back, and start our lives together."

She inhaled with a trembling breath, tears filling her eyes at the gentleness in his voice.

"Your car," she whispered. "Grant was always going on and on about that Mustang. While you were talking to Craig, I remembered how smug he acted the last time. The expression on his face. I think he might have hidden the information in that car someplace."

His eyes narrowed as he rubbed his jaw.

"He helped me put that car back together," he finally sighed. "We worked on that for months."

The painful knowledge that the man he had believed was his friend had betrayed him still lingered in his eyes, in the tight grimace in his expression as he turned away from her.

"He would have hidden it where you would never think to look," she pointed out. "He didn't expect to get killed. This was insurance in case he needed to buy his way free of a conviction," she said slowly. "The last few months, before he was killed, he was so certain he was suddenly better than you were. I never thought he would go this far."

She had thought he was insane, not criminal. She should have known better, she admitted. Grant had dropped enough hints, she just hadn't wanted to hear them.

"We'll head back to Atlanta tonight." He nodded abruptly. "The Fuentes family will know by now that I'm the one watching you. They'll be watching my house. I very seriously doubt Grant was the only spy they had in either the Atlanta Police Department or the DEA. So we'll go in quiet, check out the car, and if it's there, we'll head straight to the department from there."

"What about Craig?" she asked nervously.

Joe's broad shoulders tightened before he turned back to her.

"Craig's my backup," he sighed. "But at this point, I'm not trusting anyone else with your life." His expression hardened as he faced her. "We'll go in alone. I'm not taking any chances."

"And if the information is there?" she asked him. She could see the doubt in his eyes that it could be.

"If it's there, then we'll do just as I said." There was a fighting tension in his body now, a readiness that assured her he was planning, plotting out each move from here on out.

"And where will that leave us? Your DA, Craig, and everyone else involved will believe I knew where it was all along, Joe."

"We'll cross that bridge if we come to it," he growled. "And we won't. The DA doesn't give a shit one way or the other as long as he gets what he wants, and neither do the Feds. And I'll make certain they don't want you."

Which didn't reassure her on the fears rising inside her. But did it really matter? The main objective was to see if the information was there. If it was, then she would deal with whatever came later the best way possible. The way she had always dealt with unpleasantness. Straight ahead. She was going into this with her eyes open. Joe was here to get the information. If he believed in her, then he would trust in her. If he didn't . . . Well, if he didn't, then she would face it, and she would survive, just as she always had. The main thing was to get the proof needed and get Fuentes and his men off her back.

She nodded slowly. It was only a matter of hours before dark, and the trip to Atlanta wouldn't take long.

"Do I need to pack?"

He shook his head. "No need. If the information is there, then your part in this will be over. The DA won't need your testimony or much of a statement. I'll bring you back here until we're certain it's safe."

But where would he be? Suddenly, she felt as distant from him as she had the first day they had come here. On the periphery of his life, a job, and nothing more. And the thought of that truly terrified her.

chapter 9

joe could feel Maggie's fear. Not her guilt, just her fear. It was amazing how easily he could read her. The way her green eyes would darken to the color of shadowed moss, the frown that puckered her brow. The way she caught the corner of her lower lip between her teeth and worried it absently. That was worry, concern, not guilt.

He remembered guilt. During the months they had spent together, Joe realized he had learned quite a bit about Maggie. Things he hadn't known he had learned until this past week.

Guilt was a careful absence of expression. She had used it several times during their earlier relationship when she tried to deny that she was pushing for more—more commitment, more emotion from him. It was the way she would look down as she played with the hem of a shirt or picked at her nails. It was the shadowed tone of her voice that deepened her accent. That was guilt.

What he saw now was fear, and it wasn't fear for herself. It was the same fear she showed just before he took her virginity, staring up at him, her eyes dark, her teeth worrying that lower lip, that little frown between her brows. The fear of a broken heart, of putting herself in a place where she truly wasn't wanted.

Maggie was easy to read, unlike Grant. Grant had been trained to lie—being with the DEA demanded a certain talent in subterfuge—and Grant had always done it amazingly well. So well, in fact, that when it blended into the friendship Joe thought they had, he had never suspected.

Or maybe he had.

He remembered the uneasy feeling he had just before meeting Grant's "fiancée." The feeling that the other man was playing a carefully calculated game. Joe had pushed it behind him, especially after meeting Maggie. Little things, Joe admitted, that he should have taken into consideration long ago. Grant had shown brief spurts of mocking jealousy. It had made Joe uncomfortable at the time, though he had fought to ignore it. He should never have ignored it.

As he watched Maggie turn back to the coffee, he saw the sorrow in her eyes and knew he should do something, anything, to alleviate it.

She had no idea, even now, how much he did love her. Hell, he hadn't known himself until early this morning, until the need to tie her to him for all time had overtaken him.

Primal. He had been like an animal taking his mate, and damn if he didn't want to do it again.

He watched her, the defensive hunching of her shoulders as though expecting a blow, the careful movements as she poured her coffee. She kept her face lowered, but he swore he could feel the fear and pain radiating from her. As fiery as she could be, he knew Maggie had a core of sensitivity that was often her downfall. A sensitivity that would be breaking her heart right now. He'd bet dollars to donuts that her thoughts weren't on herself, but rather on him, and how it would look to him that she had thought of a possible place Grant could have hidden the information.

Trusting might be the biggest mistake he had made in his life, as Craig obviously believed. Joe had fought trusting her, just as he had fought loving her once before. A battle he had lost, and he hadn't even had the sense to realize it.

She lifted the coffee cup and sipped before setting it back on the counter. She knew he was behind her, and in most people that avoidance would apply to guilt. Thankfully, Maggie wasn't most people.

"Craig wasn't pleased by what he saw when I came in the room," she whispered.

Joe heard the uncertainty in her voice, the fear that Craig's misgivings could drive a wedge between them. His track record with her wasn't the best, and he admitted that getting past her fears wasn't going to be easy.

"Craig is still dealing with what happened with Grant." Hell, so was he. Out of a four-man team, only he and Craig were left. They were both still aching with the grief over Lyons's loss, as well as Grant's betrayal.

"Aren't we all?" Her painful comment had him grimacing in regret.

"It's a lesson learned," he sighed. "I trusted Grant to the point that I never ran the required security checks on him, and I pushed back doubt when I should have followed through with it. It's a mistake I won't make again."

She still didn't face him. God, he hoped she wasn't crying. He didn't think he could handle Maggie's tears; they would break his heart.

"I should have protected you better," he finally said, his voice rough with his guilt. "I was so damned jealous of what I thought he had with you that I couldn't bear coming around. If I had, I would have known something was wrong."

"So you're just going to take the blame for my marriage as well?" Her vibrant red hair rippled over her shoulders as she shook her head. "You're a glutton for punishment, Joe. And you're wrong. I would have never let you see the nightmare that marriage had turned into. I couldn't have borne it."

She set her cup down, then turned to him slowly, crossing her arms over her breasts as she stared back at him, sorrow shimmering in her eyes.

A weary smile edged his lips. "I would have known, Maggie." He would have seen it in her eyes. She wasn't a liar. Her emotions were always so clear in her eyes, so easy to read, that he had always been able to stay one step ahead of her in their previous relationship. "I would have known and I would have gone crazy with it."

"Because you loved me?" The doubt in her voice was clear.

"Because I loved you, because I've always loved you," he amended. "Because no matter how hard I've tried, you were a part of me. I knew, without seeing you, that something was wrong. For two years I avoided that house and I avoided you, and that's not like me. And I couldn't understand why I avoided it. I think a part of me always knew."

Admitting that was like cutting out his own heart. He had let her down in a way so fundamental that it ached through every portion of his being. It was bad enough that he had let her go, but he hadn't made certain she was safe.

"Grant was very good at his lies," she whispered, rubbing her hands over her arms as though to ward off a chill. "He fooled us both."

Yes, he had, and Joe would never forget that lesson. It didn't mean he was going to let Maggie pay any more than she already had.

"Maggie, have I ever taken you on a kitchen table?" The need to have her was growing by the second.

Her eyes widened in shock, as though the change in subject had come too quickly for her to process. "Do what?"

He moved closer, his hands going to the snap of her jeans, as her fingers curled over his wrists in surprised reflex.

"Have I ever fucked you on a kitchen table?" He lowered his

voice, watching the small shiver that raced over her body at the sound of it.

Maggie was a sensualist. Taste, touch, the sounds of arousal, all turned her on as much as the act itself.

As he slid the metal button of her jeans free, her eyes darkened further and a flush filled her face. Her lashes swept over her eyes as her gaze became drowsy, hungry, and suspicious.

"Sex doesn't solve everything." Her breathing was rough, causing her breasts to rise and fall in quick little movements.

Hard little nipples pressed beneath the cloth, and Joe's mouth watered to taste them. She had the softest, sweetest flesh, and the hardest nipples he had ever taken into his mouth.

"Sex doesn't solve everything, but it can sure as hell make life sweeter." He laid his forehead against hers as he slid down the zipper to her jeans. "I trusted Grant with your life once," he whispered, staring into her eyes, giving her the truth of himself, as she had always given him the truth of who and what she was. "I'll never trust another man to protect what belongs to me, or to hold what is mine to hold, Maggie. You taught me to trust you in a way Grant never did. With your heart and your soul, long before I ever learned of his betrayal."

It was the most basic truth that he knew how to give her. Two and a half years ago she had walked away from him rather than stay in half a relationship and hide what she felt, as he had been content to do. She had broken away and tried to go on, tried to live without him. Any woman greedy enough to involve herself with Grant's schemes would have never done such a thing, especially considering the cushy little life he had offered her as his mistress. And Joe had made the offer, exactly four hours before he arrived at that party with another woman on his arm.

She had shown him then what she was. Who she was. A woman willing to walk away from what she wanted most, rather than to lower herself to meet the selfish needs of someone else.

"You didn't believe me at the station," she reminded him,

though her voice broke as his hands pushed beneath her T-shirt. "I could see it in your eyes, Joe. And after we came here . . ."

"I didn't believe in me, Maggie." He lifted the shirt along her smooth stomach, over her breasts, and finally leaned back to pull it from her. "It was never you I doubted. Every instinct inside me pushed me to get you the hell out of there. It was me I doubted. For a little while."

She wore a lacy white bra that did nothing to hide the swollen mounds of her breasts, or the spiked tips of her nipples.

"Have I mentioned I love your nipples?" He released the catch between her breasts before peeling the cups back from the rapidly rising and falling mounds.

"Not in a while." She was panting now. He loved it when she panted for him. "We need to discuss things, Joe. Not have sex."

"Hmm, I'll have to remember to mention that. And nothing else matters, Maggie, not right now. The rest we'll deal with as we have to."

He lowered his head, licking over one straining tip with a slow, wet glide of his tongue, as he heard the tremulous gasp that left her lips.

That was how he liked her, soft and melting in his arms, those strangled little gasps falling from her lips as pleasure began to overwhelm her. Words would never convince her at this point that he trusted her. That trust would have to come in time, and he understood that. He expected it. But that didn't mean he couldn't edge the odds in his own favor. Her body knew what her mind hadn't yet accepted. She belonged to him just as surely as he belonged to her.

"Joe, are you sure?" Her short nails were digging into his wrists, her gaze worried, but growing hotter by the second.

"More certain than I've been of anything, baby." He laid his hand on her lower stomach, watching her closely. "Certain enough to want more with you than I have ever wanted with anyone else."

He didn't give her time to answer, or time to protest. He had never known anything as sweet or as erotic as loving Maggie. She was like a drug in his system, one he had no hope of breaking his addiction to. And God knew he had tried.

He had fought the arousal, the need, and his belief in her for nearly a week. And even as he fought it, he had known it was a losing battle. Just as he had known as he watched her interrogation through that two-way mirror.

His lips covered hers as he drew in the sobbing response to his declaration, his tongue tasting the sweetness of her passion as he pushed the bra from her shoulders before moving to her jeans.

He wanted her naked. Naked and open for him, welcoming him with all the sweet, generous fire that was so much a part of her.

Clothes were ripped, torn, pushed at, and pulled off until only bare flesh met eager hands and muted moans met open-mouthed kisses that filled the senses with aroused, imperative demands.

Hunger arced through Joe's mind as Maggie's hand attempted to wrap around the base of his cock. Her fingers didn't quite meet, but that didn't detract from the sheer pleasure of her touch.

As always, nothing mattered except pushing inside her, taking her, feeling her orgasm pulsing around him. He didn't bother with the bed or the floor. His hands moved to her buttocks and he lifted her and bore her to the table.

Maggie was fighting to breathe as the overwhelming pleasure rushed through her with a force that swept through her senses like wildfire. All she felt was the heat and demand, a need pulsing through every cell of her body as she clutched Joe to her.

She felt the cool wood of the table meet her back as Joe came over her. He didn't bother with keeping his feet on the floor. Instead, he clambered to the tabletop after her, knees bent, his hips thrusting against her, driving the hard wedge of his cock deep into the fiery heat between her thighs.

There was little grace to the act, even less finesse. The clawing hunger, fear, and desperation that spurred their passion allowed for only the most primitive response. She felt the fierce width of his erection sear the tender tissue of her vagina, and arched closer. The fiery pleasure-pain whipped through her nerve endings, ricocheting through tissue and muscle until every cell of her body was focused on one point only. The penetration of her body, the hard, fierce thrusts of his cock inside her, and the fiery sensation tightening her womb with every thrust.

Orgasm was imperative. With each stroke he threw her higher, seemed to go deeper, until every sense she possessed became focused on the steady impalement.

Perspiration gathered between their bodies, creating an exciting friction as they slid against one another. The heat building between their bodies had them both panting for air, forced to break off the kiss that had consumed them as they fought for breath.

Maggie struggled to open her eyes, staring up at Joe as his hands gripped her hips to hold her in place and the strokes pistoning his cock into her vagina increased. The cords in his neck stood out in sharp relief as the tendons of his arms and chest rippled with power.

He was as out of control now, as he had been earlier that morning. As though once lost, the power to hold himself distant, in this area at least, was gone forever.

The ability to think receded as he whispered her name, his eyes opening, his gaze spearing hers.

"I love you, Maggie." The words were torn from him, ripped from his chest in a growling, harsh sound that spiked through her womb and sent her release crashing through her.

Maggie felt the involuntary arching of her back as the wave of sensation tore through her with pleasure that bordered on violence. It exploded through every nerve ending in her body and sent convulsions crashing through her womb, as her pussy began to milk desperately at his cock. Nothing mattered but the pinnacle of pleasure, the sweeping completion she had only found in this man's arms, and a love she knew she could never survive without. Not intact. Not completely. She would live, but without Joe, Maggie knew her soul would never breathe.

In that moment, as she felt him surge inside her one last time before his own release began to spurt heatedly inside her to join her own, Maggie knew that never again could she hope for love outside of Joe's arms. Because to her heart, her soul, Joe *was* love. He was life.

chapter 10

the drive from the cabin to Atlanta was made after dark, and to Maggie it seemed as though it had taken a lifetime to accomplish. Each mile crept by despite Joe's steady speed and his attempts at a conversation. Maggie wanted nothing more than to get to his house, to check the car, and to get the hell out of there.

As Joe pulled slowly into the alley behind the two-story older home, Maggie glanced over at him nervously. She had seen the house before, though Joe rarely stayed at it, preferring the apartment he kept farther in town. The house had belonged to his father's parents, and had been their home before his grandfather struck it rich in various business enterprises.

The siding was rough wood, though in perfect condition, and sheltered by a wide front porch that gave it a charm and elegance that had always attracted Maggie. The garage that housed Joe's prized Mustang was attached to the back of the house rather than the side, and led into a large, homey kitchen.

Joe pulled the SUV into the back driveway and sat for several moments, the engine idling as he stared at the garage doors.

"Grant had a key to the garage." He ran his hand wearily over his face.

They had napped for several hours before leaving, and though he didn't look tired, he did appear weary. Much as she felt, Maggie thought. After two years of a hellish marriage to Grant, and then the past week of knowing the danger her life was in, she felt exhausted inside.

"Did he have a key to the house?" She turned back to the garage, staring at the darkened windows as her heart raced in her chest.

"No. Just the garage." He turned off the ignition but made no move to leave the vehicle.

They had driven around the block several times over the past hour. Joe had parked across from the house for what seemed like forever, before driving around again and heading for the back drive.

"Do you think someone is watching the house?" she asked, as he continued to watch the shadows.

"I have no doubt," he sighed. "If they tracked who I am, and I'm going to assume they have. As often as Grant railed about me in his journals, I'm certain he would have carried the bitch over to his new friends." The bitterness in his voice had her heart clenching in pain.

"What do we do then? How do we get in there without being seen?"

"*We* don't do anything . . ."

"I'm not staying in the vehicle, Joe." She shook her head fiercely at the thought. "It would be too easy for someone to get the jump on me."

"Leave the doors locked."

"If they had a gun to your head I'd unlock them." Her nerves were about to choke her.

He breathed in roughly. "Okay, we'll go in together, but stay on my ass and be ready to move. You jump when I say jump, don't bother asking how high."

Her lips twitched at the follow-up order.

"Don't ask how high. Got it." She nodded firmly.

"And carry this." He opened the glove box, reached in, and pulled out a small revolver. "I know you know how to use it."

Of course, she did—he had made certain she took firearms lessons the minute they had begun seeing each other years before.

"A woman's best friend." She gripped the weapon firmly.

"I thought that was diamonds?" he quipped as he scanned the area again.

"What do you think protects the diamonds?" she shot back, fighting to steady her nerves, to find at least a small measure of the calm he was displaying.

"The area is pretty sheltered here with the trees." He pointed out the large trunks of the oaks growing between his property and the houses on each side. "We should be secure as we move to the garage. Keep your ears open and stay ready, Maggie."

He reached beneath the dash, disabled the interior lights, then opened the door slowly and eased out of the vehicle. As he stood to the side, Maggie scrambled out after him, easing behind him as he pushed the door closed silently.

They moved quickly to the garage, where Joe unlocked the side door and opened it carefully before pulling her along with him.

The air in the garage was stale, rife with the scent of motor oil, a hint of paint and old grease. Maggie wrinkled her nose at the smell as her eyes struggled to adjust to the near pitch-black darkness.

A second later a small beam of light pierced the black surroundings, directing low, and angling toward the cherry red '69 Mustang Joe pampered like a baby.

"Hello, baby," he murmured as he walked to the car, patting the hood affectionately.

Maggie rolled her eyes.

"It's not a baby, Joe," she reminded him as she restrained her

grin. It was an old argument, and one of the few she often insti-
gated herself.

"'Course she is," he sighed, as his hand slid over the hood before releasing the lock and raising it slowly.

The penlight beam moved slowly over the engine, as Joe leaned
in, checking around it and inside the fender walls.

"Finding parts for her was a bitch," he said softly. "There are
very few original parts left for this model. She's a true classic."

Yeah, yeah yeah. Maggie smirked. Joe was doing more than just
checking for whatever Grant may have hidden, he was petting
and caressing that damned engine as if it it could actually feel his
touch.

"Do I need to leave the two of you alone?" she asked, keeping
her voice at a whisper as he ran his fingers in and out of the maze
of parts that made up the engine.

"You might want to look the other way," he murmured. "She
gets embarrassed if others see her naked like this."

Maggie rolled her eyes again.

Finally, he straightened from the motor with a sigh before lowering the hood back into place.

"Nothing in there." There was an edge of relief in his voice as
he moved along the side of the car.

His hand smoothed over the top before trailing down the door
and gripping the handle. "Do you know how hard it was to find
completely original parts? How many years I spent putting her
together perfectly?"

"Your dream woman, huh?"

"She doesn't back-talk me."

"She can't get on the kitchen table with you, either. I'd remember that one if I were you."

He turned back to look at her, and even in the dim glow of the
penlight, his gaze was frankly sexual.

"Oh baby, that one is just set in stone," he murmured. "You
have nothing to fear."

She rolled her eyes at him again as he turned back to the car, moving into it to begin searching the interior. Maggie drew in a deep breath, rubbing her hands against her arms as a nervous chill raced over her flesh.

The garage was damned creepy. There were too many shadows, too many places where someone could hide. She stared around the dark interior, her eyes struggling to pierce the darkness of the corners, the long shadows cast by the multitude of boxes, appliances, and only God knew what that had been stacked against the walls. If she wasn't mistaken, she had even glimpsed the hull of an old motorcycle hanging high on the far wall.

"You're a pack rat, Joe," she muttered.

He grunted from inside the car, the shadow of his large body moving in the interior as he searched each nook and cranny. He was thorough, and though her freedom depended on finding the information, she was beginning to pray it wasn't here. If it wasn't here, then she couldn't be implicated, and there would be no reason to fear Joe's distrust.

Tucking the small handgun he gave her into the back pocket of her jeans, Maggie bit her lip and waited in nervous fear as Joe took his good ole, easy time searching. He worked his way from the passenger side, back to the driver's side, searching under seats, along the sides, the carpet, the walls, anywhere that Grant could have hidden whatever it was he'd hid.

As he knelt at the driver's side door again, he ran his hands along the sides of the seat, pushing beneath it, then paused. She heard his muttered curse, heavy with bitterness, a second before he pulled a small package from beneath the seat.

"He cut my seat," Joe muttered. "Bastard. It took me two years to find that seat."

He sat back on his haunches, staring down at the dark package in his hands.

"Is that it?" She moved closer.

"Yeah." His voice was heavy with distaste. "I pretty much bet this is it. Feels like a few discs, a video, pictures." He felt around the wrapping. "I think we have it."

The garage door opened abruptly.

"And here Santiago was certain our friend Grant was such a liar."

The heavily accented voice was followed by four large bodies stepping into the garage, weapons raised, and their guns sure as hell looked bigger than hers and Joe's.

"Down."

A hard hand locked around Maggie's wrist, jerking her down, as Joe pulled her around the side of the car and toward the long shadows cast from the junk piled along the walls.

She expected gunfire. Pain. Blood.

"Get them." The order was harsh, commanding, but the sound of bodies moving behind them was the only indication that the Fuentes gang was in pursuit. The fact that they weren't firing guns yet made her even more nervous.

"I'm going to assume you are going to be difficult about this," the voice sighed as a bright light suddenly flared and began sweeping through the garage. "Don't risk your lady's life, Agent Merino. Give us the package and we will leave as quietly as we came in."

Maggie felt the tenseness of Joe's body, just as she heard the lie in the stranger's voice. They would never make it out of there alive, no matter what they did.

"Jose, kill them now. You are making Roberto's mistake in attempting to play with them," a younger voice hissed. "Finish them off and we leave."

"Shut up, Santiago. Roberto was less than the piss running down his father's leg. He had no concept of the lessons Carmelita tried to teach us, whereas I paid careful attention. I will defeat this American dog on my own terms. Is this not so, Agent Merino?" He laughed slyly. "There is no triumph in a quick death. A humiliating life is another matter."

Maggie had a feeling Jose had no intentions of allowing them either choice. She could hear it in his voice, feel it in the tension whipping through the room. She stayed down, pressed against the side of an old washer, with Joe in front of her, completely hiding her. She bit her lip, fighting back her harsh breathing, forcing herself to stay utterly silent as the flashlight swept through the garage.

Crouched low, with decades' worth of junk heaped around them, Maggie bit her lip as the sound of footsteps neared. They were searching around the stacks of accumulated boxes, appliances, and miscellaneous junk heaped six to eight feet from the sides of the large garage. It was a mess. Thank God.

She held her breath as the footsteps passed and moved away, the bright flare of the light skirting inches in front of where Joe crouched.

"Agent Merino, we can do this the easy way, or we may do it the hard way. If you make me exert effort, then I will take your woman and play with her a bit before I allow her to die. I will let you live long enough to watch. Or you can hand over the package easily, and you may just walk away."

Maggie shuddered at the offer as Joe reached back, gripped her wrist again, and they began moving slowly through the shadows, hunkered low, working around along the side of the garage toward the far wall. The direction they were going would have them coming up behind the men standing at the doorway. If they moved further into the garage, then there was a slim chance for escape.

"How disappointing," Jose finally sighed. "But I'll enjoy punishing you for the effort I must make."

Joe moved quickly along a row of boxes before pushing her between a higher stack and an old dresser. There was a maze built through the stacks of junk, haphazard and less than safe, but with a few hidden passageways that seemed more by accident than by design.

They moved into the narrow tunnel, easing slowly behind the dresser as the sound of footsteps began to near their hiding place.

Joe paused behind the dresser, crouched, and waited as the

footsteps passed before moving slowly out of the impromptu tunnel and into a mess of old clothes hanging from a long rack. Maybe being a pack rat wasn't such a bad thing after all.

"Americans are so interesting." Amusement filled the voice that spoke from just in front of the rack of clothing a second before the glare of a flashlight illuminated the floor. "Come out, my friends, let us talk for a bit."

As the rack of clothing began to move, Joe kicked into action. Before Maggie could do more than gasp he pushed her back behind the heavy dresser and opened fire.

Maggie scrambled through the unnatural tunnel, her hand fumbling behind her as she attempted to reach the revolver tucked into her back pocket.

She had just moved to the other side of the dresser when the boxes that lined the tunnel crashed around her, and cruel fingers reached in, latching into her hair.

"No!" Her fingers formed claws as she tore at the fingers holding her, fighting the grip as she was jerked from the safety of the boxes.

"Redheaded whore!" a heavily accented voice hissed at her ear as one arm was jerked behind her back, her hand pressed against her shoulder blades as she cried out in pain.

"Do you hear her cries, Merino?" the voice called out as the gunfire was silenced. "I have your whore now."

She was shaken like a rag doll as she fought against the pain ripping through her shoulders and her scalp. She was dragged through the dimly lit garage and brought to a stop next to the man she had met in her home, introduced as Juan Martinez. This was Jose Fuentes, not Martinez, and he was just as frightening now as he had been the year before, when he met with Grant.

"She's very pretty, my friend." Jose gripped her jaw in his hand, twisting her face around until she was forced to stare up at him. "I warned Grant when he married her that he had chosen one he could not tame. I was correct in this assessment, was I not?"

She fought his hold, tears filling her eyes from the burning pain tearing through her shoulder as her captor twisted her arm more forcibly behind her back.

"Let her go, Fuentes," Joe snapped. "She doesn't have what you want."

Jose Fuentes held her head in place, refusing to allow her to look over to Joe as he glanced to his side.

"Ah, there you are, Agent Merino." His smile was sickly evil, a twisted parody of humor. "It is very kind of you to join us."

"Jose, get the package from him and we will leave," Santiago snapped. "We have no time for these games."

"We have time for whatever I wish, boy. Diego is not here to listen to your sniveling. You follow my orders."

Jose tightened his grip on Maggie's face as she finally whimpered with the pain.

His teeth flashed within the expanse of scarred, dark flesh as he chuckled at the sound.

"She's a strong woman. Women such as this, they fight the drug Diego created. They are enjoyable little tramps once they succumb, both fighting and pleading for the agony to come."

Maggie shuddered at the threat as Jose released her face and stared back at her sneeringly.

"I think I will let our Agent Merino live," he sighed. "After I relieve him of the package it would appear he has dropped."

Breathing harshly, Maggie turned her head to the side, seeing the shadowed form of Joe standing tall, his hands raised behind his head as one of Jose's men stood behind him. The package was no place to be found.

"Let her go." He nodded to Maggie. "She has nothing to do with this."

"She has much to do with this." Jose ran the backs of his fingers over her cheek as she jerked back in response. He chuckled a second before backhanding her. "Grant made certain he teased us often with tales of what a cold little wife he had. I do so enjoy breaking in such women. Frigid little bitches who think their bodies are too good for a little rough, sweaty sex."

The pain ripped through her mind as the blow blinded her, nearly tearing her neck from her shoulders with the force of it. Sagging against the man holding her, Maggie fought to catch her breath as she heard the rough laughter that echoed around her.

"I will take Señora Samuels with me," Jose stated then. "The videos make us much money. She will bring quite a price from those viewers who enjoy watching the battle between the needs of the flesh and the denials of the mind. I will take her in payment for my trouble."

"Then you can forget the package."

Maggie's eyes widened as Jose's gun came up to her head.

"I can kill her now."

"Same deal. I know where the package is, you don't."

"I will find it once you are both dead," Jose snarled furiously. "I do not need you to find the package."

Joe glanced around the shadowed garage before turning back to Jose, his lips kicking into a grin. "Good luck."

A tense silence filled the garage as Jose's and Joe's eyes met in a battle of wills. Moments later, Jose bent, the hiss of a knife sliding from an ankle sheath sliding over Maggie's nerve endings like a serpent's warning.

As he rose he turned to Maggie once again, his hand lifting until the blade touched her skin. "How long would you last, my friend, as I began slicing her open, inch by inch? Her beautiful face." The knife slid down her jaw. "Or these pretty breasts." It moved to her breasts as Maggie fought to shrink back. "It would be a shame to destroy such beauty, Agent Merino."

Maggie fought to make out Joe's expression, to see through the dim light provided by the flashlight Jose had aimed more at the floor rather than Joe. It left Joe's expression in shadow to her, though she was certain Jose had the required light to watch it closely.

She shook her head slowly as Joe watched her. It wasn't worth it. The Fuentes gang would continue to kill, to rape, and to maim if they were allowed to go free. But could she bear the pain Jose could deal her? She was horribly afraid she couldn't.

"Decide now, Merino." The blade pressed into the upper portion of her breasts, pricking the flesh. "There is no time left."

In more ways than one.

As Maggie's gasp tore from her throat, light flared in the garage, brilliant and intense as sirens began to blast through the interior. Maggie felt someone's rough hands jerking her away to the side as the feel of the blade biting into her flesh had her crying out in shock.

"Stay down."

She heard Joe's fierce order at her ear as she was dragged to the other side of his precious car, the sound of bullets pinging around it sending a flash of dread through her chest.

"Sons of bitches," Joe yelled. "Be careful of my fucking car!"

The garage doors flew open as Maggie's eyes adjusted to the light, the sight of black-clad figures pouring into the interior sending jubilation rushing through her.

Within seconds it was over. Maggie rolled to her back, staring up at Joe as he leaned over her, his lips curving into a smile as she watched him in surprise.

"Looks like Craig knew me better than I thought he did," he grunted with a short laugh. "I'd have pulled that one over easy on Grant, Maggie. He would have never known I was gone until I didn't return."

"Craig did this?" Joe helped her to her feet, his arm curving around her waist as they watched the SWAT team gather up Jose, Roberto, and their henchmen, under the close supervision of Craig Allen, the district attorney, Mark Johnson, and the federal prosecutor, Andrew Jordan.

Craig turned to them slowly, his eyes watching them for long assessing moments before he lifted his hand, touched his fingers to his forehead, and nodded slowly.

"My car is ruined," Joe sighed.

Maggie jerked her gaze to the car. It was scarred with bullet holes from one end to the other.

"You can fix it." She was still breathing harshly, hardly daring to believe that it was all over. The information they needed was found, the Fuentes group was back in custody, and she was free.

"How about 'we' fix it?" He turned to her, staring down at her with sudden sobriety, his brown eyes almost black with emotion. "We could redecorate the house while we're at it."

"We?" she whispered.

"We." He nodded slowly, his fingers lifting to the bloody scratch on her chest before his gaze came back to hers. "I won't let you go again, Maggie. Ever. So for your sake, I hope you love me as much I love you, because if not, we're in for a hell of a battle."

"We're in for a hell of a battle anyway." She couldn't stop smiling. Couldn't stop crying as she threw her arms around his neck, felt his surround her, and knew, in that moment, that her dreams had come true.

She was in Joe's arms, and he was talking forever. And forever was a good thing.

epilogue

three weeks later

joe found the little plastic stick with the line running through the result window when he dragged himself out of the bed and stumbled into the bathroom.

Sleep wasn't something he had gotten a lot of the night before. Maggie, on the other hand—he had gotten a lot of her. He had taken her until he was certain sex would be the furthest thing from his mind for days. Only to reach for her again, impossibly hard, desperate to feel her coming around him.

He stared down at the home pregnancy test, hardly daring to believe what it meant. That in the weeks since he had her back in his bed, a child had developed. The child he had dreamed of having with her every fucking night she had been married to Grant.

He had lived in fear of the other man announcing pending fatherhood. Certain that the moment he heard the news, life would crumble around him. Two years he had spent in hell, aching, tormented by memories of Maggie and a hunger that never slept. A hunger that still didn't sleep.

How had one tiny woman buried herself so deeply within his heart without his knowledge of it? Yet Maggie had. He loved her in ways he had never loved his first wife. In ways that still defied his own understanding. He would die for her. Without thought. Without regret. He would die for Maggie. And now for their child.

He reached out and picked up the stick, feeling his chest clench as emotion threatened to overwhelm him. And amazingly, he felt the erection between his thighs, his cock thickening, straining as arousal began to tear through him.

Maggie was pregnant.

Joe blinked back the moisture that filled his eyes as the knowledge overwhelmed him, weakened his knees, and made him feel like whimpering in excitement and fear. Damn, he felt like a fucking teenager with his first woman now. His flesh prickled with the sudden awareness of the bond, and his chest felt too tight as his heart seemed to swell with the overabundance of emotion flooding through him.

He backed slowly from the bathroom, his eyes on that small line of color in the result box of the test stick.

"There's still time to escape."

He swung around, meeting the brilliance of Maggie's uncertain gaze. It moved from his face to his cock, her expression flickering with surprise before her eyes returned to his.

"Escape?" He winced at the sound of his own voice, hoarse, ragged. "Maggie . . ." He shook his head.

Son of a bitch, there were words he should be saying right now. Something poetic or romantic, something that would alleviate the uncertainty in her gaze. But his throat was locked with emotion, his chest heaving from it as he fought to breathe.

But he could still move, and he did so without conscious effort. He dropped the result stick, strode to her, and within seconds he had her in his arms. She wore nothing but his shirt, and he could feel the heat of her body searing him through it. Emotion threatened to overwhelm him as he stared into her eyes, saw the hope, the fears, and the love. Maggie had always stared at him with such love. Then slowly, desperate to feel her, to feel the life within her, Joe went to his knees as his arms wrapped around her hips, pulling her to him. He jerked her shirt up over her abdomen, his face pressing against the soft flesh as he felt the moisture that refused to evaporate from his eyes.

Fuck, he was a grown man. Grown men didn't cry.

"Joe?" Her voice was low, a sweet little cry filled with hope and love, joy and innocence.

He pressed his lips to her stomach, his hands moving around to grip her hips and hold her close as he imagined he felt the life growing beneath his lips, inside her precious body.

"I love you." He couldn't say the words enough as he felt a tremor rushing through him, through her. "I love you, Maggie."

Then he was pulling her to him, dragging her down to face him, staring into those beautiful green eyes and the tears that washed over her cheeks.

"I love you, Joe." Her hands touched his cheeks as he smoothed back the fiery strands of hair that had fallen across her cheeks. "I guess this means you're happy about the baby?"

Her tremulous smile had his lips quirking as he fought the shudders racing through his body.

"I want you again," he whispered, dragging the material of her shirt to her neck as he fought to remove the hated clothing she had donned.

She didn't need to wear clothes. He wanted to see her body, wanted to watch it change, to become heavy with their child. He wanted to see the pearly sheen of her skin and feel every inch of the warm satin flesh against him.

"We're going to kill each other like this." Her laughter was thick with arousal, with the same hungers that drove him as he laid her back on the carpet and came slowly over her.

Her thighs parted for him, knees bending as he settled between them, his cock lodging at the entrance to the fiery, sweetly aroused flesh awaiting him. Soft nether lips enfolded the head of his cock as he pressed against the entrance of her pussy, they caressed his sensitive flesh, the damp friction causing his teeth to grit at the subtle, torturous pleasure as he began to take her.

Maggie stared up at Joe, seeing the track of the tears he had shed on his lean cheeks, the intensity of emotion that darkened his eyes. Dark blond hair fell over his forehead, softening the savage cast of his features, and his lips appeared softer, hungry, as he stared at her.

He filled her slowly, tenderly, as though aware of the sensitivity her inner flesh held after the hunger that had raged through them the night before.

As he pressed inside her, filling her, stretching her, his fingers brushed over her cheeks, her lips, feathering over her skin as though memorizing her by touch, even as his eyes traced each feature.

"I died when I lost you." The sound of his voice shocked her. It was guttural, thick with remembered pain.

"Joe." She tried to shake her head, to halt the flow of pain she could see in his eyes.

"No. Hear me out. Now." He pressed deeper inside her and suddenly the joining of their bodies was more than just pleasure, or bonding. It was as though the embrace had become elemental, a fusion of body and soul. "I don't want to ever be that stupid again, Maggie. I don't want to ever forget the agony I felt every day that you lived under his roof, that I thought he lived in your heart. Because I don't want to ever be that stupid again, Maggie. Ever."

"As though I would let you, ever again," she whispered, a smile trembling over her lips as tears fell from her eyes. "I love you, too, Joe. And walking away isn't something I'll do again. I'm here. For always."

He moved then, as though he couldn't help himself, his hips shifting, moving against her as his erection began to thrust slow and deep inside her.

Her back arched with pleasure as a whimpering cry escaped her chest. God, she loved this, feeling him inside her, touching her, loving her in a way she knew she would never know with another man. Only Joe.

"Ah, Maggie," he groaned as his hands lowered from her face, his fingers sinking into her hair as he bent to her.

Gentle lips nipped at hers as he gazed into her eyes. She could see her reflection in the dark gaze, as well as the emotion that poured from him.

"Sweetheart, you fill my soul," he groaned as he began to thrust harder, his cock spearing into her, stroking tender nerve endings, sensitive flesh, and creating a blaze of lust as the friction increased.

Her legs lifted, wrapping around his hips as she fought to deepen the kiss, to hold him tighter to her as she felt a part of her soul lifting, lightening, melding with his as he took her with a gentleness she wouldn't have believed possible.

It seemed never-ending. He kissed her with devouring hunger, though his thrusts were tender, stretching her vagina with easy strokes as his fingers caressed her scalp. She could feel him from her lips to her ankles, his harder, stronger body moving, flexing against hers as the building pleasure began to tighten through her body.

"Joe. Oh God, it feels so good . . ." Her head thrashed against the carpet as his lips moved to her neck, his tongue licking over her flesh as he moved lower.

"Hmm. Damned good, baby. But only with you. Sweet heaven, Maggie, only with you."

Maggie fought to breathe as his lips moved to her breast, his tongue painting her tight nipple with liquid fire a second before the heat of his mouth enveloped it. The firm suckling of his mouth heralded a harsh groan from his lips before he began thrusting inside her harder, faster, fucking into her with a depth and intensity that sent her spiraling into an orgasm that swept through her soul.

Maggie was barely aware of her own cries as release raced through her, but she clearly heard Joe's. Harsh, a guttural male cry, almost animalistic, that preceded the harsh shudders that tore through his body and the feel of his release pulsing inside her.

Exhausted. Ravished. Maggie lay bonelessly on the floor as Joe collapsed to her side, breathing harshly.

"Well, that's the first time we did it on the bedroom floor." It was all she could do to form coherent words, but that thought struck her as funny.

"It was 'bout time then," he panted beside her.

His hand moved lazily to her stomach, his fingers splaying across her flesh as he turned to her then.

"I love you, Joe." There was no containing that love, or the happiness blooming inside her.

"I worship you, Maggie," he whispered. "For your sake, I hope you can live with it."

"Always, Joe." She smiled back at him tearfully. "Always."

atlanta
heat

prologue

some women a man knew to stay the hell away from. It was a self-preservation thing. Survival instinct. The lone wolf that reveled in its independence and sexual freedom knew when it was staring in the eyes of a sensual trap. A woman capable of making the male animal stand up, take notice, and tremble in his military boots.

Mason "Macey" March was a man who liked to live on the edge, though. He was all about the challenge, the risk, the excitement, whether it was a mission or a woman, or a terrorist out to destroy the world. He was a man who stared out at life with a defiant snarl and dared it to take first blood.

He was a man staring at his own destruction, and he had enough sense to recognize it, and to be equally terrified and drawn to it. Like a spectator to a train wreck. It was going to be bloody. It was going to be a mess. But he couldn't look away because she had him by his soul and he knew it. One kiss. That was all it was going to take. One touch and he was going to be a goner. He was aching to touch.

Hazel green eyes twinkled mischievously over lightly freckled cheeks. Lush lips curved enchantingly, and made a man wonder about the things that mouth could do even as it threatened the fit of his dress whites.

Softly curved, temptingly delicate, and trouble with a capital T. Messing with this woman was the ultimate insanity, but no one had ever accused him of being sane.

"You know, Lieutenant March," she drawled in a seductive Southern accent. "You could always slip out the back door. I bet the admiral won't even realize you're gone."

He stared down at her, eating up the vision of her below the neck even as he kept his gaze steady on hers. Wasn't a chance in hell he was going to let the admiral catch him leering at his god-daughter's ample breasts. The way the sapphire blue silk clung to them, held over the luscious mounds with the tiniest of straps. Her long chestnut hair fell down her back in thick soft waves, making his hands itch to touch it.

"Sweetheart, the admiral would fry important portions of my anatomy if I dared." He attempted to smile, but he was damned close to swallowing his tongue as he caught sight of those sweetly curved mounds lifting in a sigh. If he wasn't mistaken, there was a sheen of moisture popping on his brow as he fought to control the hard-on threatening beneath his slacks. This wasn't the best place to prove to the admiral that he really was nothing more than a dog panting after a pair of pretty tits, as the bastard had recently accused him of being.

He didn't pant after tits. He revered them. Worshiped them. He was nearly drooling over them. Maybe that did make him a dog.

He watched Miss Emerson Delaney smile. A playful curve of her lips that was a warning in and of itself. And beneath that silk was the faintest hint of nipples hardening.

"You know, I could help you sneak away," she whispered play-fully. "Admiral Holloran is, after all, my godfather. I'll make your excuses. You aren't looking well, you know." She was laughing at him. Playfully. In amusement. But she was getting a kick out of the fact that he didn't dare piss the admiral off at this point. He'd already been busted down in rank for one misdemeanor; he didn't need to get brought down again because Emerson was in the mood to play.

"Don't do me any favors, imp," he growled.

She pouted back at him playfully. "But Macey, doing you a favor would just make my day complete. Didn't you know that?"

He snorted. Likely story. If he didn't get the hell away from her the admiral would barbecue his ass.

"Do me a favor then and find someone else to harass, kid," he told her. "I'm in enough trouble."

He caught the narrowing of her eyes as he made his escape, quickly. Before he lost control and let his gaze drop to those incredible breasts.

Okay, so he was a tit man. He couldn't help it, and she had the most incredible set he'd ever seen.

He drew in a quick, fortifying breath as he made his way through the ballroom, the foyer, and then quickly entered the silent, empty study that the admiral made available to his men during these jackass parties his sister insisted on throwing in his name. Holloran should get married or something, to a nice shy little wife who didn't like parties, instead of letting his sister run his social life.

He stalked across the room to the bar, pulled a glass from the shelf, and splashed in a healthy dose of whisky as he heard the door snick open behind him. And he knew. Hell, he knew who was back there.

He tossed back the whisky. "Go back outside and play, little girl." He grimaced as he caught sight of her in the mirror over the bar. "You're biting off more than you can chew this time."

He'd known her for years. Known her and avoided her and lived in dread and in anticipation of the chance to touch her.

"I had a message for you." Her voice wasn't teasing this time, it was a chilly snap. A proper, aristocratic, holier-than-thou, kiss-my-ass whiplash of sound.

It made his dick hard. Made his balls draw tight in hunger and his fingers curl with the need to touch.

"So what's the message?" He rubbed his hand over his face before glancing at the mirror again.

She was leaning against the door; her eyes were glittering with anger, and those lush lips were tight with irritation.

She opened the little evening bag she carried and drew a slip of paper free, extending it to him as she crossed the room, then slapping it into his open palm.

Then, he made the biggest mistake of his life. He didn't just take the paper and tuck it in the pocket of his slacks. And he sure wasn't dumb enough to read it. Oh hell no. With his free hand, he gripped her wrist and jerked her to him, shoving the note in his pocket with the other and then curling his hand around her waist and jerking her tighter against his body.

Hell. Fuck. Son of a bitch.

Those firm mounds pressed against his lower chest, her head tipped back, shock and lust brightening her eyes as his head lowered.

He was crazy. He was destroying his career, right here, with a single kiss.

His lips took hers. Like a man starving for passion, a man suddenly, forcefully aware of the hunger tearing into his gut.

And he was hungry.

Her lips parted on a gasp and he was there, his tongue stroking past them, daring her to do her worst with those sharp little teeth. Wishing she would, because then, maybe, he could find the strength to release her.

But did she bite him? Did she rack her knee into his tortured balls as she should have? Hell no, she had lost her mind, too. Slender arms were suddenly wrapped around his neck, fingers plowing into his hair and her lips parting, taking him, her tongue tangling with his as a rough cry whispered against his lips.

She tasted like honey and spice and she went straight to his head. Kissing her was like immersing himself in addictive sweetness. He licked at her, his tongue tangled with hers, and before he realized the idiocy of his actions his hands were tearing at the little straps of her dress, dragging them down her arms. His lips tore from hers to travel down her neck, down the arch of her throat, heading for nipples that, as the pads of his thumbs stroked over them, tightened further.

Ah hell, he couldn't breathe, he couldn't think. He had to taste.

He lifted her against him, and set her on the padded barstool, his hands cupping those luscious breasts, lifting them to him as his mouth captured one tight, hot bud between his lips.

He'd have thought he could hold on at that point. He'd have thought that the sheer pleasure of finally tasting Emerson's tits would be enough to give him the control needed to hang on and enjoy it. And in doing that, he could find at least a single thought to remind him that he wasn't just playing with fire, he was playing with his own career.

But did he think? Thought washed away when she cried his name in that breathless, shocked voice. It ripped out of his head and left him in a reality where the only thing that mattered was her fingers tangled in his hair, holding him to her breast as he sucked at that tight nipple like a man drowning in lust and pleasure.

Sharp nails pricked at his scalp, pulled at his hair, dragged him close as she arched and shoved her nipple tighter between his lips.

Thought didn't control him now. His dick controlled him. Thick and hard and straining beneath his slacks. One hand dropped to her thigh and he began jerking that softer than soft evening gown up legs that he knew had to be softer.

This was what happened when a man denied himself. When he worked with no breaks to play. When he pushed back lust and refused to drown the hunger for one woman in another woman's body. This was what happened. Because then weakness became hunger, and hunger became a ravenous instinct that refused to be controlled.

Until the door to the study slammed open violently, causing his head to jerk to the mirror, his gaze to clash with the enraged gaze of the admiral. The admiral who cherished his goddaughter as most men did their own children.

Admiral Samuel Tiberian Holloran. Known as the Commodore to most of the men who served under him. A tight-assed bastard where his goddaughter was concerned.

Macey shielded Emerson with his own body, her bare breasts pressed into his chest as she struggled to straighten the bodice. He felt ice form in the pit of his soul as his gaze stayed locked with the admiral's.

"My office," the admiral snarled. "Now!"

Holloran jerked the door open, stalked out, and slammed it with enough force that Macey was surprised the frame didn't crack.

Drawing back, he stared down at Emerson. Her face was still flushed with pleasure, but her eyes were concerned.

"Thanks," he snapped as he stepped back from her, watching as she dragged the straps over her shoulders, a hint of confusion, of hurt in her face.

"For what?"

"For staying away from me like I asked you to. You're trouble, Miss Delaney. More trouble than I think I need right now."

With that, he stalked from the study and headed for the office and the bust in rank he knew was coming. Hell, he'd just been reinstated back to lieutenant, and for what? So he could go right back down because he was hungry, hungry and hurting for a woman so far out of his league that she might as well be in another universe. The one woman Macey knew Admiral Holloran would kill him over. The one woman he very much feared held his heart.

Hell, he should have stayed home.

As he entered the hall, he drew the note Emerson had just given him from his slacks pocket.

The admiral requests a meeting, ASAP, his office. Landry.

Hell. No wonder the admiral was pissed. God only knew when his aide had given Emerson that note. One thing was for sure, the admiral was out for blood now. His blood. And Macey knew he would be damned lucky if he survived.

chapter 1

three weeks later

emerson had been kidnapped.

That knowledge echoed through Macey's mind from the moment he received the admiral's phone call to the second he had received the information informing him of her location.

She had been taken from him. As the admiral had snapped in his taciturn voice, she had been stolen. And the admiral's blue eyes, chips of icy rage, had glared at Macey.

"You'll find her. Find her and hide her, Macey. You're the best, and that's what she needs now."

The best. Yeah, he was the best at this. Tracking, killing. The admiral had made certain his men were the best; he considered Macey one of his, despite their problems.

Now, Macey crouched in the corner of the shadowed warehouse and told himself it was all in a day's work. He would get through it because he didn't have a choice, and he would do it right because that was the only way he knew how to do things. Even when he fucked up, he always made it right in the end. Answering the admiral's call at midnight was his chance.

He'd fucked up last month. He hadn't just lost rank for messing with the wrong woman, but he had walked away from the woman as well. Dumb move. Hell, the admiral had had every right to be pissed when he demanded to know Macey's intentions toward his goddaughter. He had, after all, just caught Macey in a rather explicitly compromising position with her.

Unfortunately, Macey hadn't had the right answers, so to say he was surprised when the admiral called to assign him to the mission to rescue her was an understatement. But as the admiral had known, there was no keeping the information from him. There was no keeping him away from her. And that was beside the fact that the admiral knew Macey would give his own life to protect her.

It was partially his and the admiral's fault she had been kidnapped, after all. The remnants of a terrorist and white slavery organization he had helped to destroy were now striking back at the admiral because of his part in the assassination of the head of that organization. And the admiral's goddaughter was his only weak spot.

"Remind me to put your names on my birthday card list." Emerson Delaney's voice was soft and sweet, sugar-coated and so gently Southern it sounded ridiculously out of place here in the darkened warehouse. "What was your name again? Moe, Larry, or Curly?"

The sound of flesh hitting flesh sent his blood temperature rising. Fine, she was a smartass, but that was no reason to hit her, and some bastard inside that warehouse had hit her. He would kill the bastard who had dared to touch her.

"You, Miss Delaney, are in no position to sneer." The accented voice was cold, purposeful. "You will pay for your godfather's crimes."

"Melodramatics," she seemed to wheeze. "Pure melodramatics. Is that a French flaw or just your charming personality?"

The bastard hit her again. Macey knew he was going to have to move before the bastard put a bullet in her head.

Blood was going to spill tonight, and it wouldn't be Emerson's. He'd already made up his mind that the woman was his; he had only to stake his claim and convince her of it. But first they had to get her out of here. At least he had the element of surprise. The men who had kidnapped her from her bed had no clue that their route to the warehouse had been followed.

He turned to the SEAL with him, meeting the wild blue eyes of the demon stalking behind.

Nineteen months of torture and drug experimentation on Nathan had nearly broken him. It had definitely changed the SEAL for all time, but a year later, he was holding his own. Honed, savage, a creature of rage, but holding his own.

He held up three fingers. There were three guards posted at the entrance to the warehouse. He held up two more and pointed inside the warehouse. He was getting ready to give the command for Nathan to work his way around to the other side of the warehouse when the son of a bitch held up the flat of his hand and shook his head.

Before Macey could argue, Nathan was striding around the warehouse, calm, cool as hell, and crazier than a fucking loon. Son of a bitch. Macey gritted his teeth again, grinding his molars and cursing crazy Irish men to hell and back.

"Hey, dude, I need a light." Nathan's voice was ruined, slurred as he stumbled against the warehouse.

"Get the fuck out of here," one of the guards cursed.

Macey peeked around and trained his weapon on the three guards.

He saw Nathan's knife gleam in the darkness a second before he buried it in a smooth, hard upward strike at the heart of the first guard. The guard gasped, gave a shudder, then appeared to stagger with Nathan's weight, taking him closer to the other two.

Three seconds later blood coated the asphalt and three French nationals, one of whom had embassy clearance, Macey had been informed, were propped up against the wall as Nathan moved into place beside the door, his demon eyes glaring across the distance.

Who needed a whole team of SEALs? He and Nathan were enough SEALs for this job. Nathan might be a tad mentally unstable in Macey's opinion, but he was a hell of a killer. And that sucked. It used to be that Nathan shed blood only when there was no other alternative. Now, he killed without mercy, with expediency. He gave nothing or no one a chance to strike first.

"Your godfather Admiral Holloran will regret his part in the strike against our leader," the terrorist was raging, as though Emerson was going to give a damn. "He and that bitch daughter that betrayed her father. Once we have her, you will be executed, your deaths viewed by millions and cheered on by the loyal followers of Sorrell."

Sorrell, the son-of-a-bitch terrorist and white slaver they had taken down months before, was rearing his ugly head again, even after death.

"Wish you luck with that." Emerson's voice was weak. "I really wouldn't expect more than a few dozen loyal hits; the rest will be for entertainment value alone. Kind of like a train wreck." Her voice was flippant, but Macey could hear the fear in it.

Nathan smiled that demon smile of his. A hard curl of his lips, the flash of strong white teeth and cold hard death. He was a killing machine now, determined to take down the last cells of the terrorist organization that had backed Sorrell. Until it was finished, he couldn't return to his own life, couldn't reclaim his wife.

Nathan gestured, signifying that they go in low, catch the two inside off guard, and snatch the girl. Hell, it would be risky. Too fucking risky. Macey shook his head and began to gesture a less risky move when Nathan crouched, slammed the door open, and went in shooting.

"You stupid bastard!" Macey snarled, fury and an edge of fear growing in his gut as the sounds of gunfire exploded through the night.

He threw himself into the room, rolling to the chair Emerson was tied in and tipping it over. He jerked the knife from his boot and sliced the ropes holding her wrists and ankles. The two men with her lay in their own blood as Nathan moved quickly to cover Macey.

"There's more coming," Nathan hissed as Macey checked the girl quickly for injuries.

She was glaring at him. Her hazel eyes were pinpoints of fury, the green in them nearly overshadowing the brown, glittering in a rush of anger as she snarled at him. That was Emerson—fear made her angry. Made her snap and snarl and that was a hell of a lot preferable to tears. Could he handle tears from Emerson?

"We have to run for it," he warned her.

"You have to drag your heavy ass off me first," she panted. "Dammit, Macey, you weigh a ton."

"Move!" Nathan snapped behind him. "Here they come!"

Macey jerked her to her feet, ignoring her gasp, grabbed her by the wrist, and pulled her through the shadowed, cavernous building at a low run.

"I lost a shoe," she gasped.

"So lose the other one," he growled, checking behind them and praying Nathan kept up rather than dropping behind to shed more blood.

That boy was going to end up getting himself killed, if he didn't end up getting them all killed.

"I'll put those on your tab," she informed him, her voice bland despite the breathless quality of it and the fear in her eyes. "You can pay for them later."

"Sure," he snarled, jerking her around another crate as the front of the warehouse erupted in curses. "I'll go right out and buy you a new pair."

"They're very hard to find," she informed him with testy

patience as he jerked her low to the floor, within feet of the back entrance, and motioned Nathan to secure the exit.

"Should he be going out there by himself?" she leaned close to his ear and voiced the question. "The bad guys would cover the back, wouldn't they?"

Nathan gave the all-clear.

"Not this time. Shut up and run." He pulled her behind him, moving past Nathan as he collected the automatic rifle they had hidden in the back. He followed at Emerson's back, placing himself between her and any bullets that might have flown through the night.

Lights illuminated the warehouse and the lot in a flood of color, only a millisecond behind their rapid push through the chain-link fence that they had cut earlier. The truck was on the other side of the neighboring lot, less than a quarter of a mile and with plenty of cover. With any luck they were home free.

"I can't run like this," Emerson gasped behind him.

God, did he think "luck"? Didn't he remember that luck didn't exactly look favorably toward him, even at the best of times?

He looked back and nearly groaned. As she ran, those impressive, make-a-man's-mouth-water breasts were jiggling, reminding him of more than one night's worth of erotic dreams that he'd had concerning them.

"We're almost there." He pulled her to him, wrapped his arm around her waist, and half carried her as they snaked through the hulking, shadowed crates, equipment, and vehicles that filled the industrial warehouse lot they were running through.

Nathan moved quickly ahead of them now, securing the area to the truck as Macey gritted his teeth again. Her left breast was moving against his side, a firm, erotic weight that he should be shot for noticing.

Save the girl first, he reminded himself.

But it wasn't the breasts that drew him and Macey knew it. It was the woman, and that was what terrified him clear down to his combat boots. The woman could take him down, and he had a feeling he was getting ready to go down hard.

Emerson Delaney knew she was in trouble the minute hard hands jerked her from her bed and pulled her from her home. She had been driven through Atlanta surrounded by hard, cold-eyed terrorists intent on death. There hadn't been a doubt in her mind that they intended to kill her. Just as there hadn't been a doubt in her mind that Macey would be sent to rescue her.

Tall, over six feet four inches, perhaps six five, dark brown eyes, long dark hair, and a bad-boy sexy face. He was the rebel, the troublemaker. The man she couldn't stop thinking about or dreaming about. And the one she knew would come for her.

Her thoughts were interrupted when Macey March tossed her into the backseat of the dual-cab pickup, followed in after her, and gave the other man the order to drive. They eased out of the parking lot slowly, lights out, rather than tearing out of it in a scream of tires, which would have surely alerted any terrorists nearby.

The dark vehicle blended in with the shadows of hulking semis and eased out of the warehouse district and into the stream of traffic bordering it. The headlights came on then, and she wondered if it was okay to breathe yet.

She glanced over at Macey, aware that he was watching the traffic with narrow-eyed intent, his weapon held low against his thigh, his hand still pressing her shoulders against the soft leather seat, keeping her hidden from view.

"Could you pull my skirt down? It's riding up." There was a demon imp that came out every time she came in contact with the huge, taciturn SEAL. She couldn't help it. Needling him was her favorite sport.

A large, broad hand smoothed her skirt from high on her thigh back to her knees. And he did it . . . slowly. As though he were savoring the act. *She* sure as hell was. She stared up at him in the darkness, aware of the fact that he was apparently unaffected.

"Thanks, I appreciate it." She shifted her legs against his. "Next time I get kidnapped, remind me to wear panties."

His expression tightened, as did the hand on her knee. "Don't fuck with me right now."

"I'm fully dressed, Lieutenant, so 'fucking' with you is the least of your worries at the moment."

He smiled a slow, predatory smile.

"If you don't shut that smart mouth of yours, I'll have to shut it for you."

"How are you going to do that?" she whispered back. Excitement churned inside her as he leaned over her, bringing his face closer, his lips so much closer, making her mouth water.

"By cutting out your tongue. I'll blame it on the terrorists."

She sighed with dejection. "Damn. There goes that tongue ring I was going to invest in."

A rough chuckle sounded from the driver as Macey's eyes narrowed in contemplation.

"Give me trouble, Em, and you'll regret it."

"Give me lip, Macey, and I'll bite it." She snapped her teeth back at him and was rewarded with a flare of lust in his gaze. Unfortunately, the lust came with more than she expected. It came with a wolf's grin and a knowing smirk.

"Be careful, Emerson, because I've been known to bite back."

chapter 2

emerson jennifer delaney was shaking. At least on the inside. She'd be damned if she would let Macey, the big, tough, larger-than-life Navy SEAL she'd always lusted over, see her shake on the outside. She wouldn't let *anyone* see her shake on the outside if she could help it. It wasn't acceptable. Good Navy children had stiff upper lips and kept their fears to themselves. They weren't whiny babies or wimps, and if they made the mistake of being one in her family, then they learned fast the error of their ways.

So she let herself shake inside. All through the ride, while her legs remained draped over his, his large hand occasionally cupping her knees as he flicked a heated look at her.

Otherwise, he watched the traffic, kept a careful check through the back window, and talked to Nathan Malone in SEAL jargon that Emerson had only halfway learned to translate throughout her life of dealing with Navy SEALs, admirals, and various officers. Even her mother was an officer, as were her aunts on her father's side, various uncles, and cousins. Out of her entire family on her father's side, in three generations, Emerson was the only one to buck tradition and make a life and a career outside that hallowed institution.

So, translating SEAL talk wasn't easy.

She knew they were driving aimlessly around Atlanta to make certain there were no tails. Then, Lieutenant Malone was going to drop them off and report to the admiral. After that, there was something about hiding her in a cave. She hoped that was a joke, because, well, caves had bugs and bats and stuff, and she did not do bugs and bats and stuff.

"All's clear," Macey finally murmured after watching the back window for what seemed like hours. "Take us to the drop-off, then head out. Clint will be straggling back into the States around daylight. Catch up with him and let him know what's going on. Kell and Reno are OOC for a few more days."

OOC. Okay, she could handle that one. Out of Country. "Admiral's gonna wanna know your location," Nathan reminded him. His ruined voice was harsh, but there was just a hint, the slightest flavor of Ireland sneaking through. She bet his voice had been a panty-wetter before he was tortured by Sorrell and his associates.

"You don't know," Macey reminded him. "Clint doesn't know. Until I know we're secure, Nathan, I trust no one. Not even the admiral."

It was too important. Emerson was too important. And the hairs at the nape of his neck tingled at the thought of letting the location out, even to the admiral.

Nathan nodded sharply as the inner city streetlights became further apart and the dimmer, more distant lights of the residential areas threw longer, darker shadows into the truck.

"Can I sit up now?" She was tired of lying on her back and staring at Macey or the ceiling. Not that Macey wasn't a fine thing to look at, but he wasn't paying any attention to her, so it made the discomfort a bit more noticeable.

"Not yet." His hand tightened on her knee again and gave her a thrill. She was pathetic, really. Creaming her panties for a shift of fingers against her knee. How low could a woman sink?

"This is uncomfortable, Macey."

"So is death." Clipped and impersonal. She hated that voice.

"Do you believe death is uncomfortable? I'd think you'd be unaware—"

"You're going to be gagged if you don't shut up." He glowered down at her.

Emerson twitched her nose. The imp inside her was shaking in fear and staying quiet wouldn't be easy. If she wasn't talking, goading, or taunting, then she was going to start crying. And she really hated crying.

"Here we go." Macey jerked the door open, jumped out, and grabbed her legs, pulling her across the leather seat as she jerked up in response.

"Let's go," he ordered as he gripped her waist and set her down on the sidewalk of a less than reputable residential area.

"I don't have shoes," she reminded him.

He began dragging her through a row of scraggly hedges as the pickup pulled away from the curb and drove off.

She was nearly hysterical with fear, well aware of the fact that she was in a bit of trouble. After all, terrorists didn't drag you out of a bed on the spur of the moment unless they had very bad plans for you.

She shuddered at the thought and thanked God Macey was too busy dragging her through someone's backyard to notice.

"We're almost there." His voice was low, smooth, a stroke to her shattered emotions as he led her into the thick overgrowth of a neglected backyard and into the side door of a garage.

"Where are we?" she asked as he let her go and stalked through the darkness.

A second later, flashlight in hand, he moved back to her and took her arm once again.

"Watch your step here." He led her through a maze of rusted vehicle parts before they came to the back door. He pulled aside the panel of an electronic alarm, pulled out the wires, and accessed the hidden dual security panel where he punched in the security code, waited a few seconds, and reconnected the wires to the front plate before replacing it.

Dummy security plate, she thought, checking it out as he pulled her in through the door. Unusual and unexpected. Anyone who attempted to access the code, no matter the tools, jammers, or methods, would active an alarm simply by attempting to deactivate it.

The inside of the house was darker than ever, the smell a bit musty, as though it was rarely visited. There was the slide of a door, fresher air as he pulled her into a hallway, then downstairs.

Emerson tried to get her bearings. Behind her she could hear the slide of a door, then something else. A muted hum, a click, and then a burst of lights.

She brought her hand up to shield her eyes, blinking as the lights dimmed marginally.

"Sorry, I left them on full power before leaving last night." Macey stood in the center of what she assumed was the "cave."

She looked around. Across the room were a computer and server terminal, routers, secondary systems, and external hard drives. A metal cabinet held a stack of monitors that blinked up, the images showing the inside of a house. Each room and hallway was displayed and several others covered the darkness outside with infrared and heat-seeking capabilities.

Her gaze slid to Macey as he stalked to the main station, sat down in a chair she would give her eyeteeth for at work, and with his large, broad hands began a delicate series of commands over a straight keyboard.

Emerson eased closer to the command center, her eyes tracking over the electronics, both surveillance and stealth, her brows lifting at the impressive setup.

"Give me a minute to set up security and I'll show you around."

Emerson looked around and took in the small kitchen/eating area tucked into the corner beside the stairs. On the other side was an open living room with a sectional couch, plasma television with satellite reception, and a complete surround-sound speaker system. A few bookshelves. A scarred coffee table and a door that led into another room of some sort. She hoped there was a bathroom somewhere.

"Where are we?" She rubbed her hands over her arms and fought the chill beginning to invade her system.

The clock on the wall swore it was nearly five in the morning; it had felt like days rather than hours since she had been dragged from her apartment and forced into the back of a stinking van.

"The cave," he mumbled, hunched over the keyboard, his fingers working the keys with rapid motions that she would have been impressed by if it weren't for the fact that she was cold, exhausted, and standing on less than certain ground.

"I don't like caves." She bit her lip as she stared around the dark wood walls.

"Stand down, Emerson, I'll be with you in a minute." His voice was clipped again, impatient.

A frown jerked at the corners of her mouth; it had been a long night and she needed some fresh air. . . .

She came to an abrupt stop when the steps met a blank wall. Reaching out, she searched for whatever mechanism opened it. There had to be a mechanism.

"It's electronically controlled and only I have the code."

"Why isn't there a regular door?"

"It's a secured room, Emerson," he told her quietly. "No entry in or out without my command. We're on lockdown until Admiral Holloran and Nathan manage to figure this out and capture the leader of the cell of terrorists that took you from the house tonight. We're going to be roommates for a while, so you might as well come on down here and let me show you around."

"Do you have any idea when that'll happen so I can get my life back?" She watched him, feeling uncertain, off balance. Not frightened, but neither did she feel secure within herself.

"Are you going to whine over this?" He cocked his head to the side and watched her curiously. "Funny, Emerson, I didn't see you as a whiner. Come on, I'll show you the bedroom and bath. You can freshen up and get some rest."

He strode across the huge room toward the door at the far wall. Her lips parted in shock. He was ignoring her, striding away from her as though her questions were the result of a whining personality. She did *not* whine.

Her eyes narrowed to slits. "You're enjoying this, aren't you, Macey?" Each word was precise, hard.

Macey paused at the door, turned, and lifted his brow.

"Oh, yeah, Emerson, I'm really enjoying this. Instead of being on the streets searching down terrorists, or covering my buddies' backs, I'm here. With you." His gaze flicked over her body. "Where I get to sit with my thumbs up my ass, deflecting your little daggers, and praying this case breaks before the March family reunion weekend in a few weeks."

She blinked back at him in surprise. "You have family?"

"I wasn't exactly hatched."

"Neither are coyotes, but that doesn't make them domesticated," she shot back sweetly. "Does your family live close?"

"Close enough."

"Just close enough?" She turned and leaned against the wall, watching as he watched her.

"Why do you want to know, Em?"

He was the only one who called her Em. It sounded good, much better, and much more feminine than Emerson. But then, her father had wanted a son, not a daughter. They hadn't been prepared with little girl names when she had been born.

"Maybe I just want to know about you." She leaned her head against the wall, somehow enjoying how he towered over her, the way he watched her with that baffled male confusion.

"No, you don't, you want to make me crazy." His voice roughened as his gaze flicked down her body again. "That's what you're good at. Be careful, it might backfire on you this time. You're damned good at making me crazy, and that should tell you some-thing about this little deal heating up between us. You're not going to walk all over me like you do the admiral or the men you work with."

Her eyes narrowed. "I resent that remark, you know." But she had to admit she did have that habit. "Maybe I just want to find someone who can outthink me. Can you outthink me, Macey?"

"On any low country night that you want to bring on, sweet-heart."

That voice: dark, husky, male. It did something to her. It soothed the anger and the fear and it made the hunger hotter, brighter, the need for his touch almost desperate.

His head lowered as Emerson felt the familiar slow burn, the rising mind-numbing need that began to fill her. It was more than arousal, more than hunger, and it went deeper than lust. She knew lust. She had felt it often enough before Macey. No, whatever it was her body decided it wanted from this man, it was unlike anything she had ever wanted from a man before.

"Maybe it would backfire?" She stared at his lips, mesmerized, feeling her lungs struggle for oxygen as adrenaline began to pump hard and heavy through her body. She had to curl her fingers against her sides to keep from touching him, had to fight to keep from tasting his lips.

"Do you want to find out?" His lips curled into a smirk.

That smirk capped it.

"No, Macey, I want you to tease me over it," she informed him flippantly before turning away.

She would have walked away if he hadn't grabbed her. Again. If his fingers hadn't curled around her wrist and the next thing she knew her breasts were cushioned against his chest and his eyes were glittering down at her.

That look haunted her dreams. That gleam of lust and awareness that there was something between them that he couldn't fight any more than she could.

The instant his lips touched hers, it was over. She was trying to climb into his body, crawl under his skin as his lips moved to take hers.

God, this was one of the things she had loved about his first kiss. Forget an initiation or discovery. He knew what he wanted, sensed what she wanted, and gave it immediately. His lips settled over hers, his teeth nipping her lips until they parted, and his tongue rushed inside to claim territory that already belonged to him.

One large hand cupped the back of her head, and his arm tightened around her back, arching her to him. The height and breadth of his body, the powerful lean muscles, the confidence in his hold washed over her, filling her with an awareness of feminine weakness.

But fear struck her, hard and fast.

She jerked out of his hold, catching the look of surprise on his face as she stumbled away. She couldn't think. Instinct and reaction surged inside her. Her veins were pounding with the rush of blood that fueled the arousal.

What she had just experienced was even more intense than the first kiss. More fiery, harder to control.

She stared back at him, fighting to make her tongue work, to forget the feel of his against it, he smiled down at her with something akin to tenderness. Surprising, wicked tenderness.

"Gets hot, doesn't it, Em?" he crooned, moving toward her, his head lowered, his eyes dark.

Before she could consider evading him, his hands curved around her upper arms, his hold light, her response to his touch almost violent. His head lowered to her neck, his lips pressing against the throbbing vein pulsing just beneath the skin. The heated caress had her breath catching, her eyelids fluttering with sensual weakness.

"This isn't a very good idea." She licked her dry lips nervously, wondering why it was stronger, why it was hotter than that first kiss a month before, why it made her weaker, made her burn brighter.

He snorted as he raised his head. "No kidding. The last time the admiral caught me groping you I lost rank. Maybe you owe me for that, Emerson. From lieutenant to junior lieutenant isn't fun and games. I should at least get a taste of what I paid for, don't you think?"

Hurt flashed inside her. "I had nothing to do with that."

He shrugged as she jerked away from him. "The admiral might have ignored that last little infraction if he hadn't caught me devouring your tits. I think that tipped the balance."

Emerson felt the flush burning in her face and the anger blooming in her mind.

"He didn't see anything." She could feel the breath strangling in her throat at the thought of what her godfather had walked in on and the lecture he had given her hours later.

"He didn't have to see." Macey's voice dropped, the arousal that still burned in his eyes brightening as his gaze flickered over her body. "The position of my head was self-explanatory. And if you don't stop pushing me, sweetheart, you're going to find my lips there again, and next time, I won't stop. Now, go shower, crawl into bed, and stop arguing with me. Arguing with you just makes me harder."

It made him harder? It was making her wetter. And if she didn't get out of this secured basement that he called a cave and away from him, then it was going to make her jump feet-first into a relationship that she knew had the potential to break her heart.

He didn't want her, he wanted her body. He didn't want her heart, he just wanted sex. And reminding herself wasn't easy when he was standing there, his jeans straining with his erection, his gaze hot and hungry. She was terribly afraid that reminding herself was going to do very little good.

chapter 3

"come on, we both need to get some rest." Macey forced himself to ignore the hard-on torturing him. He had his pet snake to put away before she went to bed. Drack was his defense. He hated guns, and anyone with the ability to access his cave would no doubt be packing a gun. Macey didn't think Emerson would appreciate curling up with a full-grown anaconda on her first night here.

Besides, there was something in her eyes that pricked at his heart, that had him releasing her slowly and stepping back. Not exactly fear of him, but there was fear there, uncertainty, innocence. And the look didn't make sense to him.

He knew she'd had lovers before, he'd made it his business to know. He knew her medical history and the fact that she had lost her virginity between the ages of eighteen and nineteen.

She wasn't promiscuous, but he knew she wasn't a prude. Unfortunately, she might be too damned innocent for the likes of him, because the things he wanted to do with her would have had a call girl blushing.

She didn't speak as he turned away and opened the bedroom door. Flipping the lights on, Macey had to clench his teeth against the sight of the huge bed across the room: plenty large enough for two people to play some hellaciously erotic games on.

Dumb thought, he told himself, shaking his head as he felt her move into the room cautiously.

Striding to the walk-in closet, he pulled one of his T-shirts from one of the drawers built in beneath the hanging clothes. From another drawer he pulled free a pair of his sister Stacey's cotton leggings. She was always leaving clothes scattered around the upper level of the house.

Moving from the closet, he glanced at where Emerson stood in the center of the room, staring around it, resignation filling her face.

She might as well resign herself to it. Other than the bolt hole, this place was locked up tighter than Fort Knox. There was no getting in and no getting out without his help.

"Shower's in here." He moved to the door at the far end of the room, opened it, and flipped the lights on. "Towels and washrags are under the sink, fresh soap, both bar and that shower gel gunk my sister likes, is on the shelf beside the tub. Get whatever you need."

"Now you have a sister, too." She was leaning against the door frame, looking around the bathroom with hazel eyes that were gleaming a brighter green than before. "Guess you weren't hatched after all, Macey."

"Guess I wasn't," he drawled, his lips quirking as he watched white, sharp little teeth nibble at her lower lip.

She was nervous. He rarely saw Emerson nervous, and had never seen her uncertain, until now. Seeing it in her made him want to kill. It made him wish he was hunting terrorists with Nathan and drawing their blood. It plain pissed him off that Emerson would know so much as a moment of uncertainty or fear.

He watched as she backed out of the doorway and turned to the bedroom again. Her shoulders were stiff, her head held high, and as he moved around her he caught the flicker of indecision on her face. "I want you to promise me you won't try to leave while I'm trying to sleep, Em."

"I am not stupid, Macey."

"I didn't say you were stupid," he assured her. "But you're headstrong as hell. The admiral gave the orders, sweetheart; calling him or trying to run to him isn't going to do anything but endanger your life. And if I have to stand and listen to another bastard strike you, I just might have to lose my temper."

He reached out to run the backs of his fingers over the bruise that had formed on her cheek, remembering the killing rage that had swept through him when he heard the blow.

"It wouldn't do a lot for me, either," she assured him, pulling away from him as a flush brightened her cheeks and renewed arousal glittered in her eyes.

Oh, she was hot. As hot as he was and just as ready for bedroom aerobics as he was; she was just more cautious.

Macey caught her arm as she turned away from him, holding her steady as her gaze flashed back to his. Wide, wary, her eyes glittered like emeralds and threatened to ensnare him in a web of arousal.

"I told you this wasn't a good idea." Her breath hitched as he curled his arm around her waist and pulled her to his body once more.

He couldn't help it. He needed to feel her breasts against his chest again, needed the taste of her kiss going to his head like potent liquor.

"It's the only idea."

Her lips parted, whether to protest or meet his kiss he wasn't certain, so he took the kiss.

It was late. Weariness was dragging at both of them, but he couldn't help it; one more taste, one more touch, that was all he needed. His head lowered, his lips touching hers gently as he stared into her eyes. He didn't take the kiss this time, he eased into it, eased her into it. He licked at her lips until they parted further. He nipped at the lower curve and felt her ragged breath of response, watched her lashes flutter as her hands clenched on his upper arms.

And he felt that tight clench in his heart again, the one that had warned him years ago that Emerson's touch went deeper than flesh. Deeper than bone.

Macey could tell that she didn't know whether to push him away or to pull him closer to her. Her breathing was harsh, irregular, those temptingly full breasts moving against his chest heavily. He wanted to fill his hands with them, feel her hard little nipples against his tongue again. He wanted to devour her.

"Macey, please . . ." A whisper-soft plea fell from her lips as he licked over them, her eyes dilating, the small ring of green darkening in arousal.

Macey cupped her cheek with one hand, his thumb relishing the feel of satiny flesh dewed with moisture. He could feel her burning, heating up for him.

"I want to touch you, Em." He nipped at her lower lip. "I want to feel you silky and wet." His hand moved from her cheek, down her neck, her shoulder. Going lower, he watched her eyes, her expression, each nuance of emotion that flickered over her face as he gripped the material of her skirt and drew it upward.

She trembled in his arms, a delicate little ripple of response that fanned the flames inside his own body higher. He was burning for her. Touching her was addictive; the more of her soft, sweet flesh that he touched, the more he wanted to touch. The more he needed to touch.

As the material of her skirt cleared her thighs, Macey watched Emerson's lips tremble, part, fight to draw in air.

"Can I touch you, Emerson?" he whispered, his fingertips running along the elastic band of her panties as they curved around the cheek of her rear.

"Macey . . ." There was protest and hunger, fear and need resonating in the tone.

"Just a little touch," he crooned, keeping his voice soft, cajoling.

Touching her meant everything. Touching her right now was as imperative as breathing.

He moved his hand around her thigh again, sliding his fingertips over the soft damp crotch of her panties.

"Emerson." He groaned her name as his forehead rested against hers. "You're wet."

Her face flushed brighter as her hips jerked, pressing her silk-covered flesh more firmly against his fingers. She wanted, she needed, just as desperately as he did.

He moved his hand higher, slid his fingers into the low band of her panties, and a groan tore from his throat as his fingers feathered over damp curls. Sweet, heated dampness beaded on silky curls, drawing his touch, his hunger, as nothing else could have.

He couldn't stop himself. He had to have more. He wanted to see her face, watch her eyes as he took more. And he did. His fingers slid into the narrow slit, parted sweetly swollen folds, and found the nectar of the gods.

"You're hot." He was burning alive in her heat. "Hot and sweet, Emerson."

Hot and sweet. Emerson stared back at Macey, fighting to breathe, to make sense of the wild sensations tearing through her. She couldn't find the strength to pull away from him this time. She felt weak, senseless, unable to process anything but the pleasure. The feel of his fingers sliding through her pussy, parting the sensitive lips, circling the entrance to her vagina.

She lifted closer, standing on her tiptoes, desperate to encourage his fingers to delve further, to slip inside her, to ease the tight knot of pressure building in her womb.

She needed to orgasm. Oh yeah, she needed that so bad. Just this once, in his arms, to know the culmination of this pleasure.

A finger slipped inside her. Callused, firm, confident, it parted the tight muscles and sent her senses careening. Flames seared her nerve endings and she felt as though she was burning alive in his embrace, coming apart at each touch.

"This is going to be mine, Emerson," he snarled, his finger thrusting inside her, sending waves of heat and violent pleasure through every cell of her body. "You're going to be mine. You know you are."

"Macey." Her head tipped back as she fought the sensations. "You don't understand . . ."

His fingers moved inside her, fracturing her senses. But nothing could cover the feel of something . . . something smooth twining around her ankle.

She jerked, looked down. Her eyes widened. Terror ripped through her senses as a bloodcurdling scream tore from her throat.

Emerson jumped as a pointed head lifted, the flickering tongue touching her bare ankle. Nothing mattered but escape.

She was screaming, screeching, trying to crawl into Macey's body, frantic to evade a bite from the biggest, most terrifying snake she had ever seen in her life.

One minute she was climbing Macey's body, the next he was cursing and they were falling. Was he laughing?

They rolled away from the too-long, too-thick reptile, but it wasn't enough. Emerson scrambled to escape. She felt her knee hit Macey's body, heard his grunt, his strangled curse. Clawing at the wood floor, she finally managed to drag herself up on the bed, panting, certain the snake had followed.

But it was gone. It was gone and Macey was curled up on the floor, his hands cupped between his thighs as something between a laugh and a groan left his throat.

"It's a snake!" She jumped to the floor now that it seemed to be gone and tugged on his arm. "Get up, Macey. It's huge. Oh my God, it's horrible."

He was laughing?

Emerson stared around the room, caught sight of the huge

reptilian head peeking from beneath a chair, and screamed again. She was back on the bed, staring at the chair in horror.

"Macey, get up. Oh my God. Macey, get up." The head was the size of a platter, and surely its mouth was large enough to swallow an ankle whole.

"Drack." Macey groaned, pulling himself to his knees and giving a faintly wheezing cough.

"Are you crazy?" she screamed, watching the chair carefully. "Where's the gun? Tell me and I'll get it." She was terrified he wasn't going to get off the floor in time.

"Drack." He laughed; he was laughing, for pity's sake.

Emerson stared back at him, fighting the panic, the fear.

"What the hell is Drack? Macey, please get on the bed."

He laughed harder.

"What's so funny?" she cried, still keeping an eye on the chair. "Would you please get in the bed until we can find a gun."

He straightened, bent over laughing again, then restraightened.

"You just terrified my anaconda, Em. And demanned me all in the same whack. Hell, I bet you're related to Morganna." He laughed again, drawing her shocked gaze as his words began to register.

"You live with a snake?" she wheezed.

"Well, he lives here." He snickered, moved to the far wall, and pressed a lever.

And there it was, the biggest aquarium she had ever seen, ripples of water, foliage and flat stones displayed behind glass as Macey opened the door.

"Come on, Drack, time to go home."

Drack. The snake. The huge snake. The twelve-foot-long, at the very least, reptile slithered from beneath the chair with lazy ease and slid into the aquarium.

Once he was inside, Macey closed and locked the glass door before turning back to her with a grin.

"He watches the place while I'm gone."

Emerson sat down slowly, staring at the well-lit aquarium, certain her heart had stopped and she had died.

"He lives here?"

"Right in there." Macey nodded, chuckling as he pointed over his shoulder at the glass-enclosed cage.

"You should have left me with the terrorists," she said. "It would have saved them the trouble of recapturing me after I leave here. Because no way, no how, not in a million years am I staying here with a snake."

chapter 4

emerson's sleep was restless that morning, filled
with visions of a naked Macey and an anaconda twined around
his body rather than her. Flickering tongue and slitted eyes dared
her to touch his gleaming, muscular body.

She shouldn't have been bothered by him. She didn't consider
herself innocent; sometimes she considered herself too jaded, too
cynical. She had learned years ago that defending her heart wasn't
easy. She wasn't like her family. The Navy, preserving honor and
tradition, had meant more to them than trying to understand the
clumsy, too-emotional child they had found themselves stuck with.

Her parents had been overprotective, and each time she tried to
protest the restrictions, her parents had pulled the guilt card.
They were trying to protect her. They couldn't work if she was
constantly crying for their attention or arguing over their precau-
tions. So Emerson had kept her mouth shut and endured. Until her
graduation from high school, until she left on her own for college
and began carving out her own life.

But she had learned that those lessons she had missed as a child held her back now. She succeeded in her career, enjoyed it and the company she worked with. But interaction, allowing herself to be vulnerable, defenseless enough to allow herself to belong anywhere or with anyone, had become impossible.

Now, lying on Macey's big bed, that monster snake curled in the glass tank across the room, she admitted that she had never felt that loss more keenly than she did now.

She could have been curled against him, reveling in a fantasy come to life. Macey had starred in her most erotic dreams for nearly two years. But as she lay there, she realized he had somehow managed to situate himself into her heart.

If he were any other man that she desired, then she could have at least taken the physical pleasure he could give. If she hadn't hungered for more than just his touch, if she didn't crave more than just his kiss or the heated possession of his body.

Shaking her head, she forced herself from the bed, glancing at the bedside table and the clock set there. It said twelve, but if it was noon or midnight, she had no idea. There were no windows in the basement Macey called the cave, no way of telling if it were day or night.

She glanced at the glass cage and watched as the snake, Drack, Macey had called him, flicked his tongue out, his eyes slitted and displaying something akin to curiosity.

It figured Macey would own an anaconda. He couldn't do anything the easy way, could he?

"Well, he's awake," Macey spoke from behind her, his voice lazy and amused as she straightened the bed.

"Is it noon or midnight?" Whichever it was, she needed coffee before she took someone's head off.

"Noon. Sunny and in the high nineties. Weather guy said it might hit a hundred before evening. Be thankful we're nice and cool down here rather than sweltering out there."

"I like the heat."

"Yeah, I like it hot, too," he assured her. "Want me to turn off the AC?"

Emerson shook her head. "Do whatever you want to as long as you have coffee."

"I couldn't live without it. I also have lunch on the stove and ready to eat. You can shower first if you like. Homemade veggie beef soup and bread. It's one of my specialties."

She straightened and stared back at him suspiciously.

"Soup out of a can doesn't constitute homemade just because you fixed it on your own stove, Macey."

She turned and caught the flash of his smile as he leaned against the door frame, his arms crossed over his broad chest.

"Homemade means from scratch, smartass." He laughed at her. He was the only person she knew who had the nerve to actually laugh at her to her face.

"It's safe to eat?" She moved to the dresser and gathered the shirt and leggings he had left there the night before for her to wear.

"It's not safe to snarl at me when you first get up," he told her, though the vein of laughter hadn't left his voice. "Where did you come by that prickly attitude, Em? It's cute as hell most of the time, but when a man's trying to seduce you, you should soften it some."

"I do, when I want to be seduced." Her return smile was tight, but the tension whipping through her was anything but anger.

She could feel his touch. His lips on her breasts, his fingers between her thighs, and that was a very dangerous thing to remember.

"Go ahead and shower." He shook his head at her, his overly long hair brushing his shoulders as his gaze softened. "I'll put the coffee on and feed you. Maybe you'll be nicer then."

"You like that dream world you live in, don't you?" she asked him, though she had to admit she wanted to smile. It was impossible to stay mad at Macey for long. Irritated, yes. Frustrated, most often. But anger wasn't an emotion she could sustain around him when he was trying to be nice.

"Hey, baby, my dream world is what it's all about." He grinned wickedly. "Want to know the part you play?"

"No, thank you, I think I can probably figure that one out on my own."

She escaped quickly to the bathroom and the shower with his chuckle lingering in the air behind her. Damn him, he was getting under her skin and she knew it. It was bad enough that she had all these pesky emotions to deal with, but dealing with them while the object of them was around wasn't going to be easy.

She showered quickly, dried her hair, and dressed in her borrowed clothes before striding into the living room and toward the smell of coffee and homemade soup. If the smell was anything to go by, it was going to be delicious.

"On the stove." He was sitting at the computer, a security program working through several formulas and protocols, if the screen she managed to read meant anything.

"We had a bit of action around here early this morning sometime after we arrived," he told her as he pointed to two monitors off to his left.

A replay showed a black van had pulled up in the alley and four men had exited it. Dressed in overalls, they had entered the backyard and began canvassing the outside of the house.

"Did they manage to get in?" She moved to the control center and watched as Macey flipped through several commands to show each view of the house.

"They didn't get in, but only because they managed to figure out the garage alarm had a false code box." He shrugged at that. "They moved back when they saw that, seemed to be checking for signs of life. They had all their heat-seeking and sound-detection devices." He shook his head as the replay followed the men working around the house with black boxes.

"Military devices?" She leaned in to look closer. "I thought they were still in the R and D phase."

"So did I," he grunted as he rubbed his jaw and leaned back in his chair. "That means our boys have some military connections we haven't managed to pinpoint."

"Have you tried contacting anyone from the team yet?" she asked, watching one of the men, trying to pierce the shadows cast by the ball cap he had pulled low over his forehead.

He looked familiar. Something about the shape of his jaw and the way he moved made her think she had seen him someplace before.

"I'm not risking it." Macey shook his head. "Any transmissions out of the house could be tracked at this point. I have all Internet and broadband shut down for the time being. Reno knows how to get a message to me, if one is needed. Right now we're just laying low."

The monitors flipped from playback to real-time view, showing the peaceful, tree-shadowed street and kids playing in the yard next door.

"Why do you live here?" She stared at him in bemusement. "I would have figured you for a man with an apartment, not the responsibility of such a large house."

"Emerson, Emerson." He shook his head sadly. "I'm a family-type man, I told you that. The house belongs to my parents, more or less. They moved out to the farm with the grandfolks a few years back and I watch after it. I'm not an apartment sort of guy. Too many restrictions."

"Too many nosy neighbors?"

"You haven't lived on a residential block, have you, sweetheart?" He snorted. "Try block parties, someone knocking at the door at midnight to borrow a tool or to stop and chat. Old guys giving you women advice and old ladies warning you not to listen to them. Trust me, an apartment would be a hell of a lot more private."

By the tone of his voice, he didn't seem to mind the advice or the midnight visits. That should have surprised her more, she realized; the fact that it didn't worried her.

"What about you?" He swiveled around in his chair as she moved to the kitchen and the smell of coffee. "Why an apartment over a house?"

She lifted her shoulders in a shrug. "Too much room for just one person. I wanted something smaller." Too many open rooms to wander through alone would have driven her crazy, made the loneliness sharper.

She didn't glance back at him; she couldn't. Macey would see things she knew were better kept hidden, both for her peace of mind and for the state of her heart.

A heart that was rapidly beating out of control. She hadn't missed the sexual wickedness blazing in his eyes when he had stared at her moments before. She could feel it now, his gaze roaming over her back, her butt, as she fixed her coffee. She would eat later, but for now, she needed a clear head to deal with Macey.

"You don't seem to return home to Virginia a lot," he commented as he leaned back in his chair and watched her quizzically. "The admiral seemed a little put out that your parents hadn't seen you for a while."

She took her coffee to the small round table and stared back at him resentfully. She didn't want to discuss her family, but she could see the determination in his face.

"Why would the admiral mention my family?"

"He had a hard time contacting them when you were taken by those French terrorists."

"They have a life." She sipped her coffee and tried to ignore the hurt.

"They also have a daughter," he said tightly.

"A daughter who, as you said, rarely returns home. Look, Macey, we don't have family reunions; sometimes we manage to catch dinner together if I'm there on business or they're here to see the admiral about something. We aren't tied at the hip."

"You don't have to be tied at the hip to be a family," he pointed out. "You don't seem like the type of woman who would distance herself like that from family. You're close to the admiral, but not your mom and dad."

Mother and father, not mom and dad. She shook her head.

"This is really none of your business."

"I've met your parents," he said.

Emerson stared back at him directly, keeping her gaze cool. She didn't want to hear this, but she had a feeling a family-minded person like Macey would have to see her actions in a less than complimentary light.

"They're cold as hell." He sighed. "It's hard to imagine you growing up with them. Tell me they at least loved you."

"They loved me." In their own way. Bemused, irritated, often uncertain what to do with her, but they had loved her.

His expression tightened, then seemed to clear as curiosity took over. "What was the one thing you always wanted as a child and didn't get?"

The shift in the conversation threw her off balance, had her answering before she thought.

"A tree house." Regret shimmered in her voice because she couldn't stop it. "I wanted a tree house."

"Your parents owned a fifty-acre estate and you didn't have a tree house?"

"Everything had its place." Except her. She had never figured out where her place was there. "A tree house didn't fit into the scheme of things."

"Everyone needs a tree house," he said softly, rising from his chair and moving to her.

Before she could move or avoid him, he was by her chair, his hand sliding into her hair, his lips stealing a quick kiss. "Don't worry, Em, one of these days, I'll give you a tree house."

Sure he would. She shook her head and smiled at the thought as he released her and moved to get a cup of coffee for himself. She knew and understood promises and how easily they could be broken. Not just for children. She could have survived the broken promises as a child, gotten over them, gone on. But she had learned as an adult as well how easily even the most sincere promises were broken.

"I'll settle for the ability to return to my apartment. Do that for me, Macey, and you'll have my eternal gratitude."

"That and more," he stated, moving back through the kitchen to his computer. "I promise you, Emerson, I'm going to have that and more."

chapter 5

he was falling for her. Three days later Macey sat hunched over his computer keyboard and tried to make sense of his own tangled emotions.

He knew he cared too much for her; hell, he had known that for the past two years. He dreamed about her, fantasized about her, and for the past two years hadn't managed to find a single woman he wanted to fuck because none of them was Emerson.

The problem was, he didn't just want to fuck her. He wanted to give her tree houses.

And now he wondered: who would take Drack? That was sad. He'd had Drack since he was a boy. Hell, he loved that cold-hearted reptile and would have laughed at the idea of giving him up because a woman was scared of him. But instead of laughing, his first instinct was to find Drack a home, because his heart, his soul warned him that an anaconda had no place within a family.

Family.

Geez, the admiral would put a bullet between his eyes if he

even suspected what Macey was thinking, wouldn't he? Or had he already suspected it?

And God forbid if Emerson should suspect. But the fact was, she belonged to him. Didn't matter what the admiral thought about it, didn't matter the price to be paid. Though he somehow suspected the admiral was a step ahead of him here.

Emerson fit him, and he was going to make damned sure she understood that he fit her, too, before this was over.

And for the time being he was going to thank God that the admiral couldn't get ahold of him.

Complete communications blackout meant no messages transmitted to or from the team, Admiral Holloran, favorite friends, family, or associates of the dark and shadowed variety.

The blackout meant freedom from the admiral. He wasn't about to restrict his own freedoms, not when he needed information and he knew damned certain he was secure. And the information he was after pertained to the case; at least that's what he told himself. He had no intentions of letting anyone know he was checking out Emerson. Especially not Emerson herself.

He turned his head toward the bedroom door again, smirked, and pulled up her FBI file. Hell, who could have guessed Miss Goody Two-Shoes had an FBI file? My my my.

Picture. Stats. Hmm. No bra size, but he could guess that one.

A nice Macey handful. He looked at his hand, curled it just right, and felt his palm itch at the remembered feel of silky flesh.

Whew. Blowing out a hard breath, he shook his head and went back to the computer screen while keeping a careful ear out for the opening of the bedroom door.

Okay, FBI file. She even had a low-level security clearance. He scratched at his jaw, his eyebrows lifting as he scrolled down the screen and scanned the information. She worked for Diasonis, he knew that. The high-level programming, analysis, computer design, and integrations firm was a favorite with the Bureau.

He knew her college degree was in communications, design,

and integration. As he read, he pursed his lips in surprise. She was good. She'd designed several integrated programs the Bureau was currently using. Nothing compared to those on his own personal setup, but he liked to think he had equipment the Bureau couldn't touch.

He backed out of the Bureau's files before heading into Diasonis. That was a little harder. The Bureau's system was well known to him, its back doors as familiar to him as his own. Diasonis was a little more complicated.

He was working his way through the first pass when he heard the door. Damn. He backed out carefully, his fingers moving quickly over the keyboard as he exited the system, not that he'd managed to get in far, and cleared the program as she stepped into the living area.

"There's chili on the stove." He turned, tilted his head to the stove, and reactivated the virtual war game he had standing ready.

She glanced at the monitor and moved to the stove. "What time is it?"

"Nearly eight in the evening. You slept a long time, Em. Feeling rested?" He moved his player around a tree, collected a rocket launcher, and blew a tank to hell and back. A thousand points and no sound behind him.

He jerked his head around to take a quick look, and froze.

He blinked, eye level with breasts he dreamed about, covered in nothing but one of his T-shirts. She hadn't been close to him in forty-eight hours. She had maintained distance, kept a wary eye on him, and ignored most of his questions and attempts at conversation.

She had been hiding, if only inside herself, and he knew it. For the time being, he had allowed her to hide. The nice thing about his cave was the fact that sooner or later she was going to have to acknowledge him, him and the sexual tension, not to mention the emotional tension rising between them.

Two years he had waited, and she knew it. Two years too long.

"You're losing your game."

He lifted his gaze to her face, his eyes meeting her narrowed ones.

"My breasts aren't part of your game, Macey. You just lost."

A distant virtual explosion sounded behind him as she moved away. Macey sighed dejectedly and turned back to the computer. Oh well, the game was just there to hide his activities, not to actually win. He'd already beaten that sucker months ago anyway.

He swiveled around in his chair to watch as she moved across the room to the kitchenette. She was wearing one of his T-shirts and a pair of his sister's cotton sleep leggings and socks. Damn, she looked too young to be here, too young for the thoughts running through his brain.

He watched her ass as she reached up into a cabinet and pulled out a bowl. His teeth clenched in an effort to maintain control as the twin cheeks bunched and rippled when she moved back to the stove and filled the bowl with chili.

When she turned, his gaze was lifted innocently to her face as he fought every male instinct to drop his eyes to those pretty unbound breasts again.

She could have him, a little voice reminded Emerson. How many times over the past two years had he let her know just how easily she could have him?

"So when can I get out of here and back to my life? Any news yet?"

"What's the hurry? Do you have someone besides the admiral waiting for you on the outside?"

She didn't like the tone of his voice, didn't like the friendliness in it, or the silent invitation to spill her guts to him. She had no secrets; she had no reason to feel sorry for herself.

"I have a full life." She shrugged easily.

"And an empty bed." His voice lowered, the black velvet tone stroking over her senses as he moved toward her.

"My bed is none of your business, Macey. When I want a man there, I have no trouble filling it."

And how many times had she had done that? Too few. And they had been gone too quickly.

"Why are you so defensive with me, Em?" he asked then, his tone too soft, too knowing, too sexy. "You snap and snipe at me as though I've done something to hurt you. If I have, I'd be more than willing to kiss it and make it better."

He was teasing. That playful, come-hither male sexiness that she found so hard to resist. That she had to resist. Otherwise, there would be no way she could hide the feelings she had for him. Feelings that went beyond scratching a little sexual itch while they were confined together.

"If I'm so hard to be around, why did you take this job?" she asked.

"Why did I take this assignment?" He leaned close, his lips curving into a smile, his dark eyes gleaming with sexual intent. "I took this job to finally get into your pants, Em. To get you under me, around me, and to get so deep inside you that the last thing you think about is pushing me away. That's why I let your god-father maneuver me like the good little SEAL I am. Now, answer my question. Why, Emerson Delaney, do you try to push me away every damned time I get close enough to do that?"

"I don't know, Macey," she snarled. "Maybe I don't want to join the Macey's Castoffs club. Sorry, Lieutenant, but being part of the crowd never appealed to me, and being a part of *your* crowd appeals even less. So why don't you stop trying to seduce me, get on your handy-dandy made-for-spying computer, and find me a way out of this. Otherwise, we're going to end this little fiasco as enemies, rather than the fragile friendship I thought we had managed to maintain."

His brows lifted, amusement filling his expression.

"Do you let all your friends suck your hard little nipples in your godfather's study, Em? If you do, I think I'm going to need to spank you."

Flames raced through her body. Warning alarms were clanging through her head. But when his head lowered, his hand sliding into her hair to hold her still, feeling his lips on hers again, she was lost. Lost in the touch of a man she knew she could never hold, and unwilling to break free, because nothing, at no time in her life, had ever felt as right as Macey's kiss. Macey's touch. As belonging to Macey, if only for this moment.

chapter 6

he wasn't stopping this time.

Macey eased over the back of the couch, keeping his lips on Emerson's, tasting the wild passion and honeyed sweetness of her kiss, her tongue, letting himself become trapped in her pleasure and his own.

This was the snare, and he knew it. A pleasure unlike any other that he had known in his life. For the first time, he could feel his lover's pleasure as well as his own, and he was trapped within it. He wasn't touching, stroking, giving pleasure in the hopes of having that pleasure returned. Hell no. Hearing her pleasure, feeling her tremble with it, the sound of it echoing in her shaking moan, that was pleasure.

He stroked his tongue over Emerson's lips, felt them tremble as he took another short, drugging kiss. He let his hands move over her shoulders as he tried to sate himself with the sweetness of her lips and her inquisitive little tongue.

But there was no sating himself and he knew it. Had known it since that first kiss.

"Come here, Em." He lowered her to the couch as her velvety hazel green eyes opened and she stared back at him with pleasure.

"Macey." She licked her lips, and he followed suit.

He let his tongue run over them before taking another hard, quick taste of her.

"Don't think, baby," he whispered. "Let me touch you. Have you. Don't you know I'd beg for just another taste?"

"Macey." She blinked drowsily, sensually, her hands fluttering to his shoulders. He watched the hunger overcome the hesitancy in her eyes. "Why?"

"Because I can't fight it any longer."

"But you'll break my heart." He heard her breath hitch as his lips became distracted by the long, slim line of her neck. "You know you're going to break my heart."

He jerked his head up, his eyes narrowing on hers. "I take care of what's mine, Emerson. Every part of it. And whether you end up liking it or not, sweetheart, you're mine."

Her arms curved around his neck, and he set out to mark his territory. The primal need to possess had him by the balls now, and he had a feeling it wasn't going to release him anytime soon.

As his hand flattened beneath her shirt on the bare flesh of her stomach, a moan slipped past Emerson's lips into the kiss he was stealing from her soul. Callused and warm, the tips of his fingers stroking her flesh had her nerve endings howling in pleasure.

They strained together, hips arching, bearing down, the thick length of his cock pressed against her saturated core as her hands curved around his back, her nails digging into the material of his shirt.

It wasn't enough, she needed to touch his flesh, needed to feel it against her. She tore at the cloth, tugging it upward to his shoulders, revealing the tough skin and hard muscles of his back. Pleasure whipped through her palms as she stroked his flesh and felt him tense tighter against her.

"Get naked," he growled, tearing his lips from hers, lifting just enough to jerk his shirt from his body, then her shirt followed. A dark, almost black patch of chest hair arrowed along his hard abs and into the band of his jeans.

Her hands tore at the belt cinching his waist, pulling it free as his hands worked on the metal snap and zipper.

She tugged at the material, pulling it over his hips with one hand as she parted the front edges, pulling the snug boxer briefs from the thick length of flesh they covered, and felt her mouth go dry.

His cock was so hard and the skin stretched so tight it appeared painful. Heavy veins throbbed in hungry demand and the wide, dark crest pulsed with a heartbeat all its own, pushing a silky pearlescent bead of pre-cum from the narrow slit.

"Oh God, Macey," she whispered, desperation coloring her voice as she held the heavy flesh, stroking it, her pussy clenching at the thought of accommodating it.

She lifted her eyes along his tight abs, his heaving chest, to meet his dark eyes. He watched her as well, his expression tight, honed with hungry lust as she stroked the length of his erection.

"I want to taste you," she whispered. "All of you."

"For God's sake, hurry," he groaned. "If I don't touch you, taste more of you, it might kill me."

She wanted to smile at that. Had any man ever been so desperate to touch her? She knew there hadn't been.

She sat up on the couch, her legs between his spread thighs. She lowered her head, the fingers of both hands curling around the heavy shaft as she licked the little bead of creamy liquid from the head of his cock.

The savage groan that tore from his throat shocked her, excited her. Hands slid into her hair roughly, bunching it and clenching in the strands.

Fiery bursts of heat spread through her scalp. Her mouth opened, covered the swollen head, and sucked it in. She gloried in the strangled curse that fell from his lips. Her tongue swiped over the tight flesh, curled around it, and rubbed the underside, that sensitive little area just beneath the head.

"Emerson, darlin'." His voice was rough, thick and heavy with pleasure.

He was close to the edge. She could tell by the tight length of his cock, the throb of blood beneath the flesh. The fingers of one hand cupped his balls, feeling the taut sac ripple beneath her touch.

She sucked at him firmly, finding more pleasure in the act than she ever had before. He tasted male, clean and strong, vibrant and aroused. The taste could become addictive.

As she sucked, her gaze lifted to his again. A moan caught in her chest as his eyes met hers. His lips, so sensually curved, were parted, his strong, white teeth clenched tight.

"So beautiful," he groaned hoarsely. "Keep looking at me, Em. God, your eyes are beautiful. Your face. So beautiful. Your mouth so hot, so sweet."

Her mouth was filled with his flesh, with the taste of him, the heat of him.

"Do you know what you do to me, watching me like that? Sucking my dick and staring at me as though you were starving for the taste of me?"

She felt her face flush, watching the satisfaction that filled his eyes.

"Such a pretty blush. Such a wicked little mouth."

He was fucking that mouth with slow, easy strokes. He wasn't digging in or trying to ram it down her throat. He wasn't in a hurry to release. He was letting her enjoy, letting her taste, stroke.

Pleasure. It was in her eyes. She was drowning in her own pleasure right now, finding joy in touching him, even knowing she might not know the same consideration.

Love her heart, he was going to eat her alive. He was going to have her screaming in orgasm, have her begging to be fucked, to be taken, possessed before the night was over. He'd take that look out of her eyes once and for all.

He watched the head of his cock disappear into her mouth once more, bit back a curse as her mouth surrounded it, her tongue stroked it, and she sucked at it with heated hunger. Her moan was another caress, dark, rippling over the sensitive flesh and drawing his balls tighter with the need to come.

That wasn't happening. Not yet. Not nearly. First, he'd devour that sweet, sexy little body, those lush, luscious breasts. Oh yeah, he was going to gorge himself on the taste of her breasts and her sweet cherry red nipples.

"Enough, baby." He moved to draw back.

Panic flared in her eyes; her fingers tightened on the shaft of his dick and had him grimacing with the pleasure-pain of it.

"Come here, Em." He reached down, loosened her hands, and pressed her back to the couch. "It's okay, sweetheart. I just want to touch you. Don't you know how much I need to do that? Just a few minutes, that's all."

Just for the rest of his fucking life. God, the look in her eyes was killing him. Hope mixed with fear. Not the fear of physical pain, but the fear of loss. He knew that fear himself, knew how it hurt to wake up and realize that love had just been a fantasy.

Long ago, far away, when youth thought it was wise and all-knowing.

He knew better now. He knew the risk he was taking, the rewards and the possible consequences, just as he knew that he would always regret letting her slip out of his grasp if he didn't try to find her heart.

"Do you know how beautiful you are, Em?" He leaned forward, his lips feathering over hers as he touched the firm, rounded globes he dreamed about.

And he was lost. Simply lost. Oh hell yes. Clearly more than a handful, topped with cherry red, spike-hard little nipples and covered with a sprinkling of freckles.

"Damn, Em. You have paradise right here." He cupped the generous mounds, his thumbs flicking over the tight nipples. When an involuntary moan left her lips, he swore the sound went straight to his cock, wrapped around it, and stroked.

chapter 7

emerson watched in a daze as Macey's head lowered, his tongue peeking out to curl around her hard nipple. She swore she nearly orgasmed the moment it touched her.

Her hips jerked against his, rubbing the hard wedge of his cock against her core as one of his hands caught her wrists and held them over her head.

"Easy, baby," he groaned as she writhed beneath him. "Let me have you, Emerson. Just like this."

Their moans mingled as he drew her into his mouth and sucked, devoured. His teeth scraped, his tongue lashed, and heated, fiery whips of sensation wrapped around her clit. The tiny bud became more swollen, more sensitive, throbbed and threatened to explode in orgasm.

"Macey, I can't stand . . ." A desperate cry left her throat as the suckling changed, became slower, firmer, his tongue licking her nipple with relish rather than desperation.

She needed to hold back, but he wouldn't give her the chance.

And it was more destructive. So destructive that she was only barely aware of his free hand pushing at his jeans, removing them, then pulling the leggings from her hips and pushing them down her thighs before she kicked them from her legs.

She didn't care. She knew what was coming, knew and ached for it.

"You make me crazy," he groaned, releasing her wrists to cup her breasts, to kiss each nipple and suck it into his mouth in turn until the sensations were ripping through her body, the heat building in her womb and threatening to explode.

"Oh God. Macey. More. More." She forced her eyes open, to stare into the near black of his. His cock pressed against the folds of flesh between her thighs and throbbed against her clit.

"Not yet," he groaned. "Not yet, baby. Let me feel this. Let's see how good it can feel."

"I can't stand more," she protested weakly. She could feel her wetness coating his erection as she tried to move against him, to force him to finish it before he chained her body to his forever.

"God, you taste sweet," he muttered, his lips leaving her breasts, stroking down her stomach, parting her thighs. She watched as he lowered his head to the damp curls between her thighs. "Do you taste sweeter here?"

He didn't give her time to protest. Confident, hungry, his lips lowered to her clit, his tongue stroked it, and his groan, when it vibrated against her flesh, sent her senses reeling.

Her thighs fell further open, her hips lifted to him, and Emerson knew nothing had ever felt so good. He knew his way around a woman's body. Knew where to lick, where to stroke, how to flick his tongue against her narrow opening. How to make her scream and make her beg for him to take her.

She saw a smile flash across his face, sexy, certain, before his lips covered her clit and he sucked it with slow, torturous draws of his mouth as his tongue flickered around it. Never in the right spot long enough, just enough to tease, to torment, to cause her to writhe and to plead but never enough to throw her over the edge.

"Macey, it's too much," she cried out, her fingers twining in his hair, holding him to her flesh rather than pulling him away as she should have been. "I can't stand it."

"Not enough," he growled before he licked. "So sweet and hot, Emerson. I need more of you."

"Please," she panted. "I need you now. I can't wait."

"Just a few more minutes, baby," he crooned before licking lower.

His hands cupped her ass, lifted her, and a low, ragged cry filled the air as he buried his tongue in her pussy.

Emerson felt herself unraveling. Everything she had held safe inside her came loose and streamed toward him. She had managed to keep her heart sheltered through the flirty confrontations that were more a result of sexual tension than actual enmity. But this, she couldn't hold herself distant from this, from a pleasure that unlocked every shield she had placed around her emotions.

As his tongue thrust inside her, his groan vibrating against hidden tissue, she felt the explosion building inside her tighten further.

She couldn't fight it. She arched to him, begging, pleading, pulling at his hair until he loosened her hands and eased them up to her breasts.

"Touch them for me," he whispered as he lifted himself between her thighs and curled her fingers around her breasts. "Pleasure them for me, Emerson. Let me watch while I take you."

She cupped the heavy flesh, her fingers stroking over her nipples as Macey quickly tore at the foil wrapper of the condom he had pulled from his jeans.

Sheathed, his hands gripped her hips, pulling her closer as he nudged the broad head of his cock against the slick entrance to her pussy.

"Don't stop, baby, let me watch you play with your pretty breasts while I take you."

The hard crest wedged inside her, stretching her, sending rivulets of burning pleasure radiating from the slight penetration.

"Ah, that's a good girl," he whispered, his voice heavy, his breathing as labored as her own. "So pretty, Em. So damned pretty."

So erotic. Emerson stared back at him, working her nipples with her fingers, feeling the alternating sensations building inside her, burning through her nerve endings.

It was sexy, it was wicked, tempting him even as he worked the thick length of his erection inside her.

"Macey. It's so good." Her eyes closed, her fingers tightened on her nipples. It was too good, too intense, too much pleasure.

"So sweet." His voice was rough as he worked himself deeper. "So sweet and tight. Hell, Em. You're killing me."

He pressed to the hilt. The head of his erection throbbed inside her, heated and heavy, iron hard, spiking the heat burning beneath her flesh now. She felt her womb clench and ripple. Her clit, pressed solidly against his pelvis, throbbed on the brink of release.

"Macey." Trembling, she fought for the orgasm just out of reach.

"You make me lose my control," he breathed out roughly. "God, Em, I want this to be good for you. So damned good for you."

Shock shattered her. Had anyone ever cared if it was good for her? If she needed to come, or if she felt the same pleasure they did?

"It's good. So good." It was better than anything she had ever known.

His eyes narrowed on her then. "Oh baby, it's about to get so much better."

She didn't think it could get better until he began to move. She expected him to take her hard and fast, to rush to the finish line and his own release. But Macey was a sensual demon. She should have known he liked to play, liked to draw the pleasure out. He had a lazy drawl, a patient way of moving, and the sleepy sensuality in his gaze should have warned her.

"Lift your breasts to me, Emerson," he growled. "Lift those pretty nipples for me."

She cupped her breasts and offered the hard sensitive points to him, then screamed out her pleasure as his lips surrounded one tight peak.

It wasn't just the hard, heated suction of his mouth, but the thrusts of his cock, the rasp of his pelvis against her clit. It combined to push her higher, but held her back just enough to keep her locked to earth rather than flying in release.

"Not yet," he bit out, moving from one nipple to the other. "Not yet, baby. Feel good. Feel so fucking good for me."

"It's too much," she cried, trying to push past that final barrier.

"It's not enough. Not yet."

She released her breasts to grab onto his shoulders. The sensations were too much, too violent, too much pleasure. But it didn't stop him. He cupped them himself, his mouth devouring first one then the other as he began to stroke his cock inside her in a smooth, controlled rhythm.

Each thrust, each draw of his mouth stole another piece of her mind until she was nothing more than a creature of his pleasure. His pleasure, her pleasure. It whipped through her, broke through barriers she hadn't known she'd erected against him, and had her fighting for release, fighting him for her release.

His hoarse chuckle pushed her higher. The slam of his hips as she writhed against him, then his hard hands gripping her hips, his lips latching hungrily to her nipple, and his thrusts increasing.

That was what she needed. She lifted to him, her gaze filmy. Ecstasy washed through her veins, built and burned until she was screaming his name, screaming and exploding beneath him in a cataclysm of pleasure that ripped through her body.

She heard his shattered male cry, felt him tense and shudder as her arms tightened around his shoulders and the pleasure burned through her. Like lava. Like white-hot electricity shot straight to her soul.

chapter 8

she was in love with him. She might have denied it before the mind-blowing sex, but hours later, curled against him in his bed, exhausted and sated, she couldn't ignore it any longer.

Letting him go was going to bite. Watching him walk away, that careless smile on his face, would break her heart.

"This should be over in time for the March-Illison-Beckinmore family reunion." Amusement laced his voice. "The biggest damned get-together in the state of Georgia. We hold it on Grandpa's farm further south every year. And every year most of the men walk away with bruises from a fight or two, and the women walk away irritated and grumbling because they fought again. And everyone agrees it's the best year we've ever had."

Her head was pillowed on his chest as he spoke, though a frown edged her brow as he spoke of it.

"Sounds like a big family." She had no idea what a big family constituted. There were no family reunions in her family, no get-togethers outside the occasional dinner with her parents and god-father.

"One of the biggest. Over three hundred last year." His hand smoothed down her hair, her back. "Tents and RVs crowd the place for a full week, and the main farmhouse is packed with sleeping bags and overnight mattresses. Grandma March swears every year she's canceling the next one, but come June, she's the one making the calls and organizing it. The woman is seventy and runs around the place like a woman half her age. She amazes me."

"Sounds like an organizational nightmare." She could respect someone's ability to pull it together, but knew it had to be a pain. She just had no idea why Macey was telling her about it.

"Every morning for a week we pile outside for a dawn break-fast, cooked over every barbecue grill, gas grill, and fire ring on the place. Scrambled eggs, biscuits, gravy, sausage, and bacon are heaped on picnic tables and everyone eats like they're starving. For lunch the tables are piled with sandwich fixin's and pulled pork barbecue, and for dinner, good God, fresh catfish, steaks, burgers, and hot dogs. It's like a camp for the insane." But she could hear his love for it in his voice.

She just couldn't imagine Macey with a family that size. She couldn't imagine anyone with a family that size.

"How do you keep everyone straight?" she asked, confused. "Over three hundred people? That sounds more like a convention than any kind of reunion."

"It resembles one sometimes too," he chuckled. Through it all his hands stroked over her hair, her arms, her back. They were never still, always touching her.

Was it normal for him, she wondered, to want to cuddle after sex? He must be the only guy in existence who did, because it was the first time she had ever experienced it.

Hesitantly, she let the hand that lay on his chest move, to stroke over the silky hairs that grew there and enjoy the feel of them against her palm.

She hadn't imagined how much she would love his tough, hard body. The barbed wire tattoo around his left bicep, the scar on his thigh, the packed, lean muscle. Just lying against him turned her on and made her want to ignore the little aches and pains in her body and take another taste of him.

It wasn't just his body she loved, though, and that's what frightened her.

"You could go with me, you know."

Her thoughts slammed to a halt and her head jerked up. Her hand paused in the middle of the hard abdomen she had been stroking, growing ever closer to the erection stretching from between his thighs.

"Excuse me?"

"I said you could go to the family reunion with me." His eyes narrowed on her. "You'd have fun."

"I'm not part of the family."

"You're mine. That makes you family."

Emerson felt everything inside her slow to a quick stop as time seemed to take on a heavy, sluggish quality. She stared into his eyes, seeing the determination, possessiveness, and total resolve in his eyes.

"You know better than that, Macey." She had to force herself to breathe, to push back the need to believe.

"Do I, Em?"

"You should." She eased from him, wrapping a sheet around her body and moving for the doorway. "Don't make promises you can't keep. Not now. I'm not a starry-eyed teenager that needs a proposal and professions of love to excuse a little sex. You're off the hook. I won't cry on the admiral's shoulder or accuse you of taking advantage of me. So do us both a favor and don't make more out of it than what it was."

She needed her clothes, fast. She needed to shower, to wash the scent of his body from hers, and get dressed.

"Do you really think I'm going to just walk away from you, Em? For any reason?" Quiet understanding. It was in his voice, in his eyes as he stood up and walked over to her. "Did you think a one-night stand was all I wanted?"

"What else am I supposed to think?" Her heart was racing in her chest, her mouth dry with a sense of panic now. "You're not exactly known for your monogamous lifestyle, Macey."

"And you still went to bed with me?" He tilted his head, his gaze gentle as he smoothed his hands over her bare shoulders. "Why did you do that, Emerson?"

"I wanted you."

"Do you just go to bed with every man you want, Em?"

No. She stared up at him, mesmerized by the softness underlying the steel in his gaze. He was a SEAL; she knew what that meant. Filled with purpose. Determined. Slick. He knew how to get what he wanted and he didn't stop until he got it.

Emerson licked at her lips with trepidation. She could feel a trap, she just couldn't figure out where that trap lay.

"I don't sleep around." She tried to pull away from him and put distance between them.

Macey wasn't having it. His hands held her close to him, the warmth of his body enfolding her, making it harder to think, harder to resist.

"Then why a one-night stand with me? What made me so special?"

chapter 9

macey felt his heart melt, right there in the underground living room. His gaze locked with Emerson's, seeing the conflicting emotions in her eyes that shadowed the rest of her features. Panic, fear, hope, and hunger. Not sexual hunger, though that was there as well, but a hunger for more. A hunger to see where the emotions building between them would go.

He knew where they would go. He knew that within the year he'd have his ring on her finger and her soul melded with his.

But he swore he could spank her for being so damned stubborn, so unaware of her own fierce heart, and so frightened of her own emotions.

"You're not answering me, Em," he pointed out, making certain he kept his hands on her. "If you don't have one-night stands, what made me so special?"

"You don't understand. It's not like that."

"Then what's it like, sweetheart?" He lowered his head, touched her lips, kept his eyes on hers. "I love you, Emerson. Do you really expect me to walk away now that I've found the woman I've searched for my entire adult life?"

He loved her? How could he love her? She was gawky, accident-prone, and she didn't know how to love. She would mess it up. Just by being her, she would exasperate him, frustrate him, until he didn't love her any longer.

"You're wrong." Her heart was racing in her chest, making it hard to breathe. "It's just sex. It's always just sex with you. Everyone says it is. All your lovers—" She shut up, her hand clamping over her mouth as a wicked smile bloomed across his lips.

"You bothered to check me out with old lovers? I'm impressed, Emerson. I really am. Tell me, how close were you to clawing their eyes out?"

So close it had terrified her each time. But she wasn't about to admit it. "You're crazy."

"I'd hate to run into one of your past lovers." He was stalking her now, drawing closer. "I know who each one of them is, where they live, where they work, and what could destroy them. If I had to meet one of them, I'd break their bones."

Her eyes widened. He couldn't be serious. It had to be a game.

"Macey." She held one hand out as he drew closer and she blinked back her own tears. "Don't. Please. I can't handle this."

"You don't have a choice, Em. You have to face it, and you have to handle it. Because you're going to have to look me in the eye and tell me you feel nothing for me to stop this. Can you do that? Can you tell me that all you wanted was a one-night stand?"

Her lips parted, the need to tell him just that, to take the escape he was offering. But she was staring in his eyes, saw the pain in them, and the hope.

"Why are you doing this to me?" Her hands fisted in the sheet as her control broke. Years of control, the determination to never cry or ask for love again.

Her parents had always given her that vague pitying look whenever she cried, whenever she asked for hugs as a child. As though they weren't quite certain what to do with her.

"Because I won't watch you run away from me." He moved too quickly for her to avoid, pulling her into his arms before she could retreat further.

"Put your arms around me, Em." He lowered his lips to her ear as he held her against his chest. "Hold on to me. Let me hold on to you. Don't you know, when you're in my arms, I finally feel like I belong to one person rather than just having parts of me allotted out to family, friends, and the Navy? When I hold you, Em, I'm whole."

"Don't do this to me," she whispered against his chest, and wrapped her arms desperately around his neck, terrified of falling.

She was strong on her own, she knew how to do that. She knew how to be alone. She didn't know how to be a part of a couple, she had proved that.

"What am I doing to you, baby?"

"You're making me weak, Macey." Tears slipped from beneath her lashes. "Don't make me weak. I won't survive when you walk away."

"I won't walk away, Emerson." He leaned back, one hand threading through her hair to draw her head back, allowing him to stare into her eyes. "Don't you know that about me? I never walk away."

She did know that about him. Everyone knew Macey was stubborn, hardheaded, and he didn't back down.

"Why? Why do you love me?"

His lips quirked. "Why do you love me?"

Because he was funny, flirty, strong, and certain. Because looking at him made her soul ache and her heart hope. But she didn't say that; she couldn't say that.

"I love you, Em, simply because you're you, and you belong to me. Your heart belongs to me. I want your kisses and your touches, your laughter and your fantasies to belong to me."

They had belonged to him for years.

"Give us a chance, Em." He touched her cheek with the tips of his fingers, brushed her lips with his thumb. "Just a chance for more than a one-night stand. Can you do that?"

She would give him her life if he needed it.

"I don't know how to do this." She swallowed, the movement difficult with the emotions clogging her throat.

His smile was rough, rugged, and filled with sensual, wicked certainty.

"We'll learn together. Learn with me, Emerson. God, baby, learn with me."

The kiss took her by surprise, as did the roiling emotions that fired in his eyes a second before he took her lips. It was fiery, demanding, hungry. So hungry it seemed to feed her own hunger, to stoke it with ruthless licks, rough nips, and pure demand.

The sheet fell away from her body and within seconds they were back in bed.

chapter 10

drack was an unfeeling creature. He had no emotions, no loyalty, no sense of honor or dishonor. He didn't care what day it was, what part of the day it was, and he had no particular feelings for the creature that he shared his space with.

He knew he was strong. He knew that pitting his own strength against his wasn't advisable because he would only lock him into the cage when he wanted to be free to roam rather than giving him the freedom to come and go as he pleased.

He wasn't a thoughtful creature. He didn't think, plot, or plan. He didn't particularly care about anything but where the next meal was coming from and the occasional need to mate.

But there was one thing Drack did hate. Drack hated guns. He hated the scent of them, he hated the feel of them, and he particularly hated the nasty wounds they had once torn into his body. He hated them to the point that even when the creature who housed him carried one, he felt nothing more than the overriding instinct to kill. To destroy. Pain was the one memory, the one instinct that held sway when he felt the vibration of the small door open in the bathroom.

That door led to dark places, places where he could depend on a source of food if he ever reached it. Not that the creature didn't keep him well fed, but he loved the hunt.

Tonight he would hunt more than rodents or lizards. His slitted eyes narrowed, his tongue tested the air, and a hiss of rage left his throat as he butted against the glass that held him confined.

He wanted out. Why wasn't the creature who slept with his mate in the soft nest moving? He should be awakening. Didn't he smell the death moving in, the weapon held by the creature that moved into the room?

Drack watched from his glass-enclosed cage, hissed and slithered to where the door latched. His tongue flicked, testing the air, and he smelled the offensive scent of evil.

Instinct and rage converged as he lay coiled, tense, waiting. The door would open, and when it did, he would be free. When it did, the evil that had stepped into his lair would die.

He knew it would open. It always opened. No one entered for long without detection. The creature who housed him, he would give him his chance. When he did, he would kill.

Macey came awake certain in the knowledge that somehow, some way, he had managed to fuck up. How had he done it? Had he set the security parameters wrong? Had a power supply failed?

It didn't make sense. He was careful, he was always careful, especially when it came to his cave. He had one main entrance, blocked by pure steel and set with enough alarms to bring down the house. There was a bolt hole, just as heavily secured, that led to a sewer drain beneath the streets and any number of manholes scattered throughout the city.

The bolt hole should have been even harder to find than the

main entrance, but someone had managed to not only find it, but to crack his security as well. And that someone had managed to slip into the bedroom where he slept with Emerson.

He could hear Drack scraping against the door to his glass cage. A door that should have opened when either entrance was activated. But Drack was scraping against it, which meant he was still locked in. There were no alarms screaming through the cave, no lights flashing, no hard rock blaring. And he was defenseless.

"Come on, Lieutenant Junior Grade Mason March. Wakey wakey." Amused. Familiar. Deadly.

Macey opened his eyes and prayed Emerson would stay asleep just a few minutes longer as he stared into the shadowed face of the admiral's executive aide, Pierce Landry.

Hell, he had never had liked that weaselly little bastard. Macey especially didn't like him holding that automatic weapon to his head.

Macey sighed in resignation and hoped he could manage to get under the former Green Beret's guard for a second to reactivate security and release Drack.

The anaconda could smell the weapon Pierce was carrying, and he hated guns. Hated guns so much that Macey had to bar the few friends allowed access to the basement from carrying weapons.

"How did you get past the security?" he asked, hoping to stall, to find that window of opportunity. Unfortunately, he knew Landry's service record.

"All it took was finding the entrance; the security wasn't that hard. After all, I've read most of your mission reports, March; I've studied your file and your abilities. Reasoning your system out wasn't that hard." Pierce's gaze went to where Emerson appeared to still sleep against his chest. "You must have fucked her half to death. She hasn't moved."

Macey smirked. He could hear the vein of jealousy in his tone.

"What the hell are you doing here, Landry?"

"What am I doing here?" Landry's large white teeth flashed

white in the darkness of the room. The son of a bitch, Macey had always hated that smile. "Why, Macey, I'm here to carry out my assignment," he continued. "I'm here to kill Admiral Halloran's goddaughter since you so kindly fucked up the last plan to do so."

Son of a bitch. He'd missed Landry. All these years, all the leaks they were searching so hard for, and he had missed Landry.

"See, this is why I didn't just kill you when I stepped into the room," Landry sneered. "Where would the fun have been in that? You wouldn't have known who took the shot. Who got past your security. The admiral's golden child wouldn't have known who was smarter and better than he was."

Macey arched his brow mockingly despite the violence slowly gathering inside him. Emerson had woken, too, and he could feel her tension, her fear.

"You must have me mistaken for someone else, Landry. If I'm anything, it's the pain in the admiral's ass."

Landry chuckled at that, but the gun never wavered.

"He played you, Macey. He marked you for Miss Delaney's bed years ago. Though, to be honest, I believe he was hoping for a wedding ring for her rather than a romp and play between the sheets."

Macey managed to slip his hand beneath the pillows beside him to the alarm switch just below the headboard of the bed and the knife strapped to the wall. He could distract Landry, but Emerson would have to release Drack.

"The admiral's learned to accept what he can get from me." Macey tsked. "Too bad he didn't know what he was getting with you."

Macey tightened his hand on Emerson's wrist beneath the sheets, a warning he prayed she was paying attention to. When he flipped the internal alarms, Drack's cage would open. The anaconda would go for the gun. He hoped.

Macey tripped the switch. Immediately the raucous blare of sirens, screaming music, and flashing red lights tore through the room.

Landry jumped, and Macey knew the instant surprise was the only opening he would get. He tore from the bed and tackled the other man at the waist, taking them both to the floor as Emerson shot up from the bed.

Landry was strong and well trained. Macey had sparred with him on more than one occasion and had learned the other man couldn't be anticipated. He was a gutter fighter, and he was mean.

But Macey was mean too. Mean enough to slam his fist into the other man's upper thigh, his aim off just enough to distract Landry rather than curling him up on the floor.

It wasn't enough. Landry managed to roll, kick out, and throw Macey back. The gun discharged, shooting wild before Macey was on him again.

"Emerson, the cage," he screamed out as he glimpsed her from the corner of his eye. "Open the fucking cage."

Because Drack might be their only chance. The gun had shot wild, but Macey could feel the sting of a flesh wound in his side and the blood saturating his flesh now.

He was wounded and it wouldn't take him long to weaken. If they were going to survive, they just might need all the help they could get.

Open the cage? Emerson's panicked gaze swung to the glass-enclosed tank that held the anaconda. Over the past days the snake had stayed hidden amid the thick plants and shallow water basin in the stone floor, but he was out now, butting against the glass, tongue flickering, slitted eyes dilated. He looked pissed. He looked dangerous. And she was terrified of snakes. She hated them. But she loved Macey. Loved him. Trusted him.

The sirens and music were blaring through the cave. Red lights were streaking through the room. It was disorienting, as she was sure it was meant to be.

She scrambled across the room, shaking, shuddering. The

anaconda was huge. If he managed to wrap around Macey rather than Pierce Landry, then he would be dead.

Snakes had no loyalty. They couldn't be trained. They were driven by instinct, nothing more. Drack wouldn't know to attack Landry rather than Macey.

"The cage. Now!"

Her gaze swung to Macey where he struggled with Landry for possession of the gun. The other man still had it clenched in his hand, fighting to bring it around to bear on Macey.

Her gaze swung back to the snake. He was pressing against the seam of the glass door, butting against it, demanding his freedom. Emerson imagined she could feel the rage pouring from the creature.

Macey had warned her that the anaconda hated guns. Hated them so much that he had to keep them in a specially designed safe and he couldn't carry one himself within the basement because of the snake's instinctive need to kill whoever or whatever carried the weapon.

With a trembling hand she lifted the latch to the door, swung it open, and jumped aside as Drack immediately pressed out of the opening.

Drack wasn't a fast creature, but he knew where he was headed.

Pierce. Her godfather trusted him, loved him like a son. He was always extolling the warrant officer's virtues. He hadn't mentioned deceit and treason as any of those virtues, though.

She couldn't just stand here, but she couldn't look away. The anaconda was making his way across the room toward the two men struggling for the gun. Emerson was terrified the snake would go for the scent of blood rather than the scent of a weapon.

The two men were cursing, delivering hard, powerful blows even as they fought for the gun.

Emerson considered attacking Landry herself, but if he got hold of her, she knew Macey would sacrifice himself to protect her. Instead, she ran to the other side of the bed and the phone that sat at the side of it.

She glimpsed the anaconda drawing closer as she skirted the side of the bed. Had she been insane to let the creature free, despite Macey's orders? She hadn't even told him she loved him, she thought frantically as she reached the table and jerked the cordless phone from its base and began to dial.

It was ringing. Ringing. Emerson stared across the bed, watching as the two men struggled on the floor now. Macey was gloriously naked, Pierce was dressed in a black mission suit.

Macey straddled the other man, one hand locked on Landry's wrist, trying to dislodge the gun as the other hand delivered a blow to his face. Landry returned with a blow to his side, throwing Macey off as he nearly lost his grip on Landry's wrist.

They were cursing, snarling. Macey delivered another blow to Landry's jaw. When Landry's fist connected with his side again, Macey's hand broke contact with his wrist.

"Answer the phone. Answer the phone," Emerson cried out. "Oh God, where are—"

"Macey!" Her godfather's voice yelled into the line. "Secure premises. Our mole is Landry, I repeat—"

"No shit!" Emerson screamed into the line. "Get down here. Where are you? Landry's here."

A shot exploded in the room. Horrified, Emerson tried to pierce the disorienting flare of light and shadows to the two men fighting. Macey had Landry's wrist in a two-handed grip, holding the weapon, trying to turn it back on the other man as Landry's fingers tightened on the trigger again.

Macey's expression twisted savagely. Landry's wrist turned until the gun was almost trained on Macey.

She was aware of her godfather screaming in her ear, an explosion from the front of the house, and the increased blare of sirens.

It happened in slow motion, and yet so fast she couldn't make sense of it. Macey twisted Landry's hand back just as the gun fired again. The warrant officer's body jerked, spasmed, then Macey jumped back as Drack attacked.

He shot forward, slicing between Macey's body and Landry's, his mouth opening wide, teeth gleaming to clamp over the dying man's face and twine his massive girth around Landry's neck. Two more shots fired; the snake jerked, shuddered, but held his grip.

Voices were raised. Not her voice. Not Macey's. He was jerking the sheet off the bed and wrapping it around her as black-suited SEALs swarmed into the room, weapons held ready, lights slicing into the room.

"Get those fucking weapons out of here!" Macey screamed.

Amazingly, the six men rushed back into the living area and returned seconds later, weaponless, their gazes locked on the still form of Warrant Officer Pierce Landry and the anaconda attached to his head.

"Shit," Macey breathed out as he finished securing the sheet around Emerson. "Reno, hit the code on the alarms," he yelled at the suited men. "Shut this damned noise off."

Drack was dead and so was Pierce. Emerson could see the blood spreading out from beneath the creature and the aide's still form.

"Fucking bastard killed my snake." Macey's voice was weary, resigned.

The sirens cut off abruptly, the music and lights stilled, and bright normal white light lit up the room.

Macey was behind Emerson, his arms wrapped around her, his heart racing in his chest.

"You were shot." She tore her gaze from the death across the room as the six men stared over at her and Macey in varying degrees of shock.

The members of Durango Team were there, along with her godfather, and her godfather wasn't looking happy.

"Lieutenant," the admiral snapped as Emerson moved to check the crease in his side. "Are you going to live?"

"Yes, sir."

"Then find your pants, sailor. You're not dressed." The admiral's tone was clearly disapproving.

"No sir, I'm not," Macey growled, his voice, irritated, still rough from rage, cutting through the room.

"Enough." Firm, brooking no refusal, Emerson sliced her gaze back to Macey. "You need to have this seen to."

"It's nothing," he snapped. But his lips were tight and discomfort darkened his eyes as he glared at the admiral.

Emerson turned back to her godfather. "If he loses rank again, you're going to have to deal with me. Now take care of the mess in here and I'll take care of Macey."

She bent and jerked the jeans he had worn earlier from the floor where he had tossed them, before lifting her gaze to his. He still looked ready to fight.

"In the living room." She swallowed back the bile in her throat at the smell of death that had begun to permeate the room. "You can take care of Drack after I take care of you."

She led Macey back to the room, aware of the glowering looks he and her godfather exchanged. She couldn't worry about that; her godfather didn't get along with anyone, with the exception of her.

She couldn't worry about the consequences Macey might face in the short term. Because she had come to realize days before that her godfather had been matchmaking for years. In his own less-than-courteous way.

Macey would get over it. Because in a few short minutes Emerson had realized what mattered most to her, and it wasn't protecting her heart.

Macey owned her heart. And he'd better be serious about her owning his, or she was going to make Pierce Landry look like a walk in the park.

Macey belonged to her.

chapter 11

the murdering scum-sucking bastard had killed Drack. Macey still couldn't believe it. The snake had lived through one attack, years ago, by a burglar intent on stealing Macey's electronics.

At that time, the cave hadn't existed, the computer setup hadn't been as extensive, but Drack had been a full-grown anaconda. Macey had kept him locked in the computer room as an added precaution. Somehow, someone had gotten in and Drack had taken offense to a stranger in his territory. He had been very territorial.

The snake had taken six shots that had creased his hide deep enough that Macey had to take him to the vet for an extended stay. Drack had never forgotten the scent of a gun, or its consequences. And now, he had died because of one.

Snakes were unfeeling creatures, Macey knew that, but damn if he hadn't been fond of him.

But Emerson was safe.

He looked down at her as she knelt by the couch, the first-aid kit beside him as she cleaned the wound in his side.

"You need stitches." She pressed a thick piece of gauze against his side, then pressed her forehead to his jean-clad leg.

Wrapped in a sheet, her shoulders bare, her hair falling down her back, she was like a young goddess kneeling, beautiful and courageous.

Macey buried his hand in her hair and bent his head to hers, despite the pain in his side.

"I'm going to be fine, Em," he promised softly against her hair. "It's all over, baby. You're safe. That's all that matters to me."

She shook her head against his leg, and he realized that tears would begin falling soon. She had been brave and strong, but she would need to crash.

He would take her out of here, take her to a hotel room in town, someplace bright and romantic, where he could lay her back in bed and hold her through the night. Let her get used to being safe again.

"That's not all that matters." She lifted her head as he eased back, her expression pale and distressed, her sensual lips trembling. "I'm sorry. Macey, I'm so sorry. I should have told you . . ."

He laid his fingers against her lips. "You tell me later, Em. When we're safe. Where I can hold you."

"I love you, Macey. I've loved you for nearly two years. I love you so much that you terrify the hell out of me." Her voice hitched as his arms eased around her, pulled her against his chest, and felt his heart trip in joy.

Burying his head in her hair, Macey closed his eyes, fighting back the need to run away with her and hold her until he heard those words enough to fill his soul. But he didn't think he would ever hear it enough.

"Landry bypassed your security." Admiral Holloran stepped into the room, his voice scathing. "Emerson, sweetheart, Reno's getting you some clothes so you can dress upstairs . . ."

"There's a bathroom under the stairs." Macey jerked his head up and glared at the admiral. "She's not going upstairs until I can go with her."

"Macey . . ." Emerson's voice was edged with steel. It was the same tone his mother used on his father when she thought he was getting out of hand.

"Don't 'Macey' me, Em," he told her gently. "When Reno brings your clothes out, you can dress down here. This was too close." He touched her cheek, let his thumb run over her lips. "I came too close to losing you tonight. Don't separate yourself from me."

He saw the understanding in her eyes as Reno stepped from the bedroom, one of Macey's T-shirts in his hands and a pair of Stacey's leggings.

"Get dressed, baby," he whispered, ignoring the admiral for now. "We'll get out of here soon. I promise."

She turned and gave her godfather a hard look, rose to her feet, and took the clothes Reno held out to her.

"Morganna, Raven, and Emily will be here soon to take care of her," Reno told him. "We have a full night ahead of us, Macey. Cleaning this up with the local cops isn't going to be easy. Your security here will be compromised further. It won't be a secret any longer."

Macey shook his head. He'd be damned if he cared right now.

He turned his head and watched Emerson disappear into the bathroom before turning back to the admiral.

"Respectfully, sir." He clenched his teeth around the words. "Don't try to take her away from me. I'll fight it."

Admiral Holloran's eyes widened, his expression stern, though if he wasn't mistaken, Macey detected a glimmer of humor in his blue eyes.

"I expect to see a ring on her finger soon," he finally snapped. "Don't disappoint me."

Macey grunted at that and turned back to Reno. The ring would be there because that was where it belonged, not because the admiral ordered it.

"How did he get in?" he asked Reno. "He bypassed every safeguard I had."

Reno glanced disapprovingly at the admiral, his expression quiet. Macey felt his stomach sink as he turned back to Holloran.

Holloran was one of the few people who knew about the cave. He and the Durango Team. It was a secret that shouldn't have been uttered.

"I told Pierce about the cave." The admiral sighed. "This one is on my shoulders, Lieutenant; I accept responsibility for it."

He wasn't going to say anything. He really wasn't.

"Respectfully, sir," he sneered. He guessed he was going to say something after all. "That's hardly acceptable."

Holloran's lips pressed together in irritation. His arms crossed over his wide chest, his expression darkening.

"It worked out," he snapped back. "I won't be chastised by you, Lieutenant, remember that."

"Like hell! With all due respect, Admiral, your decision sucked, endangered my woman, this team, and the operation you ordered. Chastising you is the last thing I want to do."

He wanted to plant his fist in the other man's jaw.

"I want to know how we managed to miss Landry when we took this terrorist cell's leader down," Reno said.

The question from his commander had Macey turning and drawing in a hard breath as he fought to push back his anger.

"Landry managed to stay under the radar." The admiral sighed again. "He was a deep-cover mole. With the death of their leader, Sorrell, that particular cell lost its driving force. Landry wanted blood in retaliation. He messed up when he went after Emerson. It was only a matter of time before I figured out I had a spy in my own camp. Very few people were aware she was my goddaughter, rather than just a friend's daughter. On my team, only Landry knew."

And Landry would have known the admiral would figure it out after the terrorists had left the note in her apartment that they had taken his goddaughter and would kill her in retaliation for Sorrell's death.

"Yeah. Might have all worked out great if Landry hadn't known about my place," Macey snapped, glaring back at the admiral as his fists clenched.

Unfortunately, the admiral's lips twitched as that glimmer of humor returned. "Hit me and she's going to be mad. You ever seen her mad, March? I have, son, it's not comfortable."

"And I nearly lost the chance to see it," Macey fumed. "Next time you want to play patty-cake with my secrets, sir, remember this. The next time you endanger her life, you'll deal with me. And doing mad isn't my way. I do blood."

"And I do a baseball bat on stubborn male skulls," Emerson announced as she left the bathroom. "Now, can we wrap this up so I can get some real clothes on and finally get some sleep?"

She was swallowed by his T-shirt. Her legs covered in dark bronze leggings, her hair falling around her face like mussed silk, she looked like a queen to him.

She moved to Macey, gripped his arm, and pulled him back. He looked down at her, his heart softening, his soul—damn if he didn't feel his soul turning to mush at the sight of her pale face and her tired smile.

"Just hold me," she whispered as his arms surrounded her and the sound of police sirens filtered from the open entrance outside. "Just hold me, Macey."

He held her, ignoring the amusement in his friends' gazes and the admiral's scowl. He held on tight to what was his and thanked God she was safe.

His Emerson was safe and right here, in his arms, where she belonged.

epilogue

there were over three hundred people at the family reunion. There were dozens of tents in every shape and size scattered around the large farmhouse. There were bunks in the upper level of the barn and every kind of barbecue grill in existence set up beneath a covered wing off the barn. The floor of the huge shelter had been set up with dozens of picnic tables of varying sizes, and huge serving tables lined the wall.

It was an organizational nightmare, and Emerson was loving every minute of it.

Macey's parents and grandparents had welcomed her into the family with hugs and bright smiles. Brothers and sisters, cousins and aunts and uncles had all taken their turn at making her blush and hugging her fiercely.

There were so many people they could have made their own town, and their personalities, temperaments, and smiles all made her feel welcome, if a little overwhelmed.

Macey was chafing at the restrictions, though. His grandparents had placed her in a small bedroom between their room and his parents', and given Macey strict instructions to steer clear of it after she went to bed.

The pressure was wearing on him, she thought in amusement on the third day. He'd already been in two mass brawls with too many of his cousins, and sported his bruises with pride. The lot of them were rough, ready to fight, and always good-natured after trying to break each other's faces with powerful fists.

She'd tended his split lip, bruised ribs, and the wound that he had broken loose on his side. She watched as one of his cousins, a nurse, repaired the stitches that closed the wound while he glared in irritation over the inconvenience.

He was unlike any man she had ever known, even other SEALs. She knew why he had excelled in the SEALs now. A mission would be child's play compared to butting heads with the other males in his family.

And she belonged to him. She might even belong with this strange, crazy family because rather than feeling like she was drowning amid them, their easy acceptance and laughing friendliness drew her in instead.

"We gotta get out of here."

Emerson smiled as Macey's arms surrounded her from behind and his lips moved to her neck in hungry kisses.

"Stop, Macey could catch us!" She laughed as he growled.

"Macey has already caught you." He turned her in his arms, staring down at her, his dark eyes filled with laughter and arousal. Heavy arousal. He was a man skirting the edge of his control.

"Do you know what these shorts are doing to me?" His hands skimmed over the snug, low-rise shorts, smoothing over her butt and upper thighs. "They're making me crazy."

But his eyes were on another portion of her anatomy. They were gazing in rapt attention at the smooth mounds of her upper breasts as they peeked from the top of her light blue cotton shirt.

Her nipples hardened instantly, pressing against the thin material of her bra and showing through the shirt. He groaned low in his chest. "We're getting out of here." He grabbed her wrist and pulled her away from the shadow of the house toward the four-wheelers parked at the edge of the yard. Grandmother March did not allow four-wheelers in her yard.

"Where are we going?" She laughed as he gripped her waist and set her on the back passenger rack attached to the four-wheeler before swinging himself onto the front.

"Away from the mob." The smile he flashed back at her was filled with happiness, male appreciation, and more than a little lust. "A hidden place."

He started the four-wheeler and with a shift of power they were bouncing through the field that surrounded the house amid the hoots and catcalls of his male cousins and knowing smiles from the female ones.

She should have been embarrassed. There were possibly three hundred people who were going to know in a matter of minutes that Macey had made off with her for some fun sex in the sun. Somewhere. But she wasn't embarrassed, she was invigorated, energized. She could feel the emotions she had given free rein to grow inside her, filling her, pushing away the loneliness and lighting those dark places with happiness and a sense of freedom.

It was hard not to enjoy the freedom Macey gave her. The freedom to touch him, to revel in his arms surrounding her and the love growing between them.

Two weeks. It had been two weeks since Pierce Landry had tried to kill both of them. Two weeks since Macey had bulldozed his way past her shields to steal her caution and replace it with hope.

Her arms tightened around his waist as they entered the treeline and began moving deeper into the thick forest that covered the March property. She had forgotten how many hundreds of acres the senior Marches owned, but it was vast. Once a thriving cattle farm, it was now rich farmland warming beneath the sun and cool forests shadowed with secrets and a mysterious sensuality. She could imagine living here, hearing the birds sing every morning, watching the deer graze on rich, lush grass as rabbits scurried to and fro.

Maybe she wasn't the city girl she thought she was.

"Here we go," Macey called out as he parked the four-wheeler under a strand of thick trees.

"And what is this?" She kept her arms wrapped around his waist, leaning her head against his shoulder as she breathed in the scent of him and felt her hunger rising.

"Look up."

She looked up and her eyes widened in surprised pleasure.

"It's a tree house." Her smile widened at the size of it. It was built between two huge trees, the lumber weathered with age, but not with rot. It looked sturdy, natural. A part of the trees that surrounded it and comfortable with its surroundings.

"Come on, I want to show you."

Macey helped her from the back before swinging from the four-wheeler himself and leading her around one of the largest trees where a ladder had been folded down.

"It's gorgeous," she breathed. She had always wanted a tree house, but hadn't had a tree when she was younger to build one. It always seemed like such a cozy idea, the thought of the trees embracing a small shelter that embraced her. And now, Macey had one. "How long has this been here?"

"Since we were boys," he told her. "Up you go. We checked it out earlier this morning for squirrels and stuff. It's nice and safe."

Emerson glanced back at him as she moved up the ladder, nearly laughing at the piercing look he was giving her butt. He seemed particularly enamored of her breasts as well as her rear.

She giggled as his muttered "Have mercy" reached her. The sound was filled with hunger, admiration, and warmth. That warmth was what stole her heart. It wasn't just lust. It was something that was just right.

Reaching the small balcony that surrounded the tree house, Emerson stood and stared out around the forest beneath them. God it was beautiful here, quiet and peaceful, sultry and warming. She loved it.

"Let's go inside." Pulling up beside her, Macey ducked into the opening and drew her in, and her heart stopped in her chest.

A queen-sized mattress was laid out on the floor, surrounded by tapered candles. An ice chest sat in the back corner, but the mattress held her attention.

It wasn't an air mattress. It was a deep, old-fashioned feather mattress covered with quilts and heaped with pillows.

"You did this?"

"You wanted a tree house to sleep in." He looked around the small area in satisfaction. "My brothers and I built this when we were teenagers. I wanted to share it with you."

She lifted her hand to her lips as tears filled her eyes. He was giving her so much. So many dreams, so much happiness, and now, he was giving her one of the things she'd longed for as a child. A tree house.

"I love you, Emerson," he whispered, pulling her to the mattress and kneeling beside her. "I love you until sometimes I think I'm going to go insane if I don't hold you."

She shook her head, a tear falling as she stared into his face. This big tough guy, rough and ready to fight, and here he was kneeling in front of her, love shining in his dark eyes and tough face.

He lifted her hand and she stared down in shock as he slid the ring on her finger. The ring. She knew what it was. The garnet, her birthstone, gleamed fiery burgundy and curved into a rich, lustrous emerald. Macey's birthstone was emerald.

"They fit," he whispered, his thumb smoothing over the stones inset in the gold band and curving into each other. "Like we fit. Fit me forever, Em. Belong with me forever."

Her lips trembled, and tears fell from her eyes. "I like forever." Her voice shook as she met his eyes and saw all the love, all the hope and joy she could have ever prayed for. "Forever suits us."

"Belonging suits us." His head lowered, his lips taking hers with a hunger that she knew should have shocked her, but instead, it met her own.

She laid back on the mattress, their hands tearing at each other's clothes. Their lips, teeth, and tongues devoured every drop of passion and pleasure they could find.

Clothes were discarded. Naked flesh met naked flesh as desperate moans mingled and hungry hands stroked. Sweat built on their flesh, making her breasts slick, heated as his lips slid over them. When his lips covered a nipple and sucked it deep and hard, her back arched in pleasure.

She pressed the mounds together as his lips began to devour both nipples. Sucking and licking as she writhed beneath him in passion.

"I'm hungry for the taste of you," he moaned, moving from her breasts down her body.

His tongue stroked through the narrow slit of her pussy, and before Emerson could make sense of anything else she was drawn into a world of sensual hunger, heat, and longing that only built and rose until she was screaming with her orgasm and begging for more. Begging for his cock rather than his lips and tongue, pleading for him to fill her.

When he filled her, he took her with long, slow strokes, worked the pleasure to a crescendo that flung her into the heavens in a burst of brilliant, fiery waves.

It was like this with Macey. Sometimes hard and hot, sometimes slow and hot, but always hot, always building, and always drawing her deeper into the magic of his touch.

Later, as the sun began to cool and shadows began to draw deeper into the tree house, Macey moved. Champagne and two glasses were lifted from the ice chest along with a platter of cold finger foods.

They fed each other. Drank from one glass, and as darkness descended they loved again. Loved for hours until Emerson knew where she belonged, where her heart lay, and trusted in tomorrow.

In Macey's arms.

night
hawk

he wasn't exactly what she had expected. A killer shouldn't be so handsome that he made a woman's mouth water at the thought of tasting him. He shouldn't be so rugged that her heart pounded at the thought of riding him hard throughout the night. A killer shouldn't haunt her dreams, her fantasies, or her desires.

Yet this one did.

Black Jack. That was his Elite Ops code name. What his true name was, she wasn't certain. She wasn't given that information, and she knew she would likely never know who he was, or who he had once been. She was certain, though, that like her, he had once been someone far different from who or what he was today.

She watched as he entered the dark little bar she had arranged to meet him in. Mostly because it would afford her the chance to watch him walk in, to see that loose-limbed, confident stroll that drew her gaze to his thighs despite her best efforts.

He had fine, muscular thighs. They were encased in faded, soft denim, the material stretching around them, moving with each flex of hard flesh beneath. Between those thighs. She blew out a silent breath of appreciation at the way the pale denim lovingly cupped an impressive bulge. No doubt, the man had no reason to be ashamed when it came to physical endowment.

It made a woman wonder, though—as with most handsome men, was it all packaging?

She almost laughed at herself. Of course it was. It didn't even matter if the man was handsome. In most cases, ego was his best friend, and of course, he was always the best, no matter what endeavor he set out to accomplish.

Lillian Belle gave a regretful little sigh as her target moved through the shadowed room, his blue-gray eyes sweeping the darkened corners as his well-toned body moved with careful precision.

He was a man on guard, a killer who well understood the rules. But should she judge him for the fact that he did, and would kill again? After all, was she any better?

They had both signed twelve years of their lives away to the Elite Ops in exchange for another chance to live. Elite Operations agents often joked that they signed their lives away, because their missions were often nothing less than suicidal.

She had survived three years of those missions. Three years in which she had sold her soul more times than she had during the five years she had spent as an agent in Europe. She was a ghost. Not really living. She hadn't really lived in so many years. Until she met Black Jack.

Blue-gray eyes pinpointed her. Like shards of ice but also burning with an inner flame. Hot and cold, flickering over her with just enough male interest to send her hormones crashing through her system. Just enough interest to remind her that, despite the circumstances of her life at present, she was still a woman. Woman enough to want all the things that she had once promised herself she would never want again.

She didn't even know him, she told herself as he drew nearer.

She knew nothing about him. Jordan Malone, head of the Elite Operations, refused to give her any information. Her own commanding officer acted as though she were committing a sin by even asking.

She shouldn't concern herself with agents outside her own unit, she was told. Yet, she couldn't help but concern herself with this particular agent. With this particular man.

She couldn't stop her heart from beating faster. She couldn't keep her fingers from trembling in his presence, and when she slept, she couldn't help but dream.

"You're early." His voice was like aged whisky, dark and smooth, caressing the senses even as it heated them.

"I'm always early." Lillian uncrossed her legs and straightened from where she had leaned against the wall, watching him approach through the dimly lit bar. "You should be used to it by now."

His lips quirked. Lips that had to have been created with kissing a woman in mind. Finely molded, not too thin, not too full. A three-day growth of beard covered his lower face and tempted her to touch. Shades of light brown and blond blended together, giving him a rakish, wicked appearance.

"So I should be," he agreed. His voice, like all Elite Ops agents', was well-modulated. There was no hint of an accent of any sort. No hint of where he had come from or what nationality he was. There was nothing for her to hold on to, no way to identify the man she was desperate to learn more about.

Pushing her hair back from her shoulder, Lillian glanced around the bar. It was one location that she could be fairly certain was safe, but lately, even here, she couldn't shake the feeling of being watched. As though the sights of a gun were constantly on her, a finger caressing the trigger lovingly.

Paranoia? She wished she could shake off the feeling with such a simple explanation.

"Shall we go for a drive?" she asked, looking up at him as he towered over her, his six-plus feet giving him quite an advantage over her five feet and five inches.

His brow lifted curiously, though there wasn't so much as a hint of the surprise that he must surely be experiencing. After all, she had never been reluctant to hand over the information she had uncovered to him here. She had personally vetted this bar herself, become a regular, and made certain that each inch of the property was familiar and safe.

She didn't feel safe any longer.

"A drive sounds nice," he agreed as his eyes narrowed the slightest bit on her.

Then, he lifted his hand and extended it to her. As though he truly knew her, as though he wanted to touch her.

Lillian stared down at the callused palm for no more than a second before she laid her hand in his and felt his fingers curl around hers.

Just as she had known. His hand was warm and strong. His fingers encased hers as he drew her from the shadowed corner and led her through the large room.

Few of the patrons paid any attention. After all, she was well-known to them, and she had been known to meet this man here for drinks before. She wasn't an oddity, and she had stopped being a curiosity long ago.

Still, she couldn't help but search the room from beneath lowered lashes. She could feel that itch at the back of her neck, that feeling, that certainty, that to someone, she was indeed worthy of interest.

"The night's cool," Black Jack commented as they neared the door. "Did you bring a jacket?"

He glanced at her, his gaze raking over her bare shoulders as he took in the diminutive black dress she wore and flat strappy sandals.

"I'm fine."

The night was indeed cool, just as it had been earlier. Her jacket was still in her car, in the parking lot behind the bar. She hadn't wanted to cover the dress. It was one of the most flattering articles of clothing she owned. Stopping just below her thighs, the short hem showed off her tanned legs while the snug material cupped her breasts.

She'd wanted him to look at her. She'd wanted him to see her as more than a courier, a source of information. She'd wanted him to see that she was a woman.

How vain, she told herself, as he opened the door and stepped out, drawing her behind him. Instantly, her heart nearly stopped in her chest as his strong arm circled her shoulders and drew her to him.

"The car's parked in the side lot." His voice was low as he bent to her. "Were you followed?"

Always on guard. Always aware that your life could end quickly if the slightest mistake was made. She had learned that lesson already, she didn't need a reminder.

She shook her head. "Not as far as I could tell."

She wasn't an amateur, but that didn't mean she couldn't make a mistake. She was as certain as she could be, though, that she hadn't brought danger with her.

She could feel the steady watchfulness that he carried like an invisible shield. It made her want to lean into him. She wanted to soften against him, feel both arms surrounding her, holding her to his warmth.

She was losing her edge perhaps. She couldn't explain the hunger that assailed her, because it was so much more than simply a hunger for touch. Or perhaps it wasn't. Perhaps it was just the touch she needed, human warmth to combat the chill that seemed to have taken hold inside her.

"The car should still be warm," he stated as he pulled his keys from his jeans pocket and flicked the remote sensor.

Lillian remained silent as he drew her to the car, opened the passenger-side door, and helped her in. She watched as he closed the door, then loped around the front of the car to the driver's side.

She should have insisted on using her own vehicle. If she were driving, she would have felt in control, or at least a bit more in control than she was as his passenger.

"Any particular destination?" he asked as he closed his door and pushed the key into the ignition.

Lillian shook her head. "Just wherever."

"You didn't feel safe in the bar," he commented as he put the vehicle in reverse and pulled out of the parking slot. "Do we have a situation?"

Yes, they had a situation. At least she did. Her panties were getting wet. Dear Lord, she hadn't had this problem in a long time.

"We're clear." She lifted her shoulders in a shrug as she looked at his image in the window rather than turning to him. "Perhaps I'm just restless tonight."

"Perhaps, hmm?" There was a thread of amusement in his voice. "I don't think I've ever seen you restless, Night Hawk."

How she was beginning to hate that code name. She wanted to demand that he use the name she had been given after her "death." A new name for a new life that wasn't really a life after all.

She turned to him then, watching him carefully. "Do you ever get restless, Jack?"

She didn't call him Black Jack. Using the name Jack made it seem more personal to her somehow. It made him seem closer.

His lips quirked at the name. "I rarely have time to be restless." There was a hint of the same darkness in his tone that all Elite Ops agents held. A deep-seated regret, a sense of loss. They had all lost everything dear to them because of something they had been unable to control. A stark reminder that they were human, despite the arrogance that had come to them in their former lives.

For Lillian, she had been so certain that her life was charmed at one time. That she was smart enough, fast enough, lucky enough to survive the life she had led without it ever catching up with her.

How very wrong she had been.

"I get restless." She let a mocking smile tilt her lips as he glanced at her. "And the night is beautiful, you must admit."

"I admit this." He handled the car smoothly as he took a turn through the heavy St. Louis traffic and headed for the river, before he surprised her by saying, "The night isn't nearly as beautiful as you are tonight, though."

A surge of sensation shot through her stomach, tightening her womb, then traveling quickly to strike at her too-sensitive clit.

He thought she was beautiful? She stared back at him silently, her mouth dry, wishing she could come up with something flippant and teasing to return with.

"Thank you," she finally whispered.

She felt like a fish out of water with this man. On unfamiliar ground. Almost innocent. He made her feel like a teenager experiencing her first crush.

His smile, though careful, was slightly warmer now.

"You've been stationed in St. Louis for a while, haven't you?" he finally asked as he turned beneath the old bridge and followed the road that curved down to the scenic waterway.

"Occasionally." She reminded herself bitterly of the rules. She wasn't to give him personal information. She wasn't to get personal. This was part of her assignment, to relay the information she had found to her contact.

The unit Lillian worked within specialized in gathering information for the other units. In gathering certain intel she had come upon a plot that she knew was directly related to another operation Black Jack's unit was involved in.

That information was sensitive enough, imperative enough, that she hadn't been required to go through regular channels to call this meeting. For that, she was extremely happy. It meant she wouldn't be debriefed nearly as intently over this meeting. It would be a part of her report, nothing more.

They were silent then as he slowed the car and pulled into the paved parking area overlooking the edge of the water. A casino riverboat was passing by, drifting slowly as its paddle churned the water and the patrons laughed gaily from the decks.

How innocent they all looked, she thought. She hadn't realized how jaded she had become over the years.

Putting the car in park, Jack cut the motor before turning to her. She could feel his stare, the way his gaze raked over her, causing a wave of heat to flash through her body.

"You called the meet," he finally stated. "What's the problem?" All business.

Lillian lifted her lashes and let his gaze catch hers. She felt suspended then, held between duty and desire, between the rules and a hunger she couldn't explain even to herself.

"Risa Clay." She finally cleared her throat. "Daughter of Jansen Clay."

"The traitor who conspired with Sorrell." He nodded. "I know of her."

Lillian guessed there wasn't an Elite Ops member who hadn't heard of her. Jansen and his ilk were the very reasons why the Elite Ops had been created.

"There's a contract on her head," she stated. "Two million, and word is that Orion has taken the contract."

She watched his eyes then. They narrowed as his jaw tightened. It was a small reaction, but one that assured her that the search for the deadly assassin known only as Orion was still a priority with his unit.

"Why the contract?" he asked her.

"Rumor is, she's beginning to remember things that someone doesn't want her to remember. Things such as the man who conspired with her father."

"The man who raped her." His voice darkened in fury.

Risa Clay had been brutalized by her rapist, then again by her father when he'd had her drugged and institutionalized for nineteen long, horrendous months. The young woman had been freed upon her father's death, when the truth had been revealed. But nothing, Lillian thought, would ever ease the nightmares that girl must surely have.

She nodded at the statement. "The man who raped her. Evidently, he's more influential than first believed. Orion will be arriving in the States within an estimated one to two weeks. He has four weeks to complete the contract by knife."

That was Orion's preferred method of death. He'd been known to use a bullet, many times, but he normally liked to play with his victims, especially the women.

"Any hint to arrival point or his identity?" Jack asked.

Lillian shook her head. "Nothing. We're still working on it, but we've been working on it for years with nothing new. I wouldn't expect that to change in time to save her life. You know how it works, Jack. At least we have a warning this time. It's more than we usually have when men such as he accept a job. We should count ourselves lucky."

And she should know. A man such as Orion had destroyed her life, had for all intents and purposes taken her life. And now, she was wondering if the price she had paid for life might have been too high. It was a price that held her back, held her silent, and forced her to deny her need for a man who was just as dead as she.

Travis watched the woman he had long ago nicknamed "Lady Hawk." Night Hawk was her codename, and he hadn't realized how much he hated code names until he'd found a curiosity for this one woman.

Curiosity was quickly turning to desire, though. When had it started? Hell, maybe it had always been there. Staring into her emerald eyes, seeing the feminine softness, a feminine hunger, he realized it must have always been there after all.

He stored away the information she had given him. He'd arrive back at unit command tonight and relay the message to Jordan. He wouldn't mention a midnight car ride, or the fact that his cock was throbbing and his need to touch his contact was driving him crazy.

Damn. She looked like a dark angel as she sat next to him in the car, staring back at him with aching loneliness. That loneliness was easy to identify, it lived and breathed inside him as well.

"Any further information?" He forced the question past his lips. He didn't want to talk to her about death or assassins. He didn't want to talk at all, but what he did want was so forbidden that it could make him a dead man in truth. Maybe.

She shook her head, her long, dark brown hair brushing around her shoulders and upper arms, drawing his gaze, his hunger. He wanted to feel that hair on his flesh, watch it fall around his face as she lowered herself to him, kissed him, breathed her warmth into him.

"The information was sent to me directly by a contact I've been fostering for quite a while," she told him. "Orion is one of our priority missions."

Travis nodded when he wanted nothing more than to kiss the lips that were parted, glistening as her tongue swiped over them.

She wanted him, just as damned much as he wanted her.

"We'll take care of it," he told her. "Inform your unit commander that EO-1 has accepted the information as well as the assignment that will go with it."

There wasn't a chance in hell that it would be rejected by Jordan, and Travis knew it.

She nodded slowly, still watching him. Travis warned himself that he was getting into some deep shit here. He knew he was and couldn't seem to pull back.

He'd played by the rules in his former life. He'd done everything by the book, and still, he'd lost all he'd worked for. He'd fallen back into that habit with the Elite Ops. Playing by the rules. Hell, if there was a hunger worth breaking the rules for, then it was the hunger rising inside him now.

His jaw clenched as he lifted his hand and reached out to her.

His fingers brushed over her jaw as she stared back at him, surprise flickering in her gaze.

"How long have we been meeting?" he asked her then.

Night Hawk shook her head. "A couple of years."

Three years. She had been assigned to his unit as courier and information-gatherer three years ago, and Travis had tried to make certain that he was always the one who met with her.

"Three years is a long time," he said softly.

Her lips parted as the tops of her breasts began to rise and fall, her breathing becoming more uneven. In the pale light that bled into the car, he could see her nipples pressing against the snug material of her dress and saw the faint hint of a flush as it washed over the upper curves of those perfect breasts.

"Too long?" It was a question, but not about the amount of time that they had been meeting. She was questioning the amount of time they had both wondered and had never made a move to assuage the curiosity.

He'd always wondered if her lips were as soft as they looked, if her kiss would be as heated as he imagined.

His hand cupped her cheek. "We'll pay for this," he warned her.

"I've already paid," she whispered a second before his lips covered hers.

As his tongue licked over her lips, felt them part, felt the little hitch of her breath, and felt the hunger in her response, he knew this punishment was much worse.

It was a fact that he would have to leave her tonight. That he'd have to walk away. That this single moment in time was the most he could allow himself.

Then her arms twined around his neck. Her lips parted further and a small moan sizzled in the air around him. Her moan. Her need. And he wasn't about to deny it.

He was a dead man. He was a hungry man. He was a man about to take the greatest gamble of his life.

cooper's
fall

chapter 1

ethan cooper stared out the window, his expression bland. He knew it was bland. He could feel it pulling into lines of complete blank shock.

Fascination.

Lust.

He should move. He told himself to move as he clenched his fists and pressed them into the wall beside the small attic window.

He was going to move.

In just a minute.

Just as soon as he came in his jeans from the sight that met his bemused eyes.

It wasn't his fault.

He was excusing himself and he damned well knew it. He was just too . . . shell-shocked. Yeah, that was the word. Too shell-shocked to move a single muscle and drag himself away from the little window with a bird's-eye view into the neighbors' secluded backyard.

Pervert! he railed at himself.

That didn't stop him. He was transfixed. His cock was in hell. He was practically drooling on his dusty attic floor as he watched shy little priss, Miss Sarah Fox, naked as God created her.

Glistening beneath the sun, slender hands moving.

He closed his eyes. Swallowed tightly. She thought she was in the privacy of her own home. She thought that the sheltering fence she'd paid a fucking fortune to have built around her pool was tall enough to protect her. That no one could see her. That she was safe.

He opened his eyes.

He felt sweat bead on his forehead and roll down his temple as she smoothed her hands over her breasts. Cupped them. Rolled her nipples.

"Christ," he wheezed. There was a flash of gold.

Holy hell.

He felt his cock get impossibly thicker. Felt his balls tighten. His balls? Damn. He could barely breathe.

Prissy Miss Fox had nipple rings. Fucking nipple rings. Beneath those staid blouses and too-long damned skirts she wore, she was wearing fucking nipple rings?

His fists tightened as he pressed them into the window frame. He blinked back sweat, and he couldn't drag his eyes away from her.

Long, nut-brown, riotously curly hair fanned around her. A hell of a lot longer than he had imagined it was. And she was curved. Curved where a woman should be curved.

And her fingers.

He tried to swallow. Her fingers were pulling at the little gold piercings in her nipples, and her expression was filled with pleasure.

Her entire body was sheened with oil. He forced his eyes from her nipples. Down.

"God have mercy." He was breathing fast, hard.

Fine. He was a fucking pervert. He unzipped his jeans, dragged free his dick, and curled his fingers around the shaft, palming it, stroking it.

Because she was moving again. The fingers of one hand were trailing down her stomach, to her bare, waxed, glistening . . .

He leaned his forehead against the little circular window, stared, fought to breathe. There was gold there, too. Just a flash. Just enough to assure his very trained eye that Sarah Fox had a piercing at the hood of her clitoris.

And she was playing with it. Pulling at it. Stroking her clit with glistening fingers.

She didn't writhe. She wasn't arching or giving him a show. She was a woman, lost in her own fantasy, her own touch. Her teeth clenched her lower lip, perspiration beaded her skin. Oil shimmered on it. And she was stroking herself. Slowly. Enjoying it. A woman who liked to be teased. Who liked the buildup. A slow hand.

He timed the strokes on his cock with the slender fingers moving between her thighs. Fine, he was fucking hard-core into watching the coolest little piece of flesh in town touching herself.

Damn. It was good. Who knew?

He stroked his cock, feeling her fingers on his flesh, slick, oil slick. He palmed the thick crown, feeling the steel that pierced the head of his cock, stroked down the shaft, and felt his chest tightening with the release building inside his balls.

And still she played.

His gaze narrowed on her. Her expression was almost distressed. Her fingers were moving faster now, stroking. His fingers stroked. His thumb raked over the curved steel beneath the head of his cock as he imagined the piercing in her clit.

Ah hell. Damn. He couldn't handle it. He watched. Her fingers, her face, the sweat that ran into her hair, and then he blew. He felt the ragged growl that tore from his throat, the blistering curse as his cum exploded from his balls, splattering against his fingers as Sarah's hips arched and her expression twisted.

In disappointment.

Her hand slapped the cement beside her. She sat up, pushed her fingers through her hair, then jerked to her feet and stalked back into her little house as Cooper stared at her in shock.

His cum was cooling on his fingers and Sarah had been left disappointed?

He blinked down at the pool area as he absently grabbed an old T-shirt and wiped his fingers clean of his release, then his still-hard cock.

Fixing his jeans he stared out the window, narrowing his eyes. Most of the houses in the area were single story, with privacy fences built around them. It just so happened Cooper's was just a little bit taller than most to allow for a taller attic. Just tall enough, the window positioned just right to look down into her pool area.

For some unknown reason, there were few of the houses built on the same line in the little Southern Texas town. Just so happened, his was built just right.

He grinned at his luck. Then he frowned as he readjusted his jeans and moved to the door of the long attic and down the spiral metal stairs that led down to the kitchen. Damn if Miss Fox hadn't just given him the release of the year or something.

The thought of her—disappointed. Wet. Pierced.

Fuck. Pierced. Sarah Fox. The woman he assumed was a staid little virgin. At least, that was the rumor. Virgin? With those piercings? Not likely.

Satisfied was another thing entirely, and as much as he would have liked to, helping Miss Sarah find her release wasn't going to become his aim in life.

Ethan Cooper was the bad boy, and he knew it. He owned the local bar, a sometimes biker hangout and generally ill-reputed establishment. And he liked it that way.

He was ill-reputable. The local troublemaker turned bar owner after returning from the Army, where he'd served more than eight years. A bullet to his knee had put him out of the Rangers, but it

hadn't put him out of life. A few scars and heavy pins in a recon-
structed knee weren't enough to kill that untamed, sometimes
dark core inside his soul.

The Army had honed it. The Rangers had sharpened it. Life
itself may have darkened it further. But it was still there. He was
still dangerous. He was still dark. He was still footloose and fancy-
free. And he intended to stay that way.

Sarah threw the towel on her bed, pouted, and stomped to the
shower. She washed the tanning oil from her body beneath the spray
and sighed in exasperation at the need that still throbbed between
her thighs.

Twenty-four years old. She was twenty-four years old and still a
virgin. And as though everyone in this little town she had moved
to knew it, she was still known as Miss Sarah. And she was tired
of it.

She washed quickly and dried her hair vigorously before comb-
ing through the tangles and leaving the long, loose ringlets hanging
to the middle of her back, then moving back to the bedroom and
breathing out roughly.

She'd tried everything to make herself fit in here, in this little
Texas town.

Well, everything but walking into a bar and just picking up a
man, and she just couldn't bring herself to do that. Just as she
hadn't been able to bring herself to let one of the drunken frat
boys from college heave and moan over her.

She grimaced at the thought of the parties her sorority sisters
had dragged her to while in college. There had been a few boys
who hadn't been drunk. Who had flirted with her, seemed interested. In a quick little screw.

She sat down on her bed and glared at her bedroom wall. She
should have moved to a larger town. She made a damn good living
as a Web designer and computer programmer. She worked for an
excellent company. She had good benefits. She'd been damn lucky.
She didn't have to do the nine-to-five rush and could relax. She

could afford to move to Houston or Dallas. The thought had her breath trapping in her throat. So many strangers. So much noise and fear. It was quieter here in Simsburg. A little, almost unknown town outside of Corpus Christi. She could relax here.

Hide away.

Shaking her head, she rose from the bed and headed to the closet. She pulled one of the sleeveless dresses from the closet and slipped it over her head before buttoning it nearly to her neck.

She went back to the bathroom and stood in front of the mirror. She unbuttoned the dress, spread it back from her chest, and stared.

The faint white lines were still there. She should stay out of the sun, she told herself as she let her fingers trace over the thin white scars. Tanning made them worse, she reminded herself. Made them easier to see. Harder to hide.

She let her fingers trace over them. There were half a dozen, long, narrow, very thin. But they were there. They had been there since she was sixteen years old. Sixteen and stupid.

She rebuttoned her dress before moving back to the bedroom and pulling on the bronze lace panties she took from her dresser. She slid her feet into sandals, twisted up her hair, and secured it in a smooth twist at the back of her head before heading to the kitchen for her purse.

She locked the house quickly but securely as she stepped out on the front porch a few moments later. Even here, in the quaint little town, amid the little houses and friendly citizens, she didn't take chances. She kept her doors locked. Her windows locked. She kept her car locked.

Head down, she dug her keys out of her purse, raising her head just in time to see her neighbor driving into the driveway right beside hers.

The powerful steel-gray four-by-four rumbled with power as he drove into the driveway. Parking, he moved from the vehicle, then stopped and stared.

God, he was a poster boy for big, bad, and dangerous. Six four. Jeans and boots. A T-shirt that did nothing to hide the snake tattoo wrapping around his bicep.

And he was staring at her. He stopped by his pickup, folded his arms on the top of it, and just stared. Hooded dark eyes, thick lashes. Black hair, dark flesh.

She stared back, feeling her chest tighten as it did every time she saw him. She could feel her breasts suddenly swelling, her nipples pressing against the thin material of her dress. She could feel heat skimming over her body, as she felt pinned in place, held by his gaze.

His lips quirked. The lower lip was a little fuller than the upper. It was sexy, sexual. It was a wicked smile that promised he knew her secret fantasies. And knew he starred in them.

Sarah felt held. Caught. Her fingers gripped her keys, and as a breeze whispered around her, she was sure she felt his gaze like a caress. Licking over her bare legs. Up her dress.

Her breath caught.

"Miss Sarah, how are you doing today?" His voice rumbled and stroked her senses with wicked fingers of desire.

God, he was incredible.

"Just fine, Mr. Cooper. And your knee appears to be doing quite well."

He had returned from the military wounded. Sarah had done the neighborly thing for a year. Fixed soup and cookies, and a few times made certain to pick up fresh vegetables or light snacks from the store for him to eat.

He was appreciative. He always thanked her nicely. But damn if he had ever invited her to share a meal. She had done everything to make certain he was in fit, healthy shape, and he still called her Miss Sarah.

"The knee is as good as it's gonna get." He flashed her that bad-boy smile and her heart raced as though he had actually touched her.

"I'm glad you're doing better."

He made her feel jittery. He made her feel flushed and hot.

"I'm doing just fine." He tilted his head, lifted a hand, and touched two fingers to his forehead in a gesture of farewell before striding to the front door of his house, unlocking it, and moving out of sight.

Damn.

She drew in oxygen with a ragged breath, clenched her keys, and forced herself to the car. Hitting the auto door lock, she got into the sweltering confines of the car and started the engine with a hard turn of the key.

He couldn't know her fantasies. She kept all her fantasies safely locked away, along with her nightmares.

He would never know that when she touched herself, she thought of him. That when she thought of being bad, being naughty, she always thought of being naughty with him. He would never know that she had come here because of him. Because of his actions on a dark, shadowed Dallas street and her fascination with the man who her uncle had saved.

Ethan Cooper had been one of the first people she met when the realty agent showed her the little house. He had been outside, cutting the grass in his front yard, pausing to watch as she drove into the driveway with the Realtor.

He had smiled and lifted his hand in greeting before going back to his yard work. Shirtless. In jeans and boots. Dark flesh gleaming. Sweat running in narrow rivulets down his back and shoulders. Black hair lying damp along his nape.

Then he had turned his head back quickly, and grinned and winked at her while the Realtor wasn't looking, which made her respond as though he had actually touched her.

She had gotten wet instantly. Hot and wet. And she had practically been panting as she walked up the drive to the little house. As though it had been a sign, that the dreams and fantasies she had woven around him could have a chance.

He was big, tall, broad, and dangerous-looking. The Realtor said Mr. Cooper was in the military. He had disappeared several weeks later and his house had sat empty, except for the occasional motorcycle-riding, thug-looking type who came, checked over things, and then left.

A year later, Ethan Cooper had returned limping. She'd heard he'd been wounded in action. She'd watched as he worked out in the enclosed acre he owned behind his house. Weights, push-ups, sit-ups, stretches. God, he had made her crazy that year. She'd nearly killed herself trying to ease the cramp of arousal in her stomach.

During those months, she'd had a chance to get to know him. When she took him cookies or soup, he always chatted, always laughed with her. And she always came home, desperate to be touched.

She was tired of masturbating. She was tired of being alone. And she was tired of aching for that tall, broad bar owner with the sexy grin.

Perhaps it was time to do something about this, she told herself. After all, covert looks and wishing weren't going to get her anywhere. It was time to do something about it. If she was going to get Ethan Cooper to fall into her bed, then she was going to have to take the initiative.

chapter 2

he couldn't get it out of his mind. Sarah Fox, spread out on the cement by her pool, long heavy ringlets fanned around her head, her curvy body slick and hot and oh so aroused.

He jacked off to it after he got back in the house. Hell, as if he could help it. The more he thought about it, the harder he got. He hadn't been so damned hot for a woman in years. Not since his first woman, in fact.

Who would have thought it? Timid little Miss Sarah.

He shook his head again before grabbing a beer and heading to his back deck. Sarah's privacy fence was over seven feet tall and extended around the full half acre of land behind her house. His white wooden fence connected with hers at a corner and extended almost double her area.

He didn't have a pool, though. He narrowed his eyes at the back-yard and considered it before grinning and lifting the beer to his lips. He'd just end up in trouble. He'd never be able to keep his buddies out of it. It was hard enough keeping them out of his house.

He grinned, wondering if Miss Sarah would let him use her pool. Maybe while she was tanning herself beneath the hot Texas sun. All ripe and wet.

He grimaced at the thought of that. Piercings aside, luscious sweet little body aside, Miss Sarah Fox wasn't for the likes of him.

He finished his beer before heading into the bathroom to shower and change. Owning one of the roughest bars in the area could get dicey at times. He liked to be there before too late in the evening.

He was leaving the house, locking the door behind him when Sarah's compact, boring-looking little sedan pulled into her driveway.

He felt the hot lick of her gaze for just a second before the car shut off and she was moving from the vehicle. She kept her head down.

Cooper couldn't help but watch as she rounded the back of the car and opened the trunk. She pulled out a canvas bag—groceries, he assumed—and strode quickly up the drive to the house.

Ignoring him.

"Hello, Miss Sarah," he called out as she stepped up on her porch and came to a hard stop.

Her head lifted, eyes widened. "H-hello." A small smile, not hardly a smile, tipped her lips. Pouty lips. He liked pouty lips.

Cooper stepped across the drive. There wasn't much distance that separated their particular houses. The two homes had been built by two sisters, close together. The property extended out behind and beside one side of the houses, bunching them close while other neighbors were kept at a distance.

Cooper couldn't even explain why he was pushing this, except he'd already jacked off twice today because of her. He gave her one of his trademark slow smiles and watched the little flush that filled her cheeks.

She watched him carefully, making no move to unlock the door, holding her keys carefully with one hand, the canvas bag with the other, as though she hadn't known him for two years. Wary, pausing to be careful. Miss Sarah wasn't a casual person by any means.

His eyes almost narrowed. She was in a carefully disguised protective stance. Keys to slash out with, bag to hit out with. Her body was balanced, ready to flee at a moment's notice. Now, why the hell would something that tiny, that damned shy, be on guard against a neighbor?

"Can I help you, Mr. Cooper?" she asked carefully as he leaned against the side of her house.

He let his smile widen. "Yes, ma'am, you sure can." He nodded. "You can tell me why a pretty little thing like you is all alone on a Friday night. There should be a law against it."

"I'm sure there should be." There was the barest hint of cynicism in the look she gave him.

"Boys around here didn't used to be so dumb." He shook his head. "Leaving a pretty girl like you twiddling her thumbs."

"I'm into men, Mr. Cooper, not boys," she told him coolly. "And I've been a woman, not a little girl, for a long time now. Is there anything else I can help you with?"

There was no fear in her. None he could detect. Wariness, suspicion, a whole lot of arousal, but not fear.

"No, ma'am." He finally shook his head and eased back.

He wasn't going there, he decided. There was something about Miss Sarah Fox that had every male instinct inside him rioting. And he wasn't the man this delicate woman needed. No, Miss Sarah needed a forever kind of guy, and Cooper just wasn't the forever kind. "Good evening, Miss Sarah."

"Mr. Cooper." Her voice stopped him.

He turned back to her, his brow arching at the confidence, the sudden look of a woman who sees more than she ever shows the world.

"Yes, ma'am?"

"My name is Sarah. Not Miss Sarah. Or Miss Fox if you prefer.

But after two years, uncounted plates of cookies, and bowls of soup, I think you can call me by my name."

There was no censure in her voice, just quiet command. That quiet command almost had him chuckling. She wasn't a pushover and she was finally letting him know it.

"Yes, ma'am." He nodded back to her. "I'll see you around."

"'Ma'am' wasn't one of the choices," he heard her mutter as the scrape of the storm door told him she was going into the house.

It slammed behind her as he stepped into his truck and let a low burst of laughter pass his lips. Damn if she didn't have spirit. Maybe Miss Sarah wasn't the timid miss everyone had grown to believe she was since moving here. Seemed to him, she just might have a little fire in her.

Hell, he knew she had fire. Too much fire for a man to step into without giving it a hell of a lot of thought first. And for a man like Cooper, it took more than just thought on his part. More than just fire on her part.

Too damned bad. He wouldn't have minded sharing her bed, her pool, and anything else she wanted to give up to him. For a little while.

Sarah closed the door to her house and leaned back against it to let out a long, slow breath. Oh Lord, that man was seriously hot. She dropped her keys onto the side table, dropped the bag of groceries to the floor, and waved her hands over her flushed face.

Those jeans were snug. They cupped his ass. His T-shirt highlighted a six-pack that would make any woman's eyes bug out. And those arms, serious biceps; that face, rugged and tough. He wasn't a pretty boy. He looked dangerous and hard and so hot that he made her perspire.

Damn.

Just the sound of his voice had her creaming her panties. And that was so not fair, because she still just hadn't gotten the hang of masturbation. She could get to a certain point, she'd get almost there, but only sometimes did she actually manage to go over.

She had all the books. And she practiced. There had to be a trick to it. And she really wished she could find that trick, because her neighbor made her so hot she was changing panties several times a day and driving herself crazy with the arousal.

She picked up her canvas bag, slid off her sandals, and padded barefoot through the house to the large, airy kitchen in the back. There were a lot of windows spaced around the room, making it seem as though the backyard was a part of the room.

The pool had been the selling point. She loved the pool. She loved the way the sun spilled in the kitchen at dawn and how cozy and warm she felt in the house.

And it was all hers.

She put away the milk and eggs, the bag of coffee, the sugar and cream. A pack of cookies and some sweet rolls went on the counter, a carefully wrapped steak went in the fridge, with the wine and a baking potato on the counter.

Dinner.

One steak, one potato, one glass of wine, perhaps on the deck.

She stared out at the deck, bracing her arms on the counter and watching the water in the pool as she frowned and considered her neighbor Ethan Cooper. He'd introduced himself right after she moved in. Told her if she had any problems to let him know. And if any of his friends who came over sometimes bothered her or offended her, then he definitely wanted to know. And he'd been serious.

His friends weren't that bad though. They were rough-looking, funny, and always joking with her. She thought perhaps they talked to her more than Ethan had over the years. But they never flirted with her, they never came on to her. She could be everyone's kid sister for the way they treated her.

Not that she wanted his friends. She wanted Ethan. But, she glared at the pool, it was enough to make a woman wonder if perhaps she was completely unattractive to the opposite sex.

She pushed back from the counter, stared at the potato, and

sighed again. A meal alone. On a Friday night. She'd lived here for two years and had never really noticed how little other people wanted anything to do with her, until now.

And she went out every day, she made sure she did, if only to buy her dinner. She was friendly, wasn't she?

She was lonely. She trailed her fingers over the wide kitchen island, drifted through the house, and frowned at the odd feeling. She hadn't been lonely in a very long time. She'd been too busy, too concerned with surviving to worry about loneliness.

Her hand lifted to her chest as she stopped in the middle of the living room and stared at the floor. She rubbed the scars, almost as though she could feel the horrendous fear and pain that she had felt when they had been made.

She shook her head. No, she wasn't thinking about that. She had pushed it to the back of her mind and it was staying there. She had dealt with it. She had survived it. That was all that mattered. Wasn't it?

But had she survived it, really? She was still hiding. She was still keeping herself locked in her work as though each minute meant success or failure. And it didn't. Not anymore.

She had built a life for herself. In the past two years, she had picked up some great contracts within the business she was in. She didn't have to worry about going hungry, and she didn't have to worry about losing her home—her uncle Martin had made certain of that. She never had to worry about that again.

So why was she standing here like a lost puppy?

Because she didn't know how to have fun. She'd been to the bar before, but no one even asked her to dance. She had joined the business club in town, but they only met once a month and they rarely did anything but talk about how small the community was, and how high taxes were, and how the good jobs were closer to Corpus Christi.

Maybe a small town really was a bad idea. She had thought she would find it easier to fit in here; she hadn't expected it to be harder.

It was Friday night. She had a steak and a potato waiting. At least she had a few good books to go with it.

Cooper strode around the bar a week later, his eyes narrowed against the smoke and gloom, watching for drugs more than anything else. He had only a few hard, firm rules in his place. They fought in the parking lot if they wanted to use their fists. No one hit a woman, whether she was a lady or not. And no one, but no one, dealt in his place.

His bartender, an ex-Ranger like himself, was holding down the bar with the help of one of the local college kids. The boy was a hard worker, eager to learn. There were two other bouncers, ex-Rangers as well, and as hard and tough as any Cooper knew, despite their medical discharges from the service. They were all termed "disabled vets." But his men were as hard and as efficient as they had ever been in the military. Maybe just not as fast, he thought with a grin.

The Broken Bar was one of the most popular spots in the area and the only bar. Most weekdays were busy, but the weekends could turn into a madhouse if they weren't careful.

The band on the other end of the cavernous building was belting a slow country tune and couples were circling the floor. There was the usual assortment of bikers, college kids, and general bar-hoppers.

Motioning to the closest bouncer, he indicated the other man should take his spot as Cooper headed back toward the bar. As he did, he nearly came to a full-blown, hard stop.

Hell. No, he didn't need this. Not after seeing her naked, aroused, and unsatisfied.

There, standing in the doorway like a wary angel, was his intrepid little neighbor. And she wasn't wearing a dress. Or a skirt. She was wearing jeans that made her legs look like the best wet dream a man could have. Low on the hips, belted over a sleeveless blouse that was buttoned damned near to the neck, and over boots.

And her hair was down.

He felt a hard strike of jealousy at the sight of the men whose eyes found her, lusted for her, worshiped those long, wild curls.

Shit. How the hell was he supposed to get her out of here this time? This was not the place for Miss Sarah.

Pushing the fingers of one hand through his hair in irritation, he moved toward her, cutting through the room on a diagonal path as she headed for the bar.

Didn't she know the scum she could find in a damn bar? What the hell was she doing here?

And it should be damned illegal for a woman to move like that in a pair of jeans. Like they were loving every step she took in them. Like they were hugging her shapely little ass with possessive hands.

Son of a bitch.

"Hi." She smiled at his bartender. Jake damned near dropped the bottle of whisky he was holding. "Could I have a whisky, straight?"

Jake's brown eyes flickered over her. Yeah, she didn't look the whisky type.

"I have some wine coolers back here," Jake offered. "Fruity ones."

Cooper almost laughed at Jake's floored expression.

"No." She shook her head and Cooper caught her expression in the mirror behind the bar. She was one determined lady. "Just the whisky, please." Then she named her brand. "If you have it?"

Damned expensive. Oh yeah, they had it.

Cooper moved to the end of the bar, next to the stool she had snagged, leaned his forearms on it, and stared at her silently as she turned to him, her eyes widening just a little bit.

"Mr. Cooper." That little hint of a smile. A little bit of dimple.

"Just Cooper." His lips quirked as he stared back at her, watching as her gaze slid to the tattoo curling around his bicep.

She let her teeth rake over her lip before meeting his eyes again. Jake chose that moment to set the shot of whisky in front of her.

Cooper arched his brow as she lifted it, sipped as delicately as a lady would a glass of wine, then set the shot glass back on the bar without a grimace.

"It's a busy bar." She looked around. "It's been like this every time I've come. Even during the week."

Her voice lifted as she turned away. When she turned back, that little dimple peeked out again. Her smile was careful, as though she didn't quite know what to do with those pretty lips.

Cooper lifted his hand and propped his jaw in his palm as he just stared at her.

She fiddled with the shot glass for a moment, then surprised him when she lifted it and took the half shot back without a single choke or cough. Her lips tightened and he imagined the burn that hit her, his body tightening as her expression took on that relaxed, slightly pleasurable look of a woman relishing the sizzle.

Now that was a look he had never seen on a woman's face, and it made him hard. Hell. Harder. He'd been hard for her for over a week now.

"Another?" he asked, glancing at the shot glass.

"No, thank you." She shook her head, a hint of vulnerable self-consciousness entering her eyes as she stared around the bar.

She turned her gaze to the band, the dancers, her profile faintly wistful as she watched them.

"I've been here several times." She turned back to him, those wide pale blue eyes stroking over his face. Hell, it was almost a caress.

"I've seen you." He nodded.

She looked down at the shot glass, played with it for a moment, then stared back at the dance floor as the band slid into a rousing dance tune.

Damn, the look on her face. She wanted to be out there. He could see it, feel it. So what the hell was holding her back? Each time she had come into the bar, she had sat at one of the back tables, alone. She had watched, drunk a soda or wine cooler or two, and left.

She had never come to the counter. She had never drunk his finest whisky with a curl of pleasure tightening her face. He would have noticed. He always noticed Miss Sarah.

"Miss Sarah . . ."

"Sarah." Her head swung around, those wild curls feathering over her shoulder, and there was that little dimple again. "I'm not that old, Mr. Cooper."

"Cooper," he murmured, his jaw still braced on his palm as he watched her.

"Cooper." There was the slightest edge of delight in her gaze then. "Please call me Sarah."

"Yes, ma'am." He smiled back at her, just to watch her eyes flare in irritation.

She lowered her eyes again, played with the shot glass again, then lifted her gaze back to Jake and indicated another shot.

Cooper almost laughed out loud. Jake gave him a hard, disapproving glance, as though he thought Cooper could keep her from drinking.

And Miss Sarah caught that look. For a moment, Cooper saw a shattered, weary pain flash in her eyes. Then a tight smile twisted her lips.

"Forget it." She fumbled in her jeans pocket, pulled out a few bills, and slapped them on the bar. "I shouldn't have come here."

Fuck!

Cooper straightened as she slid off the bar, head held high, and all but ran toward the door. What the hell?

Following her, Cooper felt something tighten in his gut. A strange, almost tender amusement mixed with confusion. Damn it. She looked like she was going to cry when Jake didn't want to serve her the whisky. As though, somehow, she had been rejected.

"Hey, whoa. Sair. Come on, hold up." He caught up with her in the graveled parking lot, his fingers curling over an arm so damned soft it felt like heated silk. He had shortened her name. Not Miss Sarah, or Sarah. His Sair.

She jerked away from him, turned on him, her face flushed, eyes glittering. And those *were* tears.

She blinked them back furiously.

"I got the message, Mr. Cooper," she snapped. "Don't worry, I won't come back into your bar again."

"Whoa. Sair." He moved in front of her, staring down at her. "What message did you get exactly?"

Sarah stared back at him, battling her tears. "That makes half a dozen times I've been in that damned bar." She swung her arm to it. "The only bar in driving distance, mind you. Each time, I order whisky. Each time, I get some damned kid's drink. The last time, I got a soda. Now I have to have your permission to drink whisky in there? When the hell did you decide to ostracize me from this town?"

He blinked down at her. "When did I decide to do what?"

Cooper decided he was in shock. He hadn't wanted her ostracized, just protected. Nothing more.

"I walk into that bar and no one asks me to dance," she informed him frostily. "If anyone seems to be coming close to me, your bouncers waylay them and suddenly no one is speaking. And now your bartender won't serve me whisky?" She sniffed.

Ah hell. She couldn't cry on him here. Not in the damned parking lot.

Cooper rubbed the back of his neck as he stared down at her furious little face. She had guts, he had to give her that.

"That's not what it is," he finally said, grimacing.

Her arms were crossed over her breasts, her hip cocked. Damn. He was going to end up fucking her on the hood of a car if she kept this up.

"Then what, Mr. Cooper, is your problem? I'm over twenty-one. I don't believe I'm a total hag, but last I heard, even ugly women were allowed to drink whisky."

"That's not it." He hardened his voice. Hell if he wanted to explain this here.

"I just wanted to dance," she whispered, the moonlight striking her eyes, making them deeper, darker. Damn, he wanted to fuck her. "To have a drink. I just wanted to be a woman, Mr. Cooper. I'm sorry if I inconvenienced you."

She jerked her keys from her jeans pocket and turned to stalk to her car as though it were over. Son of a bitch. He should let it go. He was fucking stupid. Insane.

He caught up to her, slamming his hands against the top of the car as she reached the door, pinning her in, watching her start, feeling her sharp intake of breath as he leaned in close to her.

"This isn't a nice place," he told her softly. "This is a bar. The men who come here only want a fuck, Sair. They're not all nice, and they're sure as hell not here to share a drink and a dance and go quietly home."

He could smell the scent of her now. A little spicy, a little sweet. Whatever perfume she was wearing was going to kill him.

"My bouncers have orders. The men in that bar know me, they know what you don't. I'm a mean fucker, baby. And when I put out the order that they use extreme caution around you, they know what the hell it means."

"Why would you do that?" Breathless. A little excited, maybe. He didn't feel any fear and that was too damn bad. She should fear him more than she did anyone in that bar.

He let himself lean closer, let his nose bury in the soft fragrant silk of her hair. "Because I want to fuck you, Miss Sair," he growled. "I want to fuck you so deep and so hard that neither of us can move for hours later. And I can't have you, baby, because you sure as hell deserve better. So I'll be damned if I'm going to watch one of those sorry bastards in there taste what I know they'd never appreciate. Go home. Find a nice young man who wants forever and babies, and count yourself lucky that the devil was in a good mood tonight."

A good mood? He was so damn hard, so horny, his cock was like titanium. He could drive spikes into railroad ties with it. And it was so pressed against Sarah's lower back, the only thing separating it from her flesh was their clothes.

Clothes he wanted out of the way.

"Was he?" There was something in her voice that had the hairs standing on the back of his neck. "I don't think it was his good mood." She pulled open the door as he shifted back. "Trust me, Mr. Cooper. There's no such thing where the devil is concerned."

He watched her start the car and drive away. And he couldn't forget the little bit lost, little bit lonely look on her quiet little face. As though she had faced demons, and realized they were stronger than she had ever imagined.

"Fuck!" He propped his hands on his hips, stared after the car, and knew. Hell, he could feel it in his gut. He knew Sarah was going to rock him clear to the soles of his feet.

Before she did, he needed answers. His Sair was too wary, too damned secretive. Striding back into the bar, he made a mental note to have Jake check into exactly who Sarah Fox was.

chapter 3

sarah had learned not to cry a long time ago. She had learned how little tears helped, and she had learned how miserable they made her feel and that no one else really gave a damn anyway.

Ethan Cooper had warned men away from her at the bar. Had word of that warning gone through town? Was that the reason everyone stayed distant?

She went to the grocery store the next afternoon, as she did every day, to buy dinner for that evening. She wandered through the store, chose a few vegetables, a ripe tomato, though she had no idea what she intended to fix. She checked out a slice of watermelon, passed it by. She picked up an apple, placed it in a clear plastic bag, and laid it in her shopping basket.

She felt disconnected as she moved through the store. She didn't want steak or pork. She didn't want another chicken breast. And she had promised herself years ago that she was never eating another TV dinner in her life.

So what did she want?

She wanted to dance. She wanted to be held. She wanted to be touched. And she didn't want a stranger. She didn't want a casual fuck. She wanted something more.

She wanted Ethan Cooper.

She stopped in front of the meat aisle for the second time, frowning down at the variety. They had everything. The problem was, the hunger tearing at her had nothing to do with food and everything to do with something much more instinctive.

"The catfish is fresh."

She tensed at the sound of Cooper's voice behind her.

She tucked in a few stray strands of hair that had escaped the twist at the back of her head and stared down at the chicken.

She picked up a single-wrapped chicken breast, laid it in her basket, and moved on. Okay, an apple, a small stalk of celery, a single green pepper. There was lettuce left in the fridge. God, she so didn't want chicken.

"Are you going to forgive me, Sair?"

"My name is Sarah," she told him quietly. "Or Miss Fox if you prefer."

He breathed out heavily behind her. "No one else calls you Sair. It makes a part of you just mine."

He was close. Close enough that she could feel the heat of him against her back. Close enough that her nipples beaded, her clit grew tight and hard, and her stomach tightened with need.

"You don't want me, remember?"

Damn him. She didn't want to want him. Did he think it was voluntary?

"You won't be served sodas in the bar anymore. I promise." His voice was a quiet, dark rasp. There was a hint of amusement. A hint of something darker, deeper. "And I didn't say I didn't want you."

She lifted her shoulder in a shrug. "I won't be back in your bar, Mr. Cooper."

She moved through the dairy aisle. She could probably use another small carton of milk. Sometimes she drank it, sometimes she didn't. She placed it in the basket before selecting a small wedge of cheese she liked with the crackers she kept in the cabinet.

"You're not going to forgive me? Come on, Sair, we're neighbors. You can't hold a grudge against me." There was a tickle of laughter against the top of her head, warming her soul.

Sarah stopped and turned and her nose was nearly buried in his chest. God, he was so close. She lifted her head, stared into his amber-flecked hazel eyes, and felt all the blood rush to her face. And the damp heat of her juices rushing to prepare her vagina, filling it, seeping out to her panties.

"Am I bothering you?" she finally asked him.

His brow arched. "Hell, yeah," he murmured. "You're making me hard as a rock. And I'm tired of knowing you're mad at me."

"Very well." She turned away and resumed her journey to the checkout stand. "I won't be angry anymore."

She wasn't angry to begin with. She was hurt. She had been trying desperately to make friends in this little town. Knowing Ethan Cooper had been warning everyone against her made her feel more isolated than ever before.

She had been isolated for most of her life. She didn't want that any longer.

She heard him breathe out roughly behind her again and wanted to turn back to look at him so bad that she couldn't stand it. She loved looking at him. She could spend hours doing it.

But she'd decided it was better not to stare. It just made her want.

Cooper watched Sair as she moved away from him. Her trim, delicate figure glided, moved with a sensual unconscious grace that had his balls tightening, his cock throbbing. Hell, if he jacked off much more he was going to risk pulling off his dick.

He stayed quiet as they moved past the beverages. Pulling a six-pack of beer from the cooler at the end, he caught up with her at the checkout, remaining quiet as she spoke to the few mothers in line.

They were wary. It was a small town. Sair was the interloper and it would be years before she was fully accepted, unless someone intervened.

And he had hurt that process. The warning he had put out not to touch had somehow morphed, as it did in little towns, to a message that she was to be pushed away. Hell if he had meant for that to happen. Sometimes, he just forgot what home was like, though.

"Miss Maggie, that baby's growing." He moved behind Sair and stared over her shoulder at the precocious little boy waving his hands at Sair as she turned to amusing the baby rather than trying to push past the reserve of the mother.

Maggie's brown eyes sharpened as he all but laid his chin against Sair's shoulder. Sair was still, silent in front of him.

"Cooper, are you being bad again?" Maggie narrowed her eyes at him.

He had gone to school with Maggie. She was several years older than he was and had several kids now. She had brothers, a husband, and sons. Maggie Fallon was a damn scary woman.

"I'm always bad, Maggie." He flashed her a quick smile, his hand moving to Sair's hip to curve over it as he moved closer and made a face at the baby.

Maggie laughed and little Kyle Fallon gave him a drooling smile. The kid was cute as hell. Sair was as tense as a board.

"Has anyone warned Miss Fox about you yet?" Maggie's gaze warmed a little as she looked at Sair. "You have to be careful of that rogue behind you. He's a heartbreaker."

"So I've figured out." Sair's voice had just the right amount of husky interest in it, and wary reserve.

He wished he could see her face. Her eyes. Maggie glanced back at him with a smile and wagged her finger at him. "Ethan Cooper, don't go running off the new girls in this town with broken hearts. This town is small enough."

Cooper laughed, and he played. He let his fingers grip Sair's curved hip. His hand pressed against it and he inhaled the fresh scent of her hair, wishing he could let it down.

"If you need any advice where that wild man is concerned, Miss Fox, give me a call." Maggie shook her head at Cooper, amused indulgence filling her eyes. "I've known him since he was born."

"She likes to brag she changed my diapers," Cooper drawled in Sarah's ear, laughing at Maggie. "She was the first girl to get in my pants."

"Ethan Cooper!" Maggie was scandalized, but too amused to do much else but laugh at him. "You're getting worse in your old age."

And Sarah was blushing. He could see her profile, could see the wash of the flush rising in her cheeks.

The cashier was chortling. Mark Dempsey owned the grocery, and worked it often, along with his wife and two children.

But both Mark and Maggie were more relaxed now, their gazes more curious as they watched Sair.

Maggie paid for her purchases and Sair's moved down the conveyor belt where Mark scanned them quickly and rang up her bill.

"Thank you, Mr. Dempsey." She paid him quickly.

Were her hands shaking just a little bit? Cooper wondered.

"You're welcome, Miss Fox." Mark smiled back at her. "You watch out for that one behind you, too. Maggie's right. He's a rogue."

"I'll be sure to do that," she promised.

She must have flashed those pretty, hidden dimples, because Mark's hangdog face softened for just a minute as he gave her change back. And Sarah was walking away, quickly.

The soft dark-blue summer dress, sleeveless again and buttoned to the neck again, swished around her hips and calves as she moved from the store with her purchases.

"She seems like a nice kid." Mark was watching him expectantly. "Neighbor of yours, ain't she?"

"She's a good woman." Cooper nodded sharply. "I don't think she likes me much, though." He laughed.

Mark shook his head on a chuckle. "You need to settle down, Cooper. Ladies know a wild rouser when they meet one. She's a smart one, she seems. Bet she sees right through all that charm of yours."

Cooper arched his brow and smiled. "So she does, Mark. So she does."

Mission accomplished. He could go home and stop feeling so fucking guilty because he had almost made little Sair cry. Shit. Since when had he grown a conscience?

Sarah's next stop was the post office, where Maggie Fallon just happened to be as well. The other woman lived near Sarah, and she had rarely talked to her. But today, she kept her at the post office boxes for nearly twenty minutes, talking. Just talking.

And something inside Sarah had eased. She wasn't certain what it was, and she knew the other woman had loosened up only because of Cooper's teasing. But after Maggie finished talking to her, several other women spoke; the postmaster actually asked her how she was doing, and while she posted Sarah's packages, talked about an upcoming summer festival in the town.

Sarah left the post office with a warm glow. She had lived here for more than two years, and finally, she felt as though there might be a chance she could fit in.

She returned home, put her groceries away, and then moved to the front room as she heard Cooper's truck pull into the drive beside her own. From behind the shelter of her curtains she watched him look toward her house as he got out of his truck, then he was loping to his porch and out of sight.

She should thank him, she thought, biting at her lip. Nothing ventured, nothing gained. That was the hospitable thing to do, or so her uncle Martin had always told her.

She wiped her damp palms down the skirt of her dress and left her house, gripping her keys in her hand, and moved across her drive. A six-foot wedge of grass separated her asphalt driveway from her neighbor's.

She stepped up on the porch and moved to the door before knocking with a quick, decisive rap of her knuckles. And she waited. Holding the keys tight in her hand, one sharp point ready if need be. She jerked a little as he opened the door and stared back at her in surprise.

"Miss Sair," he drawled, leaning against the door frame. "What can I do for you?" The amber highlights in his eyes seemed to spark, flare.

"I wanted to thank you." She refused to twitch or stutter. "For what you did at the store."

His expression tightened as he lifted himself from the door frame and stood back. "Come on in."

"But I just wanted . . ."

He reached out, gripped her wrist, and pulled her in before closing the door behind her.

She never once thought to defend herself. She stood in the small foyer, a frown tugging at her brow at the thought. Had she forgotten how dangerous even innocent things could seem? She must have, because she wasn't frightened of the large, dark man looming over her.

"I didn't do anything," he said, turning away from her. "Come on out back. I was just putting lunch on the grill. You can share it with me."

"Oh, I wouldn't want to impose." But she did, she really did want to impose.

"Get your butt back here." His voice held a thread of command that had her following him slowly.

He stopped at the fridge in the kitchen, reached in, and pulled out a thick, raw steak before adding it to the platter on the table. There were vegetable kabobs, steaks, and shrimp kabobs.

"Are you expecting company?" There was a lot of food there.

"Nope. Just me." The ever-present T-shirt shifted over the hard muscles of his chest, shoulders, and biceps. The action made her mouth water, made her sex swell and come into agonizing contact with the little curved bell that pierced the hood of her clit. "Grab yourself a beer and come on out. I have to get the grill heated up before I can put on this stuff." He paused as he covered the platter and set it back in the fridge. "Or, the whisky is in the cabinet." He grinned. "Whichever you prefer."

She chose the beer, though she would have preferred the whisky, and followed him out to the deck.

The wide wooden deck matched her own. One half was covered, the other open. Cooper moved to the large grill in the uncovered corner and set the flame to it before lowering the lid and turning back to her.

She held the beer in both hands, watching him. Watched as he picked up his beer from the wooden table beside him and took a long drink, staring at her, his gaze heavy-lidded, thick black lashes framing his hazel and amber eyes.

"Are there rules in a small town?" she asked him then, for a lack of anything better to say. "No one wanted to talk to me until you made them."

He grimaced at that. "I checked around. The no-touch policy in my bar got kind of mixed up." He shrugged. "That happens sometimes. People were just a little wary, uncertain of what was going on. In little towns like this, everyone tends to watch newcomers suspiciously for a while, anyway. The twist in the order in the bar making its way around town just snowballed. I'm sorry about that."

"You must have a lot of power in town then." She frowned. She hadn't realized a small town had a power base. Rather like society. It didn't matter how much others liked you; if a prominent figure didn't, you could be ostracized immediately.

Cooper grimaced again. "I don't have a lot of power, Sair. I told you, others know what you don't about me. I'm not a nice guy."

"Maggie liked you. And children are incredibly astute. Little Kyle reached up for you several times. And the store owner seemed to like you."

"Doesn't mean anything in a town like this." He sat down on the bench as she stood watching him. "I'm a hometown boy. And

I don't take much shit. They would act like they liked me even if they didn't."

His stare was direct, honest. Sarah licked her lips and stared back at him, uncertain what to say. Her body was humming, as it always did around him. Vibrating with need. It didn't make sense. Her nipples were hard and sensitive, her breasts swollen beneath her dress.

"You're wet, aren't you?" His expression suddenly shifted, became sensual, filled with male lust. And if she hadn't been wet before, she would have been in that instant.

Sarah cleared her throat, speechless. "I'm sure a lot of women get wet around you, don't they?"

She'd surprised him. She watched his lips quirk, his eyes become more intense.

"You're messing with trouble, you know that, don't you, Sair?" His voice deepened, became graveled. Rough. "You're a nice, sweet little thing. And I'm a very, very bad boy. You sure you want to keep watching me with those hot little eyes and tempting me with that pretty body of yours? You should have a nice guy, Sair, not a man who's forgotten all the softness in life."

Was he willing to be tempted? Sarah shifted slowly and almost moaned at the feel of the little piercing at her clit rubbing against her.

"Perhaps I want to learn how to be bad," she answered him softly then. "If you're that bad, Cooper, then you could show me *how* to be bad. And I'll remind you of the softer things in life."

Pure, raw lust tore through his system. Cooper stared at her, wondering if he looked as shocked as he felt, looked as damned hungry as he knew he felt.

She stood there, her cheeks a little flushed, gripping that beer bottle with tight, nervous fingers. Her gaze was direct, though. A hint of heat, embarrassment, and something he didn't want to look too closely at, filling her eyes.

As he stared at her, a sudden thought shook him to the core.

"Shit," he muttered. "You're a virgin, aren't you?"

Her lips tilted a bit cynically. "Define virginity. Have I ever been with a man? No, I haven't. But I haven't had a hymen for years, Ethan."

She didn't call him Cooper. Fuck. She was dangerous. Because calling him Ethan struck a soft spot in him he didn't know he had. He liked the sound of it on her lips, the way her eyes softened when she said his name.

He moved toward her then. Slowly, watching her. Her gaze met his, direct, unashamed. A little quiet. A little somber. There were shadows in those pale blue eyes, shadows that made him wonder exactly what lay beneath the surface of this proud little woman.

And there was pride. Immeasurable pride.

"Why?" He moved behind her, bent his head, and brushed his nose against the hair by her ear. He wanted to hear her voice, not be distracted by the need filling her eyes. "Why haven't you been with a man, Sair?"

Her throat moved as she swallowed tightly. "I was very sheltered for a long time, and after that, I had a hard time adjusting." Sadness filled her voice. "And I was working. There was no time." And there was a little lie.

"Don't lie to me." He nipped her ear and felt her jerk. "Never lie to me, Sair. I don't tolerate it well."

She was silent for long moments. "I don't want a one-night stand. I don't want a boy who doesn't know how to touch a woman, or a man who knows only his own pleasure." She turned her head and stared at him. "I'm not looking for love, Ethan. But I want to be held. I want to be pleasured. And I want to know how to pleasure. And I've wanted you since the first day I saw you."

His cock was going to rip past the zipper on his pants, tear right through his clothes, and go for the glory. Hell.

He took her beer and set it with his on the deck railing. Here, beneath the covered porch, the lattice surrounding the enclosed area, there were no eyes to see. Not that he really cared if anyone could see. He wondered if she would care?

Turning her to him, he gripped the back of her neck, watched the pulse hammer in her throat, and stared at the way those pouty lips parted and her tongue stroked over them.

Hell. He was gonna do this. She had said the magic words, though he didn't know if he believed them. She said she didn't want love. She wanted sex. She wanted bad sex.

"Nasty sex," he whispered, lowering his lips until they feathered hers. "Hard sex, Sair. I'm a man. A hard man. And I love sex, baby."

There was the slightest little dip to her lashes and he bet she was creaming her panties. He bet when he touched that bare little pussy, he was going to find his fingers covered in her juices.

"Touch me." Her whispered entreaty tightened his balls. "However you want to, Cooper. Touch me, before I die for it."

"I won't be easy." He wrapped an arm around her hips, bent, and jerked her up to him.

Her eyes widened, innocence sparkled like incandescent lights in her pale blue eyes, and arousal flushed her face. Her lips looked poutier, ready to plunder, to taste, to explore.

Slender hands slid up his forearms as his cock throbbed behind his jeans, pressing against the soft flesh of her covered pussy. He was going to go down on her. As soon as he kissed her. As soon as he stilled the fire raging inside him for the taste of those pretty lips. He was going to lift her skirt, pull her panties aside, and devour her.

"I didn't ask for easy," she spoke against his lips, a stroke of fire, of need.

And he wasn't going to give her easy. There was something in her eyes, in the needy little catch of her voice. The memory of those piercings and the way she drank that whisky. Sweet little Sair didn't want easy at all. And that was a damned good thing, because Cooper had lost "easy" a long damn time ago.

chapter 4

sarah was swamped with sensation. Lost in it. Her fingers curled in ecstasy against strong, broad shoulders, and her lips parted beneath a kiss that was hot, hungry, and oh so good.

He held her against him effortlessly, her feet dangling above the ground, his heavy erection pressed between her thighs. She lifted her legs as his lips moved over hers, slanted across them, his tongue taking hers. She slid her legs up his—feeling the power beneath them, the bunch of the muscle beneath his jeans—until her knees were gripping his thighs, and one of his hands slid to her ass, cupping it, holding her up.

Oh, that was so good. She lost herself within the dreamy, seductive sensations flowing through her. Flames licked over her flesh, burned in her pussy. She gripped his powerful flanks, eased higher, and lowered herself, a moan tearing past their kiss at the incredible assault of sensation against the piercing rubbing her clit.

Why was it different? Why couldn't she pleasure herself with her own touch? It was the excitement, she decided. The dangerous, pulsing excitement thundering through her bloodstream, swelling in her clit and in her nipples. It was the knowledge that she was in the arms of a very dangerous man. But not a cruel man. She knew the difference. She had lived with the difference for most of her life.

The inherent dark, seductive force of the man holding her drew her. It powered through her.

"Fuck, you're like dynamite," he growled, tearing his lips from her, his head lifting, the amber in his hazel eyes almost like fire now.

It set fire to her senses. He was aroused. Really and truly aroused for her. For *her*.

"Make me explode then," she panted. "I'm certain I have a very short fuse."

Cooper stared down at her, almost shocked. Her pale blue eyes were lit with hunger, with need. Her face flushed with it. Her knees tightened at his thighs as his hand clenched in the curve of her ass.

Hell, he bet she could come over and over again. If Cooper thought he knew anything, then he knew a woman's pleasure. He'd made it his life's work. He'd put a lot of practice and research into the matter. Didn't understand their minds. Had no clue how to decipher their emotions. But he knew how to give them pleasure.

And he was betting his back teeth that he could make this little firecracker come like the fourth of July.

She was innocent, but hotter than hell. He could see it in her, and suddenly the need to know why she was innocent, why she had picked him, was rising in his head.

He'd tackle that problem later. Right now, Sarah was sweet and hot in his arms and he wanted her naked. He wanted her twisting, writhing, begging for release.

"Let's see just what it takes to make Sair come, then." He grinned down at her, watched her eyes darken.

"I want to see what makes Ethan come, too."

She'd surprised him again.

Her hands smoothed over his shoulders. Her inquisitive little face, filled with hot feminine lust, held him transfixed.

"Want to know what makes me come?" he crooned, lowering his head to touch her lips, watching her eyes flare.

"Yes," she breathed.

"Sometimes, the simplest thing." He nipped at that pouty lower lip. "I came like hell last week. In my attic. Staring down at your pool and watching you touch yourself."

Her eyes widened in shock. "You saw me?" There was the slightest hint of mortification in her voice. Just enough that he knew she was thinking more about her failed attempt to get off than she was about him seeing her.

"I jacked off watching you." He turned to the table that sat beneath the sheltered porch and sat her on it.

"You liked watching me?" There was a hint of shyness, the pleasure building back as he smoothed her dress up her legs.

"I loved watching you. And I'm going to watch you again."

She shook her head. "You touch me."

She was breathing so hard her tight little nipples were in danger of bursting through the front of her dress.

"Oh, I'm going to touch you." Just a little bit. Just enough to get her hotter, to make her wilder. "Then you're going to touch me, Sair. Let's see how hot we can make that pretty little body of yours."

He leaned back, jerked off his T-shirt, and had to clench his teeth. Her hands were there, on the thin mat of hair covering his chest and angling down the center of his body.

Then her lips.

Jesus. This wasn't a woman who wanted all the pleasure for herself.

He lifted his hands to her hair and pulled the clip from all those glorious curls, watching them fall down her back in a swath of silky ringlets. He couldn't wait to feel those fucking curls over his legs as he fucked those full, luscious lips.

"I want to touch you." Her hands moved to his belt and Cooper grimaced at the want, the need in her voice.

Not yet. Fuck, not yet. He wanted her silky and wild first. He wanted her screaming out in need.

And he sure as hell wasn't taking a virgin on a fucking picnic table. He was an asshole, but he hadn't sunk there yet.

"Not yet, baby." He picked her up, ignoring her surprised breath, loving the way her hands clenched his shoulders, her nails digging into his flesh.

He bet she was a wildcat. All claws and silky heat. He couldn't wait.

"Where are we going?"

"My fucking bed, sugar." His voice was tight; hell, his whole body was tight. "I want room to do this right."

Sarah swallowed tightly as he moved into a well-lit bedroom. The bed was huge, dark. Sunlight spilled through the sheer curtains and open blinds on the windows.

"There we go."

He laid her back on the bed, following her, stretching out beside her as he speared his fingers into her hair and held her head still for another of those deep, voracious kisses.

She loved it. Loved his lips on hers, hungry and deep, his tongue licking and stroking, pushing into her mouth and teasing her tongue until she was tasting him, too.

There was no hesitancy in him. Only hunger. Hard, male hunger.

She arched into him as the skirt of her dress slid up her thighs. His hand, big and callused, stroked her leg, sending flares of white-hot sensations racing through her bloodstream.

When his hand cupped between her thighs, she froze. Stilled. She felt her womb clench, her pussy convulse, and the pleasure. It was terrifying. She had never felt this before. Even in the darkest nights when the need had torn through her, she had never known this sensation.

His lips lifted from hers.

"Like that?"

There was knowledge in his eyes. He didn't move, just held his hand cupped over the curves of her sex.

Sarah fought to breathe. Her eyes were wide, staring back at him, her body poised at an edge she was desperate to fly over and yet terrified to experience.

"When I make you come, I'm going to make you scream my name."

His eyes were narrowed, more amber now than hazel.

"Don't stop." Her hands gripped his wrist as he pulled back.

"Easy, baby. We're not ready to go there yet."

"We are. Really." Sarah was desperate to go there. Her body was begging to go there.

His chuckle was easy, dark.

"Let's get you out of these clothes. I'm not fucking you with that skirt around your hips."

She hadn't anticipated that. "You could pull the shades," she breathed out roughly.

His smile was sexy, dark and exciting. "I like the way you look in the sunlight," he told her. "I want to see it washing over those pretty breasts."

His hands went to the buttons of her dress and Sarah froze. She watched his face as he loosened them. There were dozens, from the high bodice to the hem of the dress. Each one that slipped free filled her with more dread, knowing what he would see.

Would it turn him off? The scars were horrendous. Glaring. She felt her breath still in her lungs as she looked over his shoulder, waiting, fighting back the tears. She'd just wanted to know. She'd thought he'd take her on the deck maybe. Her skirt around her thighs. That she'd at least find release before she had to face this.

Cooper's eyes narrowed as Sarah tightened, tensed, with each tiny button that came loose. By the time he reached her stomach and pushed back the edges of the silky material, revealing her swollen, pretty breasts, she was stiff as a board.

Stiff. Almost frightened.

And he saw why. His fingers feathered over the six, very faint white lines across the tops of her breasts. As though a razor blade had sliced into the delicate skin just deep enough to scar. They weren't zagged or puckered. Almost as though someone had drawn the thin lines over the tops of each curve.

"We'll discuss these later," he told her softly.

She stared over his shoulder, her face pale now. He knew shame when he saw it, knew the fear in a woman's face when she thought something about herself was unattractive.

Watching her, he lowered his head, letting his tongue follow first one faint line, then another.

At the first touch, she flinched. At the second, he felt her forcing herself not to respond. By the time he reached the sixth, her eyes were closed, fists clenched at her sides as she fought to hold on to the arousal and the control.

"Do you think those faint little lines are going to get you out of this, Sair?" He reared up on his knees, pulling her up, dragging the dress over her hips before pulling it over her head.

Surprised, she lifted her arms, staring up at him as he pushed her back to the bed.

"Hell. God have mercy," he groaned, sliding from the bed.

He pulled her sandals off her feet, but left the little toe ring she wore. He toed off his boots and shed his jeans so fast it was a wonder he hadn't scraped his dick with the zipper.

Fuck. His hands were shaking.

She was spread out before him like the sexiest little feminine banquet he had ever laid his eyes on. Gold rings pierced her nipples. Little rings that circled the tight, hard buds. Tightening around them.

"Oh, I bet that feels good." He leaned over her, watching her eyes dilate as he lowered his head and licked over first one tight bud, then the other.

Sarah jerked, cried out. She felt the sensation clear to her womb, white-hot ribbons of pleasure striking at her, convulsing her lower stomach.

The gold rings that surrounded her nipples had never felt so good. Just the slightest pressure around the hard points. The rasp of his tongue over them. It was the most pleasure she had ever known.

Then, he covered a tip, sucked it into his mouth. Sensation slammed to her womb, arched her, convulsed her stomach. Her eyes went wide, and her fingers, almost of their own volition, rose until her nails were digging into his shoulders.

"There you go, Sair." He breathed a rough breath over her nipple. "Enjoy me, baby. I fully intend to enjoy you."

The rough sexiness of his voice destroyed her. Washed over her. Filled her senses and in the haze she forgot to be self-conscious. She forgot about the scars. Forgot about the past. All she knew was this. The man. The touch. And finally, the pleasure.

"Oh. Yes." The words escaped her lips, escaped her soul as she felt his fingers touch her between her thighs now.

Her clit was swollen as it had never been before. The little metal ball of the piercing pressed against it, creating an incredible friction.

He wasn't in a hurry. And she wished he was. She wished she could finally touch the ecstasy that always managed to stay just out of reach.

"Please," she whispered as his lips moved to her other nipple, sucked it in, drew on it.

Her skin was so sensitive. Each brush of his flesh against hers was killing her. She needed him.

"Ethan, I hurt," she panted, her head tossing, lost in the pleasure. "Oh God. I need you so bad it hurts."

Cooper almost froze. No one called him Ethan. Not since he was a boy. They called him Cooper. He was Cooper. Even his lovers called him Cooper. Until Sair.

Until today.

His head lifted. Her eyes were dark, her face damp, with perspiration? He lifted his hand, his thumb stroking beneath her eye. Tears.

"Sair?" he whispered.

"Oh God, Ethan, I need to come." She was trembling beneath him. "I can't come. No matter what I do. No matter how hard I try. Please. Please. Make it stop."

"Why haven't you found yourself a man before now, Sair?" He touched the saturated, slick folds of her pussy. She was hot. So incredibly hot. Her flesh swollen, the extent of her need telling him how long she had held back. Years. She was a woman who needed touch, yet she hadn't been touched. She hadn't been held. And he wanted to know why.

She stared up at him. "I would have."

"Why didn't you?"

Her lower lip trembled. "I saw you."

Cooper swore his cock swelled thicker, harder. Two years. He had met her the day she looked at the house. And he'd seen her eyes. The shy interest, that little hint of "want to?"

"Why me?"

He moved between her thighs. She was too hot. Too ready. For whatever reason, for him. Hell, his ego was as swollen as his dick now. No woman had ever waited for Cooper.

"Make me feel it," she whispered then, staring up at him, her gaze tortured, her eyes dark. "All of it, Ethan. I want to feel all of you."

She was twisting beneath him, her little nails digging into his biceps now. She was going to blow off his head if he didn't do something now.

He gripped her wrists and slammed them to the bed. Held her there. She arched, moaned.

"Oh yeah, you like that, don't you?"

And he liked it. But he'd be damned if he'd ever seen a sweet little thing like Sarah go for it so easily. The restraint, the wild need clawing between them now.

Hell, how had this happened so fast?

He pushed the head of his cock against the folds of her pussy.

Sweet heaven and God have mercy on his soul. Hot. Like silk, like syrup coating the head of his cock.

He blinked sweat out of his eyes. Hell, he himself had never gotten this hot this fast. What the fuck was she doing to him?

He pressed his hips closer, gritted his teeth as he felt the engorged crown of his cock press to the tiny opening of her vagina, felt the piercing tug at his cock with relentless pleasure. She was little. He wasn't huge, but he wasn't small. A fucking bruiser. Dammit, she needed someone gentle.

The piercing beneath the head of his cock lodged into the tender flesh, stroking her and him, and knotting his balls with pleasure.

Then he watched her breath catch, her nipples darken and harden impossibly as he all but shoved the thick crest just past the entrance to her pussy.

He gritted his teeth, watched her eyes.

"Ethan. More." A breath of sound. A flush of deepening arousal. Her breath catching.

Fuck. She said she'd have a short fuse, he just hadn't believed her.

Leaning over her, he grinned. The best he could do.

"You're not gonna last long, are you, baby?"

Her pussy was clenching, tightening, spasming around his cock head. Fuck. How long, was he going to last?

She was breathing hard, her eyes dilated until only a thin ring of pale blue color remained.

Oh, he knew what his little Sair needed. Right there, in that instant. Because it was his greatest fucking fantasy. Pushing in hard and deep, first stroke, and feeling his lover come from the excitement of his touch.

Every man's fantasy. His, for damned sure. A pussy so tight it was like a fist knotted around him, flexing and milking, coming and vibrating around him because she wanted him so damned much.

"Sair," he groaned her name. "I don't want to hurt you."

It was the first time in his life he had ever cursed the size of his dick. Which wasn't enormous. She was just so fucking tight.

Her lips parted. "This kind of hurt, I'll survive." She lifted, tightened, and for the first time in Cooper's life, he lost his cool with a woman. Lost his control. He lost everything but that last fragile thread of sanity that helped him pull back on his strength.

But not his dick.

He pushed into her. One hard stroke, pushing past slick, slick tissue, gripping muscle, powering into her until she screamed his name and he felt her coming around him.

Milking him. Flexing around him.

Ah, fuck. He buried in full length and son of a bitch, he was fucking coming. Pouring into her. Spurting hard and heavy without the benefit of latex, and dying with each hard flex and jet of the semen erupting from his cock.

And she was still vibrating around him, arched into him. Her clit grinding into his pelvis, her body shuddering, jerking, her eyes dazed.

Little Sair had just come apart in his arms like no other woman had ever dared. And Cooper had a feeling he might have just lost a little piece of his heart. Not to mention his sanity. Because he knew he'd forgotten the latex, and son of a bitch, he was starting to wonder if he cared.

chapter 5

"i didn't use a fucking condom." Ethan fell to his back, but he dragged her to him, draped her over his chest, and forced her to stare at him.

He should have just let her lay against him, because the look on her face was dangerous to a man who had held on to his heart for so long.

Or had he? Hell. He was starting to feel the fucking noose and it felt comfortable.

"I'm protected." A frown flitted across his brow as she lowered her lips to kiss him, and his fingers tangled in her hair to hold her back.

"How do you know I'm safe?" He narrowed his eyes back at her.

There came the dimple. A little shy. A whole lot too damned sexy.

"Your friends used to talk when I'd drop off the food while you were recovering," she admitted. "Really, Ethan. You're like a condom fanatic."

He had been.

He let her lower her lips to his. Damned if he could help it.

"I didn't get to go down on you," he growled, pulling at her hair with one hand as the hand around her neck held her to him. "You need to pay for that."

He made her pay, with her mouth. Her lips, her tongue, a kiss so deep he felt it in his balls. Hell! He needed to get away from her. She was fucking dangerous. She was stealing every fantasy he had of a woman, as though she could see inside his head and knew how to give him exactly what he needed.

Her lips were eager, her moans washing over him. Her lithe, incredible little body stroked him from breast to ankle, and he'd be damned if he wasn't harder than he was when he took her minutes before.

"I want to touch you."

He let her pull back. His head dug into the pillows when her lips moved to his jaw, his neck. She might be inexperienced, and hell yes he knew she was. He felt what he had pushed past on that first stroke. She'd been a bit wrong about that hymen. It had been weak, easy to break, but it had been there.

Now, his adventurous little virgin was running her lips over his neck, his chest. Her lips covered the flat discs of his nipples, one at a time, sucked and licked and, fuck him, burned him alive.

Then she was going down. Licking. Kissing. The closer she got to the thick shaft of his cock, the more he felt her distress. Her need. She wanted to go down on him. He could feel it, or hell, maybe he just wanted it that damned bad.

She paused, her breath washing over the head of his cock as she lifted her eyes to him.

"Help me," she breathed, her breathing hard and rough now, the need in her eyes brushing him with heat.

"Oh baby," he growled, pushing up on the pillows, reclining back. "Just love it with your mouth. A dick is pretty damned easy to please. Suck it, lick it, let it know it's loved, and it will perform all night for you."

That little dimple again. It flashed at her cheek.

"I love it a lot," she breathed, dipped her head, and licked over the heavy crown. "A whole lot, Ethan."

God, help him. She made love to his cock. With a little encouragement here and there, and a whole lot of gut-torn moans from him. He was tortured. Paying for his sins in the worst way.

This sweet little virgin was sucking his soul out of the head of his cock and he was loving every second of it.

"Yeah, baby, suck it deep." His hands bunched in the long corkscrew curls of her hair. "Christ. Yeah. Suck it like that." She tucked the head against the roof of her mouth, worked her tongue beneath it, played with the curved ball that pierced the foreskin, as he told her, and he almost lost it.

Her hands stroked, caressed. She knew the rudiments, and what she knew, she learned how to work. She loved his cock like chocolate, and he was dying from it. She licked, sucked, moaned around it. She played with the piercing beneath the head the same way he wanted to play with hers. With torturous pleasure. Until he knew, one more touch and he was going to lose it. He was going to fill her mouth when he wanted nothing more than to fill her hot little pussy again.

He lifted her away from him, pushing her back on the bed despite her erotic struggles. She was panting, breathing heavily. And when he jerked her hips forward and laid his lips to her clit, she froze.

She tasted of sweet hot woman, and himself. He wasn't a man who normally got into the taste of himself on a woman, but with this woman, hell, however he could get his lips on that hard little clit, he was all for it.

And the taste of them together—damn, it shouldn't be exciting. It shouldn't make his dick harder. But it did. And the feel of her response ripped through his senses.

Sarah bent her knees, unashamedly parting her thighs and allowing Ethan access to her intimate flesh. What he was doing was threatening to destroy her. He was playing with the little ball at the end of the curved metal piercing the hood of her clit, rolling his tongue over it, stroking it against the little bundle of nerves.

Sarah found herself so lost in the pleasure, the spiraling, the incredible hot sensations, that she could do nothing more than writhe and moan beneath him.

It was so good. Better than her dreams.

He was rolling the hard little gold ball against his tongue and stroking her clit at the same time. He sucked both into his mouth, laved around them. Sensations piled inside her. Her heart raced. Blood thundered through her veins. She felt herself—inside and out—twisting with hot licks of such incredible pleasure that she could only cry out against it.

"Easy does it, baby." Callused hands gripped her hips, held her in place against the bed. "Just let it feel good, Sair. That's my girl." He kissed her. Kissed her clit. Flicked his tongue over it. "So damned pretty. Just let me play a minute and then you can come all over me, baby. Just a minute."

She didn't want to wait a minute. Sarah whimpered out against the pleasure, her hands threading into his hair, pulling at it, trying to drag him closer.

"Come on, Sair," he whispered devilishly. "Tell me what you want."

"I want to come." Her head thrashed on the bed.

"Tell me how to make you come, baby. Come on, tell Cooper how to make you feel good."

"Ethan," she panted, a protest and a cry of need. "Oh God, Ethan, suck my clit. Suck it. Let me come."

He sucked, he lapped, but he only threw her higher, made the pleasure hotter, brighter, the need like jagged forks of electricity racing over her flesh. His tongue played with the little ring and gold ball piercing her clit. He sucked and loved it.

He teased her. Tormented her. Left her sweating, pleading, and when he began to suckle her, firmly, rapidly, his tongue playing over the little gold ball above her clit, she exploded.

She flew. She felt herself melt and went willingly into the rainbow of explosive, torrential heat.

The hard thrust of his cock inside her, the feel of his cock ring stroking her flesh, dragging over it, left her shaking, arching. Crying. And sent another orgasm crashing through her.

"Yes!"

"Fuck, Sair." He dragged her closer as he knelt over her, his hips thrusting.

The pleasure-pain. The stretching burn. The exacting, incredible ecstasy of this. How had she waited? How had she stood back from him for so long, knowing instinctively, to her soul, what being with him would mean?

Her arms wrapped around his neck, her nails bit into his flesh. She lifted and raised, cried his name, and then felt herself unraveling again.

It was too much. The pleasure. It was like dying inside and being reborn. It was like being filled with life.

Above her, inside her, she felt Ethan's release. Deep, hard spurts of his semen filling her and her breath caught at the realization that once again, he hadn't worn a condom. Hadn't one of his friends laughingly said that all his women complained because no matter how protected or safe they were, Ethan always wore latex?

Until her.

Until now.

"Oh God! You just sucked the life out of me." He collapsed beside her and once again dragged her across his chest. "Go to sleep, you little wildcat. I'll feed us later. We'll have to eat before I can giddyap and go again."

His hands were on her back. Stroking her, easing her. He was holding her. Sarah let her lashes drift closed; she let the weariness set in. Just for a minute, she told herself. She would get up in a minute. Because she didn't want to wake up in his arms, screaming in pain.

Sometimes, the nightmares were as brutal as the past itself had been.

"What did you find out?"

Cooper stood on the deck, cell phone in hand, a bottle of beer in the other as he watched the kitchen. Evening was darkening over the house, and Sarah was still sleeping. And Cooper wanted answers.

"You're not gonna believe this shit," Jake, his bartender, stated in surprise. "Man, when I finally tracked that little girl down and cut through all the bullshit, I 'bout flipped my wig."

"Fine, now flip mine," Cooper ordered him.

Jake sighed. Cooper could almost see him running his hand over his bald head as he sat back in the leather chair of the office of the bar.

"Remember that Italian mafia guy? Oh, 'bout eight years ago. Suddenly turned himself over to the Italian authorities, spilled his guts and his evidence on all the families, which caused that split through the crime families?"

"Fredrico or something like that," Cooper nodded.

"Well, man, get a load of this. What the news services didn't get an earful of is what I found out when I contacted a few friends over there at the embassy. Seems ole Giovanni Fredrico, alias Gio the Giant, had a pretty little sixteen-year-old daughter who was kidnapped when she slipped out to meet with a rival's son. She was taken, held for Gio's good behavior as they set through Italy killing off some of his strongest allies. Each time good old Gio tried to get back his baby girl, they sent him a video. A video of this tiny little teenager held down, naked from the waist up, a razor blade slicing across her breasts. The old man was going insane. Turned to the authorities. Promised them everything, but they had to get his daughter, like pronto."

Cooper lowered his head and closed his eyes. The scars across Sair's chest. Fuck.

"Okay, so get this. From what my embassy buds say, they

rescued the girl quick enough, turned her over to her daddy for a few days, then Daddy was arrested, too. Whole big trial. Threw him in prison, yada yada. We know all that. Well, six months later, little Sarita Fredrico was killed in a car bombing that took out three more of Old Man Fredrico's rivals. Or so the reports say. Start digging, and you find out that six months later, Sarah Fox emigrates from Italy by way of our good ally, Australia. Arrives with her uncle, Martin Corelli. Martin takes a security-guard job in Los Angeles, and little Sarah Fox is taking college classes. They move again a year later to Dallas. Sarah Fox goes into computer programming and graphics, and good old Martin is playing security guard again. Until four years ago. Martin dies. I talked to the coroner. He remembers the case, not because the death was anything less than natural, but because the dudes who collected the body were Italian. One grieving little mother dressed in black and a big, tall, somber young boy who managed only scattered English. They were accompanied, our coroner swears, by the Secret Service, who flashed some pretty impressive ID. The boy with the mother asks if old Corelli had other friends or family. Coroner says no, then asks the boy, How did you know he was here? The boy states, A call from a friend. Nothing more. End of story, everyone goes away. Six months later, you acquire a new neighbor. Miss Sarah Fox."

Cooper could hear the "but." It was there. Tightening in his gut.

"So?" he said carefully, glaring at the boards of the deck now.

"So, we met Corelli," Jake informed him. "Me and you, while we were in Dallas a few years back during leave. We were carousing the bars that week. Remember?"

Cooper had to sit down. Fuck, he remembered. "He just called himself Martin."

"Righto," Jake ground out. "We all drank, had us some laughs, and the dude gets up to leave, says he has to meet his niece and walk her home from nearby. Then when we left and those thugs tried to jump us outside the bar, he was there with that switch-blade like hell on fire."

"And said one day he'd take a favor in turn for the help," Cooper sighed. "That one day, if he died, he'd send me the only thing that meant anything to him. And I was to protect it." They'd been drunker than hell, Cooper remembered that. He'd laughed, told Martin he'd protect his firstborn son in exchange. And Martin had told him that what he had was much more important than his firstborn son.

"Well, here's some more good info," Jake snorted. "Corelli was here in Simsburg a few months before he died. I just got some info when I was talking to the Realtor who sold her that little house. Corelli arrived for two nights with his niece Sarah Fox. When the Realtor asked why they were looking in Simsburg, Miss Fox told her they knew someone in town."

"There was a girl there that night," Cooper mused. "After the fight. She got off the bus on the corner while we were leaning against that bar laughing our asses off."

He remembered it now, as though it were yesterday. Blue eyes in the night, the small figure, her coat hood pulled over her head. Her face had been hidden by the hood, but she'd held keys in her hand. He remembered the glitter of those keys, one sharp point held between her fingers, a laptop bag looped over her neck.

She'd been wary. On guard. But he remembered feeling her gaze go over him.

Son of a bitch.

"Corelli was her guardian. And she came here because of me."

"Actually, Martin was my uncle. And yes, I came here because I couldn't forget you."

His head jerked up at the sound of her voice. How the fuck had she managed to slip into the kitchen without him knowing?

"Shit. Your ass is in the fire now, huh, boss?" Jake groaned. "I'm gone. Good luck."

Cooper flipped the phone closed and stared back at Sarah. Her chin was held high, her dress buttoned a little crookedly. She was carrying her sandals in her hand.

Her expression was stoic. There was fear in her eyes.

He stared at her for long seconds, crossing his arms over his chest before he spoke. "Why didn't you tell me?"

She looked away from him for long seconds, then her eyes came back to him.

"Because I was tired of being someone's responsibility. For once, I wanted to be someone's woman instead," she finally said. "Thank you for today, but I think it's time I leave now."

Cooper blinked as she turned and started through the kitchen. Son of a bitch. Had she thanked him for fucking her? Then decided to leave?

He moved after her, catching her before she had taken more than half a dozen steps, and swung her around.

"Oh, it's not that easy, baby," he assured her, his voice rough.

He should be madder than hell. He should be raging. Cooper didn't do responsibility really well. The bar was the biggest weight he wanted on his shoulders, nothing more. At least, until Sarah had knocked him on his ass.

"Why didn't you tell me who you were?" He held on to her even as she tried to pull away.

"Because I wanted you, not your damned promise made to a man while you were drunk, nor did I want you to feel responsible because you flirted with me, made me want you on a night you most likely didn't even remember," she cried out. "I wanted the man I saw that night. The one that was so strong and so playful. A man who didn't hurt his attackers, just wanted them bruised a little. I wanted the man whose bar my uncle and I would slip into and watch once he learned he was dying. I wanted the man I fell in love with once I arrived here and learned he was so much more than I imagined. I wanted you to want me, Ethan. I didn't want you to feel responsible for me."

She jerked back her arm as he stared at her in shock.

"You said you didn't want love," he accused her.

"I said I wasn't looking for love." She threw him a scathing glance. "I'd already found it. I loved you. It was enough."

She shook her head, all those wild curls flowing around her.

"You're free, Ethan." She opened her arms and stepped back. "No harm. No foul. You gave me more than I dreamed you ever would. And you gave it to me, not because of the memory of a debt." There was a flash of pride in her eyes, of feminine pleasure and confidence. It made him hard. Made him want to fuck her again. Right there, in the middle of the kitchen floor.

And he was going to do it.

"We're not finished," he growled, jerking his belt loose, unzipping his jeans. "Not by a long shot."

Her eyes widened, her lips parted.

Just in case she had it on her mind to say no, he covered those pouty lips with his own, jerked her into his arms, and lifted her.

"Put your legs around me. Now." He jerked her dress to her hips, kissed her again as she tried to speak and turned, pushing her against the wall as he tore at her panties, ripping them off her hips. He heard her excitement in the moan that filled the kiss, and felt it in the way her hands dug into his hair. Her lips ate at his, her tongue fought against his.

"Hell, yeah. You love this." He pulled her closer, shifted his hips until his cock was pressing into her. "Don't you, Sair? You love my cock."

"I love you." She glared back at him.

"Tell me to fuck you."

A tear slipped from her eye. "Love me, Ethan. Just this once. Love me."

She made his knees weak.

"Damn you," he groaned. He slid the crown of his cock inside her and paused, feeling her, so silky, so hot. "Damn you, Sair."

He pushed into her, easier this time. Slower. He worked his erection into her, feeling all the little caresses, the sucking, milking ripples of her hot little pussy as she took him. So slow. So tight. So much pleasure he felt blinded by it. Felt as though he'd never have enough, could never take her enough to sate his hunger for her.

He buried his face in her hair, felt her legs locking around his back, and he took her slow and easy. Because the pleasure of it was enough to fight for, to die for.

How the hell had she managed to get past his defenses? And she had. Slid right through them and he hadn't even known it. Until he touched her. Until she asked him to show her how to be bad. Then broke through the last of his control when she asked him to love her.

"So sweet. So tight," he groaned against her neck, holding her to him, moving her on him. "God, Sair, what have you done to me?"

His arms tightened around her as he felt her juices gathering, slickening, easing his way even more as his hips began to move faster. Harder. He needed her. Needed more and more until he felt her gripping him tighter, hotter, and heard her cry out his name.

"Ethan!"

Her face buried in his neck, her pussy rippled around him, and he lost himself in her. For the third time that day, he poured himself into her. Growling. Groaning. Lost in the pleasure that burned like a supernova through his body, he spilled every ounce into her, and he knew. It wasn't just his body he gave her. It was himself.

chapter 6

it was the mother of all fuckups.

Three days later, Cooper paced his attic, stared through the little window, and saw nothing. Fucking jack shit, and it was pissing him the hell off.

Sair had walked out on him. After he pumped inside her until he thought he was going to melt to the kitchen floor, she had all but run from him.

And what the hell had he done? Stood there. Like the fool he was, he just stood in the damned kitchen and watched her go, anger rising inside him as fast and as hard as lust had.

Two years she had lived here. Two fucking years. She had brought him chicken soup while he was healing from knee surgery. Baked him fucking cookies. Talked to his friends and knew things about him she shouldn't have known. And fit him like a glove.

Hell, no woman had ever fit him like Sair did. And no woman had ever affected him as she did. He even missed her.

When was the last time he had ever missed any particular

woman? He didn't miss women. He made certain he didn't get close enough to women to miss them. So why the hell was he missing Sarah?

Well, he'd had enough of it, that was for damned sure. He looked at the clock: He had to be at the bar in a few hours. He was dressed and ready to go. He just had to get Sarah ready to go.

As though he hadn't heard the rumors of the dipshits in town hitting on her? She went to the grocery store every afternoon, everyone knew it. No less than three of the bastards had been seen coming on to her. So far, no one had mentioned her flashing that cute little dimple. He'd have been homicidal if they had. That dimple was his, by God.

And he was damned insane.

But that didn't keep him from stomping down to the main level of the house, out the front door, and over to Sair's little house.

He pounded on the door.

His arms crossed over his chest as she opened the door and stared back at him warily.

"What?" She didn't seem hospitable.

Too damned bad.

He pushed his way in between her and the door frame, turning back to glare down at her.

She was wearing another of those damned high-neck dresses. He hated those bastards.

"Get dressed," he ordered her. "We're going out."

"We are?" She closed the door, crossed her own arms over her breasts, and glared right back at him.

And that made him hard. His cock swelled in his jeans to dimensions he swore it had never attained before.

"Where exactly are we going?"

"To the grocery store first," he informed her. "Then to the bar."

God, he was a nutcase.

"And why the grocery store?" Her eyes narrowed back at him.

Cooper bent his head and growled, nose to nose. "Those bastards hitting on you at that fucking store are going to learn who the hell you belong to, starting today. Since when the hell did a grocery store become a singles' fucking meeting place?"

"It always has been actually." Her smile was tight. "You meet all kinds of people there."

"Men!" he snarled.

"If I were looking for a man, then I would have easily found one this week." She shrugged, then turned her back and moved through the house. "And I'm busy today. I bought enough groceries yesterday for dinner tonight, so I don't need to go to the store." She looked over her shoulder, those long curls falling down her back. "And I'm not in the mood for you, or your bar."

He stared at her before turning and stomping behind her. She made him stomp, dammit. She was driving him crazy.

"What do you want, Ethan?" She turned on him as they reached the kitchen. "You wanted no strings. Look, no strings." She held her arms out from her, her pale blue eyes reflecting an edge of pain. And oh yeah, there it was, a flash of arousal.

His balls went tight. They knotted up beneath the base of his cock with painful intensity.

"What do I want?" he growled silkily, advancing on her. "First, I want to show all those woman-grabbing yahoos in town that you're mine. Then I want to reinforce that little message while I rub against you on that dance floor at my bar. Once we get finished, I'm going to take you to my office, lay you back on my desk, and eat that hot little pussy like candy and hear you scream my name again. Does that answer your question?"

Her breasts were rising, falling, pushing against her dress with the panting breaths she was taking now.

"You don't want strings," she whispered.

"I fucked you without latex." He grabbed her hips and jerked her ass to him. Hell in a handbasket, he had the least amount of control in the world where she was concerned. "If that's not strings, baby, I don't know what it is."

Her hands gripped his forearms. "But I'm on birth control. There's no risk."

"Have you lost your mind, Sair?" He nipped her ear in retaliation. "I'm the condom fanatic, remember? You think I forget latex at the drop of a hat? You think I've ever trusted another woman enough to spill inside her?" He licked the little burn of the nip. "And I want to do it again. I want to watch while my cock pushes inside your tight pussy. Watch the way I stretch you open. Take you and fill you as you suck me in. Those are strings, damn you."

Sarah felt her knees weakening. She knew she should protest this. She should be screaming, throwing him out, telling him to go to hell.

He hadn't trusted her. He hadn't asked her, but had had her investigated instead. And evidently by someone who knew what the hell he was doing. Because he had found almost everything.

"Physical strings," she whispered, her eyes almost closing as he ground his erection against her rear. "You couldn't just ask me anything about me, could you, Ethan? You had to ask others."

She tried to pull away from him, but he wasn't letting go. And not letting her go, holding her firmly, rubbing his erection against her ass, was killing her.

Three days. She had been without him for three days. How was she supposed to stand this? She thought she could survive. That she would be okay. But she wasn't. She was miserable. She ached. She woke at night needing his arms around her, tormented, hot, crying out for him. And he wasn't there.

She hadn't had enough of him, she assured herself. Just a few more days, and maybe she could have sated the need that tore at her.

"It doesn't go away, baby." She jerked at the sound of his voice, as though he could read her mind. "I've jacked off until my balls are blue and it doesn't help. Nothing's going to help until I have you again."

He turned her around, his hand curved beneath her hair along the back of her neck, holding her in place while his lips covered hers.

She was supposed to fight this? Fight the pleasure that built until it felt like a fire was searing her? Tearing through her mind and melding her to him?

She was supposed to be angry at him, wasn't she? That was what she had told herself for three days. That he hadn't trusted her. Hadn't asked her about her private business but had instead had her investigated.

She should be furious, not holding on to him, her hands digging into his hair, desperate for more of him. She needed his kiss, his touch. When his fingers tore at the buttons of her dress, pulling them from their moorings, opening the material as he tore his lips from hers to rove over the tops of the swollen mounds of her breasts, her breath caught.

Yes. She needed this.

"I missed you, Sair," he groaned, lifting her until he had her on the small center island, pushing between her thighs as he pulled the shoulders of her dress over her arms, along with the straps of her bra.

His lips zeroed in on her nipples, covered them, pulled at the little rings piercing them until she felt shudders of need racing just beneath her flesh. The things he could do to her. The ways he touched her. It was unlike anything she had told herself it could be. It was potent, addictive. It was the height of pleasure.

"Damn. You make me crazy." He pulled back, jerked the edges of her dress together, and stared down at her, his gaze sensual, drowsy. "Get dressed."

"I *am* dressed." She stared back at him in confusion.

"Jeans." His hand moved over her ass. "You wear a dress to that bar and I'll end up fucking you before I get you off the dance floor. Go. I'll wait."

Sarah's lips twitched at that command in his tone. "You're bossy, Ethan."

"I'm horny, too, so watch out. Add the two and you could get more of an education in fucking me than you're ready for right now."

Her lips parted and she smiled. He obviously liked her smile because his eyes narrowed, the amber highlights darkened. "I don't know, Ethan," she drawled. "I've always been a very fast learner. Maybe you'll be the one falling behind in the lessons, rather than me."

Oh, he was falling all right, and Cooper knew it. Falling, nothing—he had already fallen, hard and fast, for that cute little dimple, those pale blue eyes, and long loose curls. Her intriguing smile and her ability to keep him intrigued. Damned if any other woman had ever done that.

"Bet me." He grinned back at her. Because this was sex talk, not love talk. Love talk would come later. As soon as he figured out exactly what it was he was supposed to say in love talk. But he was damned good at improvising.

She finally shook her head. "We need to talk before we do anything else." She sighed. "You didn't trust me, Ethan."

She stared up at him, that vulnerability, the hurt in her eyes tightening his chest.

"It wasn't a lack of trust, Sair," he promised her, letting his fingers run through the soft silk of her curls. "It was the pain in your eyes when I saw those scars. It was the knowledge that someone had hurt you and I wanted to kill them for it. But I didn't want you to see that reaction. I didn't want you to see me if the sons of bitches who did that to you were still alive."

They weren't. Even the young boy who had tricked Sair out of her father's home had died a less than easy death only a few years later. Her father's enemies had died in prison, along with her father. Anyone who would hurt Sarah was gone from this earth. And that left no one for Cooper to exact vengeance upon.

She dipped her head, moving away from him as she fixed her dress.

"It doesn't change the fact that I may want more from you than you want to give," she told him, turning back to him. "I deceived both of us, I think, to get into your bed."

"So deceive me again, Sair. Just get your ass in a pair of jeans and get back down here." He had to clench his hands and his teeth to keep from grabbing her. "For God's sake, baby, have pity on me here. I'm hard as a rock and starved for that pretty little body of yours. Let's get out of here and do what we have to do."

"Why?" Her hands went on her hips and a frown brewed at her brow. "Why does it matter if we go to the store? Or to the bar? How does it change anything other than your stamp of ownership over my head?"

He nodded decisively. "You're getting the picture there, cupcake. My stamp of ownership. Branding you in a way." He liked the sound of that enough to smile in anticipation. "And that's doing it the easy way. We could do it the hard way. I could just follow you the next time you go to the store and start knocking damned heads together when I catch those bozos sniffing after you. I'd have fun with that, but I bet you wouldn't."

Her eyes narrowed. "You're being very autocratic."

"It's one of my more advanced degrees," he snorted. "Now get dressed. You have five seconds to get your tail upstairs before I start undressing." He lowered his lashes, flicking his gaze over her. "And tomorrow I start batting heads together."

He was serious.

Sarah stared back at him, amazed, perhaps a little outraged, and a whole lot aroused.

"We're going to have to discuss your habit of ordering me around," she told him, backing out of the kitchen.

"Five. Four." He crossed his arms over his chest.

"You're being hideously arrogant."

"Three." He waited a heartbeat. "Two." He lowered his arms, his hands about his belt, as sweet little Sarah turned tail and ran.

And damn him if that wasn't the prettiest little tail.

He grinned at the sound of her running up the stairs. Grinned at the thought of the evening ahead. Then he whistled soundlessly at the thought of the night ahead.

By morning, Sarah and everyone else in this damned town would know exactly whom she belonged to.

They were being followed.

Cooper sat relaxed in his pickup, Sair pulled close to his side as he drove through town. And the little minx laughed at him because he made sure he drove through town, around the town circle, and then to the grocery store on the other side of the small town before he stopped.

"Hey, everyone needs a clear view," he told her with a laugh as he helped her out of the truck, keeping her carefully in front of him as the black sedan drove past, too damned slow.

He hustled her into the store and gave her the list for the bar. It was a list he and Jake had pulled out of their asses to make up an excuse to take her shopping. Items like celery, pepper, salt—bullshit items they had plenty of.

"Let me make sure Jake didn't forget anything." He pulled his cell phone out, hit Jake's number. Counted rings. When Jake answered, he closed the phone in a signal to Jake that there was trouble and smiled to Sair. "He must be busy."

Jake would be getting real busy right about now. He'd be calling every damned bouncer the bar hired, twelve total, and tonight every damned one of them would be on shift. Three would be at that store before Cooper and Sair left.

He was a damned paranoid man. The men who worked for him were just as paranoid. Loners. Soldiers without a war to fight because their bodies refused to do what they had to do now. They were his family. And now, they were Sarah's family.

He wandered through the store with her, his arm over her shoulders, or at her waist. He glared at the men who looked at her,

and the few who stopped and talked were treated to a possessive Cooper. Something they had evidently never seen, because
he caught the smirks.

Assholes.

He whispered dirty jokes in her ear to watch her blush, and
stopped and talked to a few of the women that he knew would
make good friends for his Sair. Women who were all safely married, happily married, and would of course tell her how great and
wonderful monogamy could be.

He had a plan. Cooper always had a plan. But first, he was going
to take care of the damned yahoos out in that dark sedan.

He was taking Sair through checkout when Casey, Iron, and
Turk entered the store. Three ex-Rangers, soldiers who looked just
as damned mean as they actually were.

"Hey, boss, Jake said don't forget to get change." Turk's voice
was a deadly growl as he moved to the register. Dressed in black
jeans and a black shirt, unruly black hair falling to his collar,
Turk's steely, cold blue eyes glanced at the store owner, Mark, before turning back to Cooper.

"Jake didn't call you," Sarah murmured.

"Jake has a weird sense of humor, sugar," Cooper drawled as he
pulled a hundred from his billfold. "Can you give me change, Mark?"

"I can, Cooper." Mark was no man's fool. The few times these
three men had run with Cooper, there had always been trouble.

Like the time that damned motorcycle gang had tried to hold up
his bar two years ago. Cooper, Turk, Iron, and Casey had walked in
and cleared the place without a single broken window. There had
been some broken bones and a few concussions, but these four
men hadn't been the ones suffering them.

Mark packed the rolls of quarters in a plastic bag and handed
them to Cooper. "You take care, Coop." He nodded before smiling at
Sarah. "And you too, Sarah. Keep this boy on the straight and narrow."

She wasn't Miss Sarah anymore. She was Sarah, Cooper's

woman. Damn, Cooper could almost feel his chest swelling with pride.

"Hey, boss, did you see that new Harley that drove through town earlier?" Casey eased in beside Sarah, Iron was in front of them, and Turk pulled up the rear. "She was a beauty with all that chrome."

Cooper kept up with the conversation, and the sedan. It eased out of the parking lot, windows tinted, but he could still glimpse three males inside. The two in the front seat wore dark glasses.

As they reached the truck, Cooper shot Iron a hard look. The other man nodded his head. He'd checked the truck and it was clean.

"Come on, darlin'." He helped Sarah into the seat via the driver's side before moving in beside her.

"You headin' to the bar?" Turk grumbled. His brown eyes were flat and hard, his scarred face resembling a junkyard dog that had won too many fights at too high a price.

"Heading that way, Turk."

Turk nodded. "See you there."

The other three men lifted their hands before loping to their motorcycles. Harleys. Bad-boy motorcycles. Cooper liked his truck.

He started the truck and eased out of the parking lot. Turk and Casey were at the lead, Iron riding behind.

Sarah was too damned quiet. The ride from the store to the bar was hell. Because as he pulled into the parking lot, he knew what the hell had to be done.

She wanted trust. Shit. He didn't like this part.

"Black sedan followed us to the store," he finally said softly.

"I know." She threaded her fingers together and took a hard, deep breath. "I'll have to leave tonight, Ethan." There were tears in her voice. "When I'm gone, they'll be gone as well."

"Like hell." He gripped her neck, pulled her face around until he could stare into her startled eyes. "You're not running, Sair. Not anymore. My town, my bar, my fucking woman. And by God, it stays that way."

Before she could protest, before the first tear could fall, his lips covered hers. The kiss shot fire through his veins, tightened every cell of his body, and left him burning for more.

His woman. For the first time in his life, Cooper loved a woman. He'd be damned if anyone was going to take her from him.

chapter 7

she'd thought she would be safe. Uncle Martin had kept track of her father's enemies. They had all died. The lieutenants who would have come after her had been arrested. Or they were gone, buried. Yet, someone had found her and was following her.

And they knew about Ethan.

Her hands were shaking as Ethan—everyone called him Cooper, but to her, he was Ethan—escorted her into the loud, crowded bar.

The Broken Bar was the hangout for every type of carouser, partier, or just plain wannabe-badass. And there were a few real badasses mixed in there, she was certain. The bouncers definitely. There had to be a dozen on duty tonight.

She picked them out instantly, most likely because there were no less than three around her and Ethan at any given time.

She pushed her fingers through her hair as she sat at the bar, tapping her fingers against the slick surface as she watched the large, cavernous room that seemed packed with twisting, drinking, gyrating, half-drunk bodies. A night of fun had never seemed so sinister.

Yes, it had. The last time she had let her fascination for a male draw her from hiding. And now, it was threatening the only man she had ever loved outside of her family.

"One of our finest." Jake pushed a glass of whisky in front of her. The little shot glass was a joke. She picked it up and tossed it back, grimacing at the pure pleasure of the burn that cascaded through her body.

"Hit me again, Jake." She set the little glass on the table as she gave the order absently, looking around, trying to make certain she couldn't recognize any of the men she knew were her father's enemies. Or could be.

He set the shot glass in front of her. She frowned and looked up at him. "How 'bout a double?"

Jake's brows lifted but he poured the shot into a glass, added to it, and handed it to her. He was watching her as though he expected her to just dunk it like she had the one before.

The first shot was for courage. This one she would sip. Drinking too fast only made her sick. She tolerated her liquor really well. What she didn't tolerate well were nerves. And she had plenty of those going on tonight.

She twisted around the bar stool and came face-to-face with Ethan's chest. She looked up the wide expanse to meet his inquisitive look from the glass to her.

"Not to worry," she sighed. "I rarely ever get drunk."

"That wasn't what I was worried about." His hazel and amber eyes were lit with amusement. "I've noticed, though. The only time I've seen you drinking is here, in my bar."

"How would you know?" She looked up at him from the corners of her eyes. "You are very rarely in the house with me, Ethan."

"But I watch you by your pool. If you were going to drink, you'd be on the patio."

Her lips twitched, and she flushed. Because he had seen her masturbating by the pool. And because, damn him, he was right.

She sipped the whisky, loving the little bit of a burn that hit the back of her throat and flowed to her stomach. It eased her nerves just enough for her to see the fun that could be had in a crowd. And at home, sometimes, a drink in the evening helped her relax for the night. Though that was rare. She didn't like sleeping at night.

"I'm not used to crowds, that's why I rarely go out," she told him.

"I figured that out. Are you ready to dance with me now?"

Sheer excitement filled her veins. "Seriously?" She looked out at the dance floor. "You'll dance with me?" He'd said he wanted to, but she hadn't been certain he meant it.

"Sair, sweetheart, I'd probably dance *for* you." He sighed, shaking his head. "Come on, you little heart stealer. Dance with me."

He pulled her out on the dance floor and he taught her the country steps, which weren't hard to follow. She laughed as he twirled her around, pulled her against him, and ground his hips against hers with the rousing country beat. Then he let her go, let her wiggle and move, mimicking the other women on the floor before he would grip her, twirl her around, her hair fanning behind her before wrapping around his shoulder, some of the curls clinging to his T-shirt.

He seemed to like that.

Then the beat slowed, became dark and intimate, and he tucked her against his chest, his chin against the top of her head as she closed her eyes and felt him in every beat of her heart.

His hands stroked up her back, over the silky blouse she wore. The one he had unbuttoned to the tops of her breasts and gazed at her. With one hand buried beneath her hair, his lips stroked over her brow, her cheek, her lips.

She whispered a sigh, her lips parting for him, feeling his kiss as she would have felt a caress clear to the depths of her spirit. He touched her that way. Just the thought of him touched her that way.

"You're mine," he whispered into the kiss as her lashes fluttered open. "Remember that, Sair. All mine."

"Always yours, Ethan." She would always belong to him, even

if she had to run to protect him. And she would have to run soon. After he fell asleep tonight, perhaps. Very soon. Because she couldn't risk allowing him to be hurt.

But for now, she could hold on to him, feel him holding her. Because this was her dream. And this man was her heart.

Cooper pulled her against him, feeling her slight form moving with him as his eyes narrowed on the entrance of the bar. The guy that stepped in was no biker, drinker, or weekend partier.

He wore black jeans, a jacket in the middle of summer, and he was packing heat. Cooper watched as three of his bouncers moved between them and the new visitor. Finally, with a grimace, the stranger left. But Cooper knew his face now. Hell, he had his face. He glanced to Jake, who caught his eye and nodded. They had him on the security camera; all they had to do was run it now. He watched as the assistant bartender took over and Jake headed to the office.

"What are you doing, Ethan?" She lifted her head now, her gaze suddenly too somber, too filled with shadows.

"Dancing with you." He touched her cheek, cupped it. "Protecting you."

She shook her head before pressing her forehead into his chest and he knew she was fighting her tears. He'd seen them glittering in her eyes, felt the shudder that raced down her spine.

"Come on." He caught her hand as the song ended. "I want to show you something."

Sarah let Ethan pull her through the dance floor, back to the bar where they moved into the narrow space Jake called his domain, and to the door at the far wall. There was no way to get back there except through Jake, and the bouncers closest to the bar.

The music became muted as he closed the door and led her through a short hall to a flight of rough wooden stairs.

"Where are we going?" she asked, loving the feel of her hand gripped in his, the warmth of it, the implied connection.

She shouldn't love him so, she thought. She should have held a part of herself back. A part of her heart.

"This is my home away from home." He unlocked the door at the top of the stairs and flipped on the switch. Soft, muted light filled the room.

There was a bed at the far end of the room. A large bed, strewn with pillows.

"And no, I've never had another woman up here." He closed the door and locked it behind him as she moved to the bank of monitors that sat over his office desk.

On one side of the room a tinted window looked out over the dance floor. She realized it was what she'd believed was a mirror on the wall above the dance floor.

There was a single shaded window by the bed, thick rugs, a table with two chairs, and a lamp hanging over it. Simple. Basic. Yes, Ethan would have come here to work, for the quiet, to brood perhaps. She could easily see him brooding here.

She turned back to him slowly.

He had stripped off his T-shirt and dropped it to the couch that sat against the wall, beside the bed. He toed his boots off, the amber in his gaze deepening as she slid her sandals from her feet and her fingers began to unbutton her shirt. Removing it, she quickly unhooked her bra and dropped it from her shoulders.

She needed him. Needed him until the ache was like talons of hunger tearing at her. She unbuttoned her jeans as he tore at the belt cinching his hips. They moved together, undressed together.

She pushed her panties and jeans down her legs as he did, stepped out of them, and stepped toward him.

"God, I missed you, Sair."

She was in his arms. He lifted her, holding her to him as he kissed her, devoured her lips, and carried her to the bed he had never shared with another woman. The bed that would only know the two of them.

The firm mattress cushioned them as he laid her back. It had been three days. She wasn't content to lie back and just be touched. She wanted to touch.

She rose up, curling her legs under her as he knelt in front of her. Her hands lifted, palms stroking along his chest, down the hard, rippling abs as her lips pressed to his hip.

She needed. Needed to love him. This one night. Enough to last forever.

She gripped the hard length of his cock, smoothed her hands over the shaft as she watched the little pearl of liquid that formed at the slit.

Her tongue touched it, tasted it. And she wanted more. She let her mouth cover the broad crest, her tongue finding the little bar piercing beneath the head, playing with it as she sucked at the crown.

"Hell, Sair." His hands burrowed in her hair, pulling, caressing the strands. "So pretty. So sweet."

She stared up at him, caught and held by his gaze. Oh God. Oh God. He was staring at her in a way she never thought he would. As though, almost as if, maybe, he cared for her?

She whimpered, her mouth filled with him, her hunger for him suddenly ravenous. She had to have him. All of him. Touch him. Learn him. Her fingers stroked the shaft; her palm moved to the tight weight of his balls and she caressed him there as well.

His shoulders looked massive from where she sat. His arms were bunched. The snake tattoo rippled across his bicep, moved, flexed, its red eyes piercing the dim light of the room.

The sight of it brought her a sense of security, not a sense of fear.

"Christ. Yeah. Suck me, Sair. Hell. Your mouth is so fucking sweet. Damn you. Tight and hot and so damned sweet."

He was blunt, explicit, and she loved it. She needed it. Her suckling strokes became deeper as she took him to her throat, moaned, and let her hands pump his shaft.

Evidently she was doing well.

"Hell. I love fucking your mouth," he bit out as the crown of his cock throbbed, seeming to swell thicker against her tongue.

His hands pulled at her hair, just enough. It sent flashes of pleasure racing through her scalp, down her spine.

"Oh yeah, suck it like that," he groaned as she took him deep, her tongue tucking against the piercing and rolling over it. "Damn, Sair. You make me hard enough to fucking cut glass with my dick." He growled the words. They rumbled from his chest, filled her senses.

She wanted to taste him, all of him.

"The hell you're gonna make me blow this fast."

She gripped his hips as he pulled back.

"Ethan, wait."

"Like hell." He pushed her back.

Before she could recover he was over her, kissing her, taking her mouth with deep plunges of his tongue. Licking and tasting her before his lips moved to her breasts.

He sucked her nipples, flicked the little rings, then tucked them back around the hard peaks. The pressure around them was heated, agonizing with pleasure.

"I love your body. So sweet and curved. Sexy as hell."

His lips moved down her stomach, kissing, licking. Sarah felt herself dissolving, losing all thoughts of everything but Ethan's touch. His lips, his tongue.

"Ethan! Oh yes. Yes, lick me there. Right there." Her hips arched, her fingers tangled in his hair, holding his head to her as his tongue stroked around her clit. He kissed it, licked around it again. Never truly touching it. Only coming close. So close.

Her legs fell farther apart, need burning inside her. She could feel her juices falling from her, heating her further, preparing her for him. Just for him. She needed him.

"Please. Please. Oh, Ethan. It's so good."

"I love your pussy," he growled. "Sweet, sweet Sair. Sweet all the hell over."

He sucked her clit into his mouth then and gave her what she needed. Rapture blazed through her. Ecstasy blazed before her eyes in rainbow hues of exploding melting color.

And he didn't wait. He didn't give her time to come down from the high. He rose over her, clasping her face in his hands as his cock pressed into her pussy.

"Look at me, Sair."

She struggled to open her eyes as her legs lifted to clasp his hips.

"Baby," he groaned, touching his forehead to hers, staring down at her as he eased inside her. Slow and easy. "I love you, Sair."

She stilled, blinked. She couldn't have heard him correctly.

"What?" Her voice trembled, hope surged through her.

"I love you, Sair. My sweet little Sair. My heart. I love you."

He pushed in deeper, stealing her breath. Her arms wrapped around his neck as pleasure turned to something brighter, hotter.

"I love you, Ethan Cooper," she cried out, arching as he took more of her. "Oh God, I love you."

He plunged deep. The hard, forceful stroke took her breath, gave her what she needed, a pleasure so rich, so destructive, nothing existed but them. No Sarah. No Ethan. Just *together*.

He pumped inside her, holding her to him, his lips covered hers, his kiss filled her. His groans met her cries, and when ecstasy exploded between them, she felt the sweet, blistering intensity. He filled her as she surrounded him. His release spurted inside her, mixing with hers as it flowed around them.

Sweat-dampened and sated, they collapsed in each other's arms.

"My woman." He pulled her against him, tipped her head up, and almost glared down at her. "You won't leave me, Sair. Do you hear me?"

She had run for so long, did she know anything else?

"Trust me, Sair." His thumb brushed her lips, his voice crooned, seductive, commanding. "Trust me to protect what belongs to me."

Did she have any other choice?

"I love you," she whispered.

"Trust me, Sair."

"I trust you." With her life, but more important, with her heart.

He dragged the comforter over them.

"Damn. Maybe I can fucking sleep now." He sighed. "You've kept me awake, Sair, missing you."

"I missed you, Ethan," she whispered, relaxing against him. "I missed you."

And she hadn't slept.

She slept now. Deep, dreamless. Held in his arms, where he protected her, even from the nightmares.

chapter 8

cooper stared at the bank of monitors over the desk, his arms crossed over his chest, the fingers of one hand stroking at the stubble over his jaw.

He'd forgotten to shave that morning and hadn't realized it until he saw the red abrasions on Sarah's sensitive skin. Now there wasn't going to be time to shave.

He watched the two men who eased up to the bar, their faces deliberately turned away so as not to allow the camera to get a clear shot. There was a third man behind them: a larger man, a ball cap pulled down over his brow.

Interesting.

They were talking to Jake as he poured drinks. Cooper watched as Jake shook his head at the two in front, then moved down the bar to serve several other customers.

One of the men looked up at the camera from beneath his lashes and Cooper's eyes narrowed. There was something about that look that he recognized. It wasn't the man, he didn't know the man, but the look itself. A sense of familiarity he couldn't place.

Grimacing, he turned and moved quickly to the bed.

"Sair." He leaned over his sleeping lover, kissed her cheek, felt her arms lift lazily and twine around his neck.

"Hm. Come back to bed," she mumbled, trying to burrow back under the covers.

"Sair, we have trouble, baby."

Her eyes opened immediately. Her arms slid from around his neck and she rolled out of the bed. Her response was too quick, too ingrained. Cooper felt his chest tighten at the knowledge that she had been forced to run too many times in her young life.

Wild, loose ringlets fell around her as she moved through the room, searching for her clothes now.

"What's wrong?" she asked as she hurriedly put on her bra and panties.

She was picking up her jeans as he pulled his T-shirt back on and glanced back to the monitors. At that moment, a red light lit up and a low buzz filled the room.

"What's that?" Sair jerked on her blouse despite the alarm that filled her face.

"That's trouble." Cooper felt his body go on alert. He shoved his socked feet into his boots and strode to the closet at the side of the room.

There, he jerked out the automatic military-issue rifle, snapped the clip in efficiently, and shoved two extra ammo clips into the band of his jeans.

The door behind the bar had just been breached, and Jake or one of his bouncers hadn't opened it willingly. He moved back to the monitors.

"Do you recognize them?" He pointed to the men moving through the short hall that led to the stairs.

Sair moved to the monitors, pulling on her sandals as she stared at the three men who kept their faces deliberately turned away from the cameras.

She shook her head. "The big guy in the back looks familiar, but I can't see his face for his ball cap."

Cooper heard the fear in her voice, felt it.

"How do we get out of here?" she whispered.

Cooper stared at the three men. Jake was in the lead, his expression furious as he glanced at the hidden cameras as they passed.

But he wasn't giving any signals. Nothing to indicate an attack. Cooper watched his face carefully as he led the men to the stairs. Nothing. Not a flicker of an eyelash, not a tightening of his lips.

"Come here." He gripped her arm and led her across the room. Slapping the side of his hand against the paneling, he stood back as the door eased open to reveal a narrow set of stairs leading down.

Coming up those stairs were Casey, Iron, and Turk. They were heavily armed, expressions set.

He pulled Sarah back as they filed into the room, the same moment a heavy knock sounded at the door.

"Jake didn't say a word, didn't even indicate trouble," Turk growled almost soundlessly. "We didn't know shit till we looked up and he was gone from the bar."

"Hey Coop, I need to talk to you." Jake knocked again as Cooper's eyes narrowed.

"Ethan?" Distressed, frightened, Sarah stared back at him. "We can't leave Jake out there with them." Her hand touched her chest, rubbing against it as though it ached. Cooper felt almost a killing rage.

"Get in here." He pushed her to the small landing behind the paneling.

"No." Gripping his arm, fear brightening her eyes, she tried to tug him in after her. "Not without you. I won't leave you here."

"Dammit, Sair."

"No. I won't protect myself while you stand in front of a bullet for me. I won't do it."

"Sarita."

Sarah froze at the sound of the voice, the name called through the door.

"Have your friend open the door for us, Sarita. I promise, there is no danger. Come, sweetheart. Let Pa-pa see your pretty face."

Her gaze swung to the door as she felt emotions—fear, hope, longing—pouring through her. She shook her head, feeling the tears that built behind her eyes at that voice.

It wasn't Pa-pa. It couldn't be. He was dead. Uncle Martin had cried when he learned the news that Pa-pa was dead.

"No." She shook her head and stared back up at Ethan in terror now. "It's a trick. He's dead. Uncle Martin knew he was dead. It's not him."

"Coop, it's cool, man. They're not armed," Jake called out. "Let's get this shit over with so I can go back to work, okay?"

"You get ready to run!" Ethan shoved his finger at her as he pushed her to the one called Casey. "Casey, if anything happens to her . . ."

"I'm dead meat and turned to sausage." Casey nodded his shaggy head as he gripped her arm and pulled her back to the landing.

Sarah felt her chest erupting with pain, with fear. Her hands gripped Ethan's arm, fear cascading through her as she felt herself shuddering, torn apart from the inside out.

"Sarita, little one. Pa-pa wants only to see his little angel. Would you deny me this?" the voice called from the other side of the door.

Sarah felt the tears that fell from her eyes. It sounded so much like Pa-pa. Her breathing hitched, the pain spearing through her heart like a double-edged sword.

"No. He's dead," she whispered, staring up at her lover, be-seeching. "We have to leave, Ethan. Please."

He touched her cheek with his fingertips. "I love you. Stay with Casey and let's see what we have here."

"No." She reached out as he pulled back from her, fighting to follow him as Casey's arm snagged around her waist and pulled her back.

"Don't get him killed, girl," Casey snapped quietly. "Let him do what he has to. Cooper doesn't run. None of us do. We stand and fight, or we're better off dead."

No. No. She couldn't do this. She knew what her father's enemies were like, the cruelties, the absolute lack of mercy. She could feel the scars on her flesh like a fresh brand now, searing her with the memory of how they used a child to force her pa-pa to do as they wanted. Until he had secretly gone to the authorities, turned himself in, and made a deal that destroyed him as well as the other crime families that had struck against him.

Her pa-pa had saved her. But she had suffered for his crimes. A part of her hated what he had been before he died, but another part of her ached for the father she had known. Loving. Strong. So kind.

At least, to those he loved. To those he didn't love, he had been a monster, not unlike those who had kidnapped her.

"Don't distract him, girl," Casey snarled at her ear as he pushed her behind him and Ethan, while Turk and Iron placed themselves at the door.

Ethan moved to the side while Turk and Iron flattened themselves against the wall on each side of the door.

"Ethan. Man. The bar is going to hell without me," Jake called out.

Ethan frowned. Every damned thing Jake was saying was a clear sign that their visitors were unarmed and unthreatening.

He moved to the table, and hit the electronic code to unlock and unbar the door. He stood back, lifting his weapon to his shoulder, bracing it, his finger caressing the trigger.

"Jake?"

"Yeah, Coop?"

"You go back to the bar. If these boys are so nice and friendly, they don't need you anymore, do they?"

Cooper glanced at the monitors and watched as Jake rolled his shoulders.

Jake stood in front of the other three at the landing of the stairs.

"Come on, Cooper," Jake's voice was irritated now. A sure sign he believed whatever crap these yahoos were giving him.

"Bring 'em on in, Jake," Cooper drawled, watching as Turk and Iron got ready.

The door swung open slowly and Jake moved in, ahead of the others. Hands held carefully to their sides, the other three men moved in behind him.

Government. The two in the front were feds, and when Cooper glimpsed the one in the back, he knew who he was dealing with. Giovanni Fredrico.

"Sarita." Fredrico pulled off the ball cap, his eyes on Sair as she stood still and silent in the entrance to the escape stairs.

He didn't look as old as Cooper knew he was. Giovanni Fredrico was fifty years old, but looked ten years younger. His black hair had only a sprinkling of white at the temples. His eyes were like Sair's, a pale blue, his skin swarthy, and he was staring at his daughter the way another man might stare at an angel.

Sarah had to fight the need to run to him. Gio the Giant, he was called. He was her pa-pa. At least, he had been, until she had learned what he was, who he was. Until she had learned he had been just as brutal, as cruel as the men who had kidnapped her.

As Ethan lowered his gun, she moved hesitantly from Casey. Skirting around the crowd now in the front part of the room, she moved slowly to Ethan. She couldn't explain the reasons why, couldn't explain why she needed to hold on to him, but the need was overwhelming. She felt as though the floor were rocking beneath her, as though the world was spinning.

When his arm slid around her and he pulled her close to his side, it felt right. And as she stared back at Gio the Giant, she fought to find in him the man who had rocked her to sleep as a child, who had sung funny songs to her, who taught her to dance and how to play hopscotch.

"Sarita." His face contorted painfully as the arms he had lifted out to her fell to his sides. "I have searched for you since you left

Dallas. Two years I looked, after your cousin and aunt learned of Martin's death. To bring you home."

"I am home." She held on to Ethan as though he were a lifeline.

She felt as though her heart were breaking in two. How she had loved her tall, strong pa-pa. Loved him so much that the news of his death, despite her anger at him, had nearly broken her. And now, to learn that that, too, was a lie . . .

He breathed in roughly, shoved his hands into the pockets of his slacks in a move that was so very characteristic of him. He stared back at her, his face more lined than it had been, his eyes shadowed.

"Your brother, he is in California searching for you. He thought perhaps you had returned there."

She shook her head. She didn't want to hear about her brother, either. Beauregard, named for an American friend, was his father's son. Not the brother she had imagined him to be.

"Go away," she whispered, feeling Ethan's arms tighten around her.

"Sair," Ethan whispered against her hair. "Let's see what he wants."

She shook her head and cried. "He wants forgiveness. Atonement. Isn't that right, Gio?" She blinked back her tears at the pain that filled his face. "It's the same thing Beau wants as well."

"I want to know my little Sarita, my angel, is safe and happy," Gio said heavily. "Forgiveness or atonement is not what I seek."

"You knew before you came here." She could feel the pain ripping at her, digging merciless claws into her chest. "You checked me out and you followed me, and you sent Beau to California. Why? Shall I tell you why?"

"Sarita," he whispered as a man stricken with grief would have whispered.

"Why, Gio?" She clenched her fists and faced him, years of anger and pain exploding inside her, cascading through her like an avalanche of sorrow and fury. "You sent Beau to California so he wouldn't kill? So he wouldn't do as he swore when I was six-teen and kill any man who dared touch me? Well, I'm no longer sixteen. And I'm no longer Sarita."

"You're still my daughter," he said softly. "The child my heart beats for."

She wanted to sneer, but it hurt. It hurt so bad.

"You killed," she whispered. "Drugs, rape, murder. Ah God." She wiped her face with her hands, shaking, shuddering with the horror of the information she had learned once her father had been arrested. "You, Uncle Martin, Beau, all of you. You were criminals. What Marco did to me when he kidnapped me was gentle com-pared to your crimes."

"I never harmed a child," Gio bellowed then, his hands pulling from his slacks, raking through his hair. "I never harmed an in-nocent, nor did I or Beau rape anyone. There were rules. Marco broke those rules when he took you."

"You should have never lied to me," she yelled back furiously. "Why didn't you just tell me you were a murdering mafia lord and that was the reason I wasn't allowed beyond the walls of our es-tate? My God in heaven, perhaps then I would have understood why they hurt me."

Gio seemed to shudder. Her pa-pa. She saw her pa-pa in this man, no matter how hard she tried not to.

"Beau was not part of that business," he finally said heavily. "It was the reason he was gone so often—he could not stomach the path I could not veer from." He shook his head slowly. "When they took you, I died inside."

"They had me six weeks," she sneered. "Six cuts, Gio. Do you remember them?"

"God, Sarita! I see them every night in my nightmares."

She was only barely aware of Ethan motioning the others out of the room. Even her father's bodyguards left silently, closing the door behind them, leaving her alone with Gio and Ethan.

"Beau was working to legitimize our holdings," he breathed

out roughly. "For him, I had agreed to turn the business over to your uncle Lucian. We were negotiating this with Lucian the night you were taken." He shook his head wearily. "I do not excuse myself, Sarita. Not what I have done, or for what I have been. But you were always my light. My precious child. More to me even than my son. And you know this."

She had been the spoiled princess. The baby. She had been loved by her father, by her brother. Cherished after the death of her mother.

"My name is Sarah," she whispered.

She didn't know what to say, how to feel. She only knew that if Ethan let go of her, she would sink to the floor in pain.

"This one, he calls you 'Sair'?" Her pa-pa nodded to Ethan behind her.

She narrowed her eyes. "Only Ethan calls me 'Sair.'"

"Ah. And only you call him 'Ethan,' when all others call him 'Cooper.'" He nodded. "Yes. It is the way of love, eh?"

She stared back at him silently as he moved and sat down in one of the large chairs that sat close to the wall.

He leaned forward, his tall, broad body almost too large, even for Ethan's furniture. His elbows rested on his knees, his hands were clasped between them as he regarded her.

"Sarah," he sighed her name. "I make no excuses for what I was. And I take full blame for how Marco terrorized you." He shook his head, and when his eyes lifted, she saw the tears in them. "For you, I would have died. Beau searched for you, and I feared he would die in the attempt to rescue you. He was enraged. So I went to the authorities. And"—he spread his hands—"I let you go. You were the only bit of innocence in my life. My sweetest daughter. And I thought I could let you fly as I knew you should, away from the ugliness of who and what I was." His expression turned fierce. "But I cannot." He rose to his feet, paced, and turned back to her. "You are my child. My daughter. You will give this man children. Blood of my blood." He thumped his chest, crossed his arms over it. "Fight me all you wish. I will move to this town if I must. I will be where you are. I will tell all, you are my daughter, who I love, who I treasure. I will not let you go as you wish." He glared at Ethan, then at her. "And my name is not Gio. My name is Ronald." He lifted his head proudly. "For my great-grandfather. Who was pure. Who was not part of that life you so abhor. I am Ronald Caspari. An immigrant." His voice lowered. "A father."

She stared back at him in shock.

"And you think it's so easy? That I can just forgive?"

He shook his head, his glance moving once again to where Ethan's arms were wrapped around her.

"Not easy," he said softly. "But I hope, perhaps in time, you can find it in yourself to remember the man who loved his Sarita. His precious angel."

That first tear slipped free. Her pa-pa never cried. He was fierce, and he was strong.

"Don't." She shook her head, feeling her eyes well with tears as well. Because she remembered her pa-pa. She remembered, and oh God, how she had missed him.

"Ronald Caspari hasn't committed any crimes, Sair," Ethan whispered.

"Don't excuse him," she cried out.

"I'm not excusing him, baby." He rubbed his chin against her head. "You're allowed the choice, Sair. It's not either-or. And hell, I'm not exactly a saint. We both know that."

"He killed."

"I protected what was perhaps not rightfully, but all the same, mine," her father breathed out roughly. "But unlike Carlos and others, Sarita, I never warred on innocents. I never kidnapped a woman or a child and brought them pain. Neither did I approve such an action. Never could I have. You were my guide, child." He shook his head. "From the day of your birth, you were my guide. Your sweetness and light ensured no child was harmed by my hand."

"Giovanni Fredrico was known as Gio the Giant. The Gentle Giant," Ethan reminded her.

"Why are you defending him?"

"Because a daughter's need for her father never goes away, Sair," he said. "You'll never stop grieving for him. And you'll tear yourself up inside. Better to pick your battles with him, and make sure he walks the path you choose for him from here on out. He's less of a threat to our peace of mind that way. Besides, someone has to give you away when we get married. I don't think Casey or Turk would look good in a tux."

She swung around. Blinked.

"Did you think I'd let you get away from me?" His smile was pure male confidence and a hint of wickedness. After all, her father was standing there.

"You didn't ask me to marry you," she pouted. "Maybe I wanted all the trimmings?"

He snorted. "Naw. You didn't. Or you wouldn't have picked the shadiest character in town to trip with that sneaky heart of yours. I've fallen, Sair. Right at your feet. I'm not asking for marriage, I'm damn well demanding it." He touched her cheek, cupped it with his palm. "And your father isn't asking for forgiveness, just a chance."

She turned back to her pa-pa, watched as he ran his hands over his face and stared back at her bleakly.

Gio the Giant was dead. Ronald Caspari might not be perfect, but she still remembered the love. Her pa-pa holding her, protecting her, laughing with her.

"Pa-pa," she whispered, shaking, realizing Ethan had slowly let her go.

Her father's lips trembled. She took a step, and then he was there. Crossing the distance to her, his hard arms wrapped around her. He lifted her against him, and the scent and sounds of her childhood washed over her.

The father she had so adored. Could she forget his crimes? She couldn't forget. But neither could she forget that he had saved her.

Given himself and all he possessed to protect her. He wasn't perfect, but he was still her pa-pa.

Ethan watched, crossed his arms over his chest, and glared at Gio. It was the look of a determined man, imposing his own will. If Sarah's father ever hurt her again, if she was ever harmed again because of him, then Gio the Giant would be dead in fact as well as in fiction. It was a look the other man well understood, and over his daughter's head, he nodded.

"I give to you my daughter," Gio said huskily as Sarah finally moved from his arms. Taking her hand, he laid it in Ethan's. "She is the light to my soul," Gio continued. "My treasure."

Ethan smiled and pulled his woman close again.

"She was mine the minute she moved here and I set eyes on her, Mr. Caspari. I tripped over my own two feet and lost my heart."

"You didn't?" Sarah stared at him, shocked. "You didn't. I would have seen it."

"I covered it damned well." He grinned. "But have no doubt, sweetheart, you were the first girl to make me fall. Head over heels."

Gio Fredrico stared at the couple. Beau, he wouldn't be pleased, but ah, his son, he was often too arrogant, too certain of life. He had wanted to protect Sarita between them. Having this man, so rough, so obviously a real man, hold his precious sister would grate on his pride.

But, his Sarita was safe. She was loved. And Gio had a feeling any man who attempted to take what Cooper deemed his would find himself perhaps knocking on the gates of hell. No, Ethan Cooper wasn't a man to cross. But he was definitely the man for Sarita.

She was his child. But she was Cooper's woman. And she was safe.

And, he brightened. Perhaps soon, there would be babies. Ah yes, Gio thought. Grandbabies. Life was perhaps about to get very, very good.

sheila's passion

prologue

vengeance.

It had been so long coming.

So many years waiting, searching.

Hating.

Ah God, the hatred.

It was like a wound festering deep within the soul, growing more tender by the year, refusing to release the acrid bitterness that filled it.

And it all centered on one man. On a monster who had destroyed countless friends and family. Who had, with a single, thoughtless decision, caused centuries of traditions to be wiped out. Destroyed as though they had never been.

And there had been no price extracted for the betrayal.

There had been no punishment, no atonement; there hadn't been so much as an "I'm sorry" or a sprig of flowers on the gravesites of those who had died because of the choices he had made.

And many had died.

A son had begun the slaughter as his father, the one so many followed, stood by, helpless, his loyalty centered on the daughter he had adored.

The daughter's life had meant more to that father than the traditions that had sustained a people for so long. That daughter had held his loyalty, his entire focus, rather than the people who trusted him with their lives.

There was a reason why marriages were arranged within their world. A reason why children were fostered out to other families throughout the years. There was a reason why fathers were often separated from their daughters and sons from their mothers.

To maintain the sanctity of tradition. To ensure family love and loyalty never came ahead of the decisions that might not be in the child's best interests.

Giovanni Fredrico had broken the trust of his people in his attempts to save the daughter he had so cherished. The child conceived with the woman he had wed after the death of his first wife—Giovanni had broken tradition and married for love. In doing so he had begun the destruction of all that had been given into his safekeeping.

Had the families known it was a love match rather than a marriage of tradition, as they and her family had sworn, it would have been dissolved with her death. She would have been killed by order of the other families immediately.

Watching Giovanni now—Gio the Giant, they had always called him—regret welled, but it hadn't paid Gio to teach his son that it was love that mattered rather than tradition. Gio, with his ready smile, his pocket of candies and coins, and his genuine love for children. He had been as treasured as any favored uncle by those who knew him. Those who lived beneath his rule gave him more loyalty than to their fathers, mothers, or kings.

And there were many who knew him, many who depended on him.

No child went hungry as long as Gio ruled the families.

No child was abused as long as Gio's punishment awaited the abuser. But in the end he had destroyed them.

The world had changed since that fateful summer when Gio had betrayed them, though. Since the day Gio had followed his heart rather than the tradition of the families, and taught his son that the heart mattered more than the unwritten laws.

The sanctity of family was no longer adhered to as it had once been. The innocence of a child mattered to no one. Abuse was rearing its ugly head, hunger was striking families who once knew prosperity, and crime was becoming an act of greed rather than a business.

Because of Gio the Giant and the son who had followed his dreams rather than destiny.

Gio had betrayed the families, the children, the wives, the fathers and brothers, sisters and mothers who had trusted in him, who had relied upon him. He had betrayed them all for the love of the child who had meant more to him and to his son than the responsibilities he had accepted when he had taken the reins of the Fredrico family and their vast holdings.

But even with all his faults, the blame did not lie with Gio alone. He had only severed the final link in a chain that had been thoughtlessly weakened by another.

The blame did not even lie with the fragile, delicate child he had betrayed them all for. The one who had suffered with her blood and with her shame as she was so carelessly used against her father, who loved her more than he loved the people.

No, the blame lay with the son.

It was the son who had set this nightmare in motion.

It was the son, Beauregard Fredrico, named for the childhood friend Gio had so missed after his death and the brother of the woman he had given his heart to.

The friend who had betrayed *his* own family as well.

Had Gio cursed his son?

Perhaps he had, for Beauregard Fredrico had followed the

example of his father and his father's friend when he had turned his back on the people who had already begun to depend upon him. He had betrayed all their honor and walked away from Italy as though the land and its people had not been burned into his soul.

Eight years.

This search had gone on for eight long, horrendous years, and finally, the end was near.

Here, in this little town called Simsburg, Texas, the prey that had eluded fate for so long had finally been located.

The selection had been narrowed to four men.

There was no doubt, it had to be one of them.

Only these four, who were a part of Gio and Sarita Fredrico's lives now, had no past to call their own.

They had not existed before that fateful summer eight years ago. Before that summer when Beauregard Fredrico had supposedly died.

Just as his sister, Sarita, and his father as well, were reported to have been killed by the remaining members of the families who eventually turned on them.

Four men.

Hardened, cold-eyed, so unlike the man Beauregard had been the last time he had been seen. Weak, uncertain of himself, angry with the world. That had been Beau as a young man.

It was not the mature male he had become.

He would be a challenge to identify and kill now, but vengeance was demanded.

So many generations of families had been destroyed because of his selfishness. So many lives lost and destroyed because of his traitorous actions.

So many lives had been wasted because of his choices.

Entire families had been lost.

And now, it was time to destroy Beauregard. No matter the new name he had taken, the man he had become, or the reasons for which he had made his choices. No matter the arguments those left behind had made for his life. None of it mattered any longer.

It was time to satisfy vengeance.

And vengeance demanded blood.

But blood demanded proof.

And there was only one way to prove Fredrico blood.

By threatening the one thing they held dearest.

The only true weakness a Fredrico was ever known to have.

The women they loved.

Beauregard, unlike Gio, had not fulfilled his responsibilities first, though. Nor had he kept the woman he had loved as a mistress. No, Beau had left Italy. He had betrayed them all, and destroyed not just his own family, but those who followed the Fredrico family as well. And he had to pay.

chapter 1

sheila was stretched on a rack of such torturous pleasure she was certain she couldn't survive it. There was no way she
would come out on the other end intact.

She always thought that at some point during the hours she
spent in Nick Casey's bed, however, that something other than her
orgasm would be found.

Each time, she swore she wouldn't allow herself to be seduced,
and each time he touched her, each time that sensual dominance
swirled in his dark chocolate eyes, she found herself seduced. Seduced. Ready. Willing. He mesmerized her with his kiss and made
her more than willing to beg for more. To plead.

Breathless. Devoured. Fucked until she was screaming mind-
lessly in a pleasure so intense she was certain she would die from
it. That was how she felt. And the pleasure became the center of
her universe.

"Oh God, Casey." She arched to him, her tone so rough and
hoarse she didn't recognize it as her own.

But oh God, his touch was so good. Everything he did to her, every kiss, every stroke, every caress was ecstasy.

Sheila spread her thighs wider, her heels digging into the mattress as she lifted for him, feeling his tongue sink into the tender flesh between the folds of her pussy.

Broad, strong hands gripped her hips, holding her in place as he licked at the sensitive flesh, then pushed inside the saturated entrance with a slow, destructive thrust.

A long, low cry tore from her lips. Casey tasted her, his tongue moving inside her, possessing and enjoying her with exquisite pleasure. Rapture suffused her senses, washing over her and racing across her nerve endings with a wave of electric intensity.

There was nothing quite like Casey's touch or the addictive sensations that tore through her.

His hard, callused hands roved over her body and stroked every response she would have kept hidden. Awakening nerve endings and hungers better off ignored. From the depths of a sensuality she hadn't known she possessed, he revealed desires she hadn't known existed inside her.

He had only to make her think he was going to touch her and her clit swelled. Her breasts became swollen, her nipples tight and hard. The very thought of the pleasure to come had her ready to explode.

His tongue slid from her pussy, flickering over the entrance, licking gently and driving her crazy with its fiery touch. Inner muscles clenched as she fought to get closer while her clit ached in a desperate need to come.

He was wicked with his touch. Diabolical.

Teasing, deliberately seductive, the tip of his tongue eased up the narrow slit as his thick, heavy lashes lifted to stare back at her.

Deliberately, with teasing, provocative licks, suckling kisses, and flickering strokes of his tongue, he began to make her insane with the lust beginning to pound through her. Heat flushed, sweat dampening her flesh and making her whole body slick.

She couldn't help but stare back at him, locked by the dark

arousal in his eyes, suspended within the swirling, nearing ecstasy he was creating.

It was exquisite.

It was so incredibly ecstatic she could barely breathe.

Fingers of powerful sensual heat raced around the swollen bud of her clit as he bestowed one of the hot suckling kisses to the sensitive nerve center.

A moan whispered from her lips as sensation clenched her pussy with rapid-fire pulses of agonizing pleasure sizzling through her senses. Her hips jerked with involuntary movements, the need racing through her, demanding she get closer.

"Casey." She moaned his name as she felt the edge of orgasm nearing. "Oh God, Casey. It's so good. So good and so hot."

She felt as though she were burning inside and out. The flames whipped over her body, searing through her flesh straight to her womb.

Her thighs tightened at his shoulders as she slid her hands from the mattress where she clutched the sheets to the heavy silk of his hair. Threading her fingers through the strands, Sheila gripped at it in desperation.

She loved his hair.

It was like silk, heated and soft to the touch.

She loved his tongue.

It rolled over her clit, licked along the slit of her pussy, fucked inside the tight clenching muscles and had her begging for release.

She loved his touch.

She loved, loved the way he made her feel. The sensuality, the intense attention he paid to ensuring her pleasure.

"Casey!" she cried out as the pleasure built, sensation washing through her as it began to tingle over her entire body.

Her nipples swelled tighter, becoming so sensitive that she slid one hand from his hair to use her fingers to ease the need for touch against them. Gripping, tugging at the thick strands, Sheila fought to ease the need for sensation that throbbed in them.

It wasn't enough.

It was never enough.

She couldn't get enough of each caress. She couldn't get enough sensation or ease the needs tearing through her.

The need for him, for every touch, for a deeper pleasure, for that something that drove her insane every time Casey touched her. Every time she even thought of him taking her. Moaning, she moved her fingers to the opposite nipple, desperate for the sensation that would push her over the edge of release.

His hands followed hers, both breasts, both nipples tightening in agony for that "sensual" touch. That sensation only came for the briefest moment, for such a shatteringly short amount of time, yet for that moment, for that flash of eternity, she was complete.

She was pure energy, pure power, and Casey was there with her, not just inside her. Not just bringing her pleasure, but bringing her such a sense of completion that she felt lost within it.

She reached for it again, desperately seeking it, willing to run headlong into complete chaos for it. Nothing else mattered.

She was becoming an addict and she freely admitted it.

Casey's addict. And she feared she could end up living only for these few precious moments.

"Please!" A broken cry left her throat, flowing around her as she lifted her hips, writhed beneath his kiss, his licks, against every luscious stroke of burgeoning ecstasy bestowed upon her.

His fingers played with her nipples, gripping and tugging, sensitizing them further when she hadn't believed they could become more sensitive. Sending pleasure streaking through them, tearing along neural pathways she had never felt before.

Casey's touch.

Each wicked little white-hot sensation detonated in her womb, clenching it, almost, just almost sending her hurtling into rapture. Just almost shooting her into the brilliant center of whatever sensation it was that had her aching every moment for one more chance to experience it again. His hands palmed her breasts, thumbs and forefingers gripped her nipples, tugged, sent fiery arcs of electrifying sensation traveling through her body and building the addiction for more.

She was grinding her pussy tighter against his lips as they surrounded her clit and sucked it inside his mouth, began to lash at it with the heat of his tongue.

"Casey—oh God, it's good. So good." Long, drawn out, the fractured moan left her lips and filled the air around them as she felt herself tightening, felt the pleasure whipping through her, building, threatening, pushing her to the very edge of pure, complete satisfaction.

Her hands tightened in his hair as his fingers tugged at her nipples, sending her rushing toward release.

Then he drew back.

He pulled her back from that edge. From the impending ecstasy.

"No!" Her eyes flared open, desperation and bemusement filling her cry as he came to his knees.

"You'll come around my dick first," he growled, moving over her, his hand gripping the hard shaft of his cock as he slid it against the wet folds between her thighs.

Her clit throbbed.

Sheila could feel her sex clenching, tightening, the muscles flexing instinctively as the broad, flared crest of his erection pressed against the entrance.

Fiery, throbbing, the heavy width began to stretch her flesh, forcing its way inside the slick, nerve-laden tissue as it stimulated and excited every cell that clasped it.

Sheila's back arched as she lifted her knees to clasp his hips, moving beneath him, lifting to him as the short, surging strokes thrust him further inside her, penetrating her deeper and creating flames that seared her nerve endings and intoxicated her senses. It was like being immersed in a sensual storm. In a wave of such intense pleasure she was helpless against it.

She felt drunk on his touch. The inebriation was like being enfolded in a world so rich with color and sensation that she never wanted to leave it.

Each inward impalement burned and excited to the point that she was certain more pleasure would destroy her. Each time he pulled back she was certain she would die from the desertion. That she couldn't bear being separated from him for even a second longer.

"Ah, babe," he groaned as he sank deeper. The sound of the pleasure in his voice had her pussy clenching, creaming, nearly coming from the sheer excitement and explicit sexuality that filled that moment. His face tightened, a dark sensual appearance overtaking it as his cock surged inside her. A harsh moan passed his lips, pleasure filling the air as the thick, heavy flesh penetrated to the hilt.

Her nails dug into his shoulders. She couldn't restrain the need to hold on to him. As he filled her, all she could do was tighten around him and lock him to her as closely as possible.

Her head tilted to the side as his head lowered, his lips finding her neck, caressing and nipping at the tender flesh. Sheila swore she lost her breath. She lost control.

Her pussy milked at his dick, the feel of that burn, that sensation that bordered pain and mixed with pleasure tearing through her as she cried out his name. It threw her higher, tossing her into a maelstrom of nearing ecstasy and mindless pleasure.

His lips sucked and nipped at her neck.

His tongue licked.

She could feel sizzling arcs and fiery trails of rapture tearing at her senses.

She wanted.

She ached.

Then, he began moving faster, harder.

If the pleasure was too much to bear before, it became an agony of sensation then.

Drawing back, he paused, a grimace tightening his lips before he pushed forward, his hips leaning into her with a heavy thrust that buried him full length inside the too-sensitized flesh. Sheila gasped, crying his name as he began to ride her harder, each thrust stealing her breath.

Each time, every time, it was more intense than the last.

There was no way to hide her response or maintain her control.

She'd lost it the moment he'd touched her. She couldn't seem to find a way to regain her balance, or to regain that part of her she could feel herself losing.

And that was the terrifying part. Though not terrifying enough to make her draw back from him. Not terrifying enough to risk never having him again.

But right there, in the center of her soul, she could feel herself opening for him, crying out his name and fighting to hold him closer, deeper. She needed to hold him as close as possible or she feared there would be nothing left to hold him to her.

Her legs wrapped around his hips as he fucked her with a force that left her dizzy. Each powerful thrust was a rocking, full-length, driving motion that sent a storm of sensations whipping through her.

Her knees lifted higher, clasping his waist, opening the sensitive depths of her pussy to him, and she was crying out hoarsely as new nerve endings were raked with the heated rasp of his cock.

Like iron covered with wet, rough silk, his erection caressed, stroked. Lit a flame of such intense pleasure inside her that it was all she could do to survive the exquisite agony of pleasure.

Pleasure and pain.

The muscles of her pussy rippled around the invading flesh. The natural, instinctive response to the pleasure he was giving her created another layer of sensation impossible to resist.

She couldn't bear it. She didn't believe she would survive the onslaught of sensation this time.

She swore each time she couldn't bear more. That before she found release she would simply explode from the need and cease to be.

Then, just as it always did, the world exploded around her instead.

The blinding response to the rapid-fire strokes, the burning stretch and possession of his cock, never failed to take her by surprise. It never failed to open her soul to him a little bit more in the process.

Unseeing, dazed, her eyes flared wide before her lashes began drifting back over her eyes in rapture. Pulsing, incredible surges of pure white-hot energy imploded through her womb. Her pussy spasmed with the pure, rapturous pleasure. The sensations wrapped around her clit and the pleasure stole reason for long, precious seconds. It overtook her, it destroyed her, and yet it filled her with life.

It seemed never-ending.

As though the release only built as it exploded again and again, drowning her in more and more ecstasy.

Then, as the pulsing waves of pleasure threatened to steal her consciousness, they began to ease. Each ripple smaller than the last until they became tremors, shuddering shivers of sensation as his own release pumped inside her and extended the heightened rapture.

Once she could function again, once time and space resumed their normal revolutions around her, Sheila found herself sprawled beneath him as he collapsed beside her, one arm pulling her to his chest as they both fought for breath. For sanity.

It was always the same.

It never mattered the position they were in. It never mattered how often she fought it or how long she went without him. Her response to his touch, to the pleasure, and to the culmination of her fiery response to him was always the same.

It was overwhelming.

It overtook her to the point that there was no way to fight it, no way to resist it. There was only the aftermath later, and the knowledge that, just as in the months past, nothing would be said of it tomorrow.

There was no relationship binding them, no promises, and no

commitments. There were no discussions of the future and no mention of tomorrow.

She never knew from one night to the next where she stood with Casey or even *if* she stood with him.

And she was beginning to hate that feeling. She didn't believe in friends with benefits or in fuck buddies. She needed more. She needed more from Casey.

As she stared up at the ceiling, she realized their nonrelationship didn't seem to be changing. She was tired of waiting on him to indicate he wanted something more, she acknowledged. She needed more. Perhaps it would be better for both of them if she found the strength to cut it off, once and for all. Otherwise her resentment could end up hurting them both.

It would definitely be better for her, because Sheila knew she was on the verge of a broken heart.

chapter 2

nick casey—just Casey to his friends—struggled to regain his senses after it seemed every one of them had pumped straight from his dick along with his cum.

Sheila did more than drain the sexual tension from his body. There were times he swore she replaced that tension with something far more dangerous to his soul. And he was damned if he wanted to delve into what that "something" was. Hell, it was such an unfamiliar feeling, he didn't even know how to describe it.

At the moment, the only thing he wanted to delve into was regaining his strength enough to fuck them both silly again.

At least, that would have been his first option. Instead, he found himself opening his eyes and watching as she rolled from him naked, as naked as sex itself, and padded to the bathroom.

Shower? He scratched at his naked chest as he peered through one eye at the door she had disappeared through. Did he have the energy to follow her? Maybe wash her back? Then other areas?

He really, really liked taking a shower with Sheila.

She made it fun.

After he convinced her to let him have fun with her.

He frowned when he didn't hear the shower running.

She was in there, but she was too quiet.

That wasn't a good thing. When she was that quiet she was thinking. Sheila thinking rarely added up to Casey having fun.

The last time she was that quiet— He was moving before he finished the thought, but hell, it was already too late.

The door opened and she stepped out. Dressed.

Son-of-a-bitch-dammit-to-hell! He felt like stomping his foot in childish petulance. He frowned at her. It was all he could do not to immediately demand she undress again and return to his bed.

She had even brushed the shoulder-length strands of her dark blond hair and had slid on her shoes. Somehow, she had gathered up her shoes and clothes before going into the bathroom while he'd been debating joining her.

Hell, he knew better than to drop his guard like that with her. She took advantage of it every friggin' time.

"Hey, baby?" He glanced down at the shoes again. "Why are you dressed?" Play it cool, he thought, maybe it wouldn't be so bad.

"Because I'm going home."

It was that bad, damn it to fucking hell! He should just lock her in his room with him.

She moved to the dresser, where she collected her purse.

How pissed would she get if he tied her to the bed?

It took a minute for him to process the fact that she was definitely leaving. He was a bit slow sometimes, he admitted. It had been a killer week and he was sleepy. One of those weary spells that invariably turned into full-fledged insomnia unless he managed to convince her to sleep in his arms. He slept like a baby whenever he could exhaust her enough to ensure she fell asleep just after release.

He made it to the door of the small apartment before she did, hoping there was some way to convince her not to leave. Naked, certain there had to be a way to accomplish keeping her there. Convince her to sleep with him. Just one night.

"Why?" He moved in front of her, blocking her way as he watched her eyes narrow on him. Those deep violet eyes held the faintest spark of anger, as though he had done something to offend her.

What the hell could he have done? Hell, he'd just made her come hard enough that her pussy had nearly strangled his dick as it tightened around him. He was more than willing to repeat the experience, too.

"Enough, Casey." There was an edge of steel in her voice, but those soft, soft violet eyes were filled with hurt. "I want to go home, not stand and argue with you." An edge of hurt lingered in her voice and he was damned if he could figure out why.

He lifted his hand, the backs of his knuckles brushing against the silk of her cheek as he stared down at her, confused.

Her gaze flickered. For a second, for just the briefest second, he saw the passion, the promise, and the incredible sensual depths of the woman in those pretty eyes. He also saw the same, confusing emotions he felt himself before they disappeared.

"Don't." She pulled back rather than leaning into him as he knew she wanted to do. She wanted him, ached as he ached for her. In her eyes he saw the need to stay, and that she wanted to return to that big bed with him.

He knew she wanted to. He didn't just see it in her gaze, he could feel it. Like a touch that was there, yet wasn't. Like a flame that connected them, licking over both their bodies.

And it made his dick damned hard. So damned hard that for a second he wondered if he really had fucked her. Or only imagined it?

In a heartbeat he was iron-hard, hot and ready to fuck, and he wondered how she could possibly find the inner strength to walk out on him when he knew she felt the same.

"Geez, Casey." Breathless, amazed, she glanced down at the erection attempting to stab into her lower belly. Fully engorged, the thick bulging head dark and throbbing, his cock was literally begging for attention. Weeping for it even.

"You make me crazy," he muttered, his hand dropping as he stared down at her before backing away. Hell, he wasn't going to beg her to stay. He sure as hell wasn't going to allow her to feel as though he were attempting to force her to stay.

She truly did make him crazy as hell. Completely insane like no other woman ever had. There was something about her that drew him, confused him, and made him feel things he didn't always understand. Things he didn't want to feel.

"I don't mean to make you crazy." She was breathless.

Damn, he loved that sexy little edge to her voice when she became breathless.

The sound of that edge of arousal in it had the power to make his balls tighten with the need to have her. The need to fuck her until there wasn't a chance in hell she could ever deny him again rose inside him.

"Hell, I can't get enough of you." He reached for her, and she backed away.

Sheila had never backed away from him before. What the hell was wrong with her?

His eyes narrowed. "What's going on, Sheila?"

Her chin lifted, and that little glimmer of feminine fire shifted from arousal to pure feminine determination.

Ah, hell. This wasn't a good thing. This meant he'd obviously done something completely male—and managed to either hurt her or piss her off.

He was in trouble now, and Casey damned well knew it.

"Nothing's going on, Casey." Her lips thinned and her eyes seemed to darken with the lie. Casey always knew when she was lying. And she only lied to him, according to her, when he should be able to answer his questions himself.

He'd never seen denial in her eyes when it came to him, though. At the moment, there was pure rejection gleaming there.

"Don't give me that shit," he growled. "We've never played games with each other. Not like this. I don't want to start now. I won't let you start now."

"I was never the one playing games."

Casey's eyes narrowed. Every man in the world knew that tone of voice.

Those violet eyes flashed again with the edge of anger, and Casey knew he was screwed.

"What the hell did I do?" Pushing his fingers through his hair, he wished the damned hard-on would abate just a little bit. It was hard as hell to be demanding when all he wanted to do was fuck the temperamental little minx.

She delighted in making him crazy, he decided. And she could make him crazy as hell faster than anyone he'd ever known.

"You didn't do anything." She lifted her shoulder in a shrug that warned him he sure as hell had done something. And he better find "her" way, to fix it fast.

See, this was what drove him crazy. It made him want to pull his own hair out because he couldn't figure out what the hell he had done. She was obviously expecting him to know this time what he had or hadn't done. Whichever, he probably had only moments to fix it before she walked out that door.

"Look, just tell me what your problem is, and I'll fix it." He glared back at her as he crossed his arms over his chest, certain his erection would deflate any second. Surely his dick would get a clue and just give it up.

It would have with any other woman giving him this kind of grief. Hell, it had never failed to deflate permanently with any other woman who dared to pull this shit on him.

Especially when he didn't know what he'd done to piss off his soon-to-be-ex-lover. So why the hell hadn't it deflated yet? Why was he still standing there like a boob trying to figure out how to get her back in his bed?

"Didn't I do something right?" he demanded when that slender little hip cocked to the side and delicate fingers curved over it. The index finger tapped against her jeans silently. He'd only seen her do that a few times, and never with him. Until now.

Yep, he was in trouble. He just wished he knew why. How. Or what to do to fix it.

"You'll fix it, will you?" she asked silkily as her thick lashes fluttered over her mocking gaze. "Why, Casey, I just can't tell you how your offer makes my little heart beat faster."

Uh huh. He could tell. He really could. She was so damned sarcastic he almost winced.

He quickly ran through the night once again, just to be certain. Just to assure himself he hadn't done anything blatantly stupid. Because he really wasn't a stupid man where woman were concerned.

Had he gotten her a drink when she showed up at the bar?

Check.

He'd bought them all drinks and sent her a plate of the seasoned fries she liked as well. She and her friends sat in the corner booth and had a nice little visit. He had made certain they had everything they needed. And he'd paid for it all himself.

He'd kissed her before he got her in the car?

Check.

Fuck, he'd been so hungry for her he hadn't been able to keep from kissing her like he was dying for her.

He'd been romantic about it?

Hell yes.

He loved the feel of her hair, so he'd slid his hand into it, along the side of her face in the way he knew she liked. He knew, because it always made her eyes a little darker, and her face flush with feminine need. And he'd started that kiss slow and easy while he'd held her on the dance floor.

Once he'd gotten her to his apartment had he offered her another drink? Check there too.

He'd even offered her a snack or a meal.

He'd turned on the music, danced with her again, easing her slowly into the deepest flames of the arousal that began to burn inside them. Just because he loved the feel of her against him. Loved the way she rubbed against him.

"Look, Casey, I just want to go home," she informed him as she stepped to the door and gripped the knob. This time, he didn't try to stop her. He wasn't going to beg her. They weren't kids. They were supposed to be adults. Adults didn't play teenage games like this. At least, they shouldn't.

"Fine, when you feel in the mood to tell me what's wrong with you, then you know where to find me."

"Of course I do." He almost winced at the sound of her voice and the mockery that filled it. "Every night."

"Pretty much," he agreed with a tight nod. "I've never been hard to find. Made sure of it where you were concerned."

That only seemed to piss her off worse. Her fingers tightened on the doorknob and for a moment he thought she just might actually say whatever the hell was on her mind. He was certain the adult in her was ready to give up the game and just be honest with him.

Then her lips thinned again; she stepped through the doorway and slammed the door closed behind her.

Casey winced at the sound of metal meeting metal.

She had slammed the door on him. Hell, he couldn't believe it.

She might be more than just a little pissed.

She was pure female pissed with a healthy dose of "done had enough" when she slammed doors. Sheila wasn't normally a door slammer.

It was cute as hell actually. It was even damned arousing, though the fact that he found it arousing confused him more than he understood.

Running his fingers through his hair again, Casey did his best to try to figure out what he'd done. The funny thing was, she hadn't even hinted at being angry until she'd left the bathroom.

There was hurt in her eyes too.

He couldn't figure out how he'd hurt her.

He was damned if he could figure any of it out.

Casey rubbed his chest before moving back to the bedroom, his gaze going over the bed critically before moving around the room as though there might be an answer there somewhere. Some way to figure out how he could have hurt her, or pissed her off.

She'd been just as hungry for him as he'd been for her when they had arrived at his apartment. Come to think of it, she had been just as eager for him as he was for her before they even left the bar.

It always amazed him how easily she matched his need. Kiss for kiss, touch for touch, pure sensual, sexual need driving them both to the brink of sanity.

Hot as fucking hell.

And it hadn't been any different than any other night. They burned each other alive.

And no matter how often he had her, it was never enough. He was always left just as hard for her as he was the first time he fucked her. And he always cursed the sunrise whenever he saw it edging through his curtains.

Because sunrise meant Sheila was going to awaken, and she was going to leave. It meant that unfamiliar warmth and the confusing yet comforting emotions he felt would disappear with her.

This time, she'd left well before sunrise, though. And there he stood, naked, hard, and rather than feeling anger he just felt . . . alone.

He heard her car start outside his window. The second floor afforded him privacy, but it also allowed him to keep his eyes and ears open.

Not that he had a lot of enemies in this new life or in this new, fairly low-key job.

He'd never seemed to make enemies as easily as he did friends, so there weren't a lot of people who wanted to hurt him, yet.

Yet, because he was involved in something that could possibly turn ugly if anyone ever figured it out. Or if they figured out exactly who Nick Casey really was.

If they did.

They hadn't yet, and it had been quite a few years since he had come to Simsburg, Texas. He'd been there for five years, ever since his days as a super-secret special operations soldier had gone to hell when an extraction had turned ugly.

He'd taken a bullet to his hip and one to his damned ankle. His reaction time was screwed then and his ability to endure the long hikes and hard runs required was forever behind him.

But he'd made enemies during those days. And once he had taken Ethan Cooper up on his job offer to handle the security at his bar, he'd learned that some men could never retire from the life of an adrenaline junkie.

Not him, not the men who worked with him at the bar, and sure as hell not his boss, Cooper.

As he threw himself back in the bed and stared up at the ceiling silently, Casey admitted that being a special operations soldier had nothing on being a covert information gatherer and tattletale. The Broken Bar, Cooper's bar, was a watering hole for the dregs of society, as well as the locals and tourists. And Cooper's men were there to scoop up the scattered whispers, rumors, and gossip left behind. Posing as bouncers and bartenders, they heard it all.

Ethan's place was the only bar or nightclub coming from Corpus Christi. It was big, always busy, and drew a damned diverse crowd. A crowd that often held customers who mixed socializing with information and dropped tidbits of those secrets as they became more intoxicated through the night. More intoxicated and more self-important than they actually were.

Iron, Turk, Casey, and Jake put that information together along with Ethan for the retired army captain who headed the southern section of the Covert Information Network.

That same army captain was the father of the woman who had

just left his bed. As though he had committed some horrible sin. A sin Casey had yet to realize was actually a sin.

He grimaced again and shifted on the bed to relieve the ache in his hip. The result of several nights working overtime, piecing together the information that had come in after a strike overseas on a terrorist cell. That strike had been the result of information the team had gathered the month before, making these past few nights even more important.

Sometimes, Casey wondered if they were even making headway despite the strikes the team was responsible for. Take one out, ten more slide in.

He was beginning to wonder what he had left behind as he chased the adrenaline dream. What had he given up all these years? What had he missed that he couldn't figure out the feeling Sheila made him feel? And what was he letting slip through his fingers now?

From that first night he and Sheila had come together, he'd felt he had finally found a cure to the restlessness that plagued him. He'd finally felt as though he belonged somewhere. Or to someone.

There was more to her than he'd had a chance to get to know, and more that swirled in that heart of hers than she allowed him to glimpse. Those secrets drew him. They made him hungrier by the day to know her better, to touch her more, to hold her tighter.

And he wanted to see it all.

Shockingly.

Casey had never wanted to delve into a woman's heart and soul at any other time. Not since the day his fiancée had cleaned out his apartment and his bank account when she'd heard he'd been wounded in action.

She hadn't stuck around to see how badly he had been hurt or cared if he had needed her. She sure as hell hadn't cared that he might need his furniture, his cash, hell, his bed, when he returned home.

Nope, she'd just cashed in everything she could and found greener pastures. His best friend's pasture.

That had been over seven years ago, nearly eight.

Sheila was different, though. From the moment he'd stared into those mysterious violet eyes, he'd known she was more different than any woman he'd ever touched. So unique he was determined to keep her as his own.

There was something about her eyes, something about the need he glimpsed in them whenever she gazed back at him that drew him. There was a warmth, a fire he longed for. All he wanted was to hold Sheila through the night.

Every night.

He rubbed his jaw, a frown working over his brow again as he wondered what had happened and why she had run on him. But even more, what was that edge of hurt he'd glimpsed in her gaze?

How had he managed to hurt her when all he'd wanted to do was make love to her until they both collapsed?

Until she didn't have the strength, the will, or the desire to leave his arms again.

chapter 3

"sheila, did we get those reports in from team two yet?" Captain Douglas Rutledge stepped from his office, his craggy face creased into a frown as he stared at her with that affronted, irritated look of a man who knows he should have something and that it wasn't there.

His hair was mussed, his clothes slept in, and it looked like his socks were mismatched again.

That was her father.

Broody, impatient, and expecting perfection though he knew he wasn't going to receive it. At least, he said he knew, she thought as she watched him fondly.

"Not yet, Captain," she assured him, using the title as her mother had before her. "I told you I'd let you know the minute they arrive."

Sheila hadn't called him dad since the day her mother told her how he enjoyed the rare times she called him captain instead.

She turned back to the computer and the completion of the final electronic copy from the past week's reports. He was her parent and she loved him, but he was as demanding as any military man could be.

Besides, things had been slow in the bars and nightclubs where the operatives under her father's command worked. He wasn't going to be happy about it either. Captain Rutledge took his job seriously and demanded results.

Reaching up to scratch at his graying head, he glared at her again, drawing her attention.

She glared right back at him. "I can't snap my fingers and get it, Captain. You're just going to have to wait for it, no matter how long it takes."

His brows lifted in surprise as she barely stopped herself from sighing in irritation. Dammit, he knew her too well, and snapping back at him never failed to start an inquisition. And that was something she really didn't need right now.

He stood staring at her, both hands buried in the pockets of his dark slacks as he continued to regard her silently. Questioningly. And she knew that look. He expected an explanation, now.

Sheila considered simply going back to the reports she was putting together. Sometimes, the best thing to do was to ignore him. She wondered if that would work today as it had in the past.

"Might as well tell me what the problem is," he grunted. "You've been out of sorts for three days and I'm tired of being your little whipping boy."

Whipping boy? Sometimes her father tended to exaggerate.

"You're not a whipping boy," she muttered. "You're a nosy old man."

She had been very, very careful not to be out of sorts. She would be damned if she would let Casey hear that she was in any way less than a terrific mood. And her father wasn't above asking everyone they knew what was wrong with her.

She simply couldn't afford it.

"Yes you have. I want to know why." Her father strode across the small office to lean against the side of her desk as he stared down at her inquisitively. He wanted an answer and she knew by the look on his face he was determined to get one.

The glare was gone, and that was an indication that the captain was now her father, and he was concerned. She could deny the captain, but it was harder to deny her father.

Besides, she didn't want him to be concerned. When he worried, he poked his nose into her life and made her crazy.

"You have reports to go over, Captain," she reminded him, barely restraining a roll of her eyes. "Not a daughter to raise. You already completed that particular mission admirably."

"You look just like your mother when you say that." Nostalgia entered his tone, his expression. "She would try to lie to me just like that, too."

A wealth of love filled his voice as he spoke, as well as that ever present shadow of pain he carried. He had loved her mother, even after her death. So much so that he had never considered remarrying. He didn't even date.

"Mom never lied to you." Sheila shook her head, barely restraining her smile. Because he was right. Her mother was very good at evasion, though not lying. And her father had always known when she was evading.

"There's no difference between an evasion and a lie," he warned her as though reading her thoughts. He simply knew her that well.

"Of course there is." She laughed back at him. "When you don't want to lie to someone, you evade. It's perfectly acceptable." That way they couldn't get angry or accuse you of deceit.

His brow arched. "So you're not lying, you're evading?"

He had no idea.

"You're funny." This time, she did roll her eyes. "I'm not evading either," she promised him. "I'm trying to get this mountain of paperwork finished."

"No, dear child, you're flat-out lying."

And at that point, she had to drop her eyes, because he was right, she was lying through her teeth and she hated it.

"My business," she told him firmly.

He watched her for long, silent moments.

"Hmm, that means it's a man," he guessed.

"It means it's my business and I prefer not discuss it with you or anyone else, Captain," she informed him.

Her father could be like a dog with a bone. She never appreciated being the bone. It was highly uncomfortable.

He glared at her again. "Then that means it's a man I'd know."

There was the displeasure. How the hell had he known?

Duh! He knew everyone she knew. There was no way to be wrong.

"No, Dad, it means someone you know might know him, and I'd prefer he be unaware of the fact that I'm displeased with him."

Not exactly a lie, not exactly the truth either.

At that point, he frowned again in confusion. "But dear, how else is your young man supposed to make the situation right and win your heart if he doesn't know why you're upset?"

Sheila leaned back in her chair, crossed her arms, and stared back at him firmly. "Dad, I don't want him to make anything right and I definitely don't want anyone else to tell him if he's done something to upset me. I prefer to take care of these things myself."

Her father reached up and scratched at his weathered cheek, and Sheila could see that he had no idea what to make of his daughter. He often lamented that she refused to fall in love and marry fast to suit him, because he had always insisted on probing into her dates' lives.

It wasn't a refusal to love, she knew how to love, it was simply a refusal to beg or to play the games she watched so many other women play. Those relationships rarely worked, she had found. It had left her friends and acquaintances with broken hearts and disillusioned lives. If a woman had to beg, plead, or hint at a need for commitment from a man, then she didn't need that man.

She didn't want that. She wanted to be like her mother. She wanted to marry once and marry a man that she not only loved, but one that loved her just as much. She didn't want to guilt Casey into loving her. Where would the satisfaction be in that?

Yet Casey had been convinced she was playing games instead.

"So, who is he?" her father asked, his tone indicating a demand for an answer.

Sheila shook her head. "Sorry, Dad, but I don't need your help in this. I'll take care of it myself. I'm rather good at that now."

She had only been young and dumb once.

His frown deepened as concern filled his eyes. "I promise to say nothing to anyone," he promised her. A huge concession from him.

"Sorry, Dad, it's not going to happen." She shook her head slowly as amusement tugged at her lips. "I know better than to tell you. You like trying to fix my life too much. And I don't need this fixed." At least, not by her father. There was nothing her father could do anyway, except make the situation worse.

He was a busybody. A loving one. A caring one. He would never do anything to hurt her. But she knew him too well. If he knew who her lover was, he would no doubt make it an order that Casey find a way to fix it.

"So why won't you let *him* fix it? Tell me that and I'll let it go," he said gently. "Otherwise, you know it will drive me crazy." Because he was her father and he felt it was his place to fix her problems. She believed differently, but she could tell him the least of what he wanted to know.

"Because, if he loved me, then he would love me enough to know what to do, Dad," she said somberly. "Like you knew with Mom."

And how many times had her father told her how he'd known the second he met her mother what she would be to him? That he had loved her from the moment he had met her and had been willing to die for her if he could have?

She wanted that kind of love as well.

Her father shook his head sadly. "Sheila, your mother led me on a merry chase. I didn't say I recognized the emotion in that first moment. It was only later I realized what I was feeling. No man that I know of recognizes love for what it is until he's absolutely forced to do so."

"So will he, if that's what he feels," she told him. "Don't mess with this, Dad."

She couldn't handle it. She wouldn't tolerate it. She wouldn't be able to bear the thought that her father had somehow "ordered" Casey to love her.

She wouldn't play games with Casey, and she wasn't going to allow her father to step in to fix this for her. Only Casey could fix it and she had a feeling that wasn't going to happen either.

She had always suspected the fact that she was Captain Rutledge's daughter had kept Casey away from her for years. If her father intervened, no doubt Casey would feel that pressure to make promises he wouldn't want to make or keep.

God, she wanted him though.

She almost wanted him—no, loved him—enough to risk it. Enough to almost consider it. She was dying for him and it was all her own stubborn fault for wanting more than he had to give.

And in all the months they had been coming together, not once had Casey suggested that there was more between them than the few nights a month they spent in his bed. He hadn't asked her out, he hadn't suggested that their relationship could ever develop into anything more serious. Just as he had never indicated to anyone else that they were together in any way.

And that hurt. As though he were ashamed of her, or too frightened of her father to risk him knowing, which she knew wasn't the case. Or perhaps he just didn't want to be a couple with her.

She was tired of it. Each time he touched her, she felt as though he had torn another part of her heart from her chest and carried it away with him. She didn't want to lose more of her heart. She didn't want to be in this relationship alone.

"You're frightened," her father finally said softly, his head tilting to the side as he regarded her with gentle admonishment.

"Frightened of what?" She couldn't believe he had said anything so ridiculous or with such fatherly chastisement.

"Of being hurt," he guessed. "You know, Sheila, I haven't heard even a whiff of a rumor that you were seeing anyone. That you were interested in anyone. You've kept him very well hidden and that makes me wonder if the problems are your fault or your unknown lover's."

Her lips thinned. "I'm not telling you who it is."

He shook his head slowly. "My dear, you wouldn't have had to tell me, if you weren't frightened of this man breaking your heart. A woman doesn't hide something so important as the man she's in love with, unless there's something holding her back. Or," his voice lowered further. "Or, she doesn't love him at all. And if that's the case, then I don't want to know who he is." He shrugged as though it didn't matter. "I only want to meet the important ones and this one obviously isn't important at all."

At that point, he straightened and moved back to his office without saying anything further, leaving Sheila to stare at his back with narrowed eyes as she wondered what game he could be playing with her. Her father could be amazingly devious when he wanted information. That was why he made such an efficient commander for the Covert Information Network.

She only wished Casey didn't matter.

She wished she didn't miss him with everything inside her; missing him was killing her.

She wished the only thing holding her back was the fear of losing the rest of her heart.

It was the fear of losing so much more than her heart that terrified her.

Because what she was beginning to feel, she felt as though it went much deeper than her heart, went much deeper than any other emotion she had ever felt.

It went clear to her soul.

Casey sat at the bar tapping his fingers against the gleaming wood. His gaze was locked on the mirror behind the bar, giving him a clear view of the entrance.

The large, cavernous building was nearly at its limit with the threat of a line forming outside once they were forced to close the doors against additional customers. Once customers arrived at the Broken Bar, they seemed to stay until last call. Which made it hard for any additional customers arriving unless the owner, Ethan Cooper, used the one-hour limit he was often forced to set.

The band, positioned along the wall at the center of the room on the opposite side of the building, was belting out another of those sensual slow tunes they were inclined to play. Broken hearts, broken loves, and beer-drinkin' nights. He was damned sick of hearing about it. Every wailing note did nothing but remind him of Sheila and the fact that he'd been waiting on her all day and half the night. He reminded himself of a lovesick teenager.

The door swung open again, but the couple that entered weren't Sheila. She should have been here by now. It was her job to pick up the information the team had acquired over the past week. Instead, he was still here waiting on her. It felt like he had been waiting on her all his life.

He glanced at his watch before his gaze lifted to the door once more. Yep, that was him: lovesick teenager.

Sheila knew he didn't work tonight. Son of a bitch, she always showed up on Tuesday nights. Tuesday nights were theirs. Slow loving and her sensual cries as they drove each other crazy with every kiss, caress, and stroke they could bestow on each other.

Casey tapped his fingers against the wood again, his teeth clenching as a surge of hunger and anger struck at his gut. She wasn't going to show up. He could feel it. She was avoiding the bar and she was avoiding him and he was damned if he was going to let her get away with it.

His jaw bunched in irritation.

If Sheila was going to cut him off like this, the least she could have done was give him a reason why she was breaking off what they had. He didn't even know what the hell was going on, what he had done, or why she had ended the relationship the other morning as she left.

Hell, he had no idea what had happened, and it wasn't as though he could talk to her about it. He couldn't even catch up with her long enough. And now, she was late arriving to pick up the files it was her job to transport to her father.

He had asked her what he had done, something he had never asked another woman and wouldn't have bothered to even care about with anyone else.

Her reply had been "nothing."

There had been an odd tone to her voice, though. One he hadn't wanted to delve into at the time. Something about the sound of her answer had immediately had his stomach clenching. Not in dread, but in an impending . . . something that still didn't make sense. What did make sense? He was dying for her.

And he had no idea how to fix any of it.

"Hey, Casey, you look down." Sarah Fox Cooper, God love her heart, his boss's wife. Trust her to get right to the point and thankfully to keep her voice down while doing so.

A charming, shy little thing, he'd once believed. Until she came out of her shell, stole Cooper's heart, and became a regular at one of the most dangerous watering holes in the state. She was like a breath of fresh air in a trash dump. Pretty as a picture she was, and from the look on her face, determined to get an answer to her question. Determined and firm, she moved through the crowd as though it were a family reunion.

Cooper was never far behind her, either. And if not Cooper, then at least two of his most trusted bouncers were planted on her ass. Cooper never, at any time, took his wife's safety for granted.

Tonight, as on most nights, it was Cooper following his wife. With an indulgent smile on his face, he kept a steady eye on the woman who had stolen his heart the summer before.

"I'm tired, Sarah," he answered. "Your husband is a slave driver."

He was tired of waiting and watching for a woman who hadn't

arrived. She had five more minutes, then he was going after her. Five minutes, that was it.

"Yeah, but such a damned sexy one," Sarah replied, her smile infectious and filled with warmth as she cast her husband a flirty look over her shoulder.

"I guess it takes a feminine eye to see the sexy part," Casey snorted as he glanced toward the entrance again and caught himself glaring at it.

"Hmm, that could be possible." Sarah shrugged as she lifted herself onto the bar stool beside him, drawing his gaze from the door. "But that doesn't tell me why you're looking such a grump this early in the week. I thought you reserved the bad moods for the weekend?"

Not lately he hadn't. Weekends had meant Sheila, too. It had meant wild, hot, explicit sex, earthy feminine moans, and sharp little nails clawing at his back.

Fuck, he was hard. His dick pulsed and throbbed in his jeans.

That fast. His erection was all but pushing past the zipper of his jeans and drawing his balls tight against the base of the shaft. It felt as though it had been years rather than days since he had fucked her.

Damn.

He glanced at his watch again. Two minutes and he was going after her.

He couldn't handle this. He wanted her to the point his back teeth ached with it.

For three nights in a row, he'd existed in a state of miserable arousal and confused anger. There was nothing worse than caring that he'd fucked up and being unable to figure out how.

"I'm fine, Sarah," he promised as he realized she was watching him expectantly.

He glanced at the door again, then his watch.

One and a half minutes and he was going after her.

"She slipped in the back entrance about three hours ago, collected the reports, and ran," Sarah leaned forward and informed him quickly, her voice low. "Ran as though the hounds of hell were nipping at her heels."

Sarah straightened in her seat then and cast her husband a teasing look as he shook his head at her. Sarah was known to matchmake. Or at least, to attempt to. It had been making all of them crazy. They indulged her, were amused by her, but seriously, she made them crazy with it.

Well, all of them except the new guy, Morgan Keane. One of the six new bouncers Cooper had been forced to hire in the past year. He was a former special forces soldier referred by one of the U.S. Marshals who were protecting Sarah's father. A former Italian mafia boss who had immigrated to America, Giovanni Fredrico.

Morgan was a brooding, grouchy son of a bitch with an attitude that managed to keep even the most aggressive jackals in the place at bay.

Nothing Sarah or anyone else did seemed to faze Keane much, though. He took it all in stride.

"Did she now?" Casey finally forced himself to mutter, irritation mixing with the lust and surging through his bloodstream with a hit of spiked adrenaline.

Yep, there it was. That shot of elixir that kept him perpetually hard whenever he thought of Sheila.

"She did." Sarah grinned. "It was all rather curious, too. I thought she was running scared, but she swore she was simply in a hurry. What do you think?"

The gleam of knowledge in her eyes was highly discomforting. It meant she was matchmaking.

"Hell if I know," he muttered, deciding in that second he didn't need her help.

"Confused on that, are you?" she asked.

He leveled a suspicious glare in her direction. It only received another of her infamous smiles. Those innocent, I've-done-nothing-wrong grins.

Bullshit. She was obviously up to something, and he had a feeling he knew what. He was getting into trouble just fine all by himself. He didn't need Sarah's help.

"I shouldn't be?" he asked softly.

She shrugged again as she brushed back one of the thick, heavy brown curls that had fallen over her shoulder.

"Well, it should have been rather obvious," Sarah sighed. "Most women of Sheila's ilk refuse to play second fiddle to anything or anyone else, Casey. They're simply too possessive to be placed in any position but first."

"She doesn't play second anything, period," he informed her. "Where are you going with this?"

Why was he letting her "go with it"? The "it" being the head game she was playing.

"It would depend on where you intend on going with things," she suggested lightly. "And perhaps that's all she's waiting on from you, to decide if you're worth risking her heart for. Sometimes, all a woman needs is to know she's wanted for more than what she provides her lover in their bed."

"Troublemaker." Cooper stepped forward, growling the accusation in a tone filled with pure adoration. He was damned crazy over the girl and everyone knew it. But he did make attempts to limit her interference in other people's lives.

"Of course I am," she admitted as she lifted her face and accepted the quick kiss he placed against her lips. "That's why you love me so dearly, though. I never let you get bored."

Casey watched their byplay until Cooper helped his wife from her seat and they headed for the door behind the bar. That door led to the stairs that would take them to the office/bedroom Cooper kept upstairs. From there, Casey didn't even want to guess what they would be doing. It was better not to.

Because then, he would start thinking of all the things he could be doing with Sheila, and it would just piss him off worse.

He glanced at the mirror again and narrowed his eyes.

He knew where Sheila was. He knew where she lived and he knew how to get to her. And he knew he was really getting tired of waiting on her.

She was his, he'd made that decision a long time before and had been forced to wait far too long to claim her. But he had claimed her, and now, letting her go wasn't something he was going to do. Not now, not ever.

chapter 4

for the third night in a row, sleep was a hard time coming. For the past months, Tuesday night was one of the three reserved for Casey. At any other time she would be in his bed.

Sheila rolled over to her back with a groan and stared up at the darkened ceiling morosely. What was he doing now? Was he alone in his bed or had he found someone else to share it with? Had she made a mistake? Had she let him go too quickly, before he could have realized she could mean something to him?

Was she letting the past influence the present in such a way that she could be harming the hopes she had for her future? Of course she was, wasn't that what she was good at? She had already proved it.

Seven years before, she hadn't demanded the commitment, or the words of love. She hadn't pressed the issue and she had learned the error of it. She'd been used by the man she'd thought she loved. Ross Mason had used her and her heart to get close to her father and to secure a military position that only Douglas Rutledge could assign.

Thankfully, her father had been smart enough to see what she hadn't, and had managed to turn Ross's game against him. When Ross had been given that position, he'd suddenly had no use for her. He'd even smiled at her and told her she had to have been aware of what he had wanted. She had just been a means to acquire it.

Not that she believed Casey was using her, because she couldn't imagine what he could want from her. But she hadn't imagined what Ross could want either, until the night he had broken off the relationship.

She wasn't going to allow that to happen to her again. She couldn't allow it, not with Casey. Already he meant too much to her.

She hadn't loved Ross, not really. She had liked him. He had been safe, or she had thought he was safe. She would have never loved him to the point that losing him could destroy her. Not like she loved Casey.

Kicking the blankets from her legs and blowing out a hard, deep breath, Sheila realized she was going to end up making herself crazy. She was already aroused. That was all the crazy she needed.

Lifting her arm from the mattress beside her, she let her fingers trail along the flesh exposed between the elastic of her low-rise panties and the white silk-and-lace cami tank top she wore to sleep in.

She missed his touch, the warmth of his arms around her, and his kiss.

Her eyes drifted closed and she saw Casey watching her. His expression heavy with lust, his gaze darkening with whatever emotion he kept hidden within his silence. The way he licked his lips the few times she had touched herself as he watched. It turned him on, made him so dominant and hungry for her that his possession stole her breath.

Innocent touches.

When she had smoothed lotion over her arms, stomach, and legs after showering, she would see his eyes narrow, his cock hardening beneath his jeans, or if he was naked, his unashamed hunger for her.

What would he have done if she had touched herself in front of him, as she did when she was alone? How intense and dominant would he have become if he had seen her touching herself when she missed him?

Or even now?

Would he enjoy watching her masturbate?

The tips of her nails rasped against the sensitive flesh of her lower stomach as she remembered his touch. His kiss. The way he would use his versatile, wicked tongue to lick and taste her skin.

She wanted to moan at the excitement that suddenly rushed through her. The silent thought that she could tease him in such a way. That the next time she saw him she would have the nerve to be the seductress she always imagined being, but hadn't yet garnered the courage to be.

Or the chance. The chance to watch his gaze darken and narrow as she touched her nipples or ran her fingers through her juices before circling her clit.

His sensuality overwhelmed her. Once he touched her, all thoughts of anything but being possessed by him, taken and ridden to exhaustion, flew from her mind. She hadn't remembered to tease him by touching herself, even though she had promised herself she would.

Her fingers trailed to the band of her panties, pushed beneath it slowly, then feathered over the short, soft curls at the top of her mound.

Below, the slick, waxed flesh felt flushed and swollen, her juices easing over it as arousal began to build within her. She could feel the inner flesh of her pussy heating, aching, needing him.

She knew better than to go further. The sheer frustration she had found over the months in masturbating was becoming ridiculous. She could never satisfy herself as she once had. She was always left aching, wanting, her pussy and her clit still throbbing despite the release she found.

Satisfaction could only be found with Casey and she knew it.

With his touch, his kiss, or the heavy, throbbing length of his cock pushing inside her, penetrating her with a slow, measured surge. Each thrust would draw a cry from her lips and stretch her to her limits. It would burn. Pleasure-pain would fill her, then ecstasy would overtake her.

She bit her lip, a surge of sexual need flooding her system and tightening through her womb.

Her fingers slid lower. Any touch would be better than none, she told herself desperately. Any release better than no release at all.

Her fingers stroked over her clit as her breath caught at the wave of sensation that rushed through her senses. Swollen and slick, the little bud throbbed in desperation as she let her fingers ease through the wet, slickened folds of her pussy.

Her hips lifted to her own touch, her fingers slid lower.

"Keep that up and I'll come in my damned jeans before I can get them off."

Sheila's eyes flew open, a gasp leaving her lips as she stared at the end of the bed where Casey stood watching her. Chocolate brown eyes looked black in the darkness as he finished unbuttoning the shirt he wore, moving slowly, giving her all the time she needed to tell him to go to hell. And that was exactly what she should do. She should never let herself weaken. She should throw him out until he decided he loved her and couldn't live without her. That was what she should do.

Instead, she let her fingers reach further, one dipping into the clenched, heated entrance of her pussy. Delicate muscles gripped her fingers, spasmed, and clenched as pleasure shot through her.

His jaw tightened and a second later he was shrugging the shirt from the powerful width of his shoulders.

Muscles rippled beneath the tough, hardened flesh. Random scars, nicks, and marks covered the broad expanse, and she knew he carried even more on his left hip and ankle from the wound that had forced his discharge from the army.

Lips parting to drag in a ragged breath, Sheila pushed her finger in deeper, aware that Casey had yet to take his eyes from where her fingers worked between her thighs. Electric sensation shot through her nerve endings as a gasp left her lips. Casey tore at the metal tab and zipper of his jeans, releasing them before pushing them from his long, powerful legs. Casey didn't wear underwear. His cock sprang free, eager to join the fun.

When he straightened, his erection stood out from his body, thick and erect, the flared crest darkened and shining with moisture.

He palmed the heavy shaft. Long, broad fingers stroked his erection as he watched her with narrowed eyes, lust gleaming in naked demand.

"Take off your panties." His voice was guttural and rough, the command heavy with hungry male intent. "Let me watch you fuck yourself with your fingers."

A chill tore up her spine before a fist clenched her womb and tightened through her pussy. A wash of juices saturated her cunt and the sizzling ache of pure sensual hunger washed through it.

Oh God, she wanted him so desperately. She needed him inside her pussy, thrusting, pushing in with the heavy thrusts she knew would throw her headfirst into ecstasy.

Feeling dazed, as though she were living in a fantasy, Sheila shed her panties, tossing them carelessly to the floor as her legs spread, giving him a clear view of her fingers sliding between the swollen lips of her pussy once again.

Sensation swept through her as he watched, sending excitement racing through her.

"Ah yes, baby," he rasped. "Let me see how pretty you are. How fucking sweet as you fuck yourself."

Stroking the hard flesh of his cock, he watched as her fingers slid once again to the snug entrance of her pussy.

She wanted him to watch. She needed him to watch. Never had her own touch filled her with such intense pleasure, such hunger.

She wanted him to ache as she ached. She wanted him as ensnared in the web created by whatever it was that flowed between them as she was. She needed him to ache, to want, to need just as badly as she needed him. In every way.

Her fingers slid back, slick and hot, her juices coating them and glistening on the curves of her pussy.

Watching him, Sheila touched, pleasured, and knew she would never be able to touch herself again without him watching. Never would she be able to find even the smallest satisfaction without Casey.

The sensations were sharper, more exciting than they had ever been without him. They sizzled through her body, burned through her clit, and tightened her womb with spasms of her approaching orgasm.

Casey licked his lips, a slow, hungry movement that mesmerized her as she circled her clit with her fingers, causing the little bud to swell harder, tighter.

Her breathing was rougher now, as though she couldn't draw enough air into her lungs.

Excitement whipped through her. As though her nerve endings were live wires, exposed and spilling their energy sensation over her flesh. And if the look on Casey's face was any indication, he was feeling it as well.

His eyes were almost black. She had only seen that when he was at his most aroused. His lips were fuller, heavier, his hard chest gleaming with sweat as he stroked the length of his cock with slow, easy strokes.

The heavily veined, pulsing erection held her attention as she slid two fingers inside the gripping, saturated flesh between her thighs once more.

It wasn't her fingers she felt.

It wasn't her own touch that held her enraptured.

It was the remembered feel, the remembered pleasure of Casey's possession that made her insane. That made her come apart at the seams.

As her fingers penetrated her pussy, it was his cock she felt. It was his possession. The echoes of it. The remembered feel of him stretching her as she parted her fingers and scissored them against the clenched muscles surrounding them.

"Casey," she whispered his name, her voice rough, filled with need as she realized her eyes had closed.

They jerked open, staring back at him in surprise as she realized he was much closer. He was kneeling between her spread knees, sitting back on his heels as he stroked his cock and watched her.

"Don't stop," he growled. "Fuck yourself, Sheila. Let me see you. Let me see how much you want me to touch you."

She wanted him to touch her bad.

Her hips lifted. A moan tore from her.

His expression tightened.

Kneeling between her knees, his gaze focused on the flesh between her thighs as she penetrated herself, her fingers gleaming with her juices as she tried to hold back her release.

"I dream of you," she gasped, feeling the release racing to her.

"What do you dream, baby?"

"Of this, sometimes," she whispered desperately. "Of you taking me, making me cry out for you, because the pleasure is so intense I can barely stand it."

She wasn't going to scream in need for it. She was going to demand he take her, that he possess her. She was going to beg him for it.

Her fingers slid back, finding her clit as his gaze lifted to hers once again.

"Fuck me, Casey," she whispered. "Please. I need you. I need you inside me so bad I don't think I can bear it."

He moved closer.

"Keep touching yourself."

He lifted her thigh, moving in, bending over her, positioning the wide head of his cock at the greedy, saturated entrance to her sex.

She caressed her clit, arching, her breasts lifting as his lips descended to one hard, tight nipple.

Sharp, ecstatic sensation tore through the sensitive tip, streaking through her body to slam into the responsive depths of her womb, then into her pussy.

He sucked the tip into his mouth as the flared head began to part the snug entrance of her pussy.

Sliding her fingers into the cool, thick strands of his hair, Sheila could only gasp his name. Sensation swirled through her senses, pleasure tore through her body. Stretching, burning, his cock worked inside her, separating her flesh as her fingers moved erratically on the swollen bud of her clit.

The intensity of the pleasure whipping through her had her senses expanding with nearing ecstasy. Sensation began to jerk through her body, to race just beneath her flesh faster.

His cock stroked inside her in short, hard thrusts, raking along the exquisitely sensitive nerve endings as she began to gasp with the sensations.

His lips, tongue, and mouth caressed her nipple, drawing on the tiny bud, tormenting it. He rasped it with his teeth as she arched to him. Her muscles tightened, clenching on his cock as it slowly invaded her.

She was dying from the pleasure.

Sensation ballooned inside her, tearing through her senses until she was arching tight beneath him. Her hips writhed on the impalement as Casey sank fully inside her. He seated himself to the hilt with one firm, possessive penetration. The thrust speared through the gripping, milking muscles of her pussy, drawing a harsh cry from her lips.

No sooner than he sank inside her, he was moving.

If pleasure was a whirlwind before, it became a cyclone. The hard, rapid motions of his hips, the heavy, deep thrusts inside her, the caress of the velvet over iron flesh impaling her was like riding a starburst.

Sensations swelled and detonated through her nerve endings, yet the release that seemed so near never seemed so far away. Moving her fingers over her clit in short, rapid motions as he shafted inside her, Sheila only increased the torturous pleasure. She couldn't stop. She was so close.

"Casey," she cried out, panting for air. "Oh God, it's killing me. Please."

His head lifted from her nipple.

"Please what, baby?" he groaned, his lips moving against the mound of her breast, his tongue licking over the damp skin he found. "Tell me what you want. I'll give it to you. You only have to ask."

"I need to come," she gasped, staring up at him, dazed, watching as a trail of sweat ran slowly down the side of his hard face. "Make me come, Casey. Make me come all over your cock. It's so thick and hard inside me . . ." she moaned.

As though she had struck a match to fuel, Casey gave a tortured moan before he began moving harder, faster.

Thrusting, shafting inside her with hard, quick strokes, his cock shuttling in and out of the tight confines of her sex, he gave her what she begged for.

Within seconds Sheila was exploding. Tossed headlong into a rapture she couldn't control and had no desire to rein in. It began in the very depths of her pussy, radiating outward to attack her clit as she stroked it in time to the hard strokes filling her cunt, and the brutal shudders that began tearing through her.

The little bud swelled quickly, harder, more sensitive than ever as she gave a wild, fractured moan and let it fling her into an ecstasy she was certain Casey had never given her before.

This one was brighter, hotter, it tore past her mind, completely obliterated thought or any belief that she could ever be the same once reality returned.

Because as that explosion ripped through her, it did more than fill her body with the most exquisite rapture she had ever known. It did more than simply satisfy that feminine ache as no other man had ever been able to do. As she exploded around the hard, fiery erection filling her, she felt him bury in deep once again, then felt his release tear through him as well.

She felt the hard, heavy spurts of his release filling her.

She felt his arms wrapping around her.

She felt his wide, muscular chest scraping against her nipples, his powerful thighs tightening.

She felt the white-hot center of her release tear a hole through the defenses she had built against him as well.

As his release jetted inside her, she swore she felt a part of *him* sink inside her soul.

He had finally possessed her.

And she knew she hadn't managed the same with him.

She knew. And she swore she felt it breaking her heart.

chapter 5

sheila remembered what it felt like when she was nineteen and she learned the man she thought she loved had only been using her to get to her father. That it hadn't been her he wanted, it had been a position that her father controlled. One that, once he'd acquired it, Douglas Rutledge couldn't take from him.

But, as her father had said, it wasn't worth taking back. It had been worth it to know he'd wanted the job rather than the daughter. And better she'd known before Sheila had messed up her life and married the man.

At the time, she hadn't seen it that way. She understood the reason he had tested the relationship by assigning the position before the proposal, but the knowledge that she'd been wanted for anything more than what her father could provide still managed to hurt.

She had never taken a love interest to meet her father since. Dates picked her up at her house, a small cottage a half mile from her father's main house. She never told her father who she was seeing, or when she was seeing them.

It was easier that way.

If anyone mentioned wanting to meet her father, it spelled the end of whatever relationship they had.

She never dated anyone her father knew.

Until Casey.

But, she excused herself, she wasn't exactly dating Casey. She was only sleeping with him, wasn't she?

Still, she was breaking one of her own rules and she knew it.

Then she had compounded that error by falling in love with him.

Yes, she was in love with him, and she knew it.

Sitting in her car outside the bar two nights later, she knew she had made that drastic mistake. A horrendous mistake. One guaranteed to break her heart in half.

Breathing out roughly, she tested the feel of the boots she wore before opening the door of her small car and stepping out.

The hollow heel still felt a little strange.

Casey had brought her the boots the night before, claiming he felt the newly designed heel would be more secure than her purse for hiding the flash drives she carried to her father twice a week.

The tiny chamber was waterproof and it would be impossible to detect the drive using any electronic means, he assured her.

He'd acted positively protective, and for a second, just a second, she'd wondered if she had been wrong, if he felt something more for her than simply lust.

"Can't have those drives getting lost or stolen if some yahoo decides to grab your purse." He'd shrugged then. "I hate wasting my time."

And her hopes had plummeted.

Dammit.

She'd thought by now he would have at least shown a few emotions besides worry over the damned flash drives.

The information on them was imperative, she knew. The tracking of terrorists, both homeland and overseas, was imperative.

Drug and weapons runners and any other criminal element that walked through the doors of the bar were fair game.

Every customer was photographed the second they entered and, using hidden remote cameras, additional pictures could be taken.

Who they met with, who they danced with, what they did in the parking lot. Rumors, gossip, and drunken bragging were recorded, saved, and then placed on the flash drive to be given to the captain. He then delivered it to the homeland security team assigned to break down the information and investigate as needed.

It was done quietly, effectively, and it had worked for eight years. Since the day Ethan Cooper had reopened the Broken Bar and brought the proposal to the captain, after he'd learned about the clientele he wouldn't be able to keep out of it.

Since that day, the bar had reigned as the only alcoholic establishment allowed within the county limits. The Broken Bar was a favorite among the locals as well as the criminal element. And Ethan Cooper ran the establishment with an iron hand.

No dealing, drugs or otherwise, was the rule, though they'd recorded it happening often enough.

The bouncers watched out for the women first, innocent men second, and they were all friends of Cooper's. Tough, hard-eyed bastards who had been discharged from the army for one reason or another.

Some honorably.

Some not so honorably.

Smoothing the skirt of her short dress, Sheila made her way from the parking spot she'd managed to snag at the side of the building and stepped up to the wood walkway that stretched around the bar.

The entrance was manned that night by Turk.

One of those hard-eyed bastards who had been not so honorably discharged.

"Miss Rutledge." He nodded as he opened the door for her.

"Thanks, Turk." She threw him a quick smile as she moved past him.

"Casey will be out in a bit, he's in a meeting with Coop."

She almost paused at the bouncer's announcement. She almost turned around and asked him why she should care. But she knew these men.

Number one, he wouldn't tell her what he knew, and there was no doubt he knew something; otherwise, he'd never have said anything.

Holding her irritation for Casey until later, she moved into the building and headed for the long, gleaming teak bar at the side of the room.

A band was belting a country-western tune on the other end. The sound of the steel guitar, the lazy sensuality in the singer's voice, and the sight of the customers swaying on the dance floor were enough to assure her she'd arrived late.

Everyone had had just enough booze to loosen inhibitions, if any existed, and lead them to the dance floor where they could rub and grind and in some cases even complete the sexual act in the dimmer areas as the sexually charged music seemed to infect them.

Her father had always warned her to beware of alcohol and slow dancing.

And he was right.

She almost grinned at the thought.

The first night she and Casey had been together, they had danced to a slow, lazy tune after the bar had closed and after they had shared more than one drink.

Her stomach clenched at the memory of that night.

There on the bar. He'd turned the cameras off and he'd taken her like a man starved for a woman.

"Hey, Sheila, you're blushing." Sarah Cooper's brows were arched as she made the accusation teasingly. "What are you thinking about that has your face all red?"

Hell.

She was half tempted to turn around and walk out rather than face the warmhearted teasing. She hoped that Casey wasn't around.

"Secrets," Sheila informed her as she took the bar stool one of the bouncers vacated.

The new guy, Morgan Keane.

Six feet four and a half inches of power and well-honed muscles. Dark blue eyes and black hair, sun-bronzed skin, and a hardened expression.

Wearing jeans and a black Broken Bar T-shirt, he looked like a man most men, let alone a woman, would be scared to run into in a back alley.

The background check her father had done on him had pretty much confirmed that impression. He wasn't a criminal, and never had been, as far as Captain Rutledge could tell. He was just a man who had treaded a thin line a little close to that element.

Even worse, and a bigger sin in the captain's eyes, Morgan Keane hadn't joined one of the military forces and served his country either.

He was a hell of a bouncer, and one Sheila knew Cooper was coming to depend upon after less than six months.

"You are not answering me." Sarah leaned forward, shy dimples peeking out from her rounded cheeks as she brushed back the incredibly long curls that fell around her.

"That's because I don't want to," Sheila answered as she leaned forward as well, ignoring the other girl's playful pout. "Where's Cooper? He's supposed to be keeping you out of trouble."

"In a meeting with your bed warmer," Sarah all but whispered as her grin widened. "Tell me, Sheila, how long did you think you would keep it quiet if you dared to challenge Casey as you did?"

Sheila's brows lifted. What in the world had Casey told Sarah? It wasn't like him to tell anyone *anything* about his private life.

To say she was shocked he had even let on that they were sleeping together was an understatement.

Sarah rolled her eyes, almost laughing back at her.

"His truck has been parked at your house the past two mornings and several of the bar's customers just happen to be working on your father's landscaping."

Sheila grimaced. She had forgotten about that. She should have thought. There were very few members of the community who hadn't been in the Broken Bar at one time or another.

"Oh well, he can deal with it then." She shrugged as though it didn't matter when she knew very well it did. She detested being gossiped about. But even worse, she knew for a fact that Casey had broken off relationships with other women for no more reason than the fact that his personal business with them had become public knowledge.

She didn't need this.

She didn't need to be forced to grapple with her own emotions and fears while wondering who in her father's employ would dare to gossip about his daughter. Because she knew every damned one of them would. It was the reason why her father employed them.

How better to stay below suspicion where the wrong men were concerned than by employing the worst gossips in the county? Men and women who knew or worked with the very men that Ethan Cooper and his bouncers watched on a nightly basis.

"So when did all this begin?" Sarah propped her cheek in her hand as she stared back at Sheila. "Come on. Give deets. Ethan so refuses to allow me to take an interest in his bouncers' buff bodies."

Sheila winced as the bouncer behind the bar, Morgan, stared at his boss's wife in amazement. He was only seconds from blushing, and Sheila had a feeling he rarely, if ever, blushed.

"I'm not giving you deets, Sarah," Sheila informed her, well aware of the fact that the other woman would be horrified if she did attempt to do so.

Sarah pretended to pout before giving Sheila a subtle wink and turning to Morgan once more. "Perhaps Morgan will satisfy our curiosity then."

Morgan lifted his gaze from where he was cleaning a whisky

glass and stared back at Sarah with an expression of baffled concern. And for the smallest second, Sheila could have sworn she saw something more there.

Did Ethan Cooper's new bouncer have a crush on Mrs. Cooper?

"Curiosity regarding what?" Morgan asked warily.

Sheila almost laughed. That wasn't concern. Morgan was bordering on fear. It was one of those rare times anything managed to bother him.

He was saved at the last second, though, as Casey and Cooper stepped from the office. Cooper took one look at Morgan's face, then at Sarah's, and shook his head with a chuckle.

"Is she causing trouble, Morgan?" Cooper drawled with an edge of laughter.

Morgan grunted. "She's dangerous, Coop. You should lock her up for our safety."

Sarah smiled back at him sweetly, but Sheila was aware that the other woman had noticed where Casey stopped. And she was very, very curious indeed.

Because Casey had stopped right behind Sheila.

Then his arms slid around her and a small kiss was pressed to the top of her head.

"Evening, sweetheart," he drawled. "Are you having fun out here with Sarah?"

She barely managed to hide her shock at the public display of possession. She had never, ever known Nick Casey to show such attachment to any other woman. Neither in public nor a hint of it having been shown in private.

"Observing Sarah is always fun," she assured him as she fought to ignore both Sarah and Cooper's curiosity.

"I live to entertain," Sarah sighed, her dimples peeking out again.

"Then you will live a very long, happy life," Sheila informed the other woman as she held back her own laugh.

It was hard to pay attention to the conversation, though, as Casey stood behind her. His hands rested low on her stomach; placed flat, they drew her closer to him, holding her firmly as her back pressed against his torso.

She could feel the strength and the warmth of him, as well as the sensuality that seemed to wrap around her. Against the small of her back she could feel the jutting arousal contained by his jeans, and in his hands, the firm strength that anchored her to him.

She had never felt that before with Casey. As though he were trying to seduce her with more than the pleasure he gave her body.

"Oh yes, Sheila—Cooper and I received our invitations to your father's barbecue this month. I can't wait. I hear the Rutledge party is the event of the year," Sarah stated happily as a glimmer of excitement filled her vivacious blue eyes.

And Sheila felt a twinge of remorse that she had been unaware Sarah had lived in the county for more than a year before Ethan had finally claimed her. Everyone in the county was invited to the Rutledge barbecue. Catered, rousing, and filled with food and laughter, the yearly party was Douglas Rutledge's way of giving back to the community his wife had loved.

It had been their hometown, but it had been Eleanor Rutledge who had wanted to come home when Douglas retired. She had died six months of a heart attack before that retirement.

"Well, it's an event, anyway," Sheila agreed, her smile almost shaking as she felt Casey settle his chin at her shoulder.

"Do you have a partner for the Rutledge party yet?" he murmured at her ear. "Or the ball?"

Sheila swallowed tightly.

The barbecue was her mother's dream, but the ball a week later was the captain's baby. Inviting officers of all the military branches as well as political and private sector law enforcement officials. The ball was the captain's excuse to be more than the stern, supposedly disillusioned army captain whose friends were generals, admirals, and senators.

It was also his chance to revel, even if privately, in the fact that the job he had accepted while in his prime, the one that had required he remain a captain rather than advancing, was succeeding.

The position of head of the National Covert Information Network.

"I don't have a date yet," she answered quietly. She had never had a date for her father's balls unless she did the inviting. She had stopped doing the inviting the summer she turned nineteen. And she'd gone alone ever since.

"You do now," Casey informed her as her eyes narrowed on him in the mirror behind the bar.

He stared back at her, his gaze heavy-lidded, his expression reminding her of the night he had taken her on the bar. That memory was seriously messing with her ability to stay angry with him.

"Do I really?" she murmured, aware of the fact that Sarah, Ethan, and Morgan were attempting to carry on another conversation despite their rabid curiosity.

"What do you think?" The look in his eyes dared her to refuse.

"I think I don't recall giving the invitation," she replied smoothly, careful to keep her voice low.

Casey smiled, his lips curving with cool warning.

"I don't wait on an invitation," he informed her, his tone warning now. "I was informing you, Sheila. You have a date. Period."

Oh, now that just wasn't going to do.

Sheila turned to him slowly.

"Choose your fights, sweetheart." If she wasn't mistaken, there was a sudden edge of anticipation in his voice. "And choose them wisely."

Her mother had warned her of that once as well. She'd told her that one day she would come across a man who didn't give a damn who her father was, or how strong she had become. He would sweep into her life and leave her heart, her mind, in disarray.

"Choose your fights, sweetheart, and choose them wisely," Eleanor had warned her. *"Otherwise, you'll destroy yourself, as well as him, fighting against him."*

But her mother hadn't known Nick Casey.

She was almost anticipating a fight with him, as much as he seemed to be anticipating one with her.

She could see it in his eyes, hear it in his voice.

Hell, she could feel it radiating in the sexual intensity that suddenly seemed to consume them both.

"They need to get a room," Cooper grunted behind Sheila.

"You are becoming such a fuddy-duddy," Sarah laughed. "Tell him, Morgan, he's becoming a prude. Nothing like the wild man I married."

Morgan was turning away as she spoke, his expression somber as he poured drinks, his eyes downcast.

"Sarah, sweetheart, you're too nosy," Casey warned her as he laughed back at her, though he didn't release Sheila, and it seemed he had no intentions of doing so.

"And you are being way too intense, Casey." Sarah shook her head.

"And this conversation is beginning to bore me," Sheila informed them all, though the look she shot Sarah was filled with an apology.

She wasn't bored, but she could definitely feel the fear beginning to travel up her spine.

Not a fear of harm. Or at least, not a fear of personal harm.

A fear of having her heart broken was another matter entirely.

"Bore you?" Casey growled. "I rather doubt it."

"Dance with me or shut the hell up, Casey," she finally demanded in exasperation. "If you're going to stand around holding on to me like a damned junkyard dog, then the least you could do is make it worth my while."

It was her mother's advice to choose her battles wisely that rang through her head as Casey led her to the dance floor. A slow, sensual beat began to fill the air, drawing couples to the floor and heating the building with the power of human lust.

At least, that was what she tried to tell herself as she felt Casey's arms wrap around her and allowed him to draw her to him. Possessively.

"What is with you and the ball-and-chain attitude?" she asked, genuinely bemused with the way he was acting.

"Trying to become a ball and chain?" he asked.

She almost stopped in the middle of the dance floor.

"Are you proposing, Casey?" She could feel her heart beginning to race in her throat. "Because if you are, then this is a lousy way to go about it."

He snorted back at her, pulling her closer once again as he bent his head against hers and swayed to the lazy, sexually charged music filling the building.

"You'll know when I'm proposing, Sheila. There will be no question about it."

Son of a bitch.

Casey was cursing silently with every four-letter word he could come up with and a few he knew were illegal in several parts of the world. Probably in the States as well.

Yeah, it was sort of a proposal.

Casey was a man who accepted what he knew he didn't have a chance in hell of changing. And the feelings for Sheila burning inside him weren't going to change.

Fidelity being the key. In the months he had been slipping in and out of her bed, not even once had he found another woman attractive. It purely, simply sucked, though, that she seemed to think he was so horrible at the whole proposal thing.

What did he have to do, anyway? Get on one knee?

He scowled back at Cooper as they swayed around the floor. This had to be his fault. That big lug had gone down on his knee to Sarah and presented her with a diamond the size of a tennis ball.

Okay, so maybe it had been slightly smaller, but that had to be where she had come up with these ideas. Sarah had to have told her.

"You're acting strange, Casey," Sheila informed him. "Like a man making a claim, and I'm not some pretty doll you can claim and expect me to fall into line with it."

"Darlin', I wouldn't expect you to fall into line with anything. We'll just keep on keepin' on till you see things my way, is all. I didn't say I expected you to agree with me overnight."

"Until I see things your way, huh?" He could hear the amusement in her tone, along with a rather vague confusion. As though she weren't entirely certain how to deal with him.

That was a good thing. Keeping Sheila off balance was always a damned good thing if a man could manage it.

"Yep," he agreed, hiding his smile in her hair. "We'll get along better that way, you'll see."

"You know, I can't decide if you're truly insane, or if you're just trying to make me crazy."

And if it were the latter, he wondered, was it working?

Of course, it could be the former as well, because God knew she had managed to turn his life upside down.

"Does it matter which?" he asked softly against her ear, feeling that little shiver of response as it raced down her back. "Tell me you really want me out of your life, Sheila. Go ahead, lie to me and I'll walk away."

Could he walk away? He didn't think it was possible. Not as long as he could feel her body heating for his, as long as he could feel that response for him in her kiss.

"No, you wouldn't, Casey," she denied as he finally felt her softening in his arms. "You'd just try to find another way to convince me."

Hell, she knew him too well.

He hadn't expected that.

"Why don't you just tell me what you want from me, Casey."

They both came to a stop as the music faded away.

His head lifted as she turned her gaze up to him, those deep violet eyes nearly drowning him in the knowledge, the sadness that filled them.

"Tell you what?" he asked her softly. "How much I want you? How hard you make me? Hell, Sheila, you already know all that."

She shook her head softly. "No, Casey. Why don't you just go ahead and tell me what you want from me, or from my father. Don't you know I still want you so desperately that I'd probably give it to you, or convince Dad to do it? You don't have to play these games with me. You never did have to play these games with me."

You never leave a lady standing on the dance floor.

Never curse a lady.

A lady was a lady even when she wasn't behaving like a lady.

Never embarrass a lady in front of friends and coworkers. Especially if she holds a position of power.

Those lessons had been drummed into him as a child before his parents' deaths.

He could remember lazy summer mornings as a young boy spent fishing on the banks of the river that eventually killed his parents and listening to the amusing assortment of rules his father had attempted to teach him where women were concerned.

Those lessons came in handy now.

He allowed his fingers to deliberately curl around her upper arm as he led her from the floor and back to the bar. He should have left her at the bar. Hell, he should have parked her right at the bar with Sarah and Cooper and left himself.

Hanging around was the worst thing he could have done. And allowing himself this confrontation with Sheila was sure a real bad decision.

He just couldn't seem to help himself.

Anger, resentment, and pure male pride had him by the throat while lust still had him by the balls.

It was a hell of a combination.

And even as he pulled her past a watchful Morgan and shouldered open the swinging door that led to the kitchen and offices, he knew he was making a damned mistake.

It might even be the biggest mistake of his life.

chapter 6

this was what she got for being honest, Sheila thought as she allowed Casey to pull her into one of the small offices. This was what she got for trying to lay to rest the doubts that filled her own mind, and to get whatever relationship they had on an equal footing.

He was pissed.

She could feel that anger vibrating through his body and threatening his control.

She didn't know whether to be frightened or turned on, because she had never seen Casey like this. She had never seen him so angry that his eyes glowed like burning chocolate, backlit with a tobacco flame.

She had a glimpse of those eyes as he swung her around at the desk, placed his hands on both sides of her, and leaned into her until they were nose to nose.

"Do I look like a fucking man whore to you?" he snarled into her face, causing her to flinch with the rage in his voice. "Do I look like someone who would fuck a woman to gain anything other than both their damned pleasure?"

His words seemed to pierce a part of her that instantly latched on to the end of his statement.

"Their pleasure," he said. As though it was a lover's pleasure and satisfaction that caused his own.

"Casey, I never meant—" She hadn't meant it to sound that way. But the rest of the words were cut off.

"The fucking hell you didn't." His nose was touching hers.

His eyes were so dark they were nearly black, body heat pouring from him in waves as rage seemed to burn through his system. "That's exactly what you meant, Sheila. Was I a fucking man whore willing to climb between your legs for a favor from you where your damned father is concerned? Do you want to know what I think of any favors your father could fucking give me? Do you, Sheila?" he all but yelled in her face.

"Not really." Weak, more submissive than she liked, her voice trembled as her gaze held his.

Not in fear, but in a variety of other emotions. Emotions she wasn't certain she knew how to adapt to.

She only wished her response to this new, volcanic Casey was fear. Fear would have been easier to handle. It would have been far easier to understand than the other emotions she felt.

Especially the lust. The hunger.

The angrier he became, the more she wanted him.

She could feel her nipples hardening and tightening, growing more sensitive by the second as he glared into her eyes.

"Not really?" he snarled back at her. "Maybe I want to tell you anyway. Just for the fucking hell of it."

"If you feel you have to." She shrugged, almost catching her breath at the feel of her nipples raking against the material of her bra.

And she wasn't the only one who felt the lust. Amid his anger, that hunger was there as well. The feel of his erection pressing wide and hard against her belly assured her of that. He wanted her just as fiercely as he wanted to rage at her.

"Then tell me, Casey," she retorted, albeit breathlessly.

Her clit was aching with a swollen intensity she didn't know if she could bear much longer. In turn, she could feel the clench and flushed arousal tightening her pussy as well as the heated, slick warmth easing through it.

Had she ever been this aroused by him?

She was certain she had never been this aroused in her life. For him or any other man. For anything or at any time.

His eyes were still blazing with fury, his expression twisted with it when she lifted her leg and let it slide up the outside of his.

The silk of her skirt slid back along her thighs, the rasp of his jeans against her sensitive inner thigh had her breath catching.

His gaze jerked down, locked on the pale flesh as her skirt slid back.

When his eyes came back to her, that rage was diluted, the smallest bit, with another fire. One of hunger and of lust.

"There's not nothing, not a single friggin' thing your father has that I want with the exception of his stubborn, wayward, completely intractable daughter."

"Completely intractable?" Her hands pushed beneath the soft cotton of his shirt and touched the iron-hard abs beneath.

With just her nails, she stroked up his abdomen, being certain to find the flat, hard points of his male nipples.

His fingers wrapped immediately around her wrists, holding her in place.

"What the hell are you up to?"

Had she ever made the first move when it came to their sexual encounters? Casey knew she hadn't. She'd always left that first step to him.

Until tonight.

Until this confrontation.

And now, she was simply hotter than hell. Hot enough to burn through his senses and make him almost, almost, forget the anger surging through him.

It was his pride. That sheer male core of the man that she had stabbed that dagger into. To dare to suggest that he wanted more than the woman he was holding in his arms was more than he could countenance.

How could anything she or her father possessed or had access to be more important?

"I could get up to many things," she whispered. "But at the moment, I'm more interested in what you're up to."

Her hips tilted upward, causing her lower stomach to press and rub against the erection barely contained by his jeans.

Releasing her wrists he allowed one hand to slide along her arm until he reached her underarm. From there, his hand skimmed down her side, to her lifted leg. Curving his fingers beneath her thigh, he reached around until he could rub the silk of her panties against her sensitive pussy.

There, he found her hot and wet, the juices of her pussy dampening her panties as he rubbed against the sensitive bare lips beneath the material.

Her head tilted back. Dark, violet eyes became drowsy, heavy-lidded as her hand smoothed back down his abs to the heavy arousal beneath his jeans.

"You make me want to bite nails." His tone was between a growl and a hungry groan. A sound he had never made before with a woman he couldn't stop wanting, no matter how often he had her.

"Is that what you want to do?" she asked softly, her fingers curving around the hard shaft pounding beneath them.

"That, among other things." Narrowing his eyes, he watched her closely, wondering how far she would go.

It was the first time she had made the first move; was she willing to continue that path? At least, for as long as he could allow it.

He was all for Sheila making her mark on him. Hell, there were nights he dreamed of it, fantasized about it.

Then, her hand slid away as disappointment began to tighten his body. But only as long as it took for him to realize those slender, delicate hands were gripping the hem of her camisole top and slowly easing it upward until she drew it over her head.

His breath caught, then he completely lost the ability to breathe as the sheer lace of her bra revealed the spiked, dark pink of her nipples as they begged so prettily for attention.

They were pert and eager for his touch, and he couldn't resist lifting his hands and framing the generous mounds that cushioned the candied perfection.

Raking his thumbs over them, he watched as her breathing roughened, a flush rushed across her face, and the drowsy sensuality in her expression increased.

Busy, industrious, and determined, her fingers hadn't forgotten their task, either.

They loosened his belt, sliding one end free of the other before they moved to each of the metal buttons. They slipped free easily, the heavy denim parting to reveal the engorged, iron-hard length of his cock.

His teeth clenched as her fingers, cool and slender, inquisitive and filled with eager pleasure, wrapped partially around the shaft and began to caress it.

"Fuck. Sheila, love, I don't know if I can stand this for long."

"Ah, poor baby," she whispered as his lips moved over hers, then brushed over them.

"I bet you think this is all the courage I have in me, too." She was laughing. Casey could hear the amusement in her voice and it only spurred his determination that tonight, in this office, he would damned well own her when they were finished.

He was sick of this damned cat-and-mouse game they kept playing. Sick of chasing after her, knowing damned good and well she wanted him clear to her soul, and yet she still refused to admit it.

"You belong to me." It was a warning, and one he hoped she took seriously.

But as he made the claim, he made certain she couldn't fight against it too hard.

As the words slipped from his lips, he slid two fingers past the elastic leg of her panties and speared into the slick, heated depths of her pussy.

A cry tore from her lips as her back arched and her head fell back weakly.

Pleasure suffused her expression, tightened her nipples further, and sent a rush of juices flowing over his fingers.

Soft, slick; he knew the taste of it, and ached for it.

He could spread her out, right there on his desk, and taste her as he craved.

But Sheila had other plans.

Surprise raced through him once again as one small hand speared into his hair, her fingers gripping the strands and pulling until his lips met hers.

And there, control became only a distant memory.

He had heard kisses described as many great and varied things over the years, but no description could come close to the sweet nectar and sensual spice that filled his senses as her lips parted beneath his.

As though starving for feminine touch, addicted and hopelessly lost to it, Casey felt his senses focus on it entirely. Her kiss, her tongue stroking back against his as he devoured her.

She devoured him in return.

The fingers of one hand tightened even more in his hair as the other stroked and caressed the violently sensitive head of his dick. He could feel himself beginning to break apart for her. His balls were tightening, the head of his cock thickening further, throbbing in an impending release when she suddenly stopped.

His head jerked back, his eyes opening, lips parting to demand an explanation when his gaze moved down again and he watched those lush, hungry lips descend to his stomach.

Like silk against roughened iron, her lips parted, and her

tongue licked out to allow herself a taste. Running down the tightening muscles, Casey could only watch, suspended in disbelief at the incredibly erotic sight of Sheila going down on him.

Without urging, without that desperation on his part, or that first moment of shyness or uncertainty on hers, she was taking what she considered hers.

Her lips covered the broad, engorged head of his cock. Curious and destructive, her tongue licked over it, learning his dick as though it were the first time for her and she wanted nothing more than to experience each sensation, each stroke of pleasure.

She was taking every part of him and loving every damned minute of it.

The furiously pounding crest was tucked against the roof of her mouth, her tongue moving against that sensitive spot just beneath the head.

A moan of feminine pleasure vibrated against the hard crest as heat began to burn his already overloaded senses. Delicate fingers moved between his thighs as one hand tugged at his jeans. He helped her push the denim down his legs, so fucking eager for her touch he would have torn them off if he needed to.

Anything to feel her palming the tight, tortured sack of his balls as his thighs tightened with the need to come. He could feel his seed beginning to heat, to boil through his system. There was no way to hold it back. There was no way to hold on to his control.

His fingers tightened in her hair, his attempt to pull her back impossible to complete. He was holding her to him instead. Staring down, watching as he fucked her swollen lips and watching her eyes darken with anticipation.

Her cheeks hollowed. Her mouth worked him with burning sensuality.

Ah God. Not yet. If he came now there wasn't a chance in hell he'd have the control to touch and taste her as well. To drive her as insane, make her as desperate for him as he was becoming for her.

And there was only one way to stop her. Only one way to ensure that his satisfaction wasn't the only one attained.

A second before it was too late, just as his balls gave that final
convulsive squeeze and sent his release spurting between her lips,
Casey pulled back.

In a single move he had his dick out of her mouth, bent, gripped
her arms, and pulled her to her feet before laying her back on the
desk.

The soft material of the skirt fell back along her thighs as he
pushed his hands beneath, gripped the elastic of her panties, and
tore them from her slender body.

In the next heartbeat, he had his head buried between her legs,
his lips circling her clit, his tongue tasting the soft spice and feminine pleasure that welled from her.

There was no time for seduction, no control left to tease. There
was only the hunger for her and the need to taste her sweet release spilling to his lips.

He should have been used to it by now, he thought. The taste of
her, the heat of her. The incredible pleasure that whipped through
his body at the knowledge that she was losing herself in the intensity and in the sensations just as he was losing himself in the giving of them.

Pushing his tongue deep inside the tight depths of her pussy
as her fingers moved to his hair, Casey licked and probed at the
sweetness. Fucking her with his tongue, his body clenching, need
raging inside him as she writhed beneath him.

Sheila fought to breathe through the wild, chaotic pleasure beginning to zip through her.

She couldn't help clenching her thighs, her legs lifting, gripping
his shoulders as a cry escaped her lips. She couldn't fight against
it. She didn't want to fight against it. She just wanted to feel him
against her, over every inch of her body.

Inside her—

A harsh, unbidden moan passed her lips as his tongue thrust

inside the clenched, snug depths of her pussy again. The rasp of his tongue against the sensitive nerve endings sent her spiraling closer to release. Spasms of sensation shot to her womb, drawing it tight as she arched and felt the warning tremors of her orgasm as they began to vibrate inside her.

So close. She was so close to coming, the need for it pounded painfully in her clit and the tormented depths of her pussy.

She was burning out of control.

Her hands clenched in his hair to hold him closer. Her hips lifted further, desperate to force his tongue deeper inside her. To increase the strokes, to make him fuck her deeper, to give her that last teasing thrust that would propel her over the edge.

And she was so close. So very close . . . when he pulled back.

chapter 7

"casey, don't stop." Sheila reached desperately for him, confused, aching with a sensual hunger that went so deep she knew it went far beyond the physical.

"I want to feel you coming on my dick, not my tongue," he groaned, as he gripped the heavy shaft and tucked it between the swollen folds of her sex.

Flames, sharp and intense, shot through her pussy, then the rest of her body as the electrical sensations continued to build between them.

Gripping her hips with his hands, his gaze locked with hers, Casey began to move, slowly at first, stretching her, working his way inside her. The heated burn of the penetration had her gasping, fighting for breath as pleasure began to build inside her with a strength she hadn't experienced with Casey so far.

It was always better than the time before.

It was always hotter.

"Good, baby?" he asked, his voice strained, the muscles standing out in his neck with his obvious fight to hold back his release.

"Oh God, Casey, it's so good," she whispered. "You know it's always so good."

"Like being wrapped in pleasure, Sheila," he agreed. "You wrap more than my dick in pleasure, baby."

Every muscle in her body seemed to clench and spasm at the explicit pleasure his words sent tearing through her body.

He pushed in deeper, an inch at a time, wedging between the tightening muscles of her clenched sex as his hips worked slow and easy, his muscles tense and powerfully restrained.

It was all she could do to keep her eyes open. Sensuality and building ecstasy had her fighting to stare up at him, to watch his expression.

At times like this, she could glimpse emotion on his face. She wasn't always certain what that emotion was, but it was there, and it fascinated her.

Just glimpses, just small hints of the emotions he might feel. Emotions she craved, feelings she needed so desperately to know he felt.

"Casey," she moaned as his cock slid into her pussy to the hilt. It sent fire raging through every cell of her body. It had her flying through sensations she didn't know how to describe or how to handle.

"Tell me, baby." Leaning closer, his head lowered, his lips moving to her neck, to her ear. "Tell me, Sheila. Do you love it? Do you love feeling me inside you? Fucking you until we both feel as though we're going to die?"

"I love it." She loved him. "It's so good, Casey." It was so past good. It was incredible.

It was flying without wings.

Moving beneath him, hips rising and writhing, grinding against his pelvis as his cock sank deep inside her, Sheila let that pleasure— let the man—have her in ways she never had before.

She was barely able to hold her eyes open, but she did, to hold his gaze. To stare into the swirls of emotion that filled them. To become ensnared in him as the heavy strokes began to quicken, lengthen.

Ecstasy began to build, to tighten and stimulate until Sheila couldn't hold back the moans and pleasure-filled cries that rose in her throat.

She couldn't bear the sharpened pleasure much longer, she knew. She couldn't get close enough to him. She couldn't move fast enough, he wasn't moving hard enough.

"Casey, please," she cried out as her legs wrapped around his hips, her arms tightening around his neck.

She had to come soon. She couldn't bear this much sensation much longer. She couldn't survive the pleasure, the building pressure that swelled the muscles of her pussy, clenching it, tightening it as Casey fucked her with ever faster strokes.

Their moans filled the air. Her nails dug into his shoulders as his teeth rasped over a torturously hard nipple. That additional stimulation sent her exploding, careening as ecstasy detonated inside her with a force that obliterated reality.

She felt the rush of her juices as Casey buried himself deep inside her. The heavy, fierce spurts of his cum filling her destroyed her senses.

The fierce throb and jetting heat amplified her ecstasy, throwing her higher, racing through her system and increasing the rapturous surges of intensity that exploded over and over and rushed through her body.

Shaking, trembling, she could only lie beneath him shuddering as Casey came above her, their bodies locked in pleasure, and in something she knew went far beyond the physical.

In a blinding second of insight, Sheila knew she had finally fallen irrevocably and totally in love.

She loved Casey in ways she had never loved when she was younger. She loved him past her heart, and into her soul. And she loved him with a power she knew she would never escape.

And she knew that as of yet, there hadn't been so much as a

hint that Casey cared more for her than for any other woman he'd taken as a lover.

She could very well be lost in this maze of emotions alone. And being there alone was a very frightening thought.

chapter 8

there was a small bathroom and shower to the side of the office that they used. The pelting water cascaded over them, washing away the perspiration that had accumulated along their bodies.

They shared the shower. Casey's larger body should have made the small space seem cramped; instead, there was a distinct feeling of comfort—perhaps protection—that Sheila welcomed.

But she was damned if she knew how *he* felt.

The past few days without him hadn't been her best, either. For some reason, she'd been more on edge than usual, nervous, almost panicky each night as she drove home from the bar with the flash drive of information collected the night before tucked in her boot.

It had never bothered her before if she saw headlights in her rearview mirror, but the last few days—it bothered her.

And it shouldn't. Other than the fact that it seemed to be happening too frequently, and those lights seemed to be the same ones nightly.

"You look worried." Rubbing a towel over his hair to get the last of the water from it, Casey watched her questioningly, his head tilted to the side as Sheila pulled her clothes back on.

She gave a quick shake of her head. "You worry me."

Pulling her shirt over her head and adjusting it over the hem of the soft skirt she had worn that night, she glanced back at Casey.

"And why do I worry you?" Tossing the towel to the counter, he turned, braced his very nicely rounded, towel-wrapped rear against the counter, and crossed his arms over his broad chest as he regarded her.

"You never do what I expect, I guess." She shrugged. "I wouldn't have expected sex in exchange for your anger earlier."

He scowled, a darkened lowering of his brows as his gaze narrowed on her. "Reminding me of that accusation you made isn't a good idea, sweetheart. We don't want to revisit that place just after we made each other feel so good."

Pushing away from the counter and dropping the towel, Casey reached for his clothing and began dressing.

Sheila watched for a moment before forcing herself to draw her gaze back from the definite eye candy he represented.

Damn, this was her problem when it came to Casey. He was simply luscious. Even the scars along his lower back and left leg didn't detract from the bronzed flesh that covered iron-hard muscles.

That always got her in trouble. Whenever she allowed herself to be distracted by that incredible body, she seemed to lose her mind, her control, and her common sense. And now, she'd gone and lost her heart.

Not a good thing.

"Of course, not a good place to revisit," she agreed softly as she turned away and headed back to the bedroom.

"Tell me, Sheila." He followed her, of course. "Why the hell do you keep fighting this relationship every step of the way? Aren't you afraid I'm going to get tired of chasing you?"

She turned to see him behind her, his hands on his hips, just above the waistband of his low-riding jeans.

Honesty. It had gotten her in trouble earlier. It wasn't going to help her now either.

"Because," she finally answered. "I haven't figured out why you want a relationship with me, Casey. Perhaps when you tell me why, I'll stop fighting it."

Hope began to fill her. She could feel it, no matter how hard she tried to fight it back. Could there be more to the sex than he was letting on? Was there more there than just a game he could be playing?

She'd heard multiple times how Casey liked to play with his lovers. He'd laugh, push them, tease them, insist on drawing them out when they wanted to remain secretive or hidden.

It was one of his gifts to his lovers. But it was a curse once he left.

"The obvious answer isn't reason enough?"

Sheila stared back at Casey silently for long moments as she tried to figure that one out.

There was an obvious answer?

She bit her lower lip, trying to figure it out. Because she knew Casey—if she asked, just out-and-out asked what that answer was, then there wasn't a chance in hell he was going to tell her.

He would turn it into a puzzle and into a game and he would make her completely insane with it. She didn't need that. Her heart had enough weight on it already.

She cared for her father.

She helped him.

She covered for him.

She scheduled for him.

She carried information for him.

And she had given up her own dreams of love the day she had learned that she was no more than a conduit to her father.

It wasn't Captain Rutledge's fault. It was her own.

But now, it was backfiring on her.

"There's an obvious answer, Casey?" She finally asked the one question she knew he wouldn't answer.

She wondered what game he would turn it into now.

"Why yes, there is, and if you haven't figured it out yet, then perhaps there's nothing left for us to talk about."

There was no anger in his tone, there was no anger in his expression or in his eyes. There was something that went beyond anger and sent her stomach clenching with dread.

"What do you mean by that?" she asked cautiously.

"When you figure out the obvious answer, Sheila, let me know," he told her with that icy calm that had come over him. "Until then, I'm tired of trying to move the mountain and I'm sure as hell tired of chasing after a woman who doesn't want me." He headed for the door. "I'm sure you can see your way out."

"I knew you would turn this into a game," she cried out as his fingers curled around the doorknob. "I know a trick question when I hear one, Casey. Is this how you break it off with all your women once you're tired of the pity fucks and the lessons in life?"

He stopped.

For a moment, Sheila wondered if perhaps she had gone too far. She had definitely exaggerated slightly, but it was *just* slightly.

Casey had a tendency to take lovers who needed to awaken, whether they wanted to or not.

"No, Sheila, I just thought this time, I'd found a woman who didn't need to be dragged kicking and screaming into life." He turned back and glanced at her for just a second. A very short, very disappointed second. "I guess I was wrong."

He opened the door and walked straight out of the room. The door closed behind him, an almost silent click that for some odd reason had Sheila flinching involuntarily.

She felt her stomach drop, then clench. Tears sprang to her eyes and she didn't understand why. She couldn't explain the dampness or the sense of agony that tore through her.

Her father had told her once, well, really, he'd told her several times that her habit of honesty was going to end up hurting her more than she was going to be able to heal.

That might have just happened, and she couldn't explain to herself why it had. All she wanted was the truth. She just wanted to know if there was a chance that he loved her. That he could love her.

Pulling her boots, on, she pushed her toes forward as she jerked the expensive leather over first one foot, then the other.

She felt the heel that contained the flash drive she had collected earlier that night. Before she had danced with Casey. Before she had asked him what he wanted from her and before she had experienced the most incredible sex of her life.

What had she done?

Shaking her head at the frustration caused by that question, Sheila moved slowly to the door and left the room as well. Rather than leaving by the public exit, Sheila moved through the dimly lit hallway to the door in the back.

Pressing the code to the back door, Sheila slipped from the building and made her way to her car. She hit the remote to unlock it and managed to get inside before the first tear fell.

How had this happened?

Call him when she figured out the obvious answer as to why he wanted a relationship with her?

What was the obvious answer?

Laying her head against the steering wheel, she let the tears fall, though she tried to hold back the sobs.

There was no obvious answer. Casey wasn't a man who held a whole lot back in that way. He threw himself into whatever endeavor he took on. Whether he was laughing, drinking, fighting, or fucking, he gave it everything he had. If the obvious answer was "love," he would have never allowed her to push him away. He would have never left the words unsaid between them.

He would have told her he loved her. Wouldn't he?

A sob shook her shoulders, surprising her. The sound had her jerking her head up, wiping the tears away, and fighting back fresh ones.

Crying didn't help, she told herself. Feeling sorry for herself sure as hell wasn't going to improve the situation.

Pushing the key into the ignition, she started her car and pulled out of the parking space. She didn't know if she could bear coming in night after night now, without Casey's touch, without his determined seduction.

How was she supposed to live without it now? How was she supposed to live without him?

Nick Casey's woman left the parking lot, but it had taken her awhile to get going. And there was the suspicion she had been crying in her car.

What had Casey done to make her cry?

If Nick Casey was truly Beauregard Fredrico, then it could be any number of things. He wasn't likely to break a tender heart, or to throw away a precious female he had seduced so effectively.

He had been much sought after in Italy before the Fredrico empire had crumbled.

Beauregard Fredrico, so handsome, so charming, and so disapproving of the families and the rules that had sustained them for so many generations.

Making his woman cry wouldn't change how he felt about her, though. And Nick Casey, despite the gossip that he cared for no woman, treated this woman far differently than any other he had taken to his bed.

Yes, there was love here, and that was surprising. He wasn't known for allowing his heart to become so involved with a woman. And neither was Beauregard Fredrico. Yet, all men loved eventually, didn't they?

And this man's heart was well and truly involved with his woman. It was proven by the fact that he stood in the shadows watching as she left, his expression heavy—was that sadness lining it as well?

It seemed this man felt much more for this woman than even he was comfortable with. How surprising. Judging by the look on his face, perhaps he and the woman had argued. Or was there a split? Because that was grief twisting his expression, and anger. Casey was not happy with his woman, or with himself. Perhaps some help was needed to draw them back together. After all, when a man and a woman loved so fiercely, such separation should not be allowed. Nothing short of, well, death, should keep them apart.

Unfortunately, despite the subtle moves that had been made to frighten his woman, Casey still appeared unconcerned, and had not made the phone call that would bring in reinforcements for only one man. Beauregard had an army at his disposal. He had only to make a single call to cash in on the vows made to him.

And yet, he had not made that call. Perhaps he needed to be convinced.

With a deft turn of the wrist, the ignition of the four-by-four pickup sprang to life.

Pulling out of the shadowed parking spot and following Miss Rutledge took only seconds. Options began to come into focus and play out. Beau wasn't getting a clue. He hadn't yet realized his woman was in danger. A danger Beau couldn't resolve on his own, and there was no chance he would tell the men he worked with about his past.

That past was too rife with blood, the sins of a family, and the choices Beau himself had made, which hadn't been exactly wise. No, his friends wouldn't know who he was, or what he had been. And he would trust only one person to protect the woman who could be endangered because of that past.

A few changes would have to be made to force that call, unfortunately. Actually striking out at Casey's woman would have to be the next move.

With that move, the danger of actually harming her was increased. And it was a danger that would have to be faced. Faced and accepted. It was one that preference would have dictated unnecessary; unfortunately preference wasn't an option any longer.

Beauregard Fredrico couldn't be allowed to escape so easily.

He had to pay.

And, just as in the past, a woman would have to pay for his crimes. Hopefully, this Nick Casey was the identity Beau had chosen. It meant no other woman would have to be endangered.

With any luck, it would end very soon.

chapter 9

one week later

sheila stood at the large picture window in the center wall of her father's office and stared out at the tall, evergreen border of trees that separated her small bungalow-style house from her father's front flower gardens.

Her mother had planted those flowers. Hundreds upon hundreds of perennials that filled the exquisite English garden her mother had created several years before her death. A garden her father worked in daily to keep it in the same pristine condition her mother had so enjoyed. Just as he kept the maid busy creating the dozens of flower arrangements that filled the house.

Cutting through the immaculate acre of fragrant blooms was a stone path that led from the evergreen wall to the side of the house. The blossoms waved in the breeze, their soft fragrance wafting through the heated Texas air and filling the office through the AC unit positioned outside.

Her father had tinkered with that unit for years to allow the fragrance from the air outside to fill the office. The office was the bedroom her mother had been confined to in the year before she had died. That bouquet from the flower gardens she worked so hard on had been her father's last gift to the woman he had loved.

The gardens had once been a source of comfort, but now, Sheila watched them with a frown, wondering if they could hold something more sinister than the precious memories she'd always had of them.

Memories of working with her mother to plant the fragrant blooms. Memories of gathering the ones her father had used to create the arrangement atop her mother's casket.

And with those memories was the one created last night. The one where she had slipped along that stone path, a feeling of trepidation breathing at her neck as panic had tightened her chest.

Someone had been in her house.

Crossing her arms over her breasts, Sheila closed her eyes and fought to control the fear.

Who would have dared to break into her home? And even if they had dared, how had they managed to break the locks her father had had installed on both the front and back doors?

She couldn't think of anyone but Casey who could do such a thing; he was simply extraordinarily well-trained in such things.

"Sheila, dammit, I can't find my glasses."

Sheila nearly jumped out of her own skin.

A squeak slipped past her lips as she jerked and turned around, facing her father breathlessly, her heart nearly choking her as it pounded out of control.

Her father paused, a scowl tightening his expression. "Are you okay, dear?"

For a moment, Sheila considered telling him about her suspicion of a break-in.

He would lose his mind, though. Protective, overly so, and filled with fatherly concern, Douglas Rutledge would put one of his guards on her twenty-four/seven and she'd never have a moment's peace.

Which wouldn't be so bad if someone had definitely broken into the house. The problem was, she just couldn't be sure. She hated worrying her father without some sort of proof, or at least her own certainty that it had happened.

Had she really walked away from her house and left the doors unlocked? Had she been so deep into her anger and need for Casey that she could have done such a thing?

"Sheila, girl, you're not answering me." There was a hint of true concern beginning to edge into his tone.

"I'm fine, Dad, just distracted."

She had just lied to her father. Sheila almost winced at the thought. Of course, it wasn't the first time. There had been the time she had slipped out to go to that party with a college boy during her senior year. She'd told her father she was staying all night with her friend Cara Cartwright. And there had been the night a few weeks ago when her father had called and asked her at the last minute to accompany him to a dinner in Corpus Christi with the city's mayor.

Sheila had told him she wasn't feeling well. At that exact moment, Casey had been undressing.

"And what has you so distracted?" He moved into the office, obviously thoughtful as he began searching the room.

Sheila walked over to him, tapped his shoulder with a smile, and then, as he turned to her, lifted the glasses from his graying hair and handed them to him.

"Hmm." He held the glasses and glared at them accusingly before looking up and giving her a sheepish smile. "I should remember to look here, huh? Your mother was always doing the same thing. She'd find them and hand them right to me."

Sheila nodded wistfully. "I remember, Dad."

"You look just like her," he sighed. "Some days, I can almost swear she's home again as I watch you move around those gardens."

She could hear the loss in his voice. For all his full and busy life, she knew her father desperately missed the woman he had called his wife. Just as she knew that he had felt no woman would ever compare to her.

He patted her on her shoulder, a gesture of affection, before dropping a kiss to the top of her head and going to his desk.

"I had a call from Cooper earlier," he told her as he slipped his glasses back on his face, sat down, and looked up at her.

"What does he need?" Sitting on the side of the desk as she had even as a young girl, she pulled her jean-clad legs up to the top of the side of the desk, crossed them, and watched her father expectantly.

"The network is doing very well." Her father sat back in his chair as his face creased thoughtfully. "Cooper's group is one of our best, and the information he's been pulling in has been damned important."

Sheila nodded. The Broken Bar wasn't the only operational location set up to gather intel on criminal and terrorist activities, and it wasn't the only location under her father's command, but as he said, it was one of the best.

"So why did he call?" she asked.

"According to Cooper, you've been slipping in, getting the intel, and slipping back out. You're not coming in at your usual time, and you're acting nervous."

Sheila looked beyond his shoulder to the gardens outside. Rather than facing the question in her father's gaze, she avoided it.

"I've been busy."

"Yeah, that heavy social life you have," he grunted with what she called his loving sarcasm. He had a way of saying things to her that let her know he was clearly disapproving and/or disappointed. Sometimes just plain disbelieving.

In this case, perhaps it was all three.

"Yeah, my social life is just all that," she agreed with the same tone.

"Yep, it's matching Casey's if my suspicions are correct."

And there it was. Sheila had wondered how long it would take her father to say something if he was aware of the relationship. Or the non-relationship. Whatever the hell it was. Or had been.

A wave of pain swept through her as she fought to keep from dragging in a ragged breath.

God, she missed him. She missed his touch, the sound of his voice, the amusement in his gaze, and that crooked smile he often carried.

"I wouldn't know," she finally said faintly.

"Yeah, avoiding him will do that." She watched him nod from the corner of her eye as he continued to watch her. "Is it working?"

She shook her head, not bothering to lie any longer.

It wasn't working.

"How did you know?" she finally asked without meeting his gaze.

"Ah yes, how did your father find out you were sleeping with one of his agents when you were so very careful to hide it?" That disappointment was there. "I've known since the first night you didn't come home because you were at his apartment," he revealed. "I swore to your mother I'd watch out for you, Sheila. I almost messed up with Ross Mason, but I haven't messed up since."

"You didn't mess up, Daddy," she sighed as she lifted her hands and began to pick at her nails rather than letting her gaze meet her father's.

If her father saw how much it hurt, he might blame himself. She didn't want that.

"I almost messed up," he reiterated. "I almost didn't introduce Mason to the general out of pride. I knew what he wanted, what he was, but seeing how it hurt you would have broken your mother's heart. I couldn't have that, you know."

A sad smile pulled at her lips as she nodded again. That was her father's way of saying it had hurt him to see her hurt.

"I got over it, Dad," she promised him.

"Not all the way," he guessed softly. "You weren't in love with him, so you got over the man, but you didn't get over the lesson, did you, baby girl?"

"Dad—" she began to protest.

He lifted his hand, silencing her immediately. As always, she clenched her teeth, irritated with herself because that one moment could immediately remind her that if she didn't quieten, then her father could refuse to speak to her for days.

It had happened once, and only once, when she had been no more than five.

"Now, look at me."

She lifted her gaze slowly, emotion clogging her throat as she met the concern and affection in her father's eyes.

He'd been a stern disciplinarian when she had been a child, but he had been a friend after she'd passed that unruly teenage stage. He was her boss and, sometimes, her sounding board, but he was always her father.

"Daddy, I don't want to talk about Casey," she stated, her tone respectful but determined. "This is my fight, not yours."

"And why is it a fight?" he asked softly. "What is it, Sheila, that has you watching the road expecting him, and yet refusing to make that first move?"

"Because I don't know what he wants from me." Frustration filled her voice now. "He wants me to guess, or to beg, I don't know," she bit out furiously. "And I can't stand not knowing."

"Maybe he just wants you," her father suggested gently.

Sheila turned her gaze back to the flowers as she shook her head. "He wants more. He has to."

"What do you want from him?"

Her gaze swung back to him in surprise. "I just want him, Dad," she whispered. "That was all I ever wanted."

"His love?"

She nodded slowly. "Just his love."

"Maybe, Sheila, you're wrong. Maybe that really is all Casey wants from you."

Her lips parted to argue the suggestion. There had to be more. Casey had to want more. No one had ever wanted just her love, and she couldn't imagine Casey did either.

"Cooper has intel ready to come in," he told her before she could argue his opinion of Casey. "He'll be waiting on you in the office tonight at nine sharp. Don't be early, Sheila, and don't be late."

She wanted to roll her eyes at the order. Her father was a stickler for punctuality.

"And what time should I be home, Daddy?" Unfolding herself from the top of the desk, she slid from the seat until she was standing beside his chair, looking down at where he pushed his glasses back atop his head.

"Getting back isn't the problem," he told her. "Cooper and his wife Sarah are leaving town tonight and want to get on the road early. Cooper knows how I am about chain of evidence."

Anyone who worked with her father knew that. Cooper was always present if he wasn't the one to turn over the flash drive.

"I'll be there at nine sharp," she promised as she turned to leave the office.

"By the way, Annie said you were at the house looking for me last night?"

Sheila composed her expression quickly before turning back to her father with a quick smile. "I was just bored."

Or scared. One or the other.

Scared, she decided. "I'm heading home, Dad. If I'm going to be there at nine sharp, then I have some things to do before I leave."

"Of course, dear. I'll see you tomorrow." He waved her away as he turned his attention to the files on his desk. "Afternoon if you don't mind. I'll be leaving in a few hours myself for Corpus Christi. A meeting with the other network commanders."

"In the morning then," she agreed, lifting her hand in a farewell wave as she left the office and headed for the front door.

If she was going to chance seeing Casey, then she was going to do what she did every night before picking up the flash drive. Shower. Choose just the right outfit. The right perfume. The right shoes.

Just in case she saw Casey.

chapter 10

was it good luck or bad luck? Fate or karma? Whichever it was, when Sheila slipped into Ethan Cooper's office, Casey was there as well, waiting.

His arms were crossed over his broad chest, his expression stoic, his gaze swirling with dark emotion. It seemed as though his emotions reached out to her, wrapped around her. Her chest tightened and the tears she had shed only in the darkest part of the night for the past week threatened to fill her eyes as their gazes met.

"Hey, Cooper, Sarah." Shoving her hands into the pockets of the light blazer she wore over the sleeveless top, she glanced toward Casey again. Clearing her throat she said, "Hello, Casey."

"Sheila." His expression didn't change, but something in his eyes did.

Dropping her gaze for a second, she turned back to Cooper and Sarah as they watched both her and Casey silently. She could see confusion in their expressions. And she understood why they felt it. After all, the last time she and Casey had been in the same room together, it was all they could do to keep their hands off each other.

They weren't having that problem now, though.

Sheila couldn't tear her eyes off his broad chest, covered by the short-sleeved denim shirt, or the powerful cut of his thighs encased in jeans and framing the hard, heavy length of his erection.

He was aroused, and the proof of it had her womb clenching, her pussy tightening, and her juices spilling to the silk of her panties.

Perhaps she shouldn't have worn the skirt. It was short, gauzy, frilly, and intensely feminine. The camisole tank and light silk blazer she wore emphasized her feeling of femininity.

The four-inch heels only topped it off.

Sitting down in the chair next to her, Sheila slid the left shoe off, pressed the small indention at the side of the heel, and watched as the tiny spring-loaded opening slid to the side to reveal the compartment just big enough to hold the tiny flash drive.

Taking the black stick that held the information gathered the night before, she tucked it into the small recess before activating the mechanism once again, closing the small hollow.

Her gaze lifted to Casey once again. He had been the one who had come up with the idea for the hiding place. It had been a hell of a decision for her to make, to allow him to cut into several pairs of her favorite shoes.

His excuse for using more than one pair of old boots was that it would throw suspicion further away from her if she altered her dress often. Any electronics created to scan her purse or clothing would miss the tiny drive nestled just beneath her heel.

He was staring at her feet, his gaze narrowing as he lifted his eyes back to her.

She felt lost in his look.

Sarah was talking, and though Sheila heard her and answered her, nothing really existed for her except Casey. Except the pure hunger and latent anger that burned in his eyes.

"Okay, that's it then," Cooper announced as Sheila signed off on the acceptance of the small card.

She used the code name her father had assigned her, just as Cooper used his.

"Yeah, that's it," she repeated, her gaze sliding to Casey once more as she rose to her feet. "Good night, Cooper. Sarah." Her lips trembled as she glanced back at Casey again. "Good night, Casey."

He inclined his head slowly and Sheila felt as though her heart had been ripped in two.

Dragging in a hard breath, she turned and strode quickly to the door, desperate to get away from him now, to find the privacy she needed to release the tears building in her eyes.

She hadn't known it would hurt this bad. She hadn't known that being without him would slice through her soul like a jagged knife, ripping past her defenses and leaving her so very vulnerable.

Holding back the tears was impossible.

By time she reached the dimly lit shadows of the building's side parking lot, the first one had escaped. Cupping her hand over her mouth, she fought to hold back the cry that would have spilled free with it. Allowing it to escape would only lead to more tears, to the pain erupting inside her like a tightly capped volcano spewing free.

She was unaware she had been followed. Unaware that the man who caused the tears was no more than a step behind her.

Casey heard the hitch of her voice, and as though the knowledge of her tears was borne in the air following a storm, he knew the pain suddenly raging inside her.

He'd never felt another person's tears or another person's emotions as he felt hers now. As though they reached out to him and pierced his chest like an arrow, shooting straight to his soul.

"Sheila." He reached for her as the door slammed behind them, the shadows of the night wrapping around them.

He gripped her shoulders, turning her, overcoming the instinctive struggle, the pride that had her stiffening against him as he pressed her body between his and the side of the building.

"God, baby, you're killing me." The words, whispered at her ear, seemed to break something inside her.

Her body slumped, her shoulders trembling as he felt the silent sobs that suddenly escaped and the tears that spilled to the thin white dress shirt he wore.

She cried silently, which was all the more heartbreaking as her fingers tightened and fisted in the shirt over his chest. Wrapping his arms around her, Casey held her as closely, as tightly to him as he could, and still, it didn't seem to be enough. He wanted her under his skin, to be a part of him, locked so tight to him that neither of them could escape.

Bending his head to her shoulder, the soft flesh bared by the thin straps of her camisole top, he let his lips press to her flesh, his tongue ease out to taste the soft, feminine taste of her.

As though that small hint of her essence only intensified the need, he allowed his lips to part further, his tongue to take more of her taste as he kissed the fragrant flesh.

"Fuck. Roses," he growled as that hint of a taste penetrated his senses.

God, he loved the taste of roses against her flesh.

His hand smoothed up her arm, lifting until he was cupping her neck, his thumb pressing beneath her chin to lift her face to where the moonlight gleamed on the damp trails of her tears.

Her eyes glittered in the darkness, filled with pain. And God knew he understood how she hurt. How the hunger and the need beat inside her soul, because it beat inside his own.

As her lips parted on a ragged breath, he couldn't resist the taste, the soft, crushed-silk feel of them.

His head lowered and he took instant advantage of the parted curves, the damp, tear-drenched saltiness, and the heat and pleasure he'd found only with his Sheila.

Her breathing hitched, but this time in response to his kiss rather than in response to the pain.

Lifting her closer as his knees bent, one hard thigh pressing in between hers, Casey pulled her to the furiously hard flesh pounding beneath his jeans.

Her skirt slid back, revealing tempting, creamy thighs in the dim light as her legs lifted, her knees bending to grip his hips and ride the cloth-covered erection raging beneath the denim.

Damn her. His body craved her like air. She was as natural to him as breathing, and he couldn't seem to exist without finding a way to see her, to touch and hold her.

He let his palm slide up her thigh, beneath the skirt. His fingers tucked beneath the tiny square of material that barely covered her sex to find her hot and wet, the silken folds drenched in sweet, feminine honey.

He was so damned hungry for her it was all he could do to keep from ripping the zipper of his jeans and impaling her with the stiff flesh of his dick.

He wanted inside her so bad he could barely think for it, barely concentrate on anything but the remembered feel of her pussy milking the cum from his dick.

As he snarled his head jerked back, his hips grinding between her thighs as a soft, desperate little moan escaped her lips.

"Tell me, Sheila." He had to hear the words. "What do you want from me? Tell me, baby, and I'll give you what we're both dying for."

He left his fingers tucked between the folds of her pussy, to rub against the snug, clenched entrance in a sensual promise to fill her if she gave him what he needed.

"Casey, just tell me."

He froze. Staring down at her he could see the confusion in her gaze, the desperation, and he could see how much she loved him.

A love so strong, so deep was what he felt for her.

No, his was stronger, deeper he decided, because he knew it for what it was, felt it for what it was, and she continued to hide from it. From him.

His fingers eased back.

"Casey, please," she cried out, her voice hoarse with tears. "What do you want from me?"

What did he want from her?

Hell.

"As strange as it may seem, baby, I want you to see without being shown." He sighed as he eased her back to her feet and steadied her until she was standing on her own. "Come on, I'll take you to your car."

Before he ended up fucking her against the wall.

That was a serious danger if he didn't get her the fuck away from him. He would end up taking her there in the shadows and he wouldn't give a damn who caught him.

"Wait." The fingers of both hands wrapped around his wrist. "Were you at the house last night? Did you come to see me?"

He could hear the need in her voice, the same desperation that he had. What the hell did she want? To ensure he made the first move?

"No, I wasn't." But he knew it wouldn't be long. He would break, and the thought of that sent a wave of anger rushing through him.

She had to know what he felt for her. She had to have realized it. No woman could be so fuckin' obtuse that she couldn't see when a man was so engulfed in her that he would gladly die for her. Or worse, kill for her.

He'd wondered several times, and prayed he was only being facetious, when he'd wondered who he had to kill to convince her he loved her?

"Oh." She released him slowly.

Catching her hand, he drew her to her car.

"Where's your key?" He couldn't keep the anger from his tone.

Pushing her fingers into the side pocket of her skirt, she pulled out the small electronic key and the snick of the door locks filled the silence.

Jerking the door open, he held it for her, watching as she moved around him to slide into the driver's seat.

"Why are you doing this?" she whispered as she stared back at him. "What kind of game are you playing with my heart, Casey?"

And that only pissed him off more. If she thought he was playing a game, then it could only be because she was playing one herself. And the thought of that lit a fuse to his temper that went straight to his lusts.

He'd find out the game she was playing.

He hadn't been at her home last night, but tonight? Oh baby, he promised her silently, he'd be there tonight.

"Go home, Sheila," he told her gently as he stepped back, gripping the edge of the door. "And think about it. I'll give you one more chance to figure it out on your own."

He closed the door before she could argue and stepped back, his gaze still connected with hers, his expression harder than she might have ever seen it.

She had him ready to explode. Not so much in anger as in pure dominant male lust. A dominance and a lust that went far beyond anything he had ever wanted to give another woman.

He wouldn't allow her to play games with what he knew existed between them. He'd be damned if he'd ever seen the love a woman felt for him in her eyes. But he'd seen it in Sheila's. Just as he'd felt her pain, her longing, her fucking confusion.

The vehicle started, and as he watched, she backed out of the parking space and turned, heading to the exit.

He watched until her taillights faded around the curve ahead and several other vehicles pulled out behind her.

And he promised himself, he silently swore to her, that before the night was over, she would know to the soles of her feet who the fuck she belonged to, and why she belonged to him.

After tonight, she'd know better than to ever again ask him what game he was playing with her heart.

chapter 11

by all accounts and research, Sheila Rutledge was a good girl.

Her heart had been broken once by Ross Mason, a young man who had used her to further his own ends. He had, at a very vulnerable time in her life, used her to get to her father and to gain an important government position within the financial sector.

The knowledge of Ross Mason's deception had caused Miss Rutledge to retreat behind a wall of frigid unconcern where men were involved. Until a man named Nick Casey had arrived in town five years before to work for Ethan Cooper at the Broken Bar.

Gossip, it appeared, had been focused on Miss Rutledge and her bouncer since the day she had met him.

And in the past nine or ten months, it had only become stronger.

Since the night Miss Rutledge had left the bar with her bouncer and spent the night at his apartment.

They were an item, despite the fact that it seemed the young miss was determined to hold on to the man whose past was shrouded in shadows.

Strange, that Captain Rutledge seemed blissfully ignorant of the fact that Nick Casey wasn't who he said he was.

Of course, Rutledge himself had a rather shady past as well. A man in his fifties and he'd never risen above captain? For all his connections and political friends, his rank should have been far higher. Which meant somewhere, in some way, Rutledge had compromised his position and his values.

Ahh, such tangled webs.

A sigh filled the pickup. Following Miss Rutledge, knowing the task ahead, weighed heavily on the shoulders.

It wouldn't be easy, terrifying her, harming her. She was a gentle person, a kind person, and forcing her to pay the price for a past she had nothing to do with would be a haunting act. It would be a memory that would haunt not just the present, but the future as well.

Hands tightened on the steering wheel. The vehicle began to accelerate. No, harming her wouldn't be easy, but what other choice was there?

Beau refused to make the call.

There was no gossip that his woman was in danger, Miss Rutledge had kept her suspicions to herself. No one else knew her home had been broken into. No one knew a vehicle followed her a little closer each night.

No one else knew about the phone message she had on her recorder.

Beau had no idea his lover had been targeted and had not yet made that all-important phone call.

It was time to ensure that all knew Miss Rutledge had a stalker. One willing to kill her to achieve whatever ideal she represented.

The vehicle accelerated further, moving steadily closer to the small car ahead and the future Sheila Rutledge might well pay the ultimate price for.

chapter 12

sheila watched in her rearview mirror as the headlights behind her accelerated at an unusual speed. They were moving faster, coming up on her at a speed that was rarely used on the back road that led to the exclusive estates outside Simsburg.

The mostly retired residents didn't drive like bats out of hell. Like the vehicle behind her and the one that had ridden her ass for the past several trips to the bar. For some reason, she never failed to miss the driver who came up on her like an Indy Car driver and, after a few seconds, zipped around her as though she weren't even there.

Tonight, though, it wasn't zipping around her.

This time, it wasn't a car but a monster four-by-four. The powerful sedan that had come up and gone around her at such high speed was absent. The chrome grille of the pickup filled her rearview mirror, the lights almost blinding as they speared into the back window.

And it wasn't trying to pull around her.

Sheila slowed down, and the truck slowed.

She sped up, and the truck sped up.

She didn't take any more chances.

With her heart in her throat, she hit the call button on the steering wheel.

"Casey." She had to fight to steady her tone for the voice-recognition software that powered the automatic calling feature of the Bluetooth connection.

The sound of the phone's ring was overly loud in the car as the truck's motor revved behind her. And it came closer. Impossibly closer.

A second ring as her gaze jerked back to the rearview mirror.

"Sheila, you okay?" Casey's voice came across the line, concern filling it.

Yeah, that was right, she never called anyone as she drove home. It was an agreement made when she first began carrying the flash drives from the bar to her father.

"I have a tail." Her voice was trembling now. "A close one, Casey."

The sound of the truck's powerful motor giving a hard, dark growl behind her sent fear pumping through her system.

"Stay on the line," he ordered. "Turk, Jake, Iron, and I are on our way. How far away are you, baby?"

She swallowed tightly at the threatening rumble of the vehicle behind her as it advanced, slowed, then advanced on her once more.

"I'm about fifteen minutes from home, Casey. I'm passing through Gator Bay now."

Gator Bay was the locals' nickname for the road she was on because of the increasing number of alligators seen on the road and along the edges of the swampy marsh further out.

"We're coming after you, sweetheart—"

At that second, the sound of the engine behind her revving and the harsh, shocking impact of the truck's grille on her bumper caused a shocked scream to escape her lips.

Her foot hit the gas harder as she fought to control the little car and edge away from the truck as it nearly rammed her again.

Casey barked out her name, the sound of loud voices and harsh orders being called out on his side of the connection echoing around her.

"Oh my God, Casey, he just hit me," she cried out as she clenched the steering wheel and fought to get more speed out of the car. "I can't outrun him, Casey. Oh God, I can't outrun him."

She was trying, but the car wasn't built for speed. They were doing seventy down the little country road and Sheila could feel the tires' grip on the road lessening with each curve she took at that speed. They threatened to skid, to throw her sideways; at one point, the back end almost fishtailed as she hit a particularly tight curve.

A curse exploded from her lips as the headlights behind her gained on her once again. A second later the impact of the truck's grille on her already abused bumper had her cheek hitting the steering wheel as she nearly lost control once again.

Sheila screamed as the car was thrown forward, the tires screaming as she fought to control the vehicle, to employ the driving lessons Casey had given her when she had first taken the job as courier from the bar to her father's office.

"Casey!" she cried out as the truck suddenly rammed the back of the car again. "Casey, I can't stay ahead of him!" she screamed.

"By God you will!" he screamed back at her. "I didn't spend those months teaching you to drive to let some asshole defeat you."

Fear was a cold, hard lump in her throat as she pressed her foot harder to the gas, barely managing to keep from being rammed again as both car and truck tires squealed going around another curve.

The car was jerked sideways as the tires lost precious traction. Fighting the steering wheel, Sheila finally managed to straighten the vehicle when another hard nudge from the back nearly had her crashing into the guardrail protecting motorists from the deep, still waters that ran alongside the road in that area.

She could feel the terror lashing at her. There were alligators in that water. They'd been driven into the area after the last tropical storms had swept through. As though they were tired of playing in the Everglades and decided to come to Texas and play there instead.

And Sheila was terrified of them.

"Casey!" she gasped as she finally sped past that danger, only to have the next heavy nudge throw the car onto the wide graveled shoulder of the road before she managed to fight the car back onto the blacktop.

The headlights stayed behind her. No matter how hard she tried, how fast she went.

"I can't take much more!" she screamed as the next nudge nearly jerked the steering wheel out of her hand. "Casey, where are you?" she cried out desperately.

"I'm coming, baby. We're passing Gator Bay. I'm almost there."

"Oh God." She pressed the gas harder.

The truck was trying to come around her.

She was afraid of what that meant, terrified of allowing the huge vehicle to come around her. It had been years since Casey had taught her the defensive driving techniques, and then, they hadn't had someone actually trying to knock them off the road.

"Casey, I can't keep him behind me," she said, feeling the tears, the terror threatening to choke her. "Oh God, Casey, I'm sorry," she sobbed. "I'm sorry I didn't understand. Casey, I'm so sorry—"

"Sheila, don't you dare let that bastard win." Casey felt his guts clenching with pure, unimagined terror as he pushed the truck as hard as he dared, speeding around the curves at a speed he had never dared before as he raced to get to her.

Beside him, Turk grabbed hold of the handgrip above him and, through the Bluetooth he wore, continued to report to Cooper and the others behind them.

Casey and Turk had managed to tear out of the bar well ahead of the others when the call had come through.

He heard her scream again, then swore insanity was only seconds away as he heard the horrifying explosion of a weapon and Sheila's agonized scream of his name as glass shattered around her.

"Fuck! Fuck! Sheila!" He was screaming her name as he pushed the truck harder, his foot landing heavily on the gas and sending the truck careening around the curves. He listened to Turk yelling out a report to Cooper as he jerked the Glock from the holster beneath the jacket he wore and checked the clip despite the wild ride Casey had him on.

"Sheila!" Casey screamed her name again as he heard an impact and the sound of what he knew was the driver's-side air bag inflating. "Sheila. *Answer* me, damn you. You will not leave me like this. I won't let you."

She wasn't answering.

Casey felt such an insane rage overcoming him that he didn't know if he could control it. God help whoever, whatever, had struck out at her. If she was harmed, if anything had happened to her, the pain he would deal out to the culprit once he found him would be unimaginable. No mercy.

"I have her." Mechanical, cold, the voice came over the line. "The past has come to collect, and the future no longer has a defense. I have taken her, and there is nothing you can do to stop me."

Casey heard the weapon cock as he slid around the curve to see the vehicles in the small clearing off the road just ahead.

A black-garbed, shadowed form took off running as Casey raced for the location.

He let it run.

The truck sped away just as Casey swung into the clearing and came to a bone-jarring stop next to Sheila's car.

He was aware of Turk sliding over and the truck racing off after Sheila's attacker as he jumped out and ran to the car.

The driver's-side door was open and his woman, his life, was slumped over the air bag, blood smearing the inflated pillow as he searched desperately for a sign of movement.

"God no! Sheila. Baby." He was terrified to touch her, fear unlike anything he had ever known in his life gripped him, took him by the throat, and strangled the sanity from him as he reached in for her.

Terrified of what he might see, Casey gripped her shoulders and eased her back carefully.

She was breathing.

Tears, honest-to-God moisture that hadn't touched his eyes in longer than he could remember, as her eyes slowly blinked open, and he watched her take a shaky, confused breath.

"Casey." The tears she held back slowly fell from her dazed, confused eyes as he lifted her from the car only to collapse to the ground beside it as he held her tight to his chest.

His head bent over hers as he shook, trembled, and felt the first rivulet of salt water ease from one eye to her hair as he rocked her, held her, and let himself believe she was alive.

"No more games." Ragged, torn, he whispered the words against her ear as he let his head lower further against her. "No more games, baby. I love you. I love you clear to my soul and beyond, Sheila. Oh God, baby." His hands stroked over her, and he found himself terrified that feeling her alive and breathing against him was only a dream. "Sweet, sweet Sheila. How I love you."

"What? Casey. What?" She forced him to pull back, to lift his head as she stared back at him blinking, her gaze confused, filled with disbelief. "Me?" She shook her head, clearly confused. "But why?"

He touched her face, desperate to feel her warmth, to feel her alive. "Why do I love you?" he laughed raggedly, cherishing her tears, her confusion, even her disbelief. Cherishing her and the fact that he could hold her, that she was in his arms where he intended to keep her. Safe, as he intended to ensure she stayed. "Because you make me warm in a place where I think I've been cold all my life, Sheila. Because the first day I saw you, I began to live. God help me, Sheila, because you're my fucking life and I think I died listening to that bastard try to kill you."

He framed her face with one hand, his thumb brushing over her tear-drenched lips as they parted in shock—and was that hope in her gaze?

"You love me?" Her hand gripped his wrist. "You love me?"

"With everything in my soul."

Her lips trembled. The scratches on her face still seeped blood, tears still filled her eyes, and she was the most beautiful thing in the world to him.

"I've always loved you," she whispered. "I thought I'd never see you again, Casey," she suddenly sobbed. "I thought I'd never get to tell you I love you. That I didn't understand, until I didn't think I'd ever see you again, that the only reason was because you loved me." Her breathing hitched as his lips touched her. "I wanted to tell you, and then there was glass exploding around me."

He laid his finger against her lips. The horror of hearing that gunshot would live in his nightmares the rest of his life.

"I have you," he swore. "I have you, Sheila, and I'll never let you go. That son of a bitch will never get the chance to touch you again."

Because Casey was determined to kill him.

His lips touched hers. Tears, a hint of blood, and the overwhelming knowledge of love filled his senses as her lips parted for him, her hands moving to his neck, his hair, as her lips met his.

"I love you," he swore again before he kissed her deeply, licked her, tasted her. He let the knowledge that she was alive seep inside him. Let the truth of it wrap around him.

Because Casey knew he couldn't have survived otherwise.

chapter 13

one week later

ross mason was led from his hotel room in Corpus Christi in handcuffs.

Once, years before, he might have been a handsome man, the man Sheila Rutledge had believed she loved, though it was rather doubtful.

A weak chin, plain brown eyes, shaggy hair, and a plump midsection—it was hard to imagine he had ever drawn the gaze of a woman as lovely as Miss Rutledge.

Though, perhaps her once-deep shyness and the loss of her mother had caused her to look beyond the surface to that weakness beneath and unconsciously believe he would be the one who would not leave her, would not betray her.

That had nothing to do with looks. Betrayal came in all shapes, sizes, races, and creeds. Betrayal came when one least expected it, when one could be destroyed by it the most.

It was a lesson that only the strong survived.

Miss Rutledge had survived that lesson and lived to find a man who might or might not know honor. Who seemed to understand it, live by it.

There was no doubt now Nick Casey wasn't Beauregard Fredrico.

Beau knew nothing of trust, honor, or true love. He knew nothing of holding a woman tight or of risking his own life to save hers, as Nick Casey had done.

No, Nick was not Beau.

The call had not been made before Ross Mason had been revealed as the attempted murderer of the young and lovely Miss Rutledge. There had been no reinforcements called out, no waiting army of loyal men willing to give their lives for the one their fathers had pledged to defend. And those sons would readily pick up arms now and travel across the seas if it meant the heir to the past would return and retake the legacy that had been meant to be his.

The past was truly dead and gone, though. There was no way to convince those men that there was no way to resurrect that past, that glory, or that wealth.

Not that the Fredricos had understood the business anyway.

Giovanni Fredrico, once known as Gio the Giant, hadn't ruled the families as he should have. There had been no blood shed for infractions, just as the whores had not been punished when they fell in love and defected, and the drug dealers had not been murdered, painfully, when they stole the product that was the lifeblood of the organization that had once ruled with a steel fist.

Once, before Giovanni had taken the mantle of leadership.

Once, before his son Beauregard had turned his nose up at the legacy that he had been honor bound to claim.

The bastard.

A fist clenched, the jaw tightened, and the familiar rage began to burn like a wildfire within a chest that had been ripped open, the very heart extracted so long ago.

No, Nick Casey was no Beauregard.

That suspicion had been there before Sheila had left the bar the night Ross Mason had followed her.

It was the reason only Ross had been following at first.

Realizing there was trouble following Miss Rutledge hadn't been easy. Diverting suspicion had been even harder.

Casey had nearly caught sight of the shadowed figure moving through the darkness to take the pictures needed.

The one of Ross Mason pointing that gun at the girl's head just seconds after firing into the car and causing the wreck would be a haunting memory.

But it was over now. The authorities had the pictures that proved Ross had been behind the assault on the woman Nick Casey now guarded so diligently.

Not that she seemed to mind. There was a smile on her face that hadn't been there before, and a joy and youth to her that would stay with her for many years to come. Because the man she loved, the man who loved her, refused to let her out of his sight.

Just as Ethan Cooper loved his Sarah, Nick Casey loved his Sheila.

That left three: Jake Murphy, Iron Donovan, and Turk Rogan.

A weary sigh filled the inside of the truck that held the eyes of the past. A tired, disillusioned sigh. It wasn't over yet. Not yet.

And there could be no peace until it was.

chapter 14

there was a heat surrounding him that Casey knew he would never escape. One he never wanted to escape.

As he lay with the woman he loved more than life itself and pulled his lips from the kiss that was pulling him headlong into a complete meltdown, he realized how he was looking forward to that final surrender to her.

Until then— He looked down at her kiss-swollen lips, the drowsy sensuality in her gaze and her flushed cheeks, and he reminded himself that getting there was just as heated, just as incredible.

Beneath him, Sheila arched closer, her lithe, naked body twisting as the blunt, heavily engorged head of his dick prodded at the swollen lips of her pussy.

Slick silk. Damn, that was what her bare, satiny pussy felt like. Like the softest, hottest syrup saturating a silk so pure and fine it could only be made in paradise.

"Casey, please," she whispered as his lips descended to her breasts. "Oh yes, lick my nipples." She arched closer yet, whimpering as his lips closed over them and he let her feel a hint of his teeth. "Suck them," she moaned. "Suck my nipples. Make me come."

Taking one of the hardened tips between his lips, Casey sucked it hungrily, the taste of her, the passion that flowed from her, making him desperate for more as her fingers fisted in his hair to hold him closer.

That slick, wet silk surrounding the head of his cock, his hips moving as he ate at the tender tip of her nipple. Slowly, with precise gentleness, he began working his cock inside her, feeling the snug muscle and tissue as it parted beneath each slow, easy thrust.

Oh God. It was like being buried, like being wrapped in pure, wild heat. Her juices eased between her flesh and his, another caress that made him ready to growl with pleasure. To snarl with the demand to come.

He'd be damned if he would let himself go that easily. If he would allow Sheila to go that easily.

He didn't want to leave the hot, milking grasp of her pussy until he had no other choice. Pushing inside the liquid heat, slowly, working his cock inside the tender portal, he had to clench his teeth to keep from riding her hard and heavy and spilling his seed inside her.

His balls were drawn tight beneath the iron-hard shaft, his muscles locked tight against the ecstasy threatening to claim him.

With his dick encased inside her, his tongue playing erotic games with her nipples, Casey knew his control wouldn't last much longer.

Her silken inner thighs caressed his flanks as her legs bent and clasped his hips. Her hips rolled against him with each thrust of his dick inside the searing depths of her pussy; each time he had to work his way past the tight muscles rather than slamming inside her.

Fuck, he wanted to ride her hard. He wanted to thrust fast and work inside her and feel her clenching on his cock, sucking his seed straight from his balls.

He wanted to fuck her with the inborn passion that he knew had only come when he touched Sheila. A hunger he'd never known before, and he knew it was a hunger he would never know for any other woman.

Giving a final lick to a cherry red nipple, Casey lifted his gaze to stare down at her.

Her head was thrown back, her hair spread around her like a dark blond halo. Small hands were clenched into fists, holding on to the sheets beneath her, her eyes staring up at him with a hunger that matched his own.

"Fuck me harder." The words slipped past kiss-swollen lips. "I dare you, Casey. Fuck me like you mean it."

For all the challenge in her voice, he also heard the love. A love Casey knew would last him until he took his final breath.

Sheila wanted to scream in pleasure. She wanted to beg, demand, and cry out with the sensations building inside the exquisitely sensitive muscles of her pussy.

Casey stretched her until he was certain she could take no more. He filled her, heated her pussy, and stroked inside it with a rhythm that was driving her insane.

She wanted more.

"Harder," she gasped, her hands lifting from the sheets to grip his shoulders, her nails biting into the hard flesh and iron-hard muscles as his hips ground against hers.

He was teasing her. Pushing her higher. He was filling her with such incredible pleasure, sensations that sizzled across her nerve endings before speeding through her system and tightening every muscle in her body with the need to orgasm.

"It's so good," she moaned, nearly incoherent with the pleasure that burned inside her. "Oh God, Casey, I love you. I love you so much." It was a plea. "Please let me come. Please, I can't stand it any longer."

Flames were building inside her, spreading outward, threatening to set the world ablaze if she didn't find her release soon. She could feel the clenching around the flesh penetrating her, tightening and spasming as the swollen bud of her clit began to throb warningly.

"Yes," she moaned. "Oh yes, Casey." Neck arching, she felt it begin, felt it rushing through her, over her, tearing into her with a force that had her trying to scream as her orgasm began to detonate inside her.

Casey wasn't but a second longer.

As he buried his cock to the hilt, Sheila felt the hard, fierce throb, the feel of the brief expansion, then the fierce, jetting spurts of his cum shooting inside her.

His release mixed with hers, burned and melded until there was no longer just Casey, no longer just Sheila. Until the two of them were suddenly joined and made whole. Made one.

"I love you," she cried out desperately. "Oh God, Casey, I love you."

With his head buried at her neck, his arms wrapped around her, his very life pumping inside her, Casey whispered, "You're my soul, Sheila. My home."

His home.

As he was hers.

And together they were creating the dream Sheila had believed she would never know.

That dream of belonging.

"I simply couldn't put it down."
—ROMANCE REVIEWS TODAY

#1 *New York Times* Bestselling Author

lora leigh

dangerous games

"Lora Leigh writes compelling, red-hot romance."
—*SACRAMENTO BOOK REVIEW*

READ ALL THE TITLES IN THE TEMPTING NAVY SEALS SERIES:
Hidden Agendas
Killer Secrets
Atlanta Heat
For Maggie's Sake
Reno's Chance

St. Martin's Griffin

Wild Card

Navy SEAL Nathan Malone's wife, Bella, was told he was never coming home. But if he can get back to his wife, can he keep the secret of who he really is . . . even as desire threatens to consume them? And as danger threatens to tear Bella from Nathan's arms once more?

Black Jack

The Secret Service can't control him. The British government can't silence him. But renegade agent Travis Caine is one loose cannon you don't want to mess with, and his new assignment is to die for.

Maverick

The only way for the Elite Ops agent to uncover an assassin—and banish the ghosts of his own dark past—is to use Risa as bait. But nothing has prepared him for her disarming blend of innocence and sensuality, or for his overwhelming need to protect her.

Renegade

Elite Ops agent Nikolai Steele, code name Renegade, is asked to pay an old comrade a favor. This friend swears he's no killer even though he's been mistaken as one by Mikayla. Nik goes to set her straight, but the moment he lays eyes her, he knows he's in too deep.

Heat Seeker

John Vincent has every reason to want to remain as dead as the obituary had proclaimed him to be. He'd left nothing behind except for one woman, and one night of unforgettable passion. Now, both will return to haunt him.

Live Wire

Captain Jordan Malone has been a silent warrior and guardian for years, leading his loyal team of Elite Ops agents to fight terror at all costs. But Tehya Talamosi, a woman with killer secrets and body to die for, will bring Jordan to his knees as they both take on the most deadly mission

ST. MARTIN'S PRESS

Midnight Sins

Cami lost her sister in the brutal murders that rocked her hometown so many years ago. Some still believe that Rafe Callahan, along with his friends Logan and Crowe, were involved. But how could Rafe—who haunted her girlish dreams, then her adult fantasies—be a killer?

Deadly Sins

A newcomer in town, Sky O'Brien is a mystery to Logan Callahan. Like him, she is a night owl. Like him, she is fighting her own demons. Like him, she hides a secret in her eyes—a fire that consumes him with every glance. Could she be the one to heal him?

Secret Sins

Sheriff Archer Tobias has watched the Callahan family struggle to find peace and acceptance in the community—despite the murders that continue to haunt them. But he is torn between duty and desire when Anna Corbin becomes the next target.

Ultimate Sins

Mia, left an orphan after her father's death, was raised amid the lies and suspicions against Crowe Callahan. But nothing could halt the fascination she feels for him, or the hunger that has risen inside her.

🐾 St. Martin's Paperbacks   📖 St. Martin's Griffin